"A good storyline...a nice read."
                                                    —*The Best Reviews*

"Impossible to put down...[Pierce is] a truly exceptional story-teller."
                                        —*Romance Reader at Heart*

TEMPTING THE HEIRESS

"Pierce does an excellent job blending danger and intrigue into the plot of her latest love story. Readers who like their Regency historicals a bit darker and spiked with realistic grit will love this wickedly sexy romance."
                                                    —*Booklist*

"Masterful storyteller Barbara Pierce pens captivating romances that are not to be missed!"
                        —Lorraine Heath, *USA Today* bestselling author
                                        of *Love with a Scandalous Lord*

"I love everything about this book. The characters are like friends you cheer for, and the story draws you in so closely you will dream about it."
                                        —*Romance Reader at Heart*

"*Tempting the Heiress* is the latest entry in the Bedegrayne family series and it is an excellent one. Known for the complexity of her characters, Barbara Pierce doesn't disappoint in this aspect of *Tempting the Heiress*...I should warn new readers to the Bedegrayne series that they will find themselves eagerly glomming the previous three novels in the series. Highly recommended!"
                                —*The Romance Reader's Connection*

SINFUL
BETWEEN
The SHEETS

BARBARA PIERCE

St. Martin's Paperbacks

This is a work of fiction. All of the characters, organizations, and events portrayed in this novel are either products of the author's imagination or are used fictitiously.

SINFUL BETWEEN THE SHEETS

Copyright © 2007 by Barbara Pierce.

Cover photo © Shirley Green

ISBN: 0-312-34822-3
EAN: 978-0-312-34822-9

Printed in the United States of America

St. Martin's Paperbacks edition / April 2007

St. Martin's Paperbacks are published by St. Martin's Press, 175 Fifth Avenue, New York, NY 10010.

10 9 8 7 6 5 4 3 2 1

For my witty and beautiful sister-in-law, Jennifer Freese

Lovers and madmen have such seething brains,
Such shaping fantasies, that apprehend
More than cool reason ever comprehends.
The lunatic, the lover, and the poet
Are of imagination all compact.

—WILLIAM SHAKESPEARE
THESEUS, IN *A MIDSUMMER NIGHT'S DREAM*,
ACT 5, SC. 1, L. 4–8

PROLOGUE

Ealkin, country house of Lord and Lady Nipping
Wiltshire County
August 5, 1808

"Kilby!"

One floor level above and hidden in the shadows of the dark stairwell, Lady Kilby Fitchwolf watched her half brother, Archer, as he kicked open a door and disappeared into the room. The breaking of glass had her cringing and shrinking deeper into the shadows. Whatever her supposed sin, her brother was determined to find her and make her pay. She stifled a cry of surprise when he staggered back into view again. From his unsteady gait, she wagered he had not stopped with the second bottle of wine she had watched him consume at supper.

"Where are you?" he raged, his body heaving in frustration. At some point since their last encounter, he had discarded his coat and had untied his cravat. Leaning heavily against one of the tables, he scowled at the closed doors, attempting to guess where she was hiding.

"Stubborn bitch. Once I get my hands on you, I'll show you how to heel." He crossed the marble hall and shoved open another door.

Kilby used the noise he made below to cover her escape. Barefoot, she raced up the flight of stairs to the next landing. A part of her knew her actions were futile. Archer seemed intent on searching every room in the house. It was only a matter of time before he discovered her. Kilby moved down the dark hall, sliding her hand along the wall as a guide. Sadly, this was not the first time she had been forced to disappear during one of Archer's drunken tirades. If she could keep away from him until he sobered, she would be moderately safe.

"Damn you, Kilby, enough of this nonsense," her brother roared from below. "Show yourself!"

"Never," she whispered softly. Her hand closed over the latch to her mother's bedchamber. As far as she knew, no one had entered the rooms since her parents had drowned in a yachting accident thirteen months earlier. Even Archer, who had inherited their father's title, Marquess of Nipping, had avoided this part of the house. With luck, he would tire of his search long before he approached the third floor.

Slowly she opened the door, praying the hinges were well oiled. They were. Kilby slipped through the narrow opening and carefully shut the door, then leaned against it. Her breathing hitched as she fought back the sudden sting of tears. The room still held the lingering scent her mother used. Kilby could almost feel her mother's arms circling around her, her warm scented flesh wrapping her in love and security.

"All will be well, my little honeybee."

Kilby wiped the tears off her cheek. How often had her mother crooned those words to her, using the special endearment she had reserved for Kilby? A thousand? Tens of thousands? When she had been a child, she had believed in the power of her mother's assurances. Her safe, happy world had never been the same since word had reached Ealkin of her parents' deaths.

And then there was her younger sister. Her given name was Evelina, but the family had endearingly dubbed her Gypsy. At age two, she had been very adept at escaping the watchful eye of the servants and roaming the house and lands at will.

Gypsy had been such a vibrant child, with a heart-shaped face, wild black hair, and laughing blue eyes. That spirited child no longer existed. The sudden loss of her parents had devastated her seven-year-old sibling. When told the news of their parents' deaths, her sister had started screaming. For hours, poor Gypsy had cried and raged at the injustice of her loss. Too dazed by her own volatile emotions, Kilby had not been able to comfort her sister. As the hours passed, she had feared for Gypsy's sanity. In desperation she had summoned a physician. By then, her sister's scream had deteriorated to a hoarse, broken hiss. The physician had dosed Gypsy with laudanum to calm her. He had promised Kilby that a few days of rest would restore her little sister.

The physician had been wrong. Gypsy had not spoken a single word from that day forward. Kilby had tried everything from rewards to threats to break Gypsy's silence. As the months passed, she realized her sister's silence was more than mere stubbornness. It was as if a part of her had died along with their parents. These days, Gypsy walked about the house like a ghost, not allowing anything, even grief, to touch her.

Kilby flinched as Archer bellowed her name again. He sounded closer. Perhaps he had moved on to the second level. Her eyes had already adjusted to the inky blackness of the room's interior. Reaching out her hands, she moved away from the door and used her hands and her memory to seek out her mother's wardrobe. The brass handles clanked together as her fingers brushed against the cold metal. Kilby opened one of the doors and slipped inside. The wardrobe was empty so she settled into it with little effort and shut the door so only a crack remained. If Archer thought to check his stepmother's bedchamber, Kilby prayed he would only give it a cursory glance as he had all the other rooms.

Kilby threaded her fingers through her hair and held them there while she rested her forehead on her raised knees. Her nerves were raw from this hide-and-seek game her brother forced her to play almost nightly. What was she going to do about Archer?

He had not always been the drunk, angry man who bullied and terrified her now. When they were children, they had been close. Archer was barely two years older than Kilby, and they had raced up and down the halls of Ealkin, playing pranks on the servants.

They did not resemble each other in looks. Kilby had inherited her straight black hair from her mother. She viewed herself unremarkable in stature and looks. What elevated her features beyond average were her eyes. Unlike her siblings, the blue eyes Kilby had been bestowed at birth had lightened to an exotic violet color. Once when she asked her father why she had violet eyes and her siblings did not, the marquess had told her that her uniqueness had been a gift from an angel.

There was nothing extraordinary about Archer. He was about the same height as their father had been. His dark blond hair curled slightly at the ends where it brushed the collar of his coats. He had blue eyes lighter than Gypsy's, and pale pink, narrow lips that hinted at his future uncompromising tendencies. Her father had always said that Archer had favored his mother in looks. The first Lady

Nipping had died giving birth to Archer's brother. The infant had died three days later.

Lost in his grief and unsure how to raise his young son alone, Lord Nipping had quickly taken a second wife. Not long after their marriage vows had been spoken, the second Lady Nipping announced that she was breeding. Kilby did not know whether necessity or love had prompted her father to marry her mother. Her parents rarely spoke of their past. What was certain, though, was that Lord Nipping and his lady were devoted to each other until the end.

Archer had been so young when his father had remarried that he had thought of Kilby's mother as his own. The troublesome changes in Archer had begun when he had been sent off to school. Kilby recalled hearing her mother and father discuss Archer's difficulties with his studies and his need for discipline. Her brother's scrapes had led to heated arguments with Lord Nipping and this eventually had created a rift between Archer and the family.

Once he had finished his schooling, her brother had moved to London, much to the dismay of their parents. Lord and Lady Nipping had always shunned London, preferring their tranquil life in the countryside. They had deemed town life too decadent for their children and the air quality unhealthy. Their parents' disapproval had made London all the more appealing to Archer.

On his rare visits to Ealkin, Kilby could see the changes in her brother and they were not flattering. Archer no longer seemed part of their little family and she had been relieved when he departed.

It was their parents' death that had forced Kilby to reach out to her wayward brother. At seventeen, she had been too young to care for the now mute Gypsy or manage the day-to-day decisions for Ealkin's upkeep. She had thought perhaps the mantle of his new title and his responsibilities to his sisters would settle her brother.

Alas, it had only brought out the worst in him.

Although Ealkin was his, Archer despised the isolation there. He had informed Kilby once that he remained only out of duty, but he did not have the patience their father had had. Alone in the library, he started drinking himself into a stupor each night. Most nights he simply passed into blissful unconsciousness.

Other nights, like tonight, he was the devil.

Lately, when his narrowed gaze settled on Kilby, his blatant, unnatural perusal sickened her. It was apparent that her brother had high ambitions for his sister, and she doubted her parents would approve. She certainly did not!

"Enough games, Kilby, my sweet sister," Archer called out, slurring his words.

His search had brought him to the third floor. Kilby lifted her head; her mouth went dry in terror. Through the crack in the wardrobe, she could see the hint of candlelight from under the door. She swallowed thickly, refusing to answer.

"Heed my words, you violet-eyed bitch. Come out of hiding or pay the consequences," he said, his booming voice echoing down the hall.

Kilby heard a distant door open and then close. She bit her lower lip to prevent herself from answering. In his present mood, she was too afraid of what he might do to her if she complied with his demands.

"Are you listening?" He paused, letting the question hang in the air. "Well, if you won't come out for me, perhaps you'll come out for our resident little mouse."

Oh, God. *Gypsy*.

Was Archer so villainous as to drag their sister from her bed and use her to gain Kilby's obedience? No. She shook her head in denial. Her brother was bluffing. Even he could not be so cruel.

"Don't believe me, eh?" he asked as if he had read her thoughts. "Let's see if I can get the mouse to squeak."

Kilby brought her hands to her mouth and sank her teeth into a knuckle. As she rocked back and forth, every passing second of silence fueled her fear and indecision.

The thin cry of a child in pain cut through Kilby like broken glass stabbing her heart. Pushing open the door of the wardrobe, she staggered out of the compartment, trying not to imagine what Archer was doing to Gypsy to make her cry out. In that moment, she hated her brother. The thought of him hurting their innocent younger sister was beyond her comprehension. Kilby shuddered, wondering what nefarious plans Archer had for her. A part of her wanted to stay hidden, stay safe. She walked over to the door and tugged on the latch. Whatever her feelings, she could not allow him to harm Gypsy.

Kilby opened the door and discovered Archer holding a terrified Gypsy by her fragile wrist. He obviously had heard her open the wardrobe. There was no one in the house who could help her and Gypsy. The servants had retired for the evening, and they had strict orders not to disturb the family. She felt so helpless and alone.

"I knew you would join me if I provided the right incentive," Archer said, tightening his grip on Gypsy's thin wrist. Her sister whined and twisted in his merciless hold.

Kilby lifted her chin in defiance. "Let her go."

The smile her brother bestowed on her in response to her harsh demand had her stomach roiling. "Why? I'm feeling playful tonight and little sisters can be so amusing when provoked." He gestured for her to lead the way.

It was difficult, but Kilby refrained from reaching out and pulling Gypsy away from Archer. Any attempt to thwart him

now would encourage him to further punish the child for
Kilby's defiance. Instead, she crossed her arms and glared at
him. "What do you want from me, Archer?"

Her brother gave her a bawdy wink. "You'll see soon
enough, pretty Kilby," he promised her. "You'll see."

CHAPTER ONE

London, April 10, 1809

The Duke of Solitea was dead.

Naturally, his widow decided to throw a ball. To the eccentric duchess, it seemed the appropriate way to herald her husband's passing. Fayne Carlisle, Marquess of Temmes, tossed back the remains of the brandy in his glass and shook his head in lingering amazement.

Christ, a ball for a dead man! No one had ever accused the Carlisles of being typical. The duchess had even wanted the deceased to join in the festivities. Fayne had balked at the outlandish suggestion and flatly refused to indulge his mother's request. He could just envision it. The duke, resplendent in his funerary finery, dominating the drawing room as he had in life, while his two beloved apricot-colored mastiffs stood guard at each end of the mahogany coffin.

God save them all from his mother's whims!

Slouched casually against one of the farthest corners of the drawing room, Fayne broodingly watched as guests flowed in and out of the room. In the center of the room, his mother had ordered that a twelve-foot-high portrait of the duke be set up for display. The painting had been a gift from the duchess, and commissioned in celebration of his father's thirtieth birthday. Oversized black and gold porcelain vases stuffed with greenery and hothouse flowers were placed around the portrait.

Fayne sipped from his glass, barely tasting the brandy. It had been a god-awful day. His stomach still roiled when he thought of the slow, stately procession he and the family had endured earlier in the day to Westminster Abbey for the interment of the Duke of Solitea. While his younger sister, Fayre, had brokenly sobbed with her face pressed into his shoulder, the duchess had sat quietly beside him, her expressionless face reminding him of pale marble. She had done her grieving in private. For days after word had reached them of the duke's passing, her wild, inconsolable sorrow had seemed inexhaustible. She had slept only because the family's physician with Fayne's unrelenting assistance had poured the apothecary's soporific tincture down her throat nightly.

Fayne had not recognized the silent, pale woman who had sat next to him in the mourning coach. He had longed to see a glimmer of his mother's former spirit, some sign that she would survive her husband's passing. It was the main reason he had even consented to the ridiculous ball at all.

Fayne watched on as a lady dropped to her knees in front of the duke's portrait and cried into her lace handkerchief. He could not see her face, but he idly wondered if the grieving lady had been one of his father's former mistresses. His gaze roved contemplatively over the dozen or more people who had positioned themselves in front of the duke's portrait. Most of them meant well, Fayne assumed. If any of them thought it necessary to speak to him, his defiant posture and intimidating expression discouraged anyone from approaching. This was fortunate, because the duchess would never forgive him if he caused a broil by punching one her unwary guests.

"Still preferring your tea cold, I see," a masculine voice said from his left, interrupting Fayne's dark musings.

Any sane individual would have had the sense to respect a grieving son's privacy. Unfortunately, that left Fayne to deal with the not-so-sane.

He rubbed his right eyebrow with his finger, giving his blond friend a vexed look. "Ramscar. I was just thinking how irked the duchess would be if I am provoked into punching some well-meaning bastard," Fayne said, in lieu of a greeting.

Fowler Knowden, Earl of Ramscar, merely grinned at the threat of violence. At the height of five feet and ten inches, the earl was several inches shorter than Fayne's six-foot-one-inch stature; however, the man's confidence and lazy graceful movements warned the observer not to underestimate him. He watched expectantly as Ramscar retrieved a decanter of brandy he had hidden behind his back and waved it before Fayne as others might use a flag of truce. "Your glass is dry, and the footmen are terrified of you. Byrchmore, Everod, and I cast lots. I was the loser," he added needlessly.

There was such an engaging sincerity to his friend's expression that it had Fayne shaking his head. Out of his three closest friends, Ramscar was the mediator of the group. The duchess had always called him the sensible one. Hidden beneath his mischievous nature were unplumbed depths of sensitivity, and a desire for fair play lurked in his intelligent hazel-colored eyes. It tended to surface at odd moments.

"You will get no argument from me." Fayne's mouth curved into a sarcastic smirk as he held out his glass. Secretly, he welcomed his friend's intrusion. In spite of the lively music playing in the ballroom, the atmosphere in the drawing room was utterly maudlin with the guests staring at his father's portrait in blank shock or sobbing uncontrollably into their handkerchiefs, like several of the female guests had done.

Fayne could not fault his mother's efforts. With the assistance of his sister, the duchess had honored the duke's request that they celebrate the life he had led, and not mourn his demise. It was a fitting sentiment for a man who many believed had enjoyed more than his fair share of decadent living.

Ramscar brought him back to the present with the clinking of crystal as he filled Fayne's glass. Muttering to himself, the man rummaged a hand into one of the inner pockets of his coat and retrieved an empty glass. He poured himself a generous portion of brandy and then placed the decanter on the floor between them.

"So what's the plan, Solitea?"

Fayne flinched. He had not given it much thought; however, the dukedom belonged to him now. From this day forward, he would no longer be thought of as Lord Temmes, but rather as the Duke of Solitea. With this new title came all its privileges—and curses. His hand was not quite steady as he brought the rim of the glass to his lips.

Ramscar shot his friend an exasperated glance. "You're the old man's heir, Carlisle. Surely you anticipated the day you'd claim that inheritance." His gaze drifted over to the duke's magnificent portrait where two young ladies were paying their respects. Regrettably, there was not a respectful bone in Ramscar's head when it came to females. As he sipped his brandy, his friend's hungry gaze gleamed appreciatively at the curvaceous backside of one of the mourners.

"Ram, my father died eight days ago. Pardon me if I find his sudden demise a bit unsettling," Fayne said dryly. A flash of color caught his attention at the open doorway. He muffled an oath as he recognized the newcomers.

Holt Cadd, Marquess of Byrchmore, and Townsend Lidsaw, Viscount Everod, approached them with the confidence born of a friendship that had begun in boyhood. Their titles and noble bloodlines made them worthy companions for a duke's heir. Through the years, they had played, fought, and studied together. Handsome, rich, and unmarried, the four had prowled London, daring the world to stop them from claiming all they desired. The *ton* affectionately referred to them as *les sauvages nobles,* the noble savages. It had been a sobriquet they had reveled in and reinforced by their drunken escapades, whoring, and reckless gambling.

"Since the furniture is still upright we assumed it was safe to approach," Cadd said, using the wall to brace his muscular form.

At four and twenty, he was the youngest—and the easiest to provoke. Once he had been a pretty lad, and this had forced him to engage in countless fights when they were in school. During one of those exchanges, Cadd had broken his nose. The injury had ruined the youth's prettiness. However, it did little to make his face less appealing. With gleaming black eyes and a slightly imperfect nose Cadd seemed to fascinate the ladies of the *ton*. Although his dark brown hair was long enough to be tied neatly into a queue, the marquess generally wore his slightly curling locks unfettered.

There was a reckless air about Cadd that always invited trouble. "What are you doing in here, Carlisle?" he asked in his provoking manner.

"Getting drunk," Fayne replied, signaling Ramscar by shaking his empty glass. He had been avoiding the ballroom for the past hour. The notion of dancing or speaking to the sympathetic and the curious held no appeal for him. His mother and sister had more patience for such nonsense.

"Mostly there, I'd wager."

Naturally, the sardonic comment was uttered by another one of his good friends, Viscount Everod. No one would ever describe the young lord as handsome. "Arresting" was a more appropriate word for him. A few inches taller than Fayne, Everod gave one the impression of a stern medieval overlord. His glossy black hair was long, the ends reaching several inches past his broad, muscular shoulders. Even the casual observer would recall the viscount's amber eyes. Ringed with light green bands, they burned with an inner fire that could be either hot or cold. Though his cravat hid most of it, he possessed a wicked scar that curved from the left side of his neck and ended on the right underside of his jaw. No one mentioned the scar; not even his friends. They knew better than most that concealed beneath Everod's biting wit, the man had a formidable temper. On numerous boisterous occasions the man's disagreeable temperament had placed him right in the thick of things, with his friends protecting his back. Fayne doubted the viscount would have wanted it any other way.

Everod stooped down and snatched the decanter off the floor before Ramscar could. He poured more brandy into Fayne's glass. At the earl's silent command, he filled that glass, too.

"A toast," Everod announced, holding the decanter up. "To the duke. May we all be so fortunate." He wobbled slightly as he brought the rim of the decanter to his firm lips and swallowed.

Cadd punched Everod in the arm, causing him to take a step back to keep his balance. "Arse! Have some bloody respect."

"Hands off." The viscount sneered, his pride bruised because Cadd had caught him unawares. The pair had a precarious friendship that usually erupted into violence at the least provocation. "I meant no disrespect. The duke was a fine gent. I'm sorry that he's dead an' all." He nodded at

Fayne while he made his apology, his amber gaze eloquent with unspoken emotion. "I was referring to *how* he died, not that he's dead. The others might not have the bollocks to speak it aloud, but there isn't a man in London who doesn't wish that death came to him so delightfully wrapped."

Damn, the duchess was not going to be pleased if that particular rumor reached her ears. The family had taken steps to keep the last hours of the duke's life private. "I do not know what you mean," Fayne smoothly lied. "My father died because his heart failed him."

"Come on, Carlisle, don't be coy," Everod said, refusing to back down. "Rumor has it that the old man was enjoying his mistress when his pump failed him. Oh, don't give me that look. Honestly, you should have realized that you couldn't silence everyone in the know. Gossip like this is too irresistible to contain."

"Most of us have the sense to keep our bloody opinions to ourselves the eventide of the funeral," Cadd muttered, pointedly glancing at Fayne. "Especially when Carlisle, here, is within arm's length."

Fayne's green eyes glittered with suppressed humor. While his family might be considered a trifle odd, he doubted his mother would forgive him if he were the instigator of a fight this evening. He could not deny the need for violence humming through him. Since he had learned of his father's death, he had been edgy and hurting, a veritable powder keg of dark fury just waiting for a proper ignition.

"Everod might on occasion be an uncouth oaf," Fayne said, ignoring the viscount's growling protest. "Regardless, I agree with him. I cannot imagine an ending more befitting the Duke of Solitea than to expire betwixt the soft thighs of his mistress." He refused to confirm or deny the *ton*'s speculation.

He lifted his glass in the direction of his father's portrait and saluted him. His friends made concurring toasts after him. Fayne glanced down at his hand, fiercely concentrating on the brandy in his glass as the unwelcome moisture filled his eyes. A Carlisle male never succumbed to the weakness of tears. If his eyes burned, it was due to the lack of proper ventilation. There were at least a hundred candles lighting up the room, fouling the air.

"The duke certainly had an eye for beauty, and I am sure his last mistress was no exception," Ramscar said, his expression becoming thoughtful. "Speaking of beauties, did any of you meet Lady Kilby Fitchwolf?"

Fayne choked on his brandy. He wondered if his friend's high opinion would change if he learned that Lady Kilby Fitchwolf was the lady his father had dallied with the night he had died. He grimaced. *Not likely.* "No, I have not had the pleasure."

That was not quite true, but it was all Fayne was willing to reveal to his friends. While he had not been formally introduced to the lady as Ramscar had been, he had seen her.

He had also met the lady's incompetent chaperone, Lady Quennell. The night his father had died, Fayne had listened to the viscountess's tearful plea for the Carlisles to quash the impending scandal by not revealing the details of the duke's death or his lover's name. He did not give a damn about Lady Kilby Fitchwolf's impressionable age, beauty, or reputation. He had swiftly agreed to remain silent on the matter because he did not want his mother to suffer any humiliating comparisons by the *ton.* It was not the duchess's fault some ambitious chit parted her thighs too easily, and that her reckless husband was unable to control his baser instincts.

Unaware of Fayne's inner turmoil, Ramscar continued. "I was briefly introduced to her several weeks ago at a card party. I believe she had mentioned that she was enjoying her first season."

Fayne had been surprised that his father had bothered

with Lady Kilby Fitchwolf. Lady Quennell had mentioned that her charge was nineteen. The lady looked even younger. It was unlike his father to choose a lady so young or innocent if the viscountess's assertions could be believed.

"Perhaps she was the young minx amusing your father in bed?" Everod interjected with a salacious wink.

Leave it to his friend with indelicate accuracy to hit upon the truth.

Ramscar grimaced at the viscount. "Highly doubtful, I say. Solitea was not the sort to seduce chits barely out of the nursery. When you encounter Lady Kilby Fitchwolf, you will understand how absurd your suggestion is."

Outward appearances are sometimes deceiving, he thought, wishing he could warn his friend not to be fooled by the lady's air of innocence. Fayne was not really surprised by his friends' speculation about his father's death. No one in his family doubted the duke had indeed bedded the lady before perishing on her fine carpet.

For generations, the dukes of Solitea were notorious for their illicit love affairs, and his father had not been the exception. While it was apparent to Fayne that his father had adored his duchess, marriage had not discouraged his sire from seeking his pleasures outside the marriage bed.

The duchess had tolerated her husband's inconstancy with amazing stoicism; although, over the years, there had been one or two of his former mistresses who had noticeably distressed her. Fayne could not blame her for finding solace in the arms of her young lovers. The duke had been aware of his duchess's affairs, but had not attempted to prohibit her from her discreet dalliances. His sister, Fayre, had always been troubled by their parents' odd, albeit amicable, arrangement. Fayne, on the other hand, had been totally indifferent.

Perhaps it was because he had understood his father's reckless inclinations, and that of his predecessors, in a manner his sister never could. The Carlisle males who claimed the Solitea title were cursed, or at least seemed to be. Family, friends, and the curious had whispered about the Solitea curse for generations.

The origins of this supposed curse were obscured by the passage of time. Some conjectured that amour propre was the family's sin. The more imaginative wondered if a vengeful mistress had summoned the dark powers of hell and cursed the Solitea heirs. Fayne did not believe in curses. However, he could not ignore the unpleasant fact that the males who inherited the Solitea title always seemed to die young. When a man grew up believing he was destined to die before his time, that man was driven to eagerly embrace all the pleasures his brief life offered—and arrogantly claim the forbidden temptations that were not rightfully his. For his father, Fayne would have definitely categorized the Lady Kilby Fitchwolf as a forbidden temptation.

"My father rarely discriminated against youth," Fayne said, feeling confident he had buried his sorrow so deep, it did not crack the calm façade he had adopted for the ball. "Nevertheless, I do concur with Ram. Despoiling innocence was not a sport the duke willingly indulged."

Lady Kilby Fitchwolf had appeared on the surface the epitome of innocence. Days before the duke had seduced her, Fayne had noticed the lady from afar. She was a tiny, slender little creature with long black hair that she had pinned up in an elaborate twist of braids. While the distance separating them had prevented him from noting the color of her eyes, it had not diminished her fresh-faced loveliness. The evening he had first glimpsed her in the crowd, she had been speaking animatedly to a female companion. Fayne, much to his chagrin, had wasted most of the night searching the crowd for glimpses of the enchanting vixen wearing the light green dress.

Even though Lady Kilby intrigued him, he had not

sought out an introduction. Despite all rumors to the contrary, Fayne had no interest in seducing young innocents who dreamed of marriage. He preferred dallying with ladies who had already been relieved of their maidenhead. The temporary lust he felt for the lady in green could be contained, or favored on a more skillful companion, if his needs overrode his common sense. Lady Kilby Fitchwolf was definitely the kind of lady who was off limits for a jaded rake like him. Or so Fayne thought, until he had learned his father had died in the lady's bedchamber.

"Fitchwolf," Everod mused aloud. "I believe I have met the lady. She is the dew-faced infant who has a fondness for silver-headed gents. I partnered her in a country dance and barely got three words out of her. Later, I noticed her chatty as a magpie with Lord Ordish. By God, the man is old enough to be her sire!"

Poor Everod. It was apparent he could still not comprehend why the lady had resisted his charms.

"Perhaps she is just particular," Cadd retorted, rubbing his upper lip with the side of his hand to conceal their bawdy discourse from the other guests. "I wager, five minutes alone in my company and I could convince her that she has been judging a man by the wrong head!"

Everod snorted in derision. "Braggart! I have unfortunately laid eyes on your less than impressive equipage, and I must say if the lady requires a stallion, she would do well to choose me. The ladies practically swoon when I mount them."

The smile Cadd gave the viscount was lacking both humor and warmth. "Their swooning probably has more to do with your forgetfulness to bathe, rather than the size of your rod!"

Fayne shook his head and his green eyes connected with Ramscar's commiserating gaze. He was relieved to drop the subject of Lady Kilby Fitchwolf. How fortunate that Cadd could never resist an opportunity to ignite Everod's temper. If someone did not intercede, the pair was likely to come to blows. Their disagreement was already drawing attention from the other guests.

"Are you prepared to wager on it?" Without breaking eye contact, Everod aggressively stepped closer to the marquess. "A thousand pounds says I can bed any lady here of your choosing."

There was a challenging glint in Cadd's black gaze as he replied softly, "Anyone? Are you certain about this, ol' man? Your arrogance will leave you shamefaced and a thousand pounds poorer come morning, if I accept."

Belatedly realizing that some boundaries were required, Everod said, "The lady must be out of the nursery and not older than my blessed mother." He hesitated, and then added thunderously, "And no bloody relatives!"

Cadd provokingly bumped the viscount with his chest. "Perhaps you should summon a footman and order a bath before I accept this wager?" The taunt provoked Everod into raising his fist.

His friends were idiots. They were definitely foxed to be placing wagers at the duke's memorial ball. Fayne cleared his throat. "Gentlemen. I know I must be drunker than I thought when I sound like the responsible one of us all. However, we are garnering nasty looks from several of the guests. I assure you, the duchess will lynch us all if one of you decides to throw a punch. Do me a favor and leash your damned tempers."

Normally, his friends' competitiveness and excessive bickering did not trouble him. There had been a time or two when he had deliberately prodded them toward violence just for amusement's sake. Fayne privately acknowledged that he was in an odd mood this evening. His father's death was a logical explanation. Deep down, nevertheless, he sensed his father's sudden death was merely an excuse for the ennui that had been plaguing him lately rather than the source.

"Damn."

The oath came from Ramscar. The earl was not referring to their friends' argument. His attention was focused on the entrance to the drawing room. Fayne tilted his head to the side to see who had caught the man's regard. His sister, Fayre, stood in the middle of the threshold with her back to the room. She cast him a frantic glance, before turning back to face the source of her agitation. *Who the devil is she arguing with?* Fayne wondered, frowning. Her arms were outspread as if she were trying to prevent someone from entering the room.

Fayne's curiosity was swiftly satisfied when a gentleman appeared in front of Fayre. The man brushed her arm aside and stepped into the room. Fayne recognized Lord Hollensworth. Four years older than Fayne, the baron had little time or patience for polite society. He preferred farming to politics. Unfortunately, Fayne knew precisely what had prompted the gentleman to leave the countryside.

Unerringly, the baron's harsh gaze fixed on Fayne's bemused one. Ignoring his sister's order to halt, Lord Hollensworth marched toward Fayne and his friends. Instead of following, his sister ran off in the opposite direction. Since Fayre had not been able to reason with their unwelcome guest, Fayne assumed she went to find her husband, Maccus Brawley. Summoning Brawley was hardly necessary. The odds were in Fayne's favor. It stung that his sister had so little faith in his abilities.

"Good evening, Hollensworth," Fayne said casually, when the baron shoved Cadd and Everod out of his way. His friends had deliberately stepped in Hollensworth's path to impede his approach. Whatever their personal differences, the two friends had put their quarrel aside for Fayne's sake. "You have journeyed far to pay your respects to my father." If the baron was embarrassed by his ill-timed appearance, he bore it well. Rage and the need for retribution were overriding any sense of civility.

Vance Mitchell, Lord Hollensworth, looked out of place in the drawing room. Several inches taller than Fayne, he had a physique that was the product of the heavy labor his lands demanded of him. Heavily muscled, his wide shoulders appeared to stretch the fabric of his coat beyond its capacity. His face was just as harsh and square as his imposing figure. He did not bother to remove his hat and tufts of pale blond hair stuck out like hay over his ears. The baron's hazel eyes narrowed menacingly on Fayne.

"Do not be coy, Carlisle," Hollensworth snarled, spittle flying in numerous directions. "Did you think that once I learned of your misdeeds that I would ignore the insult you dealt my family?"

Fayne was not surprised by the baron's presence. In fact, he had expected the man sooner. That was one of the distinct disadvantages of living in the country. One was always behind on news. How fortunate for Hollensworth that Fayne was in the mood to oblige him in a public confrontation. "What was insulting, Hollensworth, was your brother's wretched play at the tables. I did him a favor by taking his money."

Like his older brother, Hart Mitchell had never quite fit in among his peers. Embittered that his tardy birth had cheated him out of the barony, Mitchell had rejected his brother's offer to help him oversee the family's lands and tried to make his fortune at the gaming tables. Unfortunately, Mitchell's play was as reckless as the life he had chosen for himself. He had a tendency to lose heavily, and in desperation the man had tried his hand at cheating. Another sign of his abysmal luck was the fact that he had chosen Fayne's table to employ his underhanded tricks.

"In the future, it might be prudent for you to cut Mitchell's funds off, Hollensworth. It might keep him from tossing away the family fortune on games of chance," Fayne said calmly, feeling no remorse for not only claiming

Mitchell's purse and his town house, but also two of the man's best horses. All in all, Fayne had been rather generous. Another gentleman would have called the sharper out.

The suggestion enraged the baron. He tried to lunge at Fayne, but Cadd, Everod, and Ramscar held him back. "It's too late, you merciless blackguard! Hart is dead!" Hollensworth squirmed against the restraining hands holding him in place. "You killed him!"

Everyone in the room quieted as the accusation rang in Fayne's ears.

"The only killings I have done recently were at the card table," Fayne said, disregarding the unease settling in his gut. "The last time I saw your brother, he looked quite fit when he rose and left the game. I can procure witnesses testifying to that fact." He recalled the night he had trounced Mitchell at cards vividly. It was the same night he had been summoned to the family's town house and learned that his father was dead.

"He may not have died by your hand, Carlisle," the baron said, his stark face etched with grief and rage too profound to be feigned. "Nonetheless, you are responsible for his death. You lured him into deep play and it cost him everything. After Hart left you, he returned home and drew the merciless edge of a straight razor across his throat."

Mitchell was dead? Fayne had spent the past week in a blurry haze of grief and sleeplessness and if anyone had mentioned Mitchell's death in passing, he doubted he would have paid attention. Fayne lived in a profligate sphere where fortunes were won or lost every day on the turn of a single card. The losers faded away, but Fayne had never known anyone desperate enough to take his own life over a reversal of fortune. "I did not know," he said solemnly. "I regret your loss, Hollens—"

"Liar!" the man bellowed and lunged at Fayne. The baron's revelation had shocked everyone present, including

the gentlemen restraining him. He broke free of the hands
holding him back and charged at Fayne like an enraged bull.

Women shrieked and dashed to the opposite side of the
room as Fayne sidestepped his attacker. "Your brother was
a regular at the gaming hells." He danced backward into
the center of the room, avoiding Hollensworth's frenzied
swing. "And a cheat. It was a matter of time before someone spilled his blood."

Fayne regretted his words before he finished uttering
them.

An inhuman sound of anguish erupted from Hollensworth. His hazel eyes burned with hatred, promising
retribution. Ramscar seized the baron by his upper arm in a
futile attempt to stop him. The earl's reward for helping
his friend was a brutal uppercut to his jaw. Ramscar fell to
the floor without making a sound. Hollensworth rushed at
Fayne again, before the others tried to intercede.

Fayne grunted as the man's head plowed into his stomach. The momentum of Hollensworth's charge sent him
staggering backward. Time seemed to slow down for him,
which Fayne considered a very bad sign. As he fell, his
eyes locked onto his sister's pale, beautiful face. Fayre
stood in the doorway as her husband and several others
rushed forward to rescue him from his attacker.

His right elbow connected with something solid, sending
sharp pain up his arm. Shock whitened his face at the sound
of canvas ripping. With Hollensworth doing his damnedest
to pound Fayne's face into mush, the pair rended the duke's
portrait and staggered through the large .wooden frame.
Screams and the harsh cracks of the wood bracing shattering filled the air. Fayne and Hollensworth struck the floor in
a tangled heap.

The frame toppled over in the opposite direction.

Fayne was positive his back was broken. The baron, on
the other hand, was barely stunned by their fall. He slammed

his fist into Fayne's jaw once before his brother-in-law and Cadd dragged the baron off. Gingerly, Fayne touched the side of his face. Hollensworth had a fist like a sledgehammer.

He tasted blood as he sat up. A dozen faces were hovering over him, but he could not make sense of what anyone was saying. He waved everyone away. Christ, his jaw ached. It was damned humiliating to be laid flat by a single punch. As he staggered to his feet, several things became apparent. First, Hollensworth was not going to rest until he attained the justice he craved. Secondly, the duchess was going to have an apoplectic fit when she learned of what had transpired in the drawing room. Outside the drawing room, he heard his mother screech his full name. Fayne winced. Death by Hollensworth's hand was trivial in comparison to facing the duchess's ensuing wrath.

CHAPTER TWO

Two weeks later . . .

"I underestimated you, Lady Kilby," Teague Pethum, Viscount Darknell, said as he extended his hand to his two female companions, Lady Kilby Fitchwolf and Lady Lyssa Nunnick, silently inviting them to descend from their carriage. "After your compromising encounter with the Duke of Solitea, I thought your chaperone, Lady Quennell, would have had the sense to bundle you off to the safety of Ealkin, or at the very least, placed locks on the outer door to your bedchamber and bars on the windows to keep the gentlemen of the *ton* safe from your deadly wiles."

Lady Kilby slipped her hand into his, and stepped down from the carriage with his assistance. "Very charming, my lord," Lady Kilby said dryly, glancing about to see if anyone had overheard the viscount's taunting comments. "So forceful. So overtly vocal." She removed her hand from his arm and stepped out of reach. "I vow, a gentleman's oath is as stalwart as dry rot. Lyssa, remind me to have my tongue cut out if I ever contemplate revealing something in confidence to our dear friend Lord Darknell again."

Still seated in the carriage, Lady Lyssa Nunnick lifted her brows in consternation. "Really, Darknell, I expect better conduct from you. Can you not see how upsetting this subject is for our friend?"

"I was merely teasing, Fitchwolf," Lord Darknell said, coming toward Kilby only to be halted by her raised hand. He muttered an oath when she turned her head away in dismissal. "Be reasonable. No one heard me. There is no reason to fuss in this manner."

In her heart, Kilby knew the viscount meant no malice and was merely jesting. However, she could not imagine a time when she would view the fact that the Duke of Solitea had collapsed and died on the floor of her boudoir of an apparent heart attack as something humorous. She could hardly blame the man for dying, but his unexpected death was placing all her carefully thought-out plans in jeopardy. Plans she had begun outlining since the night Archer had used their sister, Gypsy, to draw her out from her hiding place. He had not beaten her as she had feared. Instead, he had revealed family secrets that almost nine months later she still could not believe.

"You are not my equal, Kilby," Archer told her, furious that she refused to recognize his authority. "Hell, you are not even my sister."

"Half," Kilby spat at him, angry with her parents for dying and leaving her and Gypsy in Archer's merciless custody. "We share a father, though I will admit when you are like this, I cannot see the connection."

Archer startled her by grabbing her and hauling her indecently close. She tilted her head back, as his lips curved into an ominous smile. "That is because, my darling Kilby, there is no connection. My father, Lord Nipping, was not your sire."

Kilby placed both of her palms on his chest and shoved

Archer away. He stumbled back, laughing at the shock and denial her pallid features revealed. "I knew you could be cruel, brother. The depths to which you have plummeted almost have me wishing it were true."

"There are letters, Kilby. I came across them while I was going through my father's papers."

"What letters?" she scoffed, not believing a word of it.

"Letters written in my stepmother's handwriting. I will credit her with being subtle in her revelations, but the truth is there for anyone who looks for it. Your mother was a lying whore. I do not know who sired you, but it wasn't my father."

Since the night of Archer's cruel revelation, Kilby had been counting the days until she could escape her brother's tyrannical guardianship. That night he had gleefully outlined his plans for her, and her fate was a grim one. Archer had confessed that he had developed an unnatural affection for Kilby. The thought of her brother lusting for a carnal union between them was utterly revolting. Nevertheless, she now understood why Archer had eagerly accepted the dissolution of any blood tie between them. While polite society might view his actions as inappropriate, bedding his stepmother's natural daughter was not a sin. There was no doubt in Kilby's mind that Archer would have dragged her into his bed that night. His disturbing, hungry gaze had revealed that much.

Fortunately, for her sake, his greed for power and money tempered his lust for her. Archer was cunning. He knew that by marrying Kilby off to a gentleman of his choosing, he would broaden his influence in society and fill his diminishing wherewithal. This handpicked gentleman would be someone Archer could use and control, a man who would readily yield his lawful place in his wife's bed to Archer. Kilby could not believe there was a man in England who would willingly allow himself to be cuckolded. Archer assured her that such men existed. He just had to be patient until the proper pawn for his ambitious plans could be found.

It was the impromptu visit of Pridwyn Hasp, Viscountess Quennell, to Ealkin that gave Kilby the first glimmer of hope that Archer's plans could be thwarted. A dear friend of her parents, Lady Quennell, or Priddy to her closest friends, had deduced in a matter of hours of observing the siblings together that Archer's keen interest in his sister was unsettling. Even if there had been an opportunity to speak openly to the viscountess, Kilby doubted she would have revealed to the lady the full extent of Archer's cruelty and guile. Just as her brother had anticipated, pride and shame stilled her tongue. If Archer had spoken the truth, and Lord Nipping was not her father, Kilby was not about to betray her mother by publicly revealing the deception.

Wholly confident in his control over Kilby, Archer arrogantly revealed to Priddy a polite version of his future marriage ambitions for his sister. Carefully watching the viscountess's expression, Kilby realized before her brother that he had made a slight miscalculation by boasting of his plans to Priddy. As a dear friend of both Lord and Lady Nipping, the viscountess naturally insisted on helping him launch Kilby into polite society. Archer tried to refuse her generous offer; however, the older woman turned a deaf ear to his excuses. If Archer wanted his sister to marry, Lady Quennell thought it was imperative that Kilby spend the season in London. She even offered to act as Kilby's chaperone and guide. Childless herself, the forty-five-year-old widow felt it was her duty to do so, since Lord and Lady Nipping could not.

It was apparent to Kilby that her brother was furious at Lady Quennell's well-meaning interference. Even so, he could not think of a polite way to refuse the offer. Reluctantly, Archer agreed that a season in town would benefit his sheltered sister.

Kilby was by no means the victor in the affair. Although Lady Quennell had masterfully outmaneuvered Archer, he was confident that he still had control over his defiant sister. Gypsy was his guarantee that Kilby would return to Ealkin once she had gained the cultured polish the viscountess maintained a lady required.

Months later, while they traveled to London, the viscountess had confessed her lack of confidence in Archer's ability to find a suitable husband for his sister. What suspicions Priddy had, she kept to herself. Still, Kilby saw her own private fears about Archer grimly reflected in the older woman's light blue eyes. Lady Quennell cheerfully promised to dedicate herself to the task of marrying Kilby off without Archer's meddling assistance. The viscountess had predicted that by the end of the season, Kilby would not be returning to Ealkin.

Everything had been going so well in London. That was, until the Duke of Solitea had literally dropped dead at her feet. Kilby was grateful that Priddy had not sent her back to Archer. Regardless, the poor woman had been despondent since she had been apprised of the duke's death. If the *ton* learned the details of the duke's death, any hopes of finding Kilby a husband this season were ruined. In a bold move to thwart the ensuing scandal, Lady Quennell had called on the Carlisle family the night the duke had died. She had managed to convince the grieving family that it was in everyone's best interest that the specifics of the Duke of Solitea's death remain secret. Whether or not it was intentional, a rumor began circulating through London's drawing rooms and ballrooms that the duke had died after visiting his mistress. Kilby had learned such speculation was not unfounded because the Duke of Solitea was renowned for having a string of mistresses. How was she supposed to know the man had been an incorrigible rake? Several names were being bandied about the *ton* as being that of the mysterious lady. Mercifully, her name was not mentioned at all.

She had told Lyssa and Darknell the truth. How could she not, when Priddy had refused to discuss the subject again, and Kilby was nigh bursting with anxiety over the duke's death? Her friends were trustworthy. They had been sharing confidences with one another for years. Her vexation with Lord Darknell would eventually wane. At the moment, his teasing comments had Kilby regretting that she had made him privy to her secrets. *He will not tell anyone the truth,* she thought. It was just unlike him to be so provoking.

She could not resist snapping at Darknell for his insensitivity. "You know there is nothing safe about Ealkin these days. Priddy understands this. I thought you did as well, my lord. Our friendship has spanned years and yet you seem to have suffered no ill effects from it." His comment about her possessing deadly wiles stung. She doubted she could deliberately flirt with a gentleman without collapsing into a fit of giggles at the absurdity of it all.

"So it would appear," Darknell said enigmatically, causing Kilby to gnash her teeth in agitation. His brows lifted in bemusement when Kilby stomped a few steps away from him. Prudently, deciding not to aggravate the lady further, the viscount turned his charming smile on Lyssa. "So what do you have to say about this business, Nunn?"

Lady Lyssa, or Nunn as her friends affectionately called her, was the daughter of the Duke and Duchess of Wildon. The first thing everyone noticed about her was that she was remarkably tall for a woman. Standing next to Lord Darknell, Kilby observed the viscount was taller barely by two inches.

While Kilby viewed Lyssa's height as an asset, her friend did not. She felt her height enhanced the illusion of a boyish figure, rather than the ideal feminine frame Lyssa often dreamed of. She had a comely face with pale blue eyes, straight teeth, and long, wavy hair the color of wheat. At nineteen, Lyssa was being pressured by her family to make an advantageous match this season. Kilby had little doubt Lyssa would receive several offers for her hand in marriage before the season had ended. Though, for her friend's sake, Kilby prayed the gentlemen seeking Lyssa's affections treasured her friend as highly as her family's connections.

The pair strolled closer to her so their private conversation could not be overheard. "I think that if you persist in taunting Kilby, you will get a deserving poke in the eye for your troubles," Lyssa said, moving away from the viscount and aligning herself with her friend. "What troubles you, Darknell? Do not tell me that you believe Kilby invited that old man up to her bedchamber?"

Darknell shifted his dark brown gaze from Lyssa to Kilby. His appraisal was too frank and contemplative for her liking. Her fingers tightened around her parasol. While the viscount might deserve a crack in the head with her parasol, she resisted the urge for violence. After all, she had begged him to join them at the rural fair east of London for a practical reason. She and Lyssa needed him to act as their escort and protector. It was not prudent for two gently reared ladies to walk about a common fair unescorted.

"No," Darknell said a few seconds later. "The Duke of Solitea had a nefarious reputation with the ladies; a fact I would have gladly shared with you, my lady, had you seen fit to reveal your plans to meet the gentleman in private."

Kilby cringed at his mild rebuke. Darknell made her sound like a brainless twit. Well, he was wrong! She would be the first to admit she was out of her element in London. Unlike her friends' families, her parents had shielded her from the boisterous town life. Whenever she had begged her father to permit her to join him on one of his trips to

London, he had refused her request. He promptly would then lecture her on the town's decadence and the subtle corruption of a person's moral character. She had grown up believing London was nothing more than a hideous cesspool of villains. Archer's callous behavior had only reinforced the impression.

It was not until she had been introduced to Lyssa at one of her parents' summer gatherings that she had been given a kinder description of the sights and delights the town offered. Since then, she had longed for a chance to visit London. The fight she had had with Archer and his angry revelations had only fueled her desire.

Archer's announcement had planted the insidious seeds of doubt within Kilby about her father. A part of her believed her brother was distorting the truth for his own twisted aims. Though he had been adamant that the letters remain in his possession, he had allowed her to read several of the more incriminating ones. It was only then Kilby had to concede that her mother had indeed been keeping a few secrets. She also knew the answers she sought could be found in London. Luckily, with Priddy's backing, she was finally here. Kilby was not about to let anyone or anything, including her own naïveté, ruin her chance to remain in town.

She twisted her parasol in agitation. Darknell was not going to drop the subject of the duke until she had to his satisfaction suffered properly for her sins. "I had not heard one unkind word about the Duke of Solitea. He seemed charming and solicitous, unlike other gentlemen of the *ton*," Kilby said, feeling defensive because flattery and a handsome face had beguiled her. "I was so grateful he was willing to discuss my parents with me, I did not question his motives when he suggested an intimate setting for our discussion. Since I do not want Priddy or anyone else to learn that I have been prying into my parents' past, his request for privacy made sense."

"Little girl, the man had every intention of bedding
you," Darknell said bluntly. "Did you have to simplify his
intent by inviting him up to your bedchamber?"

Kilby responded with a gimlet stare. She loved the man
dearly, but honestly, if he continued to remind her of her
idiocy, she was not going to be responsible for her actions.
"How many times do I have to tell you? I did not invite him
up to my bedchamber. The duke simply followed me."

Lyssa gave Kilby a sympathetic pat on her arm. "You
must have been terrified when you realized he had followed
you upstairs."

"Not really," Kilby admitted to her friends. "I thought
perhaps the poor man was confused."

Darknell snorted. "Fitchwolf," he said with affection.
"You need a keeper."

Kilby felt her cheeks color at his remark. Without a word,
she headed for the heart of the fair, not caring if Darknell
followed. Naturally, he did and Lyssa was a step behind him.
The viscount had always taken his job as their escort seriously. A little feminine temper would not dissuade him.

"I will remind you, the Duke of Solitea remained a gentleman to the end," Kilby said curtly, and then winced at her
poor choice of words. She was also lying. No one needed to
know the duke had succeeded in kissing her on the lips. She
was already in enough trouble.

"You can thank the specter of death for that small bless-
ing," Darknell shot back. He grabbed her arm, slowing her
down to a reasonable pace.

"Spare us," Lyssa muttered under her breath as she caught
up with them. She had often stepped between them in the
past when Kilby and Darknell argued.

Darknell had been insufferable from the second he had
approached their carriage. Kilby could not fathom why the
man persisted in baiting her. "I think we can all agree, the
duke paid dearly for his errors. Let him rest in peace."

"I suggest we talk about something else," Lyssa said.

"Agreed," seconded Kilby, smiling at her friend in gratitude.

The viscount released his grip on Kilby and placed his hands behind his back as they walked for a minute in silence. "Fine. I will begin. Who is your next victim, Lady Kilby?"

The fact he was using her title proved Darknell was more than a little perturbed with her. She was not going to let him goad her. "Good heavens, you make it sound like I killed the duke."

"I know you did not. Nevertheless, it is what the Carlisles are thinking," he said mildly.

Her mouth parted in astonishment. "That is ridiculous! Even the surgeon who arrived at the house agreed that the man died of natural causes."

"Fitchwolf, you are such an innocent." He sighed. "I speak of *la petite mort,* or the little death," Darknell explained, as if he were instructing a child. "I wager the entire Carlisle family believes Solitea died while pumping himself dry between your soft thighs."

Both ladies gasped at the viscount's deliberate vulgarity. Darknell's crude version of events sickened her. Kilby absently rubbed her irritated stomach. Priddy had warned her that while the duke's family had agreed the circumstances leading up to the duke's death were best kept secret, the family's private speculation about the duke's presence was beyond their control. The surgeon and the servants had been paid generously for their silence. Nevertheless, what if they talked? And what of the duke's family? Good heavens, the man had been married. Did the entire Carlisle family truly believe she had been the duke's mistress? Oh, how they must despise her!

"I am certain not everyone in the Carlisle family believes you were the duke's mistress. Do you not agree, my lord?" Lyssa asked, interrupting the direction of Kilby's distressing thoughts. Her friend was frowning at the viscount, daring him to disagree.

"Not all," Darknell conceded. His gaze softened as he noted the worried expression on Kilby's face. "You are a newcomer to polite society. Some will immediately despise you for your beauty, while others will long to claim you for their own. If the Carlisles or the servants break their oath of secrecy, your brief connection to the duke will make you a target for the gossips. Lady Quennell knows this. Surely it would be a kinder recourse if you left London, and returned next season. By then, the Carlisles will have forgotten your part in the duke's death."

"No, you are wrong," Kilby said abruptly. Darknell's frankness angered her, but she realized that he spoke out of concern. He did not think she was strong enough to face the scrutiny of the *ton* and the cruelty of the outspoken. "The Carlisles gain nothing in breaking their word. They will keep our secret. Priddy believes we can brazen this out, and I trust her judgment. Besides, I did nothing *wrong*!"

She shook her head. "Archer was manipulated by Priddy into granting his approval for this trip. If he learns that I am seeking a husband beyond his influence or, God forbid, the intimate details of the duke's death, he will drag me from London by my hair and lock me away until I am too old to care. I was told by a reliable source that a certain gentleman who knew my mother would likely be found here this afternoon. All I desire is an introduction. I beg of you, will you help me?"

The viscount stared directly into Kilby's eyes, clearly weighing the repercussions of his refusal. Darknell was a good man. He was intelligent, honorable, and above all fair. How could he refuse her?

Darknell glanced away from her pleading expression, and breathed out an exaggerated sigh. "No."

"You know, most gentlemen choose a discreet locale when engaging in a duel," Ramscar said as Fayne approached him. He leaned against the side of the phaeton and crossed his arms. "A rural fair is neither discreet nor practical when you intend to kill or maim another gentleman."

Fayne shot his friend a disgruntled look. When had his friend adopted a few scruples? His reasons for sending Hollensworth an invitation to join them at the fair had nothing to do with maiming or killing. The truth was slightly more complicated.

"As usual, I cannot fault your logic, Ram. How fortunate for me that I have no intention of engaging anyone in a duel this afternoon." Fayne frowned at his choice of words. "At least that was my original plan," he amended, as he walked around to the rear of the phaeton and knelt down to unlock the long, narrow wooden box that was strapped to a narrow shelf at the back.

Ramscar trailed after him. "Hollensworth might think otherwise."

Fayne snickered as he jiggled the key in the lock. Hollensworth wanted him dead. Since the evening of the ball, it had become apparent the baron was not particular about how he accomplished his goal. Instead of waiting for an ambush, Fayne had decided to give the man a chance to vent his rage and injustice against the man he believed stole his brother's will to live.

"The problem is Hollensworth is *not* thinking," Fayne argued. The baron's attack in front of witnesses the night of the ball hinted at the man's instability. "Before his brother's death, I had credited the man with possessing an equable disposition. Lately, his actions seem akin to a madman's."

He opened the box and withdrew a long, padded bundle. Tucking it under his arm, Fayne reached into the box again and retrieved a saber sheathed in a leather scabbard. He flung the sword hilt first at his friend who nimbly caught it. If all went according to his plan, Fayne would not need the weapon. Even so, he had no intention of giving Hollensworth any advantage.

Rising from his crouched position, he began unwrapping the layers of coarse gray wool that protected the half-dozen loose sticks no thicker than his thumb. Made of ash, each rod was unpeeled and thirty-five inches in length. To prevent the freshly cut sticks from drying out, one of the servants had bound the ends with wet linen. Once the rod was inserted into a pot or a large wicker basket that served as the hilt, he had a useful weapon for "cudgel play" or backswording.

As a boy, he had practiced swordplay and self-defense with similar primitive weapons. With practice he had gradually moved on to the foil, épée, and saber to refine his deadly skills in the fighting arts. For the sake of protection, Fayne still practiced with ash rods when sparring. Be that as it may, in the right hands, an ash stick could be just as lethal as a honed blade, especially if the end of the rod split during a match. He removed two wicker pots from the phaeton's box and tossed them at his friend.

Ramscar caught them and chuckled. "One might say the same about you, Solitea."

Fayne took pride in not visibly jolting at his new title. The dukedom and all its perquisites were chafing him like an ill-fitting collar. His father was the Duke of Solitea. Not him. Claiming the title bothered him more than he would ever reveal to anyone.

He discarded the woolen wrappings in the box. "Why? Because I have refused every challenge delivered by Hollensworth and his seconds? I thought myself rather tolerant considering the circumstances."

Nor was he a fool. Fayne sensed that if he had accepted the baron's challenge, the odds would have been against him that the duel would have been conducted fairly. He could just imagine Hollensworth's pistol discharging prematurely, leaving Fayne the victim of an unfortunate accident. If the baron succeeded in killing Fayne, his triumph would be short-lived. Ramscar, Cadd, and Everod would make certain of that.

"Tolerant?" Ramscar gaped at him, his expression a mixture of bemusement and exasperation. "Your father has been dead for how long? A fortnight?"

Fayne cleared his throat. "Twenty days to be precise."

Ramscar dismissed the correction with a wave of his hand. "In that time, you have spent most of those nights blinding yourself with drink."

Now his friend was being insulting. "There is a difference between drinking and being drunk, Ram. I have had the distinct pleasure of being both."

"You have been out every night since his death," his friend said, determined to speak his thoughts aloud.

His actions were hardly criminal. He rarely stayed at home in the evenings. The duke's death had not altered Fayne's habits. "You should know, since most nights you were by my side."

"Someone had to look after you," his friend retorted, unmoved by Fayne's misplaced humor. "Regardless, having Cadd, Everod, and me close at hand has not kept you out of trouble."

"I recovered my losses," he said stiffly. Two nights after his father had been laid to rest at Westminster Abbey, Fayne had settled down for some deep play at Moirai's Lust, a gaming hell with a well-earned reputation for its tantalizingly plump purses and the notorious losses incurred by many of the establishment's noble patrons. A night of drinking and careless betting had cost Fayne what most considered a staggering fortune. Indifferent, he had returned to the gaming hell the following evening. By morning he had recouped his losses and had added a hundred thousand pounds to it. "My actions hardly qualify as reprehensible. In fact, I recall a night or two when your losses hurt worse than your sore head the next morning."

"Carlisle," Ramscar said, briefly forgetting Fayne's new title. The lapse of protocol hinted at the extent of his concern. "Your behavior of late has been oddly volatile, even by your standards. You have refused Hollensworth's challenges, and yet you have fought four duels in the past eight days over trivial affairs."

Ah, this was the source of his friend's upset. Ramscar's father had died from a wound he had acquired while dueling. Although the man had fought several duels himself, it was not a resolution he accepted lightly. For that reason alone, Fayne had asked Cadd and Everod to be his seconds.

"The gentlemen who issued the challenges hardly thought them trivial," Fayne said mildly. He selected one of the ash rods and extended it outward, checking the length for imperfections. Finding it acceptable, Fayne switched it for another.

"Lord Pengree accused you of kicking his favorite hound."

Ramscar had been listening to the gossips. "Utterly false. The bitch attempted to urinate on my boot. I simply encouraged her to move." He had not believed the audacity of the dog or her owner for calling him out over the matter. Pengree was lucky Fayne had decided before their appointment to shoot over the man's shoulder instead of shooting his offensive animal.

"And what of Mr. Crynes? What was his transgression?"

"Crynes is a coward and an opportunist. He and I have

been tossing veiled insults back and forth for years. It is no secret that I have challenged him in the past. Instead of facing me on a dew-drenched common, he has always sent his seconds with his apologies. When he learned that I had been refusing Hollensworth's challenges, Crynes erroneously interpreted my refusal as a sign of weakness and leaped at the chance to defeat me."

"The bullet the surgeon removed from Crynes's thigh should discourage him from making the same mistake again." Ramscar seized the stick, stilling Fayne's movements. "And Mr. Nicout?"

"Like Crynes, Nicout had hopes of revenging himself over a past misdeed. He has never forgiven me for claiming his prized stallion in order to settle an old debt between us."

Ramscar scowled in puzzlement. "I recall the incident. The bargain was fair and not uncommon."

"True. My offense was not my claim on the stallion, but in selling the animal immediately at Tats. Nicout felt my haste in ridding myself of the beast was an insult to his refined taste in horseflesh."

There was a flash of humor in Ramscar's gaze. "I assume he was not aware of the outcome of your exchange with Crynes?"

Nicout had arrived at their appointment, too confident in the outcome. Fayne had not even bothered trying to persuade him to reconsider. "If he was unconvinced, I am certain the festering hole in his shoulder is proof that my aim is as accurate as my assessment of his inferior taste in horseflesh." Seconds after Fayne had discharged his pistol, the man had dropped to the ground and howled in agony. Nicout's downfall had been a pitiful sight.

His friend sighed. "I suppose Lord Burlton's reasons for challenging you were just as ridiculous?"

Fayne suddenly grinned, revealing a slight dimple in his

left cheek. "Well, actually Burlton had every right to be a trifle upset with me for bedding his sister. He claimed I had seduced an innocent and demanded satisfaction if I did not marry the chit."

"Not likely," the earl said grimly, outraged on his friend's behalf. "You abhor dallying with innocents and the sticky entanglements of their virginity. I assume the lady was not the innocent Lord Burlton claimed?"

Ramscar was correct. Fayne avoided young virgins like other gentlemen shunned dockside whores. Fortunately, the dear lady had confessed her experience in carnal matters when he had made it clear that her virtue held no appeal to him. The remainder of the evening he had spent with Miss Burlton had been exhausting and exceedingly pleasurable. "Thankfully, no. It was only later that I learned he had made similar demands of two other gents. Afterward, I was only too happy to shoot him."

"Rightly so," his friend agreed with vehemence. "Did you hit him in the shoulder or the leg?"

Fayne gestured with his hands, conveying his regret. "My aim was a bit high. The bullet grazed his head. I have been assured he will make a full recovery."

"This business with Hollensworth has placed you in a vulnerable position. Until you face him, every gentleman who has felt slighted by you will be tempted to call you out."

This was precisely why Fayne had hoped his encounter with the baron would end the hostility between them. Nevertheless, he was not squeamish about shooting idiots if they provoked him. The duchess and his sister, on the other hand, had some peculiar reservations about how he resolved his conflicts. Fayne doubted he would ever comprehend the female mind.

"If this current trend continues, a dawn appointment with me might become as coveted as a voucher for Almack's."

"How can you make light of the situation, Carlisle? Hollensworth is running all over London, vowing to spill your blood, and you have a dozen or more fools who are vying for a chance to precede him since you keep agreeing to these ridiculous duels."

"Perhaps I am fated to die one morning on the commons. The Solitea men are known for their dramatic demises. Just ask my father," he quipped, his humor laced with bitterness. "Oh, I forgot. You cannot." Fayne moved away from Ramscar. He did not want to talk about his father with anyone. A part of him wondered if he would ever be able to think of the duke without feeling the rending pain beneath his breast.

Even now, his father's deep voice resonated in his head:

"The males of our family are cursed, Tem. The Solitea name will grant your wildest desires. The title and the fortune backing it gives you power. Men will despise you for it. Countless women will beg you to fuck them in hopes of securing a portion of it for themselves. But such good fortune exacts a hefty price. Enjoy the bounty and sire your heir while you can, my son, because no Carlisle male who assumes the Duke of Solitea title lives long enough to count the silver in his hair."

His father had often mentioned what many had called the Solitea curse. The duke had not been a superstitious man, but apparently he believed the Carlisle males were cursed. While many might have accused him of squandering his wealth and talents on the frivolous, his father had lived his life on his own terms. At age fifty-four, he had lived longer than most of the heirs to the dukedom. He had even collected a full head of silver hair that he claimed no other male in the family had achieved.

The duke's longevity had supported Fayne's personal belief that there was no Solitea curse. Over the years, he had reasoned out that the Carlisle males were the victims of their own recklessness. The notion of a curse excused the family for generations of self-indulgence and excess. This knowledge did not mean that Fayne considered himself any better than his predecessors. He could be selfish, obsessed, and violent when provoked, and easily distracted by the superficial pleasures of vice and sin. His temperament had been cast at birth and encouraged by his family. Fayne had grown up daring death to claim him before his time.

Ramscar caught up with him. "This is about the curse, is it not?" The warning in Fayne's lethal glance sideways made him hesitate before he asked, "I thought you viewed the Solitea curse as histrionic prattle?"

Fayne halted and tapped the length of the one of the ash rods against his shoulder in agitation. "I do. I always have."

"Then why are you behaving slightly more cracked than I usually credit your volatile nature?" his friend demanded, his irritation showing. "The risks you've been taking by accepting those duels—" He gestured broadly at the pedestrians and tents around them. "And now this elaborate staging of a fight with Hollensworth, when you vowed never to accept his challenge."

"I have no intention of dueling a gentleman grieving his brother's suicide," Fayne said plainly.

"So you say," Ramscar shouted back. "And yet you are preparing to face the man with a weapon in your hands."

"Consider it merely a demonstration of skill."

"Then you are undeniably mad. The second Hollensworth has a stick in his grasp, he will do his best to crack open your skull."

Fayne would have been disappointed if the man did not give it his best effort. "Thank you, my friend, for your confidence in my skill in the fighting arts. As it happens, I plan on walking away from this match relatively unscathed."

The earl did not seem to hear him. "I vow, your actions of late seem to be taunting death itself."

"Oh, without a doubt, Hollensworth and Death will both try to leave their mark," Fayne said, his clear green eyes revealing his unquestionably earnest conviction that he was speaking the truth. "Unfortunately for them, they will both fail this day. I am not ready to die."

CHAPTER THREE

"Accept the inevitable, Lord Darknell, and leave us," Kilby said in chilling tones. "Your presence is no longer required." She tilted her chin defiantly and sniffed in disdain. "Or desired."

She was also lying, not that she foolishly planned on revealing such a weakness to the viscount. *Oh, the impertinence of the man!* How could he refuse such a small request? But he had, blast him. Instead of giving up and returning to her carriage as Darknell had expected, Kilby had seized Lyssa by the wrist and practically dragged the poor woman through the crowd while she sought out Lord Ursgate.

Kilby was not acquainted with the baron. Her interest in the gentleman was purely speculative. She had noted his name in one of her mother's letters before Archer had snatched the papers from her grasp.

Was the man her father?

Kilby muttered a very unladylike expletive. She was chasing a phantom. This was ludicrous. She had had a father.

A wonderful, loving father! If Archer's plan was to torment her, he was far more brilliant than she had credited him.

Nonetheless, they were already here. What harm could be done if she just took a look at the gentleman?

It had been Lord Ordish who had discreetly pointed the gentleman out to her one evening, when she had casually mentioned that he had been acquainted with her mother. If the earl had been curious about her interest in Lord Ursgate, he had been too polite to ask. Besides, it was hardly a secret that Lady Quennell was seeking a husband for her. Kilby was immensely grateful for the earl's assistance—*unlike* a certain gentleman whose name she refused to utter.

"Damn it all, Fitchwolf!" Darknell cursed and charged up behind them. "Be sensible. This is for your own good."

Breathless, Lyssa was also beginning to tire of their fierce pace. Twisting and testing Kilby's firm grip on her wrist, she said, "I was not aware you had signed us up for a race, Kilby. For the next one, I am insisting on a horse."

Full of remorse, Kilby halted abruptly, face pinched with concern. "Forgive me, Nunn. It is not fair that I have placed you in the middle of this. I just—"

Darknell grabbed hold of Lyssa's free arm to ensure they would not escape again. He glared at Kilby. "Stubborn chit! Put aside your harebrained notions for once, and use the good sense I know you possess." He took a deep breath and tried to lessen the anger in his voice. "You and Nunn cannot be traipsing through the fairgrounds unescorted. There are undesirable aspects to these amusements that only invite trouble."

"I had an escort," Kilby snapped, tugging Lyssa closer to her side. "A pity he turned out to be an unsympathetic, uncompromising boor!"

"Kilby!" exclaimed Lyssa, shocked by her friend's anger. Neither Kilby nor Darknell seemed inclined to back down, leaving Lyssa torn over her allegiance.

The viscount tugged, jerking Lyssa a step closer to him. "What has happened to you, Fitchwolf? You have shown me nothing but teeth and claws since your arrival in London." His gaze swept over her, seeking the answers in her rebellious expression. "These answers you seek about your mother's past are endangering your reputation and future, Lady Kilby. At what cost, I ask you? I doubt you will find comfort in the truth."

Pride had her straightening her spine. Darknell knew where to twist the knife. Had not the fear and uncertainty of her futile plight allowed similar traitorous thoughts to undermine her plans? She silently cursed him for speaking her fears aloud. "My lord, you have made your feelings on the subject quite clear. Pray do not trouble yourself further on my account. You are free to do as you please," she said loftily, and tugged on her friend's arm.

"Free? How can I be free?" Darknell pulled, sending Lyssa careening into his side.

Lyssa emitted a surprised squeak of pain. "Cease, both of you!" Shaking off their grips, she rubbed her abused limbs. She used the opportunity to frown at both of them. "If you want to continue arguing, you will kindly do it without me between you."

"Lyssa—" Kilby began, at a loss for words for her thoughtless actions.

The viscount grimaced, his lips forming a thin line of tension. "Forgive us, Nunn. Neither one of us was thinking about you."

"Evidently," Lyssa said tartly, causing both her friends to wince. "Now that I have your attention, I shall offer my opinion on the subject."

Kilby was prepared to accept Lyssa's dictates, since she felt guilty. As her lips parted, a gentleman caught her attention. It was Lord Ursgate! She had only glimpsed him fleetingly from a distance, but he aptly fit Lord Ordish's description as "a short, brown-haired man whose waist displayed his immense wealth." She was certain she had found her quarry. Lord Ursgate was engaged in an intense conversation with another gentleman. Leaning heavily on his walking stick, the baron and his companion were heading east.

Excited, she clutched Lyssa's arm. "Oh, Lyssa. It is him! We need to follow him." Kilby started after Lord Ursgate. Lord Ordish had been the one who had suggested shyly that if she desired an accidental encounter with the baron beyond the scrutiny of the ballroom, she should seek him out at the fair. According to the earl, Lord Ursgate enjoyed wagering on sporting events, and the baron made a habit of visiting the local fairs for pugilist matches.

Kilby glanced to her left and realized Lyssa was not beside her. Turning back, she noted her friends had not moved. "Lyssa, if we tarry, we might lose him." She did not bother addressing Darknell since he was being so obstinate.

Lyssa took a step forward, and then stopped. She cast a wary glance at Darknell. "Kilby, I know we discussed this earlier in the carriage; nonetheless, do you think it is prudent to follow Lord Ursgate? You have to admit the meeting with the Duke of Solitea ended disastrously. Besides, Mama says Lord Ursgate is a disreputable gentleman. She has even forbidden me to dance with him."

"If you refuse to heed my advice," Lord Darknell implored, standing solidly behind Lyssa, "perhaps it would do you well to listen to Nunn."

Underneath her defiant façade, Kilby knew her friends were right. Still, she could not stem her unreasonable feelings of betrayal. Neither one of them seemed to understand what her parents' unexpected deaths had cost her. Archer's unsavory plans had brought her to London in desperation of finding a husband who could protect her and Gypsy. Never once had she dreamed of gaining a husband in such a hasty, unromantic fashion! As for her attempts to dig into her mother's past, Darknell and Lyssa might view it as a fool's errand; however, she had to know whether or not the Marquess of Nipping was truly her father. Gypsy's welfare was at stake. Her thoughts returned to that horrible night.

"I despise you," Kilby said, circling around the man she had always considered her brother. She was careful to keep out of reach.

Archer had the audacity to laugh at her heartfelt declaration. "I have no doubt. However, mark my words, Kilby. Earn my displeasure and sweet Gypsy will suffer for your defiance."

Kilby went cold at his threat. "Gypsy is your sister, too, Archer."

"Then I should know what is best for our sad, little mute ghost," he said with false concern. "Cross me, and I will have Gypsy locked away in a lunatic asylum. I will do it, Kilby. Do not overestimate my affection for the girl."

No, she had no doubt that Archer would do exactly as he had promised. Ceasing her pathetic attempt to evade him, she stopped and gestured helplessly at him. "What do you want from me, Archer?"

"Offhand, this will do nicely." Without giving her a hint of his intentions, Archer lunged for her. Enclosing his hand around her neck, he pulled closer and sealed his awful promise with a brutal, punishing kiss.

Kilby shuddered in disgust, recalling how it felt to have Archer's lips pressed tightly to hers. No, her friends did not fully understand the urgency compelling her, her willingness to risk everything to prove Archer wrong and escape his tyranny. Determined to have her way, she executed a graceful curtsy. "Very well. I shall go on alone."

"Solitea, about time you made an appearance," Cadd greeted them cheerfully. "I feared you ran off to leave me and Everod to make your apologies to Hollensworth."

"Not likely," Fayne said wryly. "The pair of you would never let me live down such a disgrace."

Ramscar nodded at Cadd. "Has Everod arrived?"

"Aye," the marquess said, gesturing toward a line of carriages that circled halfway around the makeshift stage. Cupping his hand close to his mouth, he yelled, "Everod, where did you run off to? Present yourself, sir!"

Until then, Fayne had not paid much attention to the surrounding area. When he had approached the proprietor of the stage earlier, there had been very few spectators milling about. Now he estimated the number had increased to close to a hundred. There were also fifteen carriages parked nearby filled with ladies and gentlemen of the *ton*. No doubt Cadd and Everod had been spreading the news that Fayne had agreed to meet Hollensworth. Delightful. He could well imagine the lecture his mother would deliver once she learned of this latest confrontation. After his duel with Crynes, she had been sending him curt missives daily, demanding an explanation, all of which he had ignored.

"Ho, Solitea!" Everod called out, his head popping into view between the seventh and eighth carriages. "Over here, Your Grace. Several lovely devotees require an audience with you before you bash Hollensworth's skull into thick paste."

Fayne shoved the small bundle of ash sticks into Cadd's arms and went over to join Everod before his friend's boasting goaded Hollensworth into a murderous frenzy. Fayne glowered at the grinning scoundrel, who was acting rather pleased with himself. It was a pity Everod had not learned the art of discretion. The company he was keeping was proof enough.

"Lady Spryng," Fayne said, reaching for her outstretched hand and bowing gallantly over it. He released her hand. Taking up her friend's, he repeated his greeting. "Lady Silver. What a surprise." He turned slightly, giving

Everod a private glimpse of his displeasure at being lured to the side of these two particular ladies. "You have strayed far from your usual haunts this afternoon."

Velouette Whall, Countess of Spryng, and Lady Silver Meckiff were as different in appearance as they were in disposition. What they shared in common was Fayne. Everod was reacquainting him with his former mistresses. Fayne smiled politely at them, while he contemplated his friend's murder.

"Tem," Lady Spryng said huskily, using his family's affectionate abbreviation of his marquess title. "When we learned of this terrible business with Lord Hollensworth, neither Lady Silver nor I could think of anything else."

Lady Spryng was a rounded, dark-haired beauty. Her flawless dusty skin and large dark brown eyes were a charming legacy from her Spanish mother. Her mother's blood ties to the royal line had ensured a respectable match for the lady at age sixteen. The marriage had lasted four years before Lord Spryng had perished from lung fever. Loneliness had the countess yearning for someone to comfort her while she mourned her husband. Fayne had been eager to satisfy the young lady's unspoken needs.

"Ladies, there is no need to concern yourselves," Fayne assured them. "Hollensworth and I are engaging in a simple match of skills. Nothing more."

Lady Silver leaned forward, her shawl slipping out of place to reveal the generous swell of her bosom. "You are so brave, my love. Everod has told us all the sordid details about how the baron attacked you."

The daughter of an earl, Lady Silver Meckiff had been married to Colonel Perry Meckiff when she invited Fayne to share her bed. Almost six inches taller than Lady Spryng, she was blessed with the soft, curvaceous figure that Fayne generally preferred in his lovers. Lady Silver had hazel eyes that were more brown than green. She had very white skin that she was always careful to protect from the sun with veiled bonnets and parasols. Her curly hair was a luxuriant brown. It was her husband's long absences and rumored infidelities that had prompted Lady Silver to flirt outrageously with Fayne to gain his interest. They had remained lovers until her husband's return to England had ended their liaison.

"Lord Everod exaggerates the tale, I am certain," Fayne said, placing an affable hand on the viscount's shoulder and subtly squeezing. The smile on Everod's face dimmed in sincerity, the only clue to the pain Fayne was inflicting. "Now if you ladies will forgive my rudeness, I must leave you in Lord Everod's capable hands." He bowed, stepping backward to make his escape. Fayne pivoted, and headed for the stage where Cadd and Ramscar were waiting for him.

Everod caught up with him when he was barely out of earshot of the ladies. "Explain to me, Your Grace," the viscount demanded, sarcastically using his honorific. "What just happened back there?"

Absolutely nothing. If he had any sense, he would keep away from both of them. "I was polite." Fayne halted his stride, placing them halfway between his former mistresses' carriages and the stage. He did not want Ramscar and Cadd pulled into this argument. United, the three of them could be unrelenting, and he was not about to put his love life up for a majority vote.

Everod glanced at the two women they had left behind. Lady Silver waved at them. He nodded and gestured for her to be patient. "No, my friend, you were being an arse. Have you any idea what you have blithely walked away from?"

Well, having known each lady intimately, Fayne had a pretty accurate vision of what he was refusing. The realization did not improve his mood. "Everod, you are aware both of these ladies were once my mistress?"

The viscount's brow creased, revealing his puzzlement. "What does one have to do with the other?"

Fayne slapped his gloved hand against his thigh in frustration. "I have no patience for this. Hollensworth will arrive at any moment, eager for the chance to maim me, and you are concerned about who is sharing my bed this evening. Do you have any notion what has been occurring in my life, Everod?"

The viscount placed his hand on Fayne's shoulder and leaned closer. "You can have them both."

"I *have* had them both," Fayne said, rolling his eyes in disgust.

"So have I." He closed his eyes and shook his head. "Well, no, actually I have only bedded Lady Spryng," Everod amended. His random latent honesty had never ceased to bemuse his friends. Before Fayne could walk away, he tightened his hold. "*We* could have both. This evening. Two lusty ladies who want to spend the night satisfying all our desires. Do not tell me that you are not tempted."

Fayne rubbed the perspiration on his forehead with the back of his hand. Hell, he was tempted. He and his friends had shared and enjoyed women together in the past. Lady Spryng was agile and creative in bed. Lady Silver was submissive, allowing her lover to dominate and play with her body in any manner of his choosing. Everod was correct. It would be a memorable evening where he could lose himself in willing female flesh and forget his responsibilities.

Sensing Fayne was on the verge of capitulating, Everod added, "Perhaps you are not aware, but Lady Silver lost her husband over seven months ago. With a little encouragement from you, the lady is quite willing to remain in your bed beyond this one evening. Now that you are duke, I'll wager you could have them both warming your bed each night."

Fayne heard the envy in his friend's voice. Although it

was rare for a lady to refuse him, the notion of becoming his duchess enhanced his appeal with the ladies of the *ton*.

"Solitea!" Ramscar shouted and waved for him to join them. "Hollensworth has arrived!"

A tremor of nervous tension vibrated in his gut. He signaled his assent that he would join them shortly. "The baron awaits. Are you coming?"

Everod shook his head with regret. "I promised I would sit with the ladies. They will be anxious for your answer. What should I tell them?"

"Solitea!"

Hearing Ramscar call out his name again elevated his agitation. "I told you before, I do not have time to think about this."

"This isn't about thinking. It is all about taking," Everod argued. "You taking the pleasure enthusiastically offered. Just say yes. You will not regret it."

"Very well. Yes," Fayne said, though his excitement and thoughts were focused on the match with Hollensworth rather than the debauchery of an orgy.

Kilby was already regretting her brave boast to Darknell and Lyssa that she could follow Lord Ursgrate on her own. The viscount had been correct when he warned her that strolling about a fair without an escort held its own risks. Everything seemed threatening, from the curious stares of the pedestrians she passed to the vendors who called out for her to look at their wares. She did not know where Lord Ursgate was heading, but he did not seem particularly interested in any aspect of the fair.

Discreetly, studying the baron through the lace edging her parasol, Kilby could not imagine her mother befriending this gentleman or taking him as a lover. She wrinkled her nose. While his hair was dark and comparable to her own, she saw no other similarity. She silently conceded that more than nineteen years had passed since he and her mother had known each other. People change. They might have been lovers. However, Kilby doubted the man was her father.

The baron and his companion led her inadvertently to the outskirts of the fair. An impressive crowd had gathered around a stage. Some sort of event was about to commence. Lord Ordish had mentioned the baron favored wagering on sporting events.

The five shillings she handed to the man selling admission tickets a few minutes later confirmed her suspicions. Lord Ursgate was there to wager on a match. Instead of using their fists, the combatants were using singlesticks. Kilby collapsed her parasol and tucked it under her arm as she threaded her way through the crowd. She tilted her head from side to side, trying to catch a glimpse of the elusive Lord Ursgate. *This is hopeless,* she despaired. The baron had disappeared. She should admit defeat and return to the carriage where Lyssa and Darknell were waiting. They would not gloat—much.

It took mere seconds to realize that departing was impossible. A man, likely the umpire, was on the stage, calling for order so he could introduce the combatants. She had to leave. Now. Alas, there were simply too many people around her. Her pursuit of Lord Ursgate had thrown her into the very heart of the throng. Belatedly, she noticed the few women near her were not as elegantly attired as she. There were noble ladies in attendance, but they had chosen to remain in their carriages. Gritting her teeth over her blatant breach of etiquette, she decided that going back the way she came was not an option, so she pressed forward, and swiftly found herself near the stage.

The umpire called forth the first combatant, Lord Hollensworth. Kilby stilled, slightly surprised the attractive, blond-haired man on the stage was a titled gentleman. She had never attended an event like this, but she had assumed the opponents were local villagers or perhaps fighters by profession. Kilby did not know the baron, nor did she recognize any of the gentlemen or ladies sitting in the surrounding carriages. With a little luck, she might actually get through this afternoon with her reputation intact.

That cheerful thought lasted three seconds; until someone had the nerve to pinch her sharply on the backside. Kilby whirled around and glared at the men standing directly behind her. She did not trust their innocent expressions for one instant.

"The next man who pinches me will get the point of my parasol in his eye," she threatened the three men closest to her.

"Such a fierce temper, Fitchwolf," Darknell said, approaching her from the left. Lyssa was at his side. "And here we were worried about you."

Kilby was so pleased to see her friends. Giddy with relief, she gave each one a brief hug. "I knew you would not abandon me," she said, letting her resentment fade away. "I—"

"Fayne Carlisle, Duke of Solitea," the umpire yelled out over the din of the spectators. His arm arced horizontally in a grand manner, introducing Lord Hollensworth's opponent.

Kilby's mouth fell open as she recognized the man. "Him."

"Who?" Lyssa craned her neck to see who had caught her friend's interest. "Lord Ursgate?"

"No, I lost sight of him twenty minutes ago. I had already given up the chase for the day before your arrival." Kilby turned away from her friends. Incredulous, she stared up at the man on stage, raising his arms to encourage the cheers he received from the throng. This man was the old duke's heir. "*That* is the new Duke of Solitea," she said, glancing back at her friends for confirmation.

"Yes," Lyssa said, equally startled to see two gentlemen on the wooden stage.

Darknell seemed rather displeased by the young duke's presence. "If I had known of your interest, I could have arranged an introduction."

Kilby lifted her brows. If she had not been so intimately acquainted with the viscount, she might have thought he was jealous. "I do not desire an introduction. I was merely curious. After all, his father died in my arms. I have often wondered what his family thought of—well, the strange circumstances in which he died."

In truth, she was telling Darknell a tiny fib. It was not simply curiosity about the family that held her attention. It was *him*. Kilby had seen this gentleman before. It mattered little how many weeks had passed since that night. The new Duke of Solitea, like his father, was not the sort of gentleman a lady easily forgot. She had noticed him immediately when he entered the ballroom.

He was very striking in appearance. Tall, lean, with a hint of muscle in his broad shoulders, the man had entered the room as if he had claimed it for his own. There had been several other gentlemen at his side, but they were not as fascinating as the man who had intrigued her. It had been difficult not to boldly admire him. Priddy had explained that such behavior was too brazen. The viscountess had her practicing in front of a mirror for hours the discreet art of observing without being observed; the cunning and graceful use of her fan. The hours of repetition had been tedious. However, Priddy had been satisfied with the results. Kilby too saw the benefits of honing such skills. It allowed her to move through polite society, discreetly observing the gentlemen of the *ton* without overtly doing so.

It had also given her the distinct pleasure of admiring the man, who she now knew was the heir to the Solitea dukedom. She liked the way he moved as he circulated the large room speaking to various groups of people. His graceful masculine gait revealed a quiet strength with a hint of dominating arrogance. She did not particularly care for arrogant gentlemen, but she supposed the young duke could not avoid this trait. Sophistication and arrogance were in his blood.

Kilby had also been enthralled with his hair. He wore it long. The wavy length was tied neatly at his nape, but it reached the middle of his back. And what an unusual color! His hair was a thick, burnished chestnut that, even restrained, gleamed with an inner fire. Kilby had often wondered about the color of his eyes. Were they blue, black, hazel, brown, or green? Although tempted, she never strolled close enough to discover the answer.

He had watched her, too. A woman sensed when she had a man's interest. He had spent the entire evening watching her, and yet he had not approached her. How many times had they circled the ballroom that night? She had felt a pang of disappointment when he had abruptly left the ballroom and had not returned. Oh, if she had bothered to point him out, Priddy would have eagerly made the appropriate introductions. Despite her interest, Kilby had refrained. The heir to a dukedom was too lofty an aspiration for a lady whose paternity was being called into question by a member of her own family.

"What are they doing?" Lyssa asked, drawing Kilby back to the present.

Darknell looked grim. "Backswording." They all watched as the combatants removed their coats and handed them to their respective friends. He lashed both women with his heated glare. "Neither of you have any business being here. These battles can get rather bloody."

Kilby felt the full weight of his disapproval settle on her slender shoulders. "Well, we are stuck with our misadventure, my lord. It is impossible to escape this mob. Perhaps

the brutality of two men pummeling one another with
wooden rods is a fitting punishment."

She had never seen two men engaged in backswording.
However, they were using rods instead of genuine swords.
And these men were *gentlemen*—such a battle could not be
so dangerous.

"Do not be so certain," Darknell said.

Kilby returned her attention to the stage. The man who
had sold her a ticket had called this match a demonstration
of skills. Kilby was beginning to have her doubts as she
observed the Duke of Solitea tense in response to something Lord Hollenworth said. This was not a friendly
match between two friends. They looked like they wanted
to kill each other.

"We are leaving," Darknell said, grabbing both ladies
by the upper arm. "Now."

"My lord, pray be sensible," Kilby begged, struggling in
his harsh grasp. She was not about to be dragged off like an
errant child in front of all these people. "Darknell, you are
calling undue attention to us. We are too close to the stage
to move in any direction and the way out is through at least
two hundred people! You will have to let Lyssa and I endure this noble display of masculine ferocity. If either of us
feels dizzy, you can waft my vinaigrette under our noses.
You will find it in my reticule." She gave her arm an unladylike jerk to free herself.

"A favor," the duke's voice rang out, the low rousing
quality of it slipping beneath her skin and making her
shiver. "I demand a lady's favor. Who shall claim me as her
champion?"

Women all around Kilby cried out, pleading with His
Grace to take their tokens. Craning her neck back and agilely poised on her toes, she noticed even the ladies of the
ton, elegantly draped in their carriages, were vying for the
duke's attention. Bits of lace, colorful ribbons, and silk

scarves were brandished in the air. Kilby was too busy staring at the ladies in the carriages trying to guess which one
the duke would choose, so she did not notice he had
jumped down from the stage and was standing behind the
lady he had selected.

"Lady Kilby Fitchwolf." The Duke of Solitea said her
name in a low, provocative drawl. "Will you favor me?"

CHAPTER FOUR

Fayne could not believe his good fortune. While he stood on the stage, listening to Hollensworth snarl insults at him before the match, his roaming gaze had alighted on the elusive Lady Kilby Fitchwolf. What was she doing here? Had she come because she had learned of the match? Fayne was not truly interested in the reasons that brought his father's mistress to him.

Lady Kilby was here. Staring down into her wary face, Fayne realized he did have the answer to a question that had haunted him since the night he had seen her at the ball. The lady had violet-colored eyes. Intriguing. He had the sudden urge to glide the tip of his tongue lightly over her dark lashes, tracing the almond shape of her exotic eyes.

This was the first time he was standing close enough to touch her face. And yet, he had picked her out of a crowd. It was as if the elegant curve of her spine, the flirtatious tilt of her stunning face, and her black tresses had been imprinted on his brain.

Lady Kilby seemed charmingly flustered by his question.

"A favor," she repeated, frantically touching the brim of her small bonnet, the cuffs of her sleeves, and hem of her bluish-gray silk shawl as she tried to comply with his request.

She was wearing a white muslin dress with lace trimming. The dress was demure in comparison to the one Lady Silver wore that afternoon. Between the two, Fayne would have never thought modesty could be so stimulating.

"The lady has nothing to offer, Your Grace," her male companion growled. It was apparent the gentleman viewed Fayne's presence as trespassing. "There are others who will gladly give you what you seek."

Fayne was not intimidated. Her scowling friend was not the first man who thought to challenge him over a woman. If Lady Kilby returned his interest, she would be well worth the inconvenience of a duel.

Lady Kilby looked startled by her friend's rude dismissal. Fayne noted the heightened color flowering in her cheeks. If she had not invited his father to her boudoir, he would have thought her an innocent.

"Lord Darknell speaks truthfully," she said apologetically. "I have nothing that is not stitched, pinned—"

Fayne placed a finger on her soft lips. Without breaking eye contact, he brushed his fingers against the gauzy bluish-gray aerophane crepe bow poised so irresistibly on the front of her bodice. Grasping one of the nearly transparent tails, he collapsed the pretty bow with a decisive tug. Fayne grinned mischieviously as her beautiful violet eyes crossed at his brashness. "There, you see? You have something to offer, my lady."

Wrapping one of the ends around his fingers, he slowly pulled the long, wispy band of crepe that had been threaded through the fabric loops framing the edge of her rounded bodice until it was free. Without the modesty of the bow, he was treated to an enticing glimpse of her breasts. The spell broken between them, Lady Kilby gasped and slapped her hand over her bodice. Clutching his prize, Fayne longed to press his tongue against her soft flesh and taste. She took a retreating step back as if sensing his lustful thoughts.

"Don't rush off," he entreated, amused by her sudden coyness. His father would not have been attracted to a timid creature. He held up the length of crepe. "Will you honor me by tying your favor to my arm?"

Lady Kilby's forehead furrowed at his polite request. He thought at first that she might refuse him. Ignoring her friends, she moved closer and took the gauzy scarf from his hand.

"Very well. If you insist, Your Grace," she softly said, and began winding the length of fabric several times around his upper arm before tying the ends into a secure knot.

Fayne grimaced at the clearly feminine trimming on his arm. She stepped away from him, pleased with her accomplishment. Noting her smile, the complaint forming on his lips faded. His reputation would not be outdone by a lady's scarf. Her male companion was certainly not pleased with her. If his grim expression was any indication, Fayne would be facing another dawn appointment if he pursued her.

"You intrigue me, Lady Kilby," Fayne quietly confessed. It was the only warning he could give her.

Startled by his admission, she hastily glanced at her companions. "It is not my intention to do so, Your Grace."

"And yet I seem unable to resist." Fayne shrugged, hearing another summons coming from the stage. "And what about you, my lady? Do you require courting or do you prefer a man who just takes?"

He did not give her a chance to reply. Alas, the Lady Kilby Fitchwolf would have to wait for another opportunity when they could privately discuss their mutual desires. Hollensworth was impatiently awaiting his return.

＊ ＊ ＊

Kilby's gaze rested on the Duke of Solitea's back as he accepted another gentleman's hand and hauled himself back onto the stage. *What just happened?* she wondered, lightly touching her right temple with her fingertips. Had she been bewitched? What had possessed her to stand there docilely while the young duke had untied the bow on her bodice and with confidence born of practice removed the threaded length that framed her bosom?

The combatants were preparing for the match. Coatless and hatless, they wore no padding to protect themselves from the stinging blows of the sticks. Each had what appeared to be a wicker guard in their grasp. The ash rods were inserted into the hilt, creating a wooden sword. In their opposing hand they held a length of rope that was looped between their legs and the two ends were held rigidly in place by their hand. The rope was designed to hinder the movement of that arm. Each man could lift their bent elbow high enough to protect their face, but the arm could not block a ruthless strike to the head.

"Encouraging that particular man will lead only to disgrace," Darknell warned. "The duke is not thinking how to court you, of taking you as his bride. He is wondering how quickly you will tumble into his bed, my naïve Fitchwolf."

Kilby clenched her teeth at his chastisement. She was not *that* dimwitted. Given time, she would reason out the duke's motives on her own. "Silence, my lord. You are becoming positively tedious. My ears are still ringing from your previous lectures." She was being intentionally rude, guaranteeing that the viscount would refrain from speaking to her.

Kilby did not owe her friends an explanation about her reaction to the duke. She was not even certain what had occurred between them. The Duke of Solitea had looked down at her with those penetrating green eyes of his, a slightly amused expression on his face. When he had asked her to tie the favor to his arm, how could she refuse the innocent request?

Kilby mentally shook off the lingering effects of the duke's proximity. She was still flabbergasted he had approached her so daringly in public. The man had called her by name and openly flirted with her. His actions completely baffled her. If he knew her name, he knew she had been with his father when he had collapsed and died in her arms. Although the Carlisles had agreed that Kilby's connection to the duke should not be revealed, Priddy had hinted that the family did so not for her sake—they cared little for her fate—but to avoid a scandal. If this was true, why had he not cut her dead?

Kilby jolted at the thwacking sounds of the ash rods connecting. Lord Hollensworth and His Grace had begun the match. The brief affable respite of having them search for a lady's favor had not dimmed their thirst for battle. Glancing at the scrap of white lace tied to his arm, she surmised that the baron had found a lady to favor him. Kilby had been too focused on the duke to witness which one of the ladies had bestowed her favor.

As she watched them, the speed and grace with which the two men attacked and parried was extraordinary. This was definitely not a sport for the fainthearted. The duke took a solid hit on his arm. The man did not even grimace. He swiftly returned the hit by striking the baron on the shoulder and again on his upper right thigh. A small red spot of blood appeared on the shoulder of Lord Hollensworth's white linen shirt, and the crowd cheered. The duke circled and Kilby noticed a larger bloodstain ruined his sleeve, too.

"Oh, I cannot watch," Lyssa complained, covering her eyes. "Tell me when they have finished."

Kilby brought the handle of the parasol to her lips. She wanted to look away, too. "What is the point? Thrash one another until each is bloody and senseless?"

She had not realized she had spoken aloud until Darknell replied quietly, "A singlestick can be as damaging to the flesh as a sword. These types of matches can get quite gory."

She cringed as the duke parried twice and then took a stunning blow to his lower back. He used the forward momentum to crouch low and spin around for a countering attack. His Grace tripped the baron and the man landed hard on his back. Lord Hollensworth froze when the duke pressed the tip of his singlestick against the man's breast.

"Surrender," the duke demanded. He was drenched in sweat and breathless, his white linen shirt was marked in half a dozen places with his blood.

Lord Hollensworth sneered and batted the stick away with his own weapon. "Mercy from a Carlisle? What a laughable notion! Are you finally feeling remorse over my brother's death, you bastard? Surrender? Ha! Never to you."

Extremely winded from their battle, he staggered to his feet, never taking his hate-filled gaze off his opponent. He swung his singlestick wildly, aiming at his opponent's head. The duke jumped back, dodging the blow.

"Getting careless, Hollensworth?" His Grace taunted. "Tasting blood, are you?"

"Only yours," the baron replied, feinting left and then blocking his opponent's hit. "Since you are too cowardly to accept my challenges, I will gladly use this staged mockery to bleed you dry."

Her close proximity to the stage allowed her to hear their angry discourse. None of it made sense to Kilby. Something terrible had occurred and the baron was determined to take his revenge on the duke.

The duke used the side of his arm to blot the sweat on his face. "Looks like you are bleeding your fair share, sir!"

The baron reversed their direction and aggressively lashed out at the slight opening his opponent presented. The duke must have predicted this move, since he turned his body, using his bent arm to block. Blood instantly soaked the duke's forearm.

Lord Hollensworth howled in fury at his opponent's apparent skill and agility. As he kicked out, his foot connected with the duke's knee.

"No!" Kilby shouted, clutching her parasol in a stranglehold as she watched the duke's face contort with pain.

Solitea stumbled backward to find his footing. The baron did not hesitate. He lunged and drove the point of his singlestick into the duke's chest.

"Unfair!" Darknell unexpectedly called out beside her.

The crowd was also booing and jeering their disapproval. Kilby did not know the rules of this bloodthirsty game, but it was apparent Lord Hollensworth had acted dishonorably.

His Grace glared at the baron in disbelief. The point of the stick had pierced the meat of his ribs. Furious, he grasped the offending rod and jerked the tip out of his chest. A bright splash of red appeared on the front of his shirt. The duke tossed aside his singlestick and released the rope confining his other hand. "To hell with good intentions, you miserable, sanctimonious devil!" He slammed his fist into the baron's jaw and sent the man flying backward. "I'm through playing. Let's settle this. I call for sabers!"

The bastard had impaled him with a stick! Unbelievable. His friends had been right all along. He should have accepted Hollensworth's challenge and been done with it. This was his reward for allowing guilt for his minor part in

Hart Mitchell's suicide to interfere with his dealings with the grieving brother. When Hollensworth had first challenged him, he should have accepted, and then callously fired a bullet into him to discourage him from ever picking up the gauntlet of revenge.

Fayne deliberately turned his back on the baron and marched over to his friends. It was Cadd who offered up his saber. If Hollensworth dared to attack him while his back was turned, Fayne *would* kill him. There were hundreds of witnesses present who would verify that he had acted in self-defense.

"Solitea," Ramscar greeted him, his face a mask of concern. "How badly are you wounded?"

Fayne glared at the bloodstain on the front of his shirt that had a circumference larger than his hand. "I'll live. I give even odds for Hollensworth after his cowardly deed." The baron's ash rod must have split at the tip some time during their frenzied clashes. The point had been as lethal as an unbuttoned foil. Fayne had felt the tip slide into his muscle. The only reason why he was not lying on the ground fighting for his life was that the rod had struck one of his ribs.

"You are deservedly furious, Solitea," Cadd said, handing him the saber. "All the same, you do not want to commit murder in such a public fashion."

Fayne sent his friend a look of annoyance. Cadd had acted as one of his seconds for every duel he had ever fought. He was generally the bloodthirsty one of their group. "God spare us all," he muttered. "Cadd spouting sagacity. I thought you at least would be standing on my side."

He turned away from his friends, not waiting for a response. Fayne was livid, and a healthy portion was directed at himself. The wind picked up and teased the gauzy bluish-gray fabric tied to his arm. The ends fluttered on the breeze, reminding him of the lady who had given it to him.

His hot gaze latched on to her pale face within seconds. Lady Kilby was clutching her collapsed parasol to her as if it were a shield. Her violet gaze met his, and he sensed her fear for him even at this distance.

The mob was cheering his name. He let their energy flow over him, through him. Dismissing her, he faced his adversary. "You made a mistake, Hollensworth."

"How so?" the baron scoffed. "I am not the one with the hole in his chest."

He refused to be baited. "My skills at backswording are merely above average. My skills with a saber . . ." He passed the hilt of the sword from one hand to the other, smiling evilly. "Are exceptional."

Fayne raised his sword, acknowledging his opponent, and then attacked.

Kilby brought her fist up to her mouth, completely undone by the brutality she was witnessing. Both men seemed oblivious to their wounds as they circled, lunged, and parried in a terrifying *danse macabre*. The singing clash of steel set her on edge. There was a horrifying beauty to the violence that made it difficult for her to glance away.

The Duke of Solitea was a lethal extension of his weapon. He did not hesitate to trip the baron when there was an opening or use his fist to land a well-deserved punch. Lord Hollensworth's mouth and nose were bleeding and his defensive parries made it clear the duke had been holding back. The man's eyes seemed to glow with an inner green fire as he pursued the baron around the stage. Each movement he executed was another step closer to the other man's defeat.

It was evident Lord Hollensworth was succumbing to fatigue. Even to Kilby's untutored eye, the man's technique was clumsy and desperate. She could hear Darknell quietly comforting Lyssa, but she did not spare them a glance. All her attention was centered on the stage.

Suddenly, the baron slipped. Sweat and blood from both combatants had splattered the wooden planks, making them perilous in places. Whether by design or accident, the baron's foot had backstepped into a wet patch and he lost his balance. The crowd's roar was deafening.

The duke pressed the tip of the saber into Lord Hollensworth's ribs. The man's eyes widened in fear, knowing his life was literally in his opponent's hands.

"Pray I do not slip, Hollensworth," the duke mocked, unmoved by the impressive bloodstain forming on the man's shirt. "At this range, my blade will not miss puncturing your lung. What say you?"

The Duke of Solitea waited patiently for the baron's response while the mob circling the stage chanted for the man's death. Kilby closed her eyes, unable to watch any more.

"I—I yield!" Lord Hollensworth cried out. "Your Grace, I yield!"

The frenzied mob cheered the victor.

Someone shoved Kilby into Lyssa and Darknell as many of the spectators tried to move closer to the stage. She could not help smiling as she watched the duke graciously offer his hand to the man so determined to hurt him. Playing to the crowd, the Duke of Solitea raised his saber in triumph and caused them to cheer louder for him. The man certainly had a flair for the theatrical.

Darknell leaned his head close to Kilby's ear. "We should leave."

Kilby nodded in agreement; though she was unconvinced their departure would be simple. She turned away from the stage and waited for the viscount to clear a path for them.

A heavy hand kept her in place. She looked back and was amazed to see the young duke grinning at her. Despite all the blood and sweat mottling his white shirt, he seemed unharmed. In his hand was the diaphanous scarf he had taken from her bodice.

"This brought me luck," he shouted over the din of the crowd. "I suppose you want it back."

"Yes. Thank you," Kilby said, surprised he would have bothered returning the bit of fabric to her. She offered him her hand. "I hope yo— Oh!"

Instead of giving her the length of crepe, the Duke of Solitea seized her hand and tugged her closer. *Good heavens, he was not so bold as to think of kissing her?* She stared at the large, strong hand imprisoning her. Kilby was close enough that she could feel the heat from his exertion rolling off him. She could smell the musk of his sweat, the recognizable scent of blood. Twisting her palm up, the duke brought her hand up until it was poised inches from his lips.

He waited.

For what?

The anticipation was too much. Curious, Kilby lifted her lowered lashes, her wary gaze meeting his, which burned with confidence and triumph. Using his thumb to peel down her kid glove, he exposed her wrist with a practiced gesture. Kilby inhaled sharply at the touch of his lips against her flesh. His mouth on her felt like hot silk and she trembled under his tender assault.

She had been kissed before. Her parents' summer house parties had provided opportunities over the years for daring young gentlemen to steal a kiss or two from her in the gardens. Those kisses had been sweetly innocent. Archer's drunken assault in Ealkin's library by comparison had made her sick to her stomach.

The duke's kiss on her inner wrist was a new experience

entirely. He had taken what should have been an innocent kiss on the hand to new heights. As he pulled away, the light fluttering in her stomach expanded as the sensation ascended into her breasts. She wanted to lift herself up on her toes, and see what it felt like to have those searing lips pressed against her mouth.

Grunting his satisfaction, the duke curtly bowed over her hand. His green eyes had a feverish cast to them. He leaned closer and whispered in her ear. "Come with me. I want to finish this in a soft bed."

Kilby whipped her head up, wide-eyed and staggered by his offer. The man was assuming a great deal from one little kiss. "Thank you, Your Grace, for your lovely invitation. Nonetheless, I must respectfully decline," she said, keeping her voice even. There was nothing she could do about her blush. If Darknell guessed what the duke had indecently proposed, the viscount would have felt obligated to call the man out.

"Does your refusal have anything do with my father?" The Duke of Solitea smirked, giving her a shrewd look. "I assure you, I am not bothered in the least that he had you first."

"How very tolerant you are," Kilby said, blinking in mock admiration. The pleasure she had felt from his kiss dissipated with the understanding that he viewed her as no better than a doxy. She resisted the urge to rub the spot where his hot breath and lips had caressed her wrist. "I still must decline. You asked me for the favor. The only one you shall have from me is gripped in your hand. Good day."

Kilby walked away, pretending not to see Darknell's censuring stare as she passed him. The viscount stepped in front of the Duke of Solitea, a clear warning that he was not to follow.

Fayne let her escape. Pursuing her meant taking on her guard dog, Darknell, and he was still hurting from his fight

with Hollensworth. "Run, Lady Kilby Fitchwolf." He raised
her scarf to his nose and inhaled the subtle scent. "I have
claimed one favor from you, and I hunger still. I shall not be
appeased until I have tasted all of you."

... ...

CHAPTER FIVE

"Did you enjoy your afternoon outing with Lady Lyssa?"
Lady Quennell asked Kilby several hours later. Grimacing,
the viscountess braced her hands on a chair and sucked in
her stomach as two maids behind her tugged on the lacings
of her corset. Priddy was an attractive woman with an enviable, shapely body. She was too pretty to live the remainder of her life as a widow. Slightly taller than Kilby, she had
vivid light blue eyes and short dark brown hair, which she
often wore curled. There was a sprinkling of freckles across
her nose and cheeks, revealing her joy of the outdoors.
Whereas most ladies her age were beginning to glimpse the
aging lines of time, the viscountess's oval face was still
youthful.

Kilby had sought Priddy out, directly after she had returned from the fair. Her chaperone had retired upstairs in
her bedchamber, preparing for the evening. Tonight they
were spending part of the evening at the Sans Pareil Theater. Afterward they were having a late supper at Lord Guttrey's town house.

"Very much so," Kilby said, sitting down on one of the chairs the viscountess had scattered about her boudoir for entertaining close friends.

Once the maids had finished securing the ties of Priddy's corset, she straightened and gingerly exhaled. "This morning you mentioned that you and Lady Lyssa were contemplating visiting Mrs. Ripley's literary circle? Did you attend?"

Kilby had debated if she should confess that she and Lyssa had spent part of the afternoon at the fair. If her friend's family viewed Lord Ursgate as a disreputable character, she assumed the viscountess would be equally distressed by the notion of Kilby casually conversing with the gentleman. "Our plans changed somewhat. We met up with Lord Darknell and decided to visit one of the fairs outside London."

Priddy made a face. "Heavens, a rural fair. What was Lord Darknell thinking?" She made a soft disapproving noise with her tongue. "We need to tread carefully. If people were to learn that you were alone with the Duke of Solitea when his heart failed him . . ."

Kilby lowered her head and played with the lace at her wrist. In hindsight, she viewed her encounter with the new Duke of Solitea as potentially disastrous. She had rejected his insulting invitation. What would she do if His Grace took his revenge and broke his oath, thus revealing her connection to his father? If anyone recognized her as the lady he had demanded a favor from this afternoon, she doubted there was any hope of the quelling speculation.

As she noticed her young charge's utter misery, the severe expression softened on the viscountess's face. She raised her arms and held still while one of the maids pulled the dress over her head. "Kilby, dearest, I must caution you about such amusements. These lesser fairs are always popping up like mushrooms on the outskirts of town." Her head and arms appeared through the openings. Giving her skirts a shake, she helped the maid smooth the fabric into place. "They are generally organized to give young gentlemen the opportunity of participating and wagering on a multitude of sporting events."

Kilby could not disagree with the viscountess's opinion. "Well, there is no call for concern. Lyssa and I had Darknell to protect us," she said, hoping to reassure her. "Besides, we noted numerous stately carriages, some bearing ladies of distinction."

Priddy cocked her head in her direction, on odd expression on her face. Moving away from the maid who was buttoning the back of her dress, she laid her hand affectionately on Kilby's cheek. "What is this? You speak as if you stand apart from these ladies, *ma petite.*"

Kilby gently touched the viscountess's hand. Priddy had been so kind to her since her parents' deaths. "You told Archer that I needed the polish only London could provide. When I compare myself to the other ladies of the *ton,* I feel like a duck among swans." Kilby was aware she lacked the sophistication and confidence she had noted in other ladies close to her age.

"Nonsense." Priddy took Kilby's hand and pulled her to her feet. Guiding her to the cheval mirror in the corner of the room, the viscountess stood behind her. "You are a beautiful young woman with a respectable pedigree. When I spoke of your needing polish, I was telling Archer what he needed to hear so he would agree to this trip."

It had taken the viscountess several visits and countless discussions with Archer to gain his consent. Afterward, her brother had, up until the day she had left Ealkin, threatened to forbid Kilby's departure. Eventually, he had let her go because he knew Kilby would return home for Gypsy's sake. "Archer was becoming . . . difficult. I cannot fathom how you convinced him. Nevertheless, I am grateful."

Priddy's brilliant light blue eyes knowingly met Kilby's gaze in the mirror. "We both are aware that it is time for you to permanently leave Ealkin. You need a home of your own, and a husband's protection. With your cooperation, I vow to accomplish the deed before the season's end. It is the least I can do for the daughter of my dearest friends."

Although she had not revealed Archer's cruel accusations about her mother, the viscountess had deduced that Kilby was not safe in her brother's care. And what of Gypsy's fate? Archer was not denouncing their blood ties, but Kilby feared he was fully capable of locking his young sister in a lunatic asylum. She felt like one of the rope-walkers she had seen at the fair. A single misstep could lead to her downfall.

Kilby gave Priddy a strained smile, and the hint of tears sparkled on her dark lashes. The notion of marrying a stranger just for protection sounded as frightening as returning to Archer. "Marriage. I think Mama and Papa would approve."

"Word reached me, Mother, that you were on your deathbed," Fayne said, entering her drawing room confident that his casual stride would not betray the injuries he had received from Hollensworth.

His mother was sitting on the sofa, stuffing a generous piece of cake in her mouth. His sister, Fayre, was standing at the rectangular tea table pouring tea into a cup. The fraud! "For a soon-to-be-corpse, you seem quite animated."

After the surgeon had cleaned and bandaged the worst of his wounds, Fayne had returned to his house, hoping to medicate the stiffness setting in with brandy. The wish had been futile. On his arrival, his manservant had presented him with a distressing note from the duchess claiming that she had collapsed. Sensing a ruse, Fayne had remained at his house long enough to bathe and dress before he drove to the family town house.

Fayre's brows came together as if she disapproved of his bizarre humor. Unlike their mother, who was wearing a cheerful green and yellow striped dress, his sister was looking properly tragic in mourning black crepe. "Stop it, Fayne. You are deliberately being provoking."

He kissed her on the cheek. "And spoil all my fun? God forbid!" he mocked, winking at his mother. The duchess understood and accepted his jocular disposition.

Fayre, by Carlisle standards, was a tad too staid, though his sister had showed brief spirited flickers of the family's outrageous tendencies. Two years ago, she had managed to stir up the family when she had given her heart and body to an ambitious scoundrel who seduced her for nefarious reasons. The family had been recovering from the scandal when she abruptly announced that she intended to marry a wealthy commoner, Maccus Brawley.

Unremorseful, the duchess now beckoned Fayne to join them. She put her plate of cake aside and opened her arms so she could embrace him. "Come here, you ungrateful rogue. You ignored all my other notes. I was left with no choice but to resort to desperate measures."

Fayne bent over and pressed the side of his face firmly against her dark cinnamon tresses bound up into a fussy knot. She felt fragile in his arms. He pulled back and studied her face. The spark of mischief, so akin to his own, still gleamed in her bluish-green eyes. Even so, the duke's death had marked her face. The lines around her eyes and mouth seemed pinched from lack of sleep. Despite their odd marriage, Fayne was positive his mother was mourning the duke in her own unique manner.

"You look healthy," he lied.

The duchess responded by poking with alarming precision the stab wound Hollensworth had delivered with his singlestick. He yelped and placed a protective hand over his chest.

"You, on the other hand, do not," his mother said smugly.

Concerned by his sudden paleness, Fayre pushed him down onto the sofa beside their sadistic mother. "Are you hurt?" she asked, her green gaze searching him from head to toe for additional signs of injury.

Fayne glared bitterly at his mother. Someone had already told her about his fight with Hollensworth. "Vicious harpy, how did you know?"

"Know what?" his sister demanded, her eyes narrowing in suspicion. "No. Not again."

Magnificent. Now he would have both Carlisle women bullying him. This was the main reason why he had been avoiding his mother in the first place. "Again? Listening to gossip, dear sister? When do you find the time? I thought Brawley kept you on a tight leash these days."

Fayre's face flushed almost as brightly as her cinnamon-colored curls. Her mouth tightened at his taunt. "According to my husband, you are the one who needs a leash, Fayne," she said tersely, using his given name instead of calling him Tem as was her preference. It was a clear indicator of her annoyance. "Or the lash."

"Dueling," the duchess moaned, retrieving a lace handkerchief from a hidden pocket in her gown. She dabbed the corners of her eyes. "How many have you fought? Three? Four?"

The duchess had such a pathetic expression on her face. He refused to allow her to reprimand him as if he were still a boy. "Are we counting the number of duels I have fought in my life, Mother, or just the tally this week?" he sarcastically quipped.

The duchess held her chin up, appearing brave. "I wish

your father were alive. I evidently do not understand this violent aspect of you, my son."

His father, had he lived, would have been proud. The duke had fought a fair amount of duels in his youth. The Carlisle men were taught from the cradle to fight for what they wanted. Glancing from his sister to his mother, he sensed no amount of arguing would convince them of the necessity of violence.

Still, he could not resist trying. "Would it ease your mind, Mother, if I told you that each gentleman I fought deserved it?"

The duchess furiously dabbed at her eyes and shook her head. If she was truly mopping up actual tears, she was going to need to wring out her handkerchief soon. "No, I do not believe it does, Tem."

"Good heavens," Fayre exclaimed at his impudence. "That is the best you can do?"

He glowered at his sister's interference. "Why don't you go home? Isn't Brawley waiting for you at home?"

"No, he is not. Maccus is at the 'Change."

"Perhaps you should leave anyway. You are upsetting the duchess."

The duchess saw where her children were heading, and the inevitable explosive finale. "Tem . . . Fayre—really—"

"Me?" Fayre replied, her voice thick with outrage. "I am not the one who is treating dawn appointments as if he were paying social calls. How many wounds are you concealing underneath your coat, Fayne? How many times has a surgeon bled you?"

Sometimes his sister saw too much. "My business, not yours, sister mine," he growled.

"It will be our business if you get yourself killed!" she yelled back at him. It was so rare for Fayre to raise her voice in anger that Fayne found the experience rather disquieting. "We just laid our beloved father to rest. How soon before your recklessness obliges us to mourn you, as well?" she demanded.

Fayne winced at her genuine tears. "No. None of that," he ordered, feeling something akin to panic. Fayre's lower lip quivered before she started sobbing. "Aw, hell, Fayre."

He pulled her onto his lap and cuddled her against him. He sent a mute appeal to his mother, but she was concentrating on blowing her nose into her handkerchief. Fayne shut his eyes in disgust. "See here, Fayre. Brawley is going to want to rip my head off for making you cry. If you value my life, you will dry up those waterworks immediately."

With her face pressed into his shoulder, his sister sniffed and then giggled.

Fayne lifted his brows, perplexed. "You scream at me for dueling, and yet the thought of your husband throttling me amuses you," he mused, pressing a kiss into her hair. "Pondering the feminine intellect leaves me at sixes and sevens."

Fayre pulled her face from his shoulder, laughing. Wiping the wetness from her cheeks, she said, "No, silly, the thought of you and my husband fighting never amuses me. I was just remembering that Maccus had a similar worry about you when we announced our betrothal."

The duchess gasped, probably recalling how her husband had reacted to the news that Mr. Brawley had *ruined* his daughter. Twisting the damp linen in her hands into a contorted mess, she said, "Tem, pray tell me that you did not attack Mr. Brawley?"

"Why would I?" Fayne countered, seeing no reason to admit that he and Brawley had had a private chat the day after their betrothal was announced. "Father had the situation well in hand."

"Well in hand?" The duchess expelled a breathy laugh. It was the first glint of humor he had seen on his mother's face since his arrival. "Oh, what a night! The duke murdered half a dozen doors in the house trying to get to Fayre's poor Mr. Brawley."

Fayne chuckled. "And a harpsichord, if I recall the tale correctly." His father had been so livid about the damage he had wrecked on his daughter's behalf that he sent Brawley the bill. Fortunately for all, Brawley had settled the debt without a whimper.

His sister tugged at his cravat impishly and climbed off his lap. Retrieving their mother's empty teacup, she went over to the tea table to refill it. "Papa was very agreeable about our match, once Maccus paid for all the damages," Fayre said, blissfully unaware that she had the men in her life wrapped around her little finger. If she ever learned the truth, she would be insufferable.

"Yes, he did," the duchess cheerfully agreed. "I think Brawley has been an interesting addition to our little family."

His disagreement with his sister had distracted their mother from her earlier worry over his dueling and her mood had lightened tremendously. If luck was on his side, she would not recall why she had summoned him until after he had departed.

"Speaking of paying one's debts," his mother said, switching topics. She smiled and accepted the cup of tea Fayre offered her. "Tem, do you recall your promise that you would escort me if I required it?"

Fayne's green gaze narrowed slightly. "Yes. Vaguely." He had made the hasty promise right after Hollensworth had shoved them both through the duke's portrait, rending it beyond repair. The duchess had been so distressed afterward that he would have sold his soul to the devil to appease her.

"I have need of you tonight," she said crisply, raising the edge of the cup to her lips. The duchess gave his sister a sly sideways glance, which Fayne returned with an arrogant smirk.

Belatedly, he sensed the trap before it snapped shut. The Carlisle women had hatched a plan to keep him out of trouble—at least for the evening—and their execution was short of brilliant. He had never been hoodwinked by a woman before, let alone two.

Suitably impressed, Fayne surrendered wordlessly.

CHAPTER SIX

The supper at Lord Guttrey's was a small gathering, comprising thirty or so guests. The viscount was nearing his seventieth birthday, and the majority of his guests were considerably older than Kilby. There was one lady, however, a Mrs. Du Toy, who at twenty-six was the closest to Kilby's age. The five-foot-nine-inch blonde had taken one dismissive glance at her, and then moved on to converse with several gentlemen she seemed to be acquainted with.

Resigned that her supper companion was likely to be a gentleman forty years her senior, she left Priddy to discuss politics with their host's brother and his wife and wandered on her own. The drawing room connected to the music room. She did not linger in the music room. Beyond the door she found herself in an outer hall that led to the stairs. The viscountess had warned her earlier at the theater that Lord Guttrey would be asking her later to play the pianoforte. Her parents had ensured that her skills with the instrument were competent, so she was not worried about disgracing herself or Lady Quennell.

"Lady Kilby, is that you, my dear girl?"

She glanced down from the balustrade and saw Lord Ordish poised on the stairs. "Why, good evening, my lord," she said pleasantly. "I did not know you were joining the festivities this evening."

The earl looked a little sheepish. "In truth, I am not. Guttrey and I had some late-night business to conclude. I was hoping to leave before anyone noticed my presence and insisted that I remain for supper." He leaned heavily on his walking stick and grimaced. "By Jove, I am too old to be cavorting about at these hours. The night is for the young."

Kilby hid her smile as she glanced back at the open doorways. Lord Ordish could not be older than fifty, but acted as if he had the poor constitution of someone near seventy. She wagered half of Guttrey's guests were older than the earl and she had not heard them complaining about the hour. It was a pity. He was a fine-looking gentleman. If he was not so rigid, he might have made a perfect companion for Lady Quennell. Descending the stairs to draw less attention to their conversation, she said, "Well, do not concern yourself. I will not tell a soul I have seen you."

The earl formally bowed over her hand. "You are a sweet girl. I knew I could count on you." He beckoned her closer. "Actually, finding you here is a prodigious coincidence," he said in a conspiring tone. "You had asked me about some of the gentlemen who courted your mother in her youth."

Pleased he had been thinking about their previous conversation, she confided, "Yes, the last time we spoke on the matter, you had mentioned Lord Ursgate. I took your advice and tried to seek him out at the fair. Regrettably, my efforts were unfruitful." There was no reason to confess that she had forgotten all about the man after she had encountered the Duke of Solitea.

Lord Ordish patted her hand sympathetically. "Just as

well. First, I must beg your forgiveness. In hindsight, I must confess I directed you to the wrong gentleman."

Kilby was frankly relieved to cross the baron off her list of gentlemen to interview. Lyssa had warned her that Lord Ursgate was an unsavory character. She preferred to heed her friend's advice. "There was no harm done. Whom should I add to my list?"

"Tulley. Rutger Elliot, Earl of Tulley." Lord Ordish smiled blandly at her. "He was quite a bit younger than the crowd he ran with in those days. Tulley has done well for himself. Inheriting the title added twenty-six thousand pounds annually to his income, and the ladies seem to think his visage fair."

"Why, Lord Ordish, are you playing matchmaker?" Kilby teased.

"I would never be so presumptuous," he replied with feigned indignation. "It just seems a shame someone as lovely as you is spending her time in London seeking out old friends of her parents instead of flirting with a dozen beaux."

She laughed lightly. Her friends had given her similar advice. "Never fear, my lord. Lady Quennell has taken up the challenge to have me married off before the season ends. Personally, I think she is being overly ambitious." Kilby shrugged, unwilling to share with the earl the truth behind her chaperone's dedicated efforts. "We are out almost every night, and there has been a never-ending stream of introductions, so that I no longer can recall anyone's name."

Lord Ordish's gray eyes warmed with amused sympathy. Together they walked to the front door. One of the footmen opened the door. "It sounds like your Lady Quennell is determined."

The gentleman had no idea what a veritable whirlwind of enthusiasm Priddy was when she settled on a project. "She is. If you can stay longer, I could introduce you?" Kilby asked, guessing the earl would refuse her invitation.

Although she liked both Lord Ordish and Lady Quennell, at this delicate stage of her search into her mother's life, she was somewhat reluctant for the couple to meet. The earl might innocently reveal to the viscountess Kilby's interest in her parents' old friends. Priddy had been very close to both her parents during their years of seclusion at Ealkin, and she was protective of their memory. If the older woman learned their eldest daughter was stirring up the past with her questions, she might abruptly end their stay in London. No, it was best to keep Priddy and Lord Ordish from encountering one another.

"Another time, perhaps. I really must be off," the earl promised, bowing stiffly. "Besides, I am keeping you from flirting with all the young gentlemen who undoubtedly desire your company."

She fluttered her lashes at her companion's flattery. The man was just being kind. "Well, the best-looking gentleman is leaving, so I will just have to set my sights on Lord Guttrey."

Lord Ordish's cheeks reddened at her compliment. His bark of laughter was dry and hoarse. "Careful with that old scoundrel. He will be offering for your hand on the morrow if you smile more than once at him."

Kilby smiled and waved farewell to the earl. Lord Ordish was merely jesting about his concern regarding any genuine interest her host might have in her. Lord Guttrey had cataracts in both eyes and moved at a snail's pace. Receiving a marriage proposal from the gentleman was unlikely, and the least of her concerns.

"Now that he's gone, mayhap you will settle for second best?" the Duke of Solitea said behind her.

Fayne's green eyes gleamed with unconcealed pleasure as Lady Kilby whirled around and gaped in amazement at him. After his mother had bullied him into escorting her this evening, he had never guessed he would feel gratitude to be sharing supper with a bunch of old fossils; especially when he compared the staid event with his original plans of going off with two of his former mistresses and Everod.

An evening with Lady Kilby Fitchwolf was worth the sacrifice. She looked delectable wearing a fine white muslin dress. The front was cut low, offering him a tantalizing glimpse of her breasts. The pleated back was high, with ribbon bows adorning the back from waist to train. The sleeves were puffed and two bows matching the back one were attached. Her black tresses were pulled high and the ends curled. A wreath of greenery and small purple flowers adorned her crown. Amethyst and gold jewelry gleamed from her ears, throat, and wrists.

Her deep violet eyes narrowed on him suspiciously. "What are you doing here?"

"Eventually having supper, if Guttrey ever manages to pull his guests from the card tables," he said casually, suddenly wishing he were not escorting his mother. Fayne loved the duchess dearly; however, the model of a dedicated son was not overtly part of the wicked reputation he had garnered over the years.

Without a hint of conceit, he knew Lady Kilby desired him. Like the countless ladies before her, she had the keen eye to admire his masculine beauty, the intelligence to covet his title and wealth, and the ambition to claim a part of him for herself. Fayne was usually attracted to ladies who were not afraid of their passions and were bold enough to take what they wanted. He would be only too happy to oblige this particular lady.

Nevertheless, Fayne had a strict rule about flaunting his lovers in front of his family. And Lady Kilby Fitchwolf would soon be in his bed.

"What about your injuries?" she asked, her gaze drifting

unerringly down to the wound on his chest. "There was so much blood, I thought you would be abed."

If he had managed earlier at the fair to lure her away from her friends, he would have cheerfully surrendered to her tender mercies and enjoyed the evening with her in bed. He liked sharing secrets with her. Not even his mother knew the extent of his injuries. Fayne smiled, basking in the concern she expressed on his behalf. Taking her arm, he escorted her past the library toward the conservatory. "Most of my wounds were superficial. The surgeon on hand was actually pleased that the worst ones bled so freely as to prevent the risk of infection."

Fayne opened the glass doors to the conservatory and gallantly bowed. "My lady." His initial response when he had seen her giggling and whispering to Lord Ordish was jealousy. The strange reaction was a first for him. He had laid claim to her this afternoon, and he was not about to permit a gentleman old enough to be his father to steal away a lady he deemed as his. Lady Kilby was fortunate that she had not inadvertently provoked him further by leaving with the gentleman. This newly discovered possessive side to his nature was unpredictable. He wanted the lady to be wary of him, but not terrified.

Someone had lit the lanterns within the conservatory, but the lush, earth-scented interior was gloomy and mysterious to the less adventurous. "We really should not be wandering about Lord Guttrey's house like this. Everyone is upstairs."

"Not everyone, my dear lady," he said, pleased they were alone. "Come. No one will miss us."

"Do not be so certain," she said, placing her hand on his arm as they descended the four wave-shaped steps into the conservatory. "With the exception of Mrs. Du Toy, I believe we are the youngest guests present. That alone makes it difficult for us to be inconspicuous."

"Morrigan Du Toy is here?" he asked innocently. Before her marriage and very public divorce to one of the royal court physicians, Fayne and Morrigan had indulged in a spectacularly unforgettable affair one hot summer. He had not spoken to her privately since the House of Lords had dissolved her marriage. However, Ramscar and Cadd had told him that the statuesque blonde had expressed a desire to see him again. Fayne had resisted calling on her. The passion he had shared with her had burned out years ago. As pleasurable as their time together had been, he was not interested in rekindling the friendship.

Lady Kilby halted and looked at him sharply. "You are acquainted with Mrs. Du Toy?"

"Not really. I haven't seen the lady in years," he said, giving her the partial truth. She seemed relieved by his admission.

Fayne only hoped Morrigan would behave herself this evening. No doubt she would try to use their meeting to her advantage. In many ways, the lady was a lot like him. He pulled Lady Kilby away from the entrance, taking her deeper into an alcove of potted orange trees.

"I have never been to Lord Guttrey's house," she admitted shyly, her voice just above a whisper. "Someone in the drawing room commented on his impressive conservatory, and upon seeing it, I must concur."

"You can speak aloud. This is not a place of worship," he said, teasing her into smiling up at him.

As he recalled the brief taste of her flesh when he kissed her wrist at the fair, his green gaze was contemplative as it dropped down to her lips. A man who generally indulged his impulses, he did not question his motives as he pulled her into his arms. Lady Kilby was shorter than the ladies he usually chose for lovers. She also did not have the curvaceous figure he preferred. These differences did not seem to matter when he touched her. When he pulled her against his lean, muscular torso, the lady fit him perfectly.

He did not ask for permission. Her eyes and the subtle tilt of her face revealed she wanted his mouth on hers. Fayne gently brushed his lips teasingly against her full lips. Lady Kilby shivered at his brief contact. She had a generous mouth, just begging to be kissed. If she was so responsive to such a light touch, he could not wait until he had her naked in his bed.

"I stand corrected," he murmured against her mouth. He laved her upper lip with the tip of his tongue.

"How so?" Her lips parted at his tongue's coaxing.

Fayne grinned impishly at her. "With you in my arms, this is a place where I will gladly worship."

Kilby moaned as his agile tongue slipped between her parted lips, savoring her taste. The feel of his rough tongue mating against hers seemed to bring her body to life. A tingling awareness coursed through her entire body. Oh, the taste of him! There was a sweet decadence in the way he moved his mouth thoroughly over hers, his tongue sizzling over her sensitive lips. Despite her limited experience with males, she sensed the duke was unlike most gentlemen.

"We should—oh—we should stop. Go back upstairs," she said breathlessly. Fayne's questing mouth glided down to her neck. If she were honest with herself, she knew she did not mean a single word. He nipped the tender flesh above the gold and amethyst dangle earring she wore, and then laved the inner recess of her ear. Clutching him tightly on the arms, she expelled a melodiously sound against his cheek.

Fayne pulled back and grinned roguishly at her uninhibited response. "I prefer your company, little wolf."

Kilby pressed her face into his shoulder, a little mortified by his teasing endearment. It was not her last name that prompted the nickname, but rather her unbidden reaction to his loving caresses. She *had* sounded like a wild animal. The man was too dangerous.

He backed her up until she felt the abrasive surface of one of the brick pilasters designed as a structural buttress for the large interior. Anyone entering the conservatory would not be able to see them. She was grateful no one could see her wanton position. The sensible side of her was urging her to break away from her ardent companion and return to the safety of the drawing room. Her body was not listening to reason. All she could do was turn her face to the side, giving him access to the bared flesh above her corset.

"This is a new experience for me," he murmured, laving the swells of her breasts.

Kilby tangled her fingers in the long length of dark cinnamon hair he had tied into a queue. Unlike the man, his hair was luxuriantly soft to the touch. She was tempted to untie his queue, needing to feel the texture against her warm skin. "It is the same for me." Never had a gentleman handled her so intimately, so skillfully.

"This might come as a surprise to most," he said, pulling the edge of her bodice forward and revealing more of her right breast. "We Carlisles have a few rules regarding our passions, you know. Never coveting one of my father's women is one I have always adhered to, until I saw you."

Bewildered and slightly hurt, Kilby locked her elbows, deliberately holding him away from her. "Your Grace, I thought you understood. I was never your father's mistress. Good heavens, I had just met him. He was old enough to be my father! The night he—" Kilby bit her lip in hesitation. She did not want to ruin what they had shared with unhappy thoughts. "He only visited me to continue a discussion we had begun the previous evening. You have to believe me. Nothing untoward occurred between the Duke of Solitea and—"

He silenced her with an abrupt rough kiss. "You do not have to explain anything to me." Fayne seared her soul with his smoldering green gaze. "I prefer conversing with you in other, more gratifying ways."

To prove his point, he slid his hand underneath Lady Kilby's chemise and stiff corset, cupping her right breast. The warm globe fit easily in his hand. She was less voluptuous than the sort of lady who usually caught his eye; however, he was pleasantly surprised by the firm texture of her breast. His mouth salivated at the thought of laving the plump nipple stabbing into his palm. Despite the lady's suggestions that they leave, she was aroused and panting for his deft caresses.

"You are correct. We cannot let this go too far this evening." He exposed her rosy nipple. His cock jerked in response. If he had any sense, he would cease tormenting them both. "A taste. There is no harm in sampling the passion between us." Fayne lowered his head and teased the beckoning bud with his tongue.

"Your Grace!" she gasped, her hands pulling at his hair. She was tugging him closer, not pushing him away.

"Call me by my name," he said impulsively, not wanting her to use the variations of his titles. He craved a level of intimacy he had not sought with other women. Gently, he suckled her nipple. It reminded him of a ripe succulent berry. "Fayne. Say my name, little wolf."

Kilby shuddered as he peeled back her bodice, coaxing her left breast into view. "Fayne. No . . . no, this is not right. Not like this," she hissed, when he set his teeth into her skin. He wanted to mark her flesh, so later she would see his claim on her.

Fayne had never been so aroused for a woman. His cock ached, straining for release from his breeches. What they were doing was risky. Unfortunately, passion tended to overrule good sense.

He worked his way up the graceful line of her throat to her jaw. Hungrily, he nipped her chin. "Ah, Kilby, what you do to a man's good intentions. Guttrey's conservatory is not exactly the place I would have chosen for lovemaking." His hand grazed the front of her skirts, unerringly pressing against the juncture between her legs. Her body jerked at his touch. He imagined that if he lifted her skirts and plunged his fingers into the moist heat of her womanly sheath, he would discover she was ready for him.

They both froze at the sound of a door opening.

No!

"Kilby, my girl, are you in here?" Lady Quennell descended the four steps, expecting a reply.

Kilby's violet eyes widened in horror at their awkward predicament. Fayne removed the hand he had buried in her skirts and put a hand over his rigid cock. If the viscountess was as adventurous as her young charge, she was going to get an eyeful. Hastily, Kilby began stuffing her breasts into her bodice. She gestured helplessly at him, demanding him to do something. Fayne held a finger to his lips, warning her to be silent. He respected her wish to keep their friendship a secret. For now, he did not mind sneaking around. His mother was a tolerant lady, but even he was not certain how she would react if she saw Kilby.

Ah, yes.

The viscountess's sudden search for Kilby was abundantly clear. Fayne leaned close to her ear and whispered, "Did I forget to mention that I am my mother's escort this evening?" Noticing her panicked expression, he assumed he had not. He held her against the brick pilaster to prevent her from bolting into the open.

They listened to Lady Quennell's retreat and the door closing behind her.

Kilby shoved him away. "You are here with your mother? Good grief, your mother!"

"Do not sound so shocked," he said defensively, in reaction to her appalled tone. "I occasionally act as the duchess's escort. It has been a disconcerting time for her with the duke's death and all."

"I *know*. You—you simpleton!" She lifted her hands up in supplication and started to move toward the door. "What am I doing here with you?" she asked herself. "You are the last person in this entire country I should be kissing . . . and such."

He was too amused to be offended. "I hope to do more of the 'and such' you mentioned," Fayne said, finding Kilby's nervous fluttering about the duchess's presence endearing. Without a doubt, his mother would certainly disapprove of his soon-to-be mistress. Nevertheless, it did not deter him from wanting the lady. If she did not believe his sincerity, all she had to do was look at the front of his breeches. "When can we meet again?"

Kilby halted at the steps and whirled around to confront him. "What? Are you daft? We can never meet again."

Fayne frowned slightly at her. He was not used to having anyone refuse him. "Of course we can," he said reasonably. "Tonight got a trifle out of hand, I will admit. Next time, we shall strive for a less public place to display our affections."

"I have to find Priddy before she returns upstairs," Kilby muttered, already concentrating on the lie she planned to use to explain her absence. "Forgive me, Your Grace. As much as I find you appealing, I did not come to London for a blithe flirtation. Undoubtedly, you will be able to quickly stumble on a half dozen ladies more agreeable to your amorous purposes."

Lady Kilby Fitchwolf left him. Standing alone in the conservatory, Fayne was burdened with an arousal that had him wondering if it would ever wane. So Kilby thought she could dismiss him so easily? Obviously, she was as used to getting her way as he was. It was a battle she was bound to lose. He had tasted her passion. When she forgot how improper it was to take both father and son as lovers, she was beautifully responsive. Fayne now understood why the duke had made an exception and chosen Kilby above his usual type of mistress. He had discovered that his predilection in women had altered, too.

Moving to one of the stone benches near the front, he sat down and gingerly adjusted his arousal. Perhaps it was for the best that Kilby escaped with Lady Quennell. Fayne chuckled humorlessly at the thought of the duchess's reaction if he arrived in the dining room in his present uncomfortable condition.

He never had a chance to tell her, but he doubted Kilby would fare much better. One look at her face and the viscountess would know her charge had been up to some pleasurable mischief. His kisses had left Kilby's lips red and swollen, and her dress had been delightfully rumpled. Fayne wished he could see the lady's reaction when she noticed the love bite he had bestowed on her left breast.

His cock swelled at his musings. Fayne pressed his fingers to his brow and groaned. Just thinking about Kilby had him craving her. He was going to have to get his unruly body under control, else he would be spending the night on the cold stone bench.

CHAPTER SEVEN

"It was a near thing at Guttrey's, do you not agree?" Priddy asked Kilby the following day as they entered the perfumery on Jermyn Street. Kilby watched her companion summon a clerk and send him scurrying to find her special order. They had not spoken about the incident so Kilby was surprised the older woman had brought up the subject. The pair had spent the afternoon shopping. The sunny day and gusting spring breeze had made their walk a pleasant one.

Priddy returned to her while they awaited her package. "The Carlisles are an eccentric clan. Honestly, no one could have predicted that the dowager Duchess of Solitea would have attended Lord Guttrey's supper so soon after her husband's death. It just isn't done," the viscountess said, shaking her head in wonderment. "We were fortunate I was elsewhere when the dowager was announced."

Since her son had been prowling around downstairs, Kilby assumed she had just missed encountering the lady. "If Her Grace believes half the things Darknell suggested she might, giving me the cut direct would be the kindest greeting I could expect."

"I disagree," the viscountess countered. "I have met the duchess on several occasions and know her to have a liberal disposition. Still, the intimate setting of the supper and your regrettable connection with the duke had me questioning the sagacity of remaining."

"You made the correct decision for a very awkward situation," Kilby assured her friend. The thought of sitting across the table from Fayne's mother was the stuff of nightmares. "If we had remained, and something was said, the gossips would have certainly rewritten the encounter in a fashion so ugly it does not bear contemplating."

"I must agree." Priddy smiled at the clerk approaching with a large wrapped package and a smaller one balanced on top. She signaled her footman forward to carry the boxes for them. "I trust you carried out my instructions to the letter?"

The clerk nodded, handing the boxes to the servant. "Yes, Lady Quennell. I checked each piece myself. You will be pleased with the results."

Priddy sniffed, unconvinced by the man's assurances. "I should hope so. The proprietor will be hearing from me, if I am not satisfied." She inclined her head. "Come along, my dear. I am weary from shopping. Besides, the London merchants have collected enough of Quennell's gold this afternoon."

Kilby followed the older woman out the door. "What do the boxes contain?"

"A surprise," Priddy said enigmatically. Her light blue eyes sparkled with merriment. "For you."

"Me?" she replied, stunned by the viscountess's generosity. "Oh no, Priddy. I cannot accept another gift from you. You have been by far too generous."

"Fiddle-faddle! It is always my pleasure to spoil you,

Kilby," the older woman said warmly. "My only regret is that your mother could not be here to share in our adventure."

Kilby's heart swelled with emotion to the point of bursting. "As is mine," she said sadly. "Oh, Priddy, sometimes I cannot believe they are lost to us. I think it must all have been a terrible mistake." Her father had always been so disparaging of London. What would he think of Priddy's lofty ambition to see her rushed into marriage this season with no thought of courtship or even love?

Priddy pulled her into her arms, reminding Kilby of her mother. "I know," the viscountess crooned, rocking Kilby tenderly in her arms. "Ermina and Weldon were so proud of you. You were their bright violet-eyed angel. How they loved you and your sister so."

She drew away first. Kilby ignored the pang of guilt that stirred within her each time she questioned her parents' honor because of her brother's cruel accusation. He had set her on a path that even had her lying to the viscountess. "Do you think my parents would have approved of me coming to London to hunt for a husband? Papa rarely had anything kind to say about the *ton*. I cannot help but wonder—"

"Cease wondering, little one. Weldon might not have supported your mingling with the *ton*. Regardless, even he respected their influence," Priddy explained as they reached their carriage. "They would have brought you themselves last season if they had not died."

She nodded, knowing her friend spoke the truth. Kilby climbed into the carriage with the assistance of the footman. The viscountess studied her young charge with a speculative expression on her lovely face. Making up her mind, the woman ordered the footman to get her the boxes they had just picked up from the perfumery.

"Here," Priddy said, offering Kilby the smaller box. "You are the closest I have to a daughter, Kilby. I would never presume to replace your mother. However, I pray our time together can help ease your loss."

She was touched by Lady Quennell's words. It was a pity the lady's beloved viscount had died before they had children. Priddy would have been a good mother. "You have been so kind to me. I will never be able to repay you."

Priddy delicately wiped away a tear. "Repayment is not necessary, my girl. Just be happy. It is what Ermina and Weldon would have desired most for you."

Kilby untied the cording on the box and opened the lid. Inside was a magnificent scent bottle. Cylindrical in shape, it was made of hand-carved gold filigree that covered a rock crystal bottle. "Priddy, I have never owned anything so lovely." She turned the bottle in her hands, examining the detailing of the filigree. Within the scrolling leaves were tiny roses. There was a large scroll that almost looked like a heart lying on its side. A lady in Grecian costume danced beneath a tree. On the opposite side, the larger scroll framed a unicorn.

Giddy with excitement, Priddy said, "Open the top and reveal the stopper."

She opened the filigree lid as instructed. Removing the stopper, Kilby brought the scent bottle to her nose and inhaled. The scent was a mix of citrus, perhaps lemon and jasmine. "The scent is heavenly."

Priddy beamed in delight. "I am so pleased you like it. I had the perfumer create a scent especially for you. You always seemed to enjoy the scents Ermina wore. I had them concoct a variation of one of her favorites."

Kilby wrapped her arms around the viscountess before she had settled on the bench and fiercely hugged her. "Thank you. It is a wondrous gift." She returned the scent bottle to the box and stuffed it into her reticule.

The footman handed Priddy the larger box. In turn, she

offered it to Kilby. "What is this? It is heavy." Tugging on the cord, she removed the box from its coarse canvas wrapping. She gasped in awe at what she beheld. "Is this what I think it is?"

"I suppose; it depends on your guess," the viscountess teased.

On her lap was a toilet table box made out of black japanned iron that had been gilded. The edges of the lid were decorated with a repeating diamond design containing an inner narrower shell pattern. Within the center was a painted enamel plaque. The painting expanded on the images carved in filigree on the scent bottle. The limbs of the tree spread out gracefully across the top, while the dark-haired beauty took advantage of its shade. The lady's hand was extended as she patiently coaxed the unicorn to her.

"The lady is so lovely," Kilby murmured in awe as she caressed the lid. "And the workmanship of the box is so detailed."

Priddy beamed with delight. "Look inside."

Needing no further encouragement, Kilby turned the small key in the lock and opened the lid. On the inside of the lid was a polished metal mirror. Within the box, there was a hairbrush with boar bristles, a tortoiseshell comb, a hand mirror, a button hook, a glove stretcher, and a shoe horn. Each silver piece was decorated with the scrolling filigree with dainty roses that matched the scent bottle.

"Thank you, Priddy. The box contains a veritable treasure," Kilby said, kissing the older woman on the cheek.

"No, my dear Kilby," the viscountess countered gently. "The rarest treasure is you."

"Trouble?"

"That was what I was trying to decipher." With his hand braced on the saddle, Fayne squinted up at Lord Everod as he approached on horseback. Waiting for the man to dismount, he gestured at his horse. "Moments ago, the animal bolted unexpectedly. Whatever ails the creature persists." It had taken all his strength and skill to get the agitated horse to halt.

Everod crouched down and examined the horse's left leg. "A bee sting?"

"Perhaps," Fayne said, his hand stroking the animal's smooth, gleaming croup affectionately. "I was fortunate the incident occurred in the park, instead of a busy street. Someone might have been injured."

Like me, for instance.

Murmuring assurances to the edgy horse, Everod moved around to check the right hind leg. He paused and scowled at Fayne. "Where were you two nights past?" the viscount demanded, suddenly recalling the reason that had him combing London for his errant friend. "What happened? Was the wound Hollensworth delivered worse than you let on at the fair?"

The chest wound was healing. There was no sign of infection. His arms, legs, and torso, on the other hand, had some impressive bruising. "No, I am quite fit despite Hollensworth's clumsy attempts with a single stick."

Fayne had not seen any of his friends since the afternoon at the fair. Nor had he seen Kilby. He had decided to ride through Hyde Park in hopes of encountering her there. She was a beautiful lady. Most of the ladies he was acquainted with took great pleasure in displaying themselves at the park. This was the second afternoon he had ridden his bay in the park. There had been no sign of the lady or her friends.

"Do you see any sign of injury?" Fayne asked.

"Nothing." Everod cleared his throat. "The ladies were disappointed that you did not join us at my house. Lady Sprying, in particular, was rather vocal regarding her dismay."

Ah, Fayne mused, the dusky-skinned Velouette. With a distant fondness, he recalled thoroughly enjoying her lusty

appetite. He shrugged off the reminiscence. These days, he
hungered for a violet-eyed little wolf. "My friend, I had
every confidence that you could keep those ladies amused
without any assistance from me."

The viscount laughed heartily and stood. "Indeed. Savoring the company of two ladies at once was a pleasurable
means to pass an evening. It certainly surpassed getting
foxed with you, Cadd, and Ramscar."

"If it isn't, then you are doing something wrong!" Fayne
sardonically quipped.

Everod just gazed distantly ahead with a faint grin on
his face.

Most likely, the man was recalling the particulars of his
pleasurable evening. Fayne had a similar expression on his
face whenever he thought about tasting Kilby's flawless
breasts.

The viscount snapped out of his private musings. "If it
wasn't your injuries, what kept you from coming to the
house?"

"The duchess," Fayne said, wearily sighing. Naturally,
his petulance was only for appearances. No self-respecting
gentleman would admit that the two ladies in his family had
him wrapped around their little fingers. "She and Fayre had
learned of the duels I had participated in, and fussed over
my injuries. Later that evening, the duchess wanted to attend a late supper at Lord Guttrey's. With my father gone, I
felt obliged to offer her an escort."

The viscount scowled, his brows pinching together. "Guttrey? He's still alive?"

Fayne grinned at his friend's puzzled amazement. "Apparently so. And he entertains on occasion, too."

The highlight of the entire evening had been the pre-
cious minutes he had spent with Kilby in the conservatory.
It had been difficult to let her go. As he had guessed, Lady
Quennell had whisked the lady away to avoid any awkward

confrontation with his mother. In truth, he had been more alarmed that Kilby had encountered his former mistress, Morrigan Du Toy than he had been about her meeting the duchess.

He had seen Morrigan when he finally joined the other guests in the drawing room. Once they could speak openly the widow had expressed a desire to rekindle their old friendship. He had caught his mother observing their quiet discourse. She had been shaking her head in dismay. Clearly, Mrs. Du Toy was not a suitable candidate for the next Duchess of Solitea. Fayne privately agreed. Then again, when they had been lovers, marriage had not even glimmered in his ardent thoughts.

"Well, I benefited nicely from your duty," Everod said smugly. He went low and ran his hand along the underside of the bay. "I am tempted to send your mother a token of my appreciation."

Fayne snickered. "Please refrain from doing so. You will only encourage her." Sending the duchess gifts was trouble his friend did not want. Everod was a bit younger than his mother's usual lovers. For some reason, he suspected the duchess would make an exception for his bawdy friend. The prospect of the viscount and his mother together was really disturbing.

"Hold. What's this?" The viscount cursed and straightened. "I think I found the reason your bay bolted."

Fayne circled around the head of the gelding, giving its neck a pat as he crouched low to see what Everod had found. He noticed the three-inch crease on the horse's right flank. The wound was raw looking, but there was little blood loss.

He sighed. "I think we can rule out a bee sting."

Everod chuckled. "I would have to agree. I'd wager a flying piece of stone was the culprit." He walked over to his horse that had been idly nibbling on the grass. "It could have been worse."

Fayne agreed. A little healing salve and a few days of being spoiled by one of the grooms and the bay would be fine. "Even so, I find it peculiar since our gait was too slow to—" He broke off, distracted by the carriage to the right of them. It was the couple within who had caught Fayne's attention. The dark-haired gentleman looked vaguely familiar. The blonde hair he glimpsed beneath the lady's bonnet even more so.

"Another problem?" Everod politely inquired. Curious, he glanced at the couple who had obtained his friend's rapt interest.

"No," Fayne said, grinning like a fool. If the woman in the carriage ahead was Lady Lyssa Nunnick, his luck had changed in his favor.

He was in the card room.

Exhilarated by her discovery, it was all Kilby could do to stop herself from brazenly introducing herself to Lord Tulley. Discreetly, she admired him from the respectful distance she kept between them.

Lord Ordish had told her that he was younger than the other gentlemen he had singled out as men who had once courted her mother's affections. According to snippets of information she had gathered from Lyssa, Priddy, and several others, Rutger Elliot, Earl of Tulley, was forty-two years old and had been married once eight years ago. His countess had died three months into their marriage. The details of her demise were rather sketchy, and no one dared to speak of the lady in front of the earl.

Good grief, could this man possibly be her father? No. She immediately discarded the notion. It was impossible to view any of the gentlemen she had encountered as her father. Weldon Fitchwolf, Marquess of Nipping, was her father. Kilby sensed it wholly in her heart. Archer had to be lying to her and she refused to let him take her family from her to justify his selfish ambitions.

Although Lord Tulley was clearly too old for her, she thought he was a handsome gentleman. His dark brown hair, just shy of black, was cut stylishly short. Observing his profile while he sipped his drink, she noticed his lips were full and his nose straight. He looked slightly bored with either his companions or the game he played with them. Kilby took a deep breath, wondering if she had the courage to approach him on her own.

"Little wolf," the Duke of Solitea murmured in her ear. "Care to dance?"

Lady Kilby shivered as his hot breath teased her ear. As she tilted her head in his direction, Fayne got the impression the lady was not pleased to see him. "I beg you, never call me that silly name ever again," she said curtly, opening her fan with a practiced snap of her wrist. "What if someone heard you?"

She was stylishly attired in a dress of mulberry sarcenet. Draped over the dress was a diaphanous robe of white net that fluttered about her; the front of it was cut diagonally, making the sheer covering longer at the back. Around her neck and on her upper arms she wore a double strand of carnelian and silver beads. Matching earrings dangled pertly from her earlobes.

"I am the only one who knows you howl softly when pleasured," he said, turning her so she concentrated on him instead of whatever had intrigued her in the card room. He was anticipating getting her alone to see if he could coax those impassioned husky cries out of her again. "If anyone overheard us, they would assume it was an endearing abbreviation of your family name. Of course, they would also know we shared an intimate connection."

One he hoped to share again with her soon. Their hosts, Lord and Lady Sallis, resided in one of the older town squares. The house was huge in comparison to some of the newer residences being built. With so many rooms, Fayne was certain he and Kilby could disappear without anyone noticing their absence.

"I told you four days ago that what happened in Lord Guttrey's conservatory was an aberration," she said primly behind her fan. "By the bye, how is your mother? Is she here this evening?"

Fayne was not going to allow Kilby to escape him so easily. The day he and Everod were riding together in Hyde Park, the lady in the carriage had indeed been Lady Lyssa Nunnick. Regrettably, her male companion had been Lord Darknell. For obvious reasons, both he and the viscount had taken a mutual dislike to each other. While Everod distracted Darknell with idle conversation, Fayne had charmed what information he could about Kilby's plans for the week out of her friend. His plans to seek out the lady had failed miserably when he had missed her on two other occasions. He had almost convinced himself Lady Lyssa had deceived him about Kilby's whereabouts when he espied her in the Sallis's ballroom.

"If I said yes would you dash out of here as you did at Guttrey's supper?" Fayne asked, prepared to chase after her this time.

"Of course," she said, crossing her eyes at him for his intentional obtuseness. "Perhaps it is uncouth of me for mentioning your father so soon after your loss; however, you force me to speak plainly. I know what was said the night Lady Quennell visited your family, the accusations that questioned my good character. Priddy related to me the family's confusion regarding my friendship with your father."

"You must forgive us, my lady, it was a—difficult night,"

Fayne quietly said, recalling the rage and grief that had struck them all when they realized the duke was dead. "Accusations might have been uttered in the blind heat of torment. I suffer no such confusion now."

"You are merely being kind," she replied, looking unconvinced. "And so am I. Despite what your family might think, I am not so unfeeling as to cause your mother any unnecessary anguish."

Fayne sensed Kilby's earnestness. He was still trying to understand the lady who had captured his father's interest in his last days. A part of him envied his father for having claimed her first. Had she loved him? He had already gathered she was neither thoughtlessly ambitious nor cruel. "There is no need for you to run from me this evening," he confessed, pleased his mother had decided that she did not need his services once she was satisfied that his recent recklessness had left him unharmed. "I am wholly yours if you desire it."

Kilby looked away and glanced curiously at the card room. "And . . . how many ladies have received this generous offer from you?"

A dangerous question. Answering it truthfully would never get him what he wanted from the lady. "This very evening or in the past year?" he asked mischievously.

Amused, she glanced back at him, searing him with her violet eyes. "I thought as much. How many have refused you?"

He was not certain of the game she was playing with him, but he did not mind the challenge. "Why, absolutely none, my lady." He blatantly lied.

"Really?" she marveled, her eyes flashing with indulgence. "It is a shame, though."

"Not from my perspective," he said, wondering how she would react if he suggested they leave the ballroom now. "I savored every pleasurable moment."

"No, you incorrigible man, I meant it is a shame I must ruin your perfect record by refusing your kind offer." She blithely ignored his stunned expression. "I meant it when I told you that I was not interested in pursuing our friendship further, Your Grace."

A surge of unjustifiable resentment rose and exploded in his chest. "Give me a few minutes alone with you in the Sallises' gardens," he said with terse impatience. "And then refuse me."

Kilby's features darkened with regret. "You tempt me, Your Grace. It is a challenge I would be unwise to accept."

CHAPTER EIGHT

Kilby forced herself to walk away from the Duke of Solitea. It was a difficult task when every nerve in her body was so aware of him. When the man stared at her with those beguiling green eyes, she felt her will to resist him weaken. If he sensed the full depth of her desire to explore the passion between them, he would have whisked her out of the ballroom and she would have been helpless to deny him.

"Oh, I see, His Grace found you," Lyssa said, greeting her with a brief hug. At Kilby's puzzled expression, her friend nodded at something behind her.

She turned back and saw Fayne broodingly staring at her. His burning regard was arrogant and transparently possessive. Her body trembled in response. The duke was going to have to stop looking at her in that manner. Someone was bound to notice.

"How did you know he was looking for me?" she asked, deliberately turning away.

"His Grace approached Darknell and me while we were driving in Hyde Park several days ago," Lyssa confided, thrilled with the notion that her friend had gained the attention of a duke. "Darknell, naturally, warned me not to reveal your whereabouts to him. Nevertheless, while the duke's companion distracted our mutual friend, I did reveal to His Grace that you would be attending the Sallises' ball this evening. Did I do something wrong? I thought you would be pleased."

From Lyssa's perspective, the young duke was everything Kilby should be seeking in a husband. He was handsome, wealthy, and his position in polite society far eclipsed Archer's. He was perfect—well, almost.

It was a pity he was Solitea's heir.

Kilby did not blame her friend for her hasty attempt at matchmaking. If Fayne were so determined to seek her out that he approached her friends, he would have eventually found her on his own. He might have even sought out Priddy's assistance. Kilby could well imagine how thrilled the viscountess would have been by that prospect.

"You did nothing wrong," Kilby said cheerfully. She could feel the weight of Fayne's stare on her. Becoming increasingly agitated, she gripped Lyssa's hands. "I need to leave the ballroom for a few minutes. Will you let Priddy know if she asks after me?"

Her delicate brows furrowed in concern. "Are you ill?" Lyssa asked, holding on to Kilby before she could escape.

"Not really. I am unused to so many people. I just need a few minutes alone."

"You might try the informal parlor. No one should be there," her friend helpfully suggested. "I could sit with you, if you like?"

Kilby wrinkled her nose. "No. Stay and enjoy the ball. I will not be gone for long." Releasing Lyssa's hand, she pivoted and headed out of the ballroom. Fayne had disappeared. If she had any sense, she would leave the Sallises' house and wait for Priddy at home. However, Fitchwolfs were made of sterner stuff. Once she calmed down and composed herself, she would focus on her task of meeting Lord Tulley and forget all about the flirtatious Duke of Solitea and his sinful kisses.

"She was the pretty wench you were flirting with at the fair," Cadd nonchalantly remarked as Fayne observed Kilby depart the ballroom. "The lady who gave you the gossamer frippery, the favor."

"Who was Solitea flirting with?" Everod asked, shouldering himself in between the two men.

Fayne saw no point in hiding his growing obsession. Everod had been with him the afternoon he had approached Lady Lyssa Nunnick. One of them was bound to discover her name. "Lady Kilby Fitchwolf," he said, his tone warning them off.

The viscount cocked his head, trying to glimpse more than the back of her head. "Ho-ho! What's this? Are you keeping secrets from your friends?"

He accepted his friend's teasing with his usual sarcastic manner. "Not much of a secret when you gents are involved, is it?"

Cadd shoved him boisterously on the upper arm. "Sweet Christ, she is the one, isn't she?" Realizing his voice had drawn the interest of nearby guests, he leaned in closer. "The lady your father was tupping when he—" The earl illustrated his point by clutching his heart and staggering.

"Nice one, Cadd." Everod smirked, shaking his head at his companion's insensitivity. "Perhaps later we can break into the abbey and crack open Solitea's crypt for a lark."

Fayne rubbed his brow in exasperation. He wished Ramscar had joined them. The earl was a better mediator when his demented companions started fighting than he was. Personally, he was tempted to let them come to blows.

A bloody match would keep them from prying into his business.

The marquess glared murderously at Everod. "Very amusing, you horse's arse. I was just saying—"

"I know what you meant, Cadd," Fayne interjected, resigned that his friends had guessed the truth. He was surprised they had not figured it out sooner. "Yes. The lady I demanded a favor from at the fair was with the duke when he died." He gave them a harsh look. "This is family business, gents. If I hear Lady Kilby's name uttered in connection with my father, I will know the source and deal with you both accordingly."

"Don't be an arse! You have our oaths if you require them. I just thought you had a hard rule about not fuc—" Everod halted and grimaced. Recalling where he was, he cleared his throat, and said in a quieter voice, "A rule about not dallying with any of your father's mistresses."

"I do," Fayne snapped, not liking that his friends were reminding him that he was not abiding by a rule that ages ago, he had deemed not only sensible, but necessary in keeping the peace among the Carlisles. The duchess and his sister would have been devastated if father and son had come to blows over a mistress. His father had quietly honored his side of the unspoken bargain, as well.

"The rule applied when my father was alive," he said, switching his gaze from Everod to Cadd, daring either one of them to argue. Christ, he could not believe he was getting lectured by a man who bedded two ladies in one night! "Now that the duke is dead, I see no reason why his former mistress cannot find solace in my bed."

Unapologetic, the viscount grinned at him. "You do not have to convince me, my friend. Lady Quennell introduced me to Lady Kilby Fitchwolf when she first arrived in town. The wench has a bewitching face and a lithe body to tempt

even the devil himself," he said, his enthusiasm for his subject reflecting on his handsome features.

Fayne glowered at his friend. Everod had no business
looking at Kilby.

"I'll admit that I have considered calling on the Quennell residence," Cadd confessed, surprising both of his
companions. "The viscountess has high hopes of marrying
the girl off this season. A man could do worse for a bride."

It was worse than he thought. Fayne not only had to
worry about Lady Quennell finding some insipid, foppish
suiter for Kilby, but he had to watch out for his friends'
amorous intentions.

Fayne let his companions feel the impact of his unwavering green gaze. "Forget about courting Lady Kilby, gents.
She's a Carlisle woman, whether she knows it or not."

Everod stepped in front of him, blocking his view of the
doorway. "You have bigger problems than worrying about
someone usurping your place in the lady's bed."

Cadd glanced in the general direction and swore. "Hollensworth. I thought the man left town."

Damn. Fayne was in a tense, volatile mood. It would not
take much prodding from the baron to incite him to violence. "I hope this business between us is settled. If he persists, I might have to kill him."

"Nay," Everod drawled, clapping Fayne on the shoulder. "He hasn't seen you. Nor does he have to, unless you
want to openly challenge him." The viscount was always
ready for a fight.

"We could distract him while you leave the ballroom,"
Cadd offered, subtly shifting so Fayne was effectively hidden from view from the doorway.

Fayne broodingly contemplated his options. If Hollensworth was still seeking a fight, he was willing to oblige
him. Or . . . his second option was more appealing. He

could go after Kilby. Enough time had passed since she had quit the ballroom. If anyone noticed his departure, he doubted they would connect his leaving with Kilby's.

"Distract him," he ordered his friends. His green eyes heated as he thought of the impending chase. Once he had bedded Kilby, she would understand the full extent of his claim on her. "I have a little wolf to tame."

Kilby had strayed far from the ballroom in search of an empty room. The house was large enough that most of the staff was stationed in the wing where the ballroom was located. Where she had wandered was lit, but she had encountered very few people.

Initially, she had gone upstairs to find an uninhabited bedchamber to relax in. The three rooms she had checked had definitely been occupied. She had seen enough of one gentleman's bared backside that she could not bring herself to open a fourth.

She went down one landing in the opposite direction of the ballroom. The hall split, giving her a choice in direction. Kilby chose to turn right, but quickly discovered this way opened into a kidney-shaped room. On the paneled walls were so many mirrors of differing shape and sizes, it must have been a collection. The odd-shaped room was furnished with gilded black chairs softened by green cushions, scarlet sofas with frills, and gold fauteuils. She started to step into the room, noticing a mosaic center table as she entered.

The sound of a lady's voice had her quietly backing out of the room.

"I almost declined Lady Sallis's invitation," the unknown woman continued. "Last week I noticed her cheating at cards. Can you believe it?"

"My word, no," was her friend's faint retort.

"My companions, naturally, begged me not to confront

the pathetic woman. I was prepared to cry off when I heard Carlisle was planning to attend."

She realized the woman was talking about Fayne. She glanced in one of the mirrors and immediately recognized the tall, voluptuous blonde. It was Mrs. Du Toy. Her companion was a darker blonde whom Kilby was not acquainted with. A swift insight had her bringing a hand to her mouth in horror. If she could see the lady in the mirror, Kilby could be seen, too. Silently, she retreated farther down the hallway.

The darker blonde spoke, but her voice was not as distinct as her companion's.

"Oh, he is feigning reluctance," Mrs. Du Toy said in response. "Our parting was frightfully violent. It was my fault, really. I devastated poor Carlisle when I announced I was accepting Du Toy's offer of marriage and could no longer continue our affair."

The lying fiend! Kilby fumed. He was only distantly acquainted with her, he had implied. He had not seen the lady in years. *Ha!* That rude woman had been his lover. How many other ladies that the duke considered his *distant* friend were present at the Sallises' ball? she wondered. She took another retreating step. Jealousy was an ugly emotion. Kilby despised both Fayne and Mrs. Du Toy for evoking it within her.

"To be expected, the tragic death of his father has upset him."

The other woman spoke. Kilby thought she heard her utter, "Solitea curse," although she was not positive she had heard the woman correctly.

"Do not believe the gossips. The Carlisles never do. They are an amazingly arrogant clan," Mrs. Du Toy said, laughing. "Then most dukes are. If Carlisle behaves himself this time, I might even let him convince me to become his duchess."

Kilby had heard enough. She retraced her steps to the intersection and then continued straight down the unexplored hall. Even if Fayne had told her the truth about him not seeing Mrs. Du Toy in years, the widow had apparently made up for lost time after Kilby and Priddy departed Lord Guttrey's house. His former mistress had lofty ambitions of becoming his duchess. She wondered if Fayne would be pleased by the news.

Kilby tried the first door on the right and discovered it was locked. The second closed door opened. She stepped inside, and not too soon, for she heard the voices of Mrs. Du Toy and her companion as they left the mirror room. Listening to their footfalls through the crack in the door, she finally allowed herself to breathe again when their voices faded off in the distance.

"Close the door, my lady of mystery."

Kilby visibly started at the command. She turned around to see Lord Tulley sitting on an indigo and crimson striped sofa with a flask in his hand. The room she had stumbled into appeared to be a small parlor.

"Good evening, my lord," she said, curtsying. "Forgive me for disturbing you. I thought I was alone."

"Did you?" the man drawled lazily, urging her to sit beside him on the sofa. He tucked his flask in an inner pocket of his frock coat. "Earlier, I could not help but notice your keen regard while I sat contemplating my cards. I anticipated that a lady who watched a gentleman so boldly would also defy propriety by approaching me. When you did not, I decided to seek you out. I thought a private setting for our introduction would be more to your liking."

She sat gingerly down on the sofa, keeping a respectable distance between them. His profile did not do Lord Tulley justice. Age had added lines around his murky blue eyes, but he still retained the handsomeness bestowed upon him in his youth. His dark brown hair on closer inspection was feathered with fine strokes of silver. It did diminish her initial impression of his male beauty. Nevertheless, there was a hardness to his features that was absent at a distance.

"Lord Tulley—" she began.

"Ah, I see you are aware of who I am," he said, pleased he had correctly deduced her interest. He also had not released her hand.

Kilby hastily nodded. "Yes. Since we are alone, permit me to introduce myself. I am Lady Kilby Fitchwolf. I was under the impression you knew my parents, the Marquess and Marchioness of Nipping."

The earl frowned upon hearing her parents' titles. "Nipping." He digested her revelation. Recognition sparked in his blue gaze. "You are Ermina's daughter? I had not realized she had had a child."

"Two daughters, actually." Kilby fidgeted, wondering how she could extract her hand without offending the gentleman. "My sister Gypsy recently turned eight." She doubted Lord Tulley would be interested in her family's problems.

"Awful news about Ermina's and your father's deaths," he murmured, coincidentally picking up her melancholy thoughts. "You and your sister have my condolences." He bowed his head and tenderly caressed her hand.

Kilby shuddered, concealing the revulsion his light touch provoked. The heavy scent of the spirits he had been imbibing before her arrival had her nose wrinkling.

"If you know my name, then I can assume you are aware that I too have suffered an indisputable loss," he said, his downcast gaze moving up the graceful line of her arm and lingering speculatively on her bodice.

Her expression softened with empathy. She understood loss intimately. "Forgive me if speaking of it has stirred your sorrow. Yes, I was told you lost your wife eight years ago."

"Are we not a pair?" Lord Tulley laughed bitterly. Shaking his head, he said, "Two unhappy souls mourning what we cannot have, and refusing to accept solace when it is so sweetly offered."

A thread of fear vibrated in her spine like the plucked string of a harp, when the earl lifted his lowered gaze to her face. Not caring how he interpreted her actions, Kilby rose off the sofa, tugging her hand free from his grasp.

"Perhaps you misunderstand me, my lord." She walked away from him, pretending to study one of the small paintings on the wall. "I am happy. While I might grieve for my loss, I continue to embrace life. That does not mean I have forgotten them." She seized the moment to explain why she had sought him out. Being alone with Lord Tulley was disconcerting, and she wanted to leave him to his solitude. "It was why I had wanted to meet you. I was told that you knew my mother in her youth. I had hoped that you might share what you recall of the lady you knew."

The earl had the stealth of a sleek jungle cat. Kilby stifled her squeak of surprise when she realized he was standing behind her. She turned, attempting to put a respectable distance between them. Her efforts found her flat against the wall with the earl holding her in place with his body.

Lord Tulley smiled; his eyes gleamed in anticipation of his nefarious intent. "Why discuss the past, my lady, when the present is so fascinating?"

Where has Kilby run off to? Fayne wondered crossly for the thousandth time. The Sallises' town house was too large for a cursory search. He stood on the second landing and peered up into the shadowy stairwell, wondering if Kilby had ventured upstairs. Before he left his friends, he had noted that Lady Quennell was still in the ballroom, chatting with several of her friends. Kilby would not have left the house without alerting her chaperone to her plans.

A muffled scraping sound overhead was his only warning of the impending disaster. He threw himself backward seconds before a large piece of plaster struck the railing he had been leaning over and shattered. His heart pounding, he glanced up at the blackness and then down at the broken remains of a muse's face that had adorned the ceiling several stories higher.

A precise blow to the head, and that hunk of plaster might have killed me.

It was a sobering thought. "I wonder if Sallis knows his bloody house is falling apart!"

Staying clear of the stairs, Fayne continued toward the opposite side of the house, assuming Kilby was trying to put distance between them. It frustrated him that she refused to acknowledge the unbidden passion that electrified the air whenever they were in proximity of each other. Hell, he did not even need to see her. Fayne had reclined in his bed alone night after night, craving the violet-eyed witch. When the yearning overwhelmed him, he closed his hand around the rigid ache she had caused, stroking his cock until his seed pumped vigorously into his palm. It had been simple for him to conjure her beautiful face during that blinding moment of ecstasy, to imagine his straining cock was pumping into her wet, tight sheath.

Fayne cursed, forgetting the potency of his idle thoughts when they centered on Kilby. It was going to be awkward explaining away his arousal if someone happened upon him in the hall.

Just minutes earlier, he had nearly collided with Morrigan Du Toy and her friend. Like a thief, he had ducked into a shadowed corner and prayed he would escape unnoticed. The ladies had walked by him, gossiping about their hostess.

The hallway he now strode down split off to the right and left. Fayne heard a muffled thump coming from the left. Assuming he had nothing to lose, he headed for the source of the sound. Perhaps Kilby was hiding from the women, too.

Opening the door, Fayne was unprepared for neither what he stumbled upon nor the eruption of the rage that had been simmering just below the surface. Inside the small parlor, an unidentified man had Kilby pinned against the opposite wall with her arms over her head. He seemed to be devouring her mouth as his hips rhythmically thrust against her.

Kilby moaned, and Fayne wanted to throttle her. The lady had been denying him for days, and yet she spread her thighs for this stranger. It was ridiculous to feel betrayed, but his feelings toward the deceitful bitch had never seemed rational. He wanted to tear the man off Kilby and demand explanations he never would have asked from his former lovers.

Kilby turned away from her lover and gasped. "My lord . . . please . . . let go!"

Glowering at the entwined couple, Fayne almost backed out of the room. The lady had made her choice. Carlisles never begged. However, her words echoed softly in his head.

Let go.

Fayne had held Kilby in his arms, tasted her desire. She might have told him to stop, but she had never begged him to let go of her. He marched up to the straining couple. If he was wrong about the situation, he was gentleman enough to apologize for his error. If her lover's honor demanded satisfaction, Fayne would gladly put a bullet in the smug bastard's chest.

Grabbing the man by the shoulder, Fayne pulled him away from Kilby. The man staggered out of reach. He collided with a chair and both went tumbling.

"Fayne, thank heavens!" Kilby sobbed, sagging against the wall. Her relief was so evident, he felt physically ill to realize that he had so badly misjudged her.

"Did he hurt you?"

She shook her head, too overcome to speak. Her hand went to her throat. The skin around her neck was reddened as if the man had been strangling her to gain her compliance.

Fayne was going to kill him. Hauling the man to his feet, he recognized Lord Tulley. The fact the earl seemed to match Kilby's preference for an older lover only made Fayne want to punch the bastard harder.

"Fayne! No!" Kilby cried out.

It was the wrong thing to say. He slammed his fist into the earl's jaw, sending the man sprawling. Fayne was mad at himself as much as he was at the earl for believing even for a minute that Kilby had chosen this man to be her lover. As for Tulley, he was the unfortunate focus of Fayne's punishing ire.

"Get up!" he curtly ordered.

When Tulley tried to roll onto all fours, he kicked the man in the underbelly. The earl grunted, curling his knees into his chest. Nothing was going to save the man for touching Kilby.

He pulled the man up by his cravat. Using the fancy knot to hold him in place, Fayne repeatedly struck the man in the face until his fist was slick with blood. Tulley's eyes rolled upward until only the white was showing. Distantly, he heard Kilby frantically calling to him.

"Stop! You are going to kill him!"

Fayne felt Kilby's hand on his arm. He shrugged off her touch and dragged the earl to the door. "Tulley, can you hear me?" He impatiently slapped the man in the face to make certain he was paying attention.

"Yesh," the man said, slurring the word.

Fayne kicked open the door with his foot. "Good. Consider yourself challenged. My seconds will call on you to-morrow."

He threw the man out of the room, watching dispassion-ately as he crashed into the wall opposite the door. "Tulley, do me the courtesy of not coming to your senses, and issuing an apology. If I hear word that you have linked Lady Kilby's name to our regrettable disagreement, I will make certain the bullet I fire into your worthless body is positioned so that you languish for days in feverish agony. Do I make myself clear?"

At Tulley's sluggish nod, Fayne said, "Good."

He slammed the door and locked it. Pivoting slowly, Fayne confronted the lady who was determined to drive him mad. He took out his handkerchief and wiped Tulley's blood from his hand. "Have I ever mentioned to you that your choice in lovers is atrocious?"

Dry-eyed, Kilby ignored his question. "Fayne, you cannot challenge him."

"No?" He was rather skillful at evasion, too. "Then perhaps you should stop running away from what's between us and choose me."

"I beg of you, do not challenge Lord Tulley," Kilby said, clutching his arm.

He moved away from her. "Do not dare defend the man to me!" Fayne paced in front of her, reminding her of a hungry lion in a cage. "He had you pressed against the wall. His hands were on your throat. Tulley had every intention of taking you by force. If I hadn't found you—"

She crossed her arms over her chest and hugged herself. "Yet you did. Lord Tulley did not harm me. Please let it go."

In mid-stride he switched directions and lunged for her. Kilby shrieked as he backed her against the wall. Earlier when they had spoken in the ballroom, she had sensed the dark, unpredictable emotions simmering beneath his affable mask. The earl's attack had cracked his fragile veneer, placing her in a very precarious position.

"Have I misunderstood, Kilby?" Fayne held her against the wall with his body, calculatingly re-creating the scene from which he had just rescued her. Gently, he placed his hand on her bruised throat. "Did I interrupt something you desired?"

"That is an outrageous suggestion!" she snapped, angry that he could believe she wanted the earl's hands on her. Especially when she had been valiantly resisting Fayne. "I never encouraged Lord Tulley!"

"Are you so certain?" he asked, the hand at her throat tightening imperceptibly. "I have watched you for weeks, flitting from one gentleman to the next."

She rolled her eyes at his reasoning. "As is every other unmarried lady this season. Lady Quennell has made no secret that she hopes to secure a match for me before I return to Ealkin. There is nothing criminal in my actions."

"It depends on your perspective, I suppose," Fayne conceded, curling his fingers against her throat and stroking her neck. "When you gaze at me through those haunting violet eyes, I see within them an unspoken promise."

"An illusion," she blurted out, suddenly uncomfortable with the way he was staring at her. For some reason, it had become awfully warm in the room. Unable to hold his gaze, Kilby turned her face away.

Fayne grazed his lips along the line of her jaw. "Perhaps," he absently murmured. "Let us test your conjecture."

Kilby could barely breathe as his hand left her throat and slid down the slope of her breast. Fayne did not need his hands to restrain her. He used his hard, lean body to pin her in place. His hands jumped from her waist to her arms. The sensation of his fingers on her bare flesh made her shiver.

Her nipples constricted painfully in response to his touch. She squirmed against him. "Fayne," she huskily pleaded, no longer thinking about Lord Tulley.

A tremor went through him at the sound of his name on her lips. The tender stroking ceased. Fayne caged both her wrists and winged them up over her head. He leaned into her body, reminding her who was touching her, who had control.

Although fully clothed, Kilby felt vulnerable stretched out like a sacrifice against the wall. "You have proven your point, Fayne. Release me."

"Is that truly what you want, little wolf?" He covered her mouth with his, lingering so that she still felt the scorching heat after he withdrew.

"Yes!" Well, not exactly. She liked kissing him, but his dominating manner was unfair.

Fayne expertly spun her around, so that her front was facing the wall. Holding her wrists above her head, he used his mouth to nuzzle her sensitive neck. "I think you are lying. The real question is, which one of us are you trying to fool?"

Without warning, one of his hands seized the edge of her bodice and tore open the back. She cried out as a hail of glass buttons from her dress struck the floor, scattering in all directions. Kilby bucked against him, but he managed to hold her in place one-handed, using his hip as a brace.

"I am not trying to fool anyone," she said, gritting her teeth. The blasted man was too strong from her vulnerable position.

"No, Kilby, you're not." His hip dug into her back and he slid lower. She realized he was groping for something from his boot. The pressure eased slightly as he straightened.

She sucked in her breath when she glimpsed a small knife in his hand. "Are you planning to kill me, Your Grace?" He had told her that he did not blame her for his father's death. As she eyed the knife, it occurred to her that he could have been lying to her all along.

Fayne heartily laughed. "You occasionally annoy me, Kilby. However, I can think of a more pleasurable means of retribution."

Kilby felt the edge of the blade at her lower back. Fayne

tugged roughly. The tension of her corset suddenly eased. With her relief came outrage. "Are you mad? You are cutting my laces?"

Fayne was not listening to her. She felt his hand move up her back as he ruthlessly sawed through the bindings holding her corset together. Once he was finished ruining her corset, he slipped the blade under the tapes at her waist and cut them. Her petticoats slithered down her legs to the floor.

He discarded the knife.

"Stop cutting up my undergarments!" If she ever got her hands on that knife, she intended to shred his clothes into rags.

"I'll buy you new ones," he promised, licking the line of her spine at her nape.

Fayne surprised her by next doing the unexpected. He released her arms and stepped back. Relief soared through her. Letting her arms fall to her sides, she inadvertently did precisely what he had wanted her to do. Wordlessly, he hooked his fingers under the sleeves of her dress, and stripped her, corset and all. He had left her wearing only a chemise, stockings, and slippers.

Enough was enough! Kneeling at her feet, he lifted his head and grinned. The scoundrel was toying with her. When he stood and reached for her, she seized her chance to retaliate. Attempting to burrow her face into his hand, she sank her sharp teeth deeply into the soft flesh between his thumb and first finger.

A very satisfying yelp erupted from him, which he followed with some particularly nasty expletives. "Bloodthirsty wench!" he said, eyeing her sullenly while he shook the sting from his hand.

Kilby dropped down and gathered up her discarded clothing circled at her feet. Her thoughts were centered on the door across the room. Once she had put some distance from Fayne, she would worry about her ruined dress, which she clutched to her chest.

"Kilby. You cannot leave this room undressed."

No, of course she could not. She had him to thank for that! That did not mean she could not stay out of arm's reach. With a haughty toss of her head, Kilby intended to remove herself to the opposite side of the room. Or she would have if she had not tripped on a section of her petticoat that had slipped out of her hands. On a muffled oath, she stumbled forward. Fayne reached out to catch her, but his added weight prevented her from regaining her balance. Together they hit the back of the sofa, rolled across the top and landed on the cushions.

Naturally, she was on the bottom.

Fayne stared down at her with a positively fiendish grin. "Intent on seducing me, eh?"

Kilby gaped at him, surprised by his outrageous question. "You are delusional," she muttered to herself. Fruitlessly, she tried to shove him off the sofa.

Fayne had no interest in moving, now that fate had placed him exactly where he wanted to be—right between the lady's thighs. He bounced his pelvis against her, testing the cushions. "This is much better than the wall, do you not think?"

"I hope your hand is bleeding," she snarled, delighting him with her burst of temper. "Get off me."

Fayne might have obeyed if he was wholly certain Kilby truly wanted him to back away. Staring down at her face, he noticed her cheeks were flushed with passion and her eyes had dilated to thin violet rings. It revealed that although Kilby was wary of him, she also desired him. Fayne blamed himself for her conflicting emotions. Earlier, he had been so angry because she had spent most of the evening avoiding him, that when he found her in the arms of Lord Tulley, he had been tempted to throttle them both.

His temper had not improved after she begged him not to challenge Lord Tulley. Fayne had considered himself a patient man, but Lady Kilby had a dangerous habit of provoking him. Pride and anger had prompted him to press her against the wall and reenact the scene he had witnessed when he had discovered her with Tulley. Once he had put his hands on her, felt how her body fitted his so perfectly, his half-baked notion of punishing her faded as need overtook him. There was nothing preventing either of them from indulging their desires.

"Listen to me," she demanded, pinching him on his arm. "You have to let me up. What if someone discovers us?"

"Then we will have to be quiet." Fayne was not concerned. His passionate nature had placed him in some rather awkward predicaments over the years, and he had survived them relatively unscathed. Since he doubted such an explanation would ease her distress, he added, "The door is locked. No one will bother us."

"But—"

Fayne silenced her with a sizzling kiss. Kilby stiffened in his arms momentarily, before she sighed and surrendered to the hunger his touch always seemed to elicit. He slid his hand under her head and deepened the kiss. She moaned against his mouth. Kilby was a puzzling mix of contrasts. Every time she opened her mouth, she was telling him that she was uninterested in having an affair with him. Her body, on the other hand, told a different story. The way she responded to his questing touch revealed that she did want him. Fayne could not understand why she put so much effort into denying what they both desired.

Nothing could stop him from claiming her now. Tonight.

• • •

Kilby was dreaming. It had to be a dream. Kissing Fayne, the comforting sensation of his weight pressing her into the sofa transcended all pleasures she had experienced up until that moment. He was a dangerous temptation. It would be so easy for her to forget the reasons that had brought her to London and just enjoy the sensual tide of pleasures he offered.

Fayne pulled away from her lips. "I am being selfish," he said, tugging at the complicated knot of his cravat. "No, do not move—yet." He winked and removed his coat.

"I believe you tossed your knife over there," she said, shocked all the way to her toes that she sitting there so calmly while a gentleman disrobed in front of her. "Shall I fetch it for you?"

He laughed and shook his head. Her gaze dropped to the front of his waist as he casually unfastened his breeches. "Not in this life," he teased, kneeling on the floor beside her. "Now that I have witnessed your fearsome temper firsthand—"

Kilby sat up on her elbows. "I am a very agreeable person. No temper to speak of in the slightest."

Fayne made a sound of disagreement in his throat. "Just keep away from the knife."

"No, truly—"

He rolled his eyes heavenward. "No temper, she claims," he complained, gesturing to the ceiling. "And still she argues with me when there are other, more pleasing diversions within our grasp." To add credence to his words, Fayne took her hand and slipped her fingers into the opening of his breeches.

Kilby's mouth went dry. Belatedly, she wondered if he had been baiting her about her temper because he sensed she was nervous and thought the brief distraction would calm her. She almost snatched her hand back when her fingers

connected with the heated flesh nestled on a bed of coarse
hair within. The fleshy rod seemed to swell beneath her hesitant caress. "Am I—does this hurt?" she asked hoarsely.
Her hand trembled as she tried to make sense of what she
touched. She had never seen or touched a man's rod before,
although she had a basic understanding of lovemaking.

"Only in a good way, little wolf," he replied, his green
gaze fixed on her face. "Like this."

Fayne glided his hand over her knee and under her chemise. Unlike Kilby's, his touch was not hesitant. He parted
the cleft between her legs and skillfully plunged a finger
into her. She sucked in her breath, half expecting some discomfort, but her body had been anticipating him all along.
He had briefly touched her like this in Guttrey's conservatory before Lady Quennell's ill-timed appeared had broken
the sensual spell. Nevertheless, it appeared the encounter
had left her body instinctively craving more.

"You are as hungry as I am, eh?" he rasped, his expression one of stark need. "We have circled around each other
long enough, have we not?"

His thumb expertly found and coaxed the sensitive nub
hidden within her womanly folds. Kilby squirmed against
his hand. Fayne was thoroughly aroused by her response. His
manhood thickened and twitched, demanding to mate.
That part of him was so large. She began to worry that she
was too small to accommodate him.

Using his other hand, Fayne gently removed her hand
from his breeches. "Having you caress my cock is torture I
cannot bear, especially when your body beckons."

Withdrawing his hand from between her legs, he met
and held her gaze. Kilby watched mutely as he tasted her
desire. "Like sweet wild honey."

Fayne then leaned over her. He shoved his breeches
down over his hips and kicked them off to the side. Bracing
his hands on either side of her prone figure, he crawled up

until his face hovered above hers. "Kilby, forgive me, I cannot wait."

His purpose was unmistakable when he pushed her chemise higher and the tip of his manhood pressed firmly against her cleft. Kilby felt her body softening, anointing the broad hood of his arousal to ease his path. It was not an unpleasant sensation, she decided, relaxing slightly. "I like the weight of you on top of me," she shyly confessed.

Fayne bit her on the neck playfully and smiled mischievously. "Then it would be cruel to deny you the chance to experience it fully." Arching his back, he imbedded himself into her tight sheath with a single energetic thrust.

Kilby cried out, more from his startling invasion than pain. The pain was there, however, a persistent stinging and overwhelming tightness that made her think she was stretched beyond what nature intended. "You have to stop. I am too small," she said, near tears.

Fayne also seemed shaken. His expression was bleak incredulity. "A virgin," he said, his voice becoming accusatory. "You're a damn virgin!"

His anger perplexed her. "Of course I am. I told you . . ." She trailed off as the truth hit her. Kilby's violet eyes hardened. "I told you the truth. I was never your father's mistress." She bit her lower lip to conceal its slight tremor. "You did not believe me."

He pounded the side of the sofa with his fist. "What I believed does not matter now," he hedged.

The cretin had lied to her. He had claimed that he believed her so he could bed her himself. Confound it! And she had let him. She punched him in the shoulder. "Off. Get . . . off . . . *now!*" Kilby punctuated each word by pounding her fist into his muscled arm.

"Damn it, Kilby. Hold still," Fayne demanded harshly.

Her angry struggles were not helping the situation. Each time she bucked up against him, the motion plunged him deeper into her. Fayne groaned as if she were the one hurting *him*. If there was pain, she was too angry with him to feel it. The painful stretching his abrupt invasion had caused had eased significantly. In fact, she slowly became aware that with each abbreviated stroke their movements became even more fluid. A curious tension began to build inside her.

Fayne must have felt it, too. Suddenly, his fingers curled into fists. His features were taut and his mouth grim as he stared down at her. There was a mute apology in his green eyes. "I—" Strangling on the word, he fiercely rocked his pelvis against her and then he froze. Fayne clamped his eyes shut in agony as air hissed through his lips.

A second later, Kilby felt the foreign heat as his seed filled her. Kilby held Fayne while he shuddered in her embrace. Her hand covered her eyes in resignation.

Well, it was official.

She was truly the Duke of Solitea's mistress.

CHAPTER NINE

"A virgin!"

Fayne had been lamenting those two words aloud ever since he had callously breached Kilby's maidenhead hours earlier, her violet eyes wide with accusation and pain. Realizing the ramifications of her innocence, he felt like the vilest rogue, and comparable to the gentleman who, two years earlier, had seduced his innocent sister and heartlessly abandoned her. Fayne had wanted to murder Lord Thatcher Standish for his cruelty. Finding himself inadvertently cast into Standish's dastardly position had made him queasy and very irked at Kilby.

"I would have never touched her had I known she was a virgin," Fayne sullenly confessed.

It was his fault that they had parted awkwardly. Since she refused to speak to him—and he had his pride—Fayne had helped her dress, repairing the damage to her clothing the best he could. Angry and disillusioned, Kilby had left him alone in the room.

"It is an affliction many young ladies suffer from."

Ramscar picked up the bottle of wine placed between them and refilled his friend's glass. "As men, I consider it our solemn duty to relieve them of it."

The earl had been playing cards at White's when Fayne had stormed into the room, his brooding expression daring one and all to challenge him. Knowing his friend well, Ramscar foresaw the inevitable explosive conclusion if Fayne remained at the club. Bidding farewell to his companions, the earl had nudged his friend into a coach and driven him to the Red Satyr, a tavern known for its rotgut liquor and nightly violence.

A flicker of annoyance flared in Fayne's green eyes. "Not me," he muttered, picking up his glass and swallowing. He grimaced. Whatever they were drinking was nasty and potent. "Bedding virgins. Troublesome business." He knew firsthand.

"Bah, if you ask me, it is a stupid rule," scoffed the earl, pointing a finger at him. "What good is it? If you were not so damned honorable, you would be bouncing on your delectable virgin this very minute instead of getting drunk with me."

He doubted Kilby was thinking highly of his abilities as a lover. Setting down his wine, he scrubbed his face roughly with his hand. He had bungled everything with her.

"Your optimism overwhelms me," he snorted into his glass.

Fayne blamed himself entirely. He should have believed her when she denied being his father's mistress. If he had paid attention, there had been subtle clues hinting of her innocence. In his arrogance, Fayne had ignored them, letting his father's notorious reputation incriminate her. Kilby had been alone in her boudoir with his father the night he had his fatal heart attack. Virile and charismatic, the duke had spent his entire life seducing and bedding every lady who had caught his eye. Fayne could hardly blame Kilby for succumbing to her passions. The moment he had seen her standing in the ballroom, he wanted to claim that passion for himself.

"Honestly, I do not understand your quandary, Solitea," Ramscar said, obviously musing over what Fayne had told him. "So the young lady is not your father's former mistress. While your discovery, in itself, is a tiny infraction of your rigid rule about bedding innocents, your lapse has successfully nullified her virginity. If you want Lady Kilby, and the lady is willing, I say enjoy her."

Fayne doubted Kilby would allow him to touch her again after his hasty claiming of her maidenhead. He was still rattled by his discovery. Kilby had not seemed innocent. She had been so curious and responsive to his caresses. Her arousing wetness had clung to his fingers as he teased her womanly flesh. When he finally had her naked and squirming underneath him, he thought only of claiming her.

"Willing?" Fayne shook his head at the impossibility. "Ram, the lady is a trifle upset with me. I expect any day her male relatives will be pounding on my door and demanding satisfaction."

The precise moment he had swiftly buried himself into her welcoming channel had played over and over again in his mind. The tearing of her maidenhead had jolted both of them. While it might have been gentlemanly to stop just then, the primitive desire to claim her and the basic laws of gravity impelled him gratifyingly to the hilt.

Oblivious to his friend's thoughts, Ramscar flirted with a brown-haired barmaid who was serving a table across the room. "You are in luck. Curious about the lady who seems to have befuddled one of my closest friends so magnificently, I made some casual inquiries about Lady Kilby Fitchwolf. The parents are dead. They drowned in some unfortunate tragedy. I heard she has an older brother, but he is not in town."

"A brother." He gripped the empty glass in his hand and glowered into the bottom. "Aye, no trouble there," he muttered sarcastically. "The man will be tickled to learn I have tupped his sister."

In hindsight, Fayne realized he should have stopped, withdrawn completely, when he realized Kilby was a virgin. He had every intention of doing so, but Kilby had started struggling to get free. Her frenetic movements bumped her hips against his as she tried to dislodge him. He had tried to warn her, had ordered her to stop. She had ignored him. Her movements pummeled the head of his cock against her womb.

Although she was innocent, her body and nature had coaxed their union to its predictable conclusion. The sensation of her wet channel constricted around his cock was his undoing. For the first time in his life, he surrendered to the instinctive need to mate and released his seed into Kilby.

"Well, it will not be the first time a man has challenged you for sullying his virginal sister," Ramscar said pragmatically.

Fayne picked up the bottle, refilling his friend's glass and then his own. "It will be the first occasion I deserve it!"

"I suppose you could always marry the chit," Ramscar suggested absently. The barmaid was gesturing for him to join her at the bar. "Excuse me. I will return shortly." His friend stood up, hoping to engage the pretty maid in a tryst later.

Fayne barely noticed Ramscar's departure. His thoughts were centered on Kilby. In the past, he had always been careful about denying his lover his seed. Though the family rarely discussed his father's infidelities, it was known the duke had sired a son with one of his married lovers, Lady Dening. She delivered the infant nine months after Fayne had been born.

Fayne did not know the specifics, but he was certain

there must have been a confrontation between the duke and Lord Dening. In the end, the earl had claimed the boy as his heir.

The undeniable proof of her husband's unfaithfulness had shattered his mother's heart. Since her husband could not recognize the boy as a Carlisle, the duchess had felt bound by duty to visit the Denings each year and see Lord Jerrett on the duke's behalf. Both he and his sister, Fayre, knew how painful those visits were for their mother. It was an anguish he had vowed never to burden his future wife with.

And yet, he had spilled himself into Kilby like an uncouth lad mounting his first mistress. Fayne had always prided himself on being a skillful lover. There was little doubt Kilby had not enjoyed his fumbling efforts. Fayne's mouth went dry at his next thought.

What if Kilby is carrying my heir?

He closed his eyes, recalling the blissful pinnacle of his orgasm. Fayne could not summon up any real regret that Kilby had been the one who had pierced his restraint. Just thinking about her made his cock swell with anticipation. He craved her. The small taste of her body had whetted his appetite.

Kilby was rightfully angry and disappointed, but Fayne was confident he could persuade her to forgive him. Once he was back in her good graces, he planned to seduce her into his bed again. This time he would do it properly. Fayne looked forward to tempting her with pleasure. He planned on coaxing and tormenting her until she thought of nothing else but him.

"Did you hear the news?" Lyssa asked Kilby as she approached, her blue eyes sparkling with excitement.

"I have heard several things this evening," Kilby replied, smiling indulgently. Three days had passed since Fayne had pried her out of Lord Tulley's vile embrace. Three days since she had happily surrendered her virginity to the cad. "Let me think. Hmmm . . . Lady Ambridge is reportedly considering accepting Lord Drakefield's marriage proposal . . . Mr. Favero was so foxed last evening that he used Lord Kibblewhite's high-crowned beaver as a privy . . . oh, and the very married Countess of Sarell had a public row with her lover."

"No, I heard something else. I—" Lyssa paused, thinking about her friend's revelations. "Mr. Favero piddled in Lord Kibblewhite's hat?" She wrinkled her nose in revulsion, dismissing her question with the wave of a hand. "Never mind. I heard something even better. It appears the Duke of Solitea has fought yet another duel. According to my source, Lord Tulley had insulted a very good friend of His Grace's. Words and cards were exchanged a few nights ago. Lord Tulley refused to apologize so they settled their differences this morning at dawn." Lyssa looked expectantly at Kilby, daring her friend to best her news.

Kilby was appalled by the news. The reckless ne'er-do-well! So Fayne had challenged Lord Tulley despite her wishes after all. Kilby was not really surprised. The duke apparently did whatever he wanted. He had chased her mercilessly around London for weeks, seduced her at first opportunity, and then let her walk away without a single word to her in three days. Three days! If he was not already dead, she was tempted to borrow a pistol from Darknell, and shoot him herself.

"I assume this tale has a happy ending?"

Lyssa furrowed her brow at Kilby's waspish tone. "I suppose it depends on whose side you choose. Lord Tulley fired first. The bullet missed His Grace, but managed to put a hole in the left sleeve of his shirt."

Kilby had not realized she had been holding her breath until a wave of dizziness assailed her. Pressing her fist to

her stomach, she slowly exhaled. Fayne was unhurt. If he
had died for defending her honor, she would have never
forgiven him. Her friend was giving her an odd look so
Kilby smiled brightly and said, "A ruined shirt. His Grace
has more lives than a cat."

Lyssa concurred with a quick nod. "The Duke of Solitea
fired next. His shot hit the earl in the collarbone, breaking
it in two places. I was told that Lord Tulley was conscious
long enough to apologize to His Grace before the surgeon
had him carried to his coach."

"An amazing tale," Kilby said faintly. "And the woman—
the woman whom the Duke of Solitea was defending. Does
anyone know her identity?"

Lyssa fanned herself slowly in contemplation. "No."
She frowned. "No, I do not believe the lady's name was
mentioned. The Duke of Solitea's accuracy with a pistol
should keep Lord Tulley silent on the matter."

Fayne had taken an incredible risk, challenging the earl.
If Lord Tulley had spun a sordid tale about her as he had
threatened, there was little doubt her reputation would have
suffered greatly. While Kilby did not agree with Fayne's
resorting to violent measures on her behalf, she had to admit his resolution was exceedingly effective.

Lyssa raised her fan to cover the lower half of her face
as she leaned over to speak confidentially. "You have spoken to His Grace on several occasions. Who do you think
his mysterious lady is?"

Kilby had never kept secrets from Lyssa. She trusted
her friend unequivocally. Be that as it may, Fayne had gone
to great lengths to protect her. She owed him her discretion. "I have no clue," she lied guilelessly.

Damn Lady Quennell and her never-ending hunt for a husband for her young charge! The viscountess did not understand the trouble she was causing. Fayne had trailed Kilby

and the viscountess to three residences this evening and at each stop he had missed them by minutes. He had the disconcerting pleasure of encountering the dozen or more gentlemen his lady had beguiled with a kind word, a dance, or a flirtatious smile. Lady Kilby Fitchwolf was a bewitching menace! Two of the gentlemen, Viscount Milyard and Mr. Edison Linsacre, had brazenly announced at one gathering that each intended to marry Lady Kilby Fitchwolf. This was a shock to both gentlemen, who each claimed he had procured Lady Kilby's affections. The viscount shoved Linsacre and soon a full-blown fight erupted. By the time Fayne had found someone who had known their whereabouts, the two ladies had already driven off to their next diversion.

For the past three days, he had resisted calling on Kilby. Their parting had been awkward, and he accepted the blame for it. He also knew she would be angry once she learned that he had formally issued a challenge to Lord Tulley. Kilby's complete lack of faith in his fighting skills stung his pride. He was perfectly capable of dealing with an ill-mannered bruiser like Tulley. Her concern, however, had given Fayne hope. Perhaps the lady cared about him more than she was willing to admit aloud.

Fayne was wagering his entire future on it.

Gaining admittance to Lord and Lady Wasbrough's ball without an invitation in hand had proved to be simpler than he had first thought. Initially, their insolent butler with a face like a bulldog had been troublesome. Fortunately, one of the arriving guests had vouched for him and he was free to search the house for his errant lady.

As he entered the ballroom, Fayne breathed a sigh of relief. Kilby was standing near one of the open windows. Her friend Lady Lyssa was at her side. There was no sign of Lord Darknell, thankfully. Despite Kilby's claims that the gentleman was only a dear friend, Fayne recognized a rival when he saw one. The viscount desired more than friend-ship from her.

Fayne's expression softened tenderly as he observed the ladies share confidences. Kilby had once told him that she was unsophisticated in comparison to the other ladies in the ballroom. He disagreed. Lady Quennell had impecca-ble taste, and Kilby's attire reflected the viscountess's in-fluence. Tonight she was wearing a dress of fine muslin. Across the bust and down the front diagonally, dainty flow-ers and scrolling vines had been elegantly embroidered. All the edges of the dress were trimmed in dark blue ribbon. Kilby's black tresses were piled high on her head. White gloves and matching slippers completed the costume.

Fayne thought she looked delectable as he drew closer.

From her stunned expression, it was obvious Kilby had not expected him to boldly approach her in public. He smiled indulgently as her cheeks turned a deep pink. "Y-your Grace," she stuttered. "What a coincidence! Lady Lyssa was just telling me the details of your remarkable morning."

Ah, so that explained why she was so undone by his presence. He had caught her gossiping. He was heartened to see that the anger and disappointment he had seen in her violet gaze at their last encounter was absent.

"Not particularly. I actually found the entire business te-dious," he confessed nonchalantly.

Although he had ruthlessly convinced Lord Tulley not to mention Kilby's name in polite society, there was little he or anyone else could do about the gossips.

Fayne bowed formally to each of the ladies. "Forgive me for intruding. Lady Kilby, I pray you will honor me with a dance?"

Kilby was bursting with questions as Fayne escorted her to-ward the dancing. "I am surprised to see you, Your Grace," she said, addressing him formally for appearance's sake.

His green eyes flickered enigmatically over her face, before coolly replying, "Then you have underestimated me."

There was no doubt in Kilby's mind. While Kilby had been caught up in Lady Quennell's quest to find her a husband, Fayne had been pursuing his own selfish interests. Neither spoke as they circled the perimeter made up of onlookers. Fayne made no attempt to join the other dancers. Kilby assumed he had used the excuse as a ruse to separate her from Lyssa. A few minutes later, he confirmed her suspicions when he dragged her away from the dancing and toward the open doors to the gardens.

"Where are we going?" she demanded, thinking of the trouble she had gotten herself into the last time she had slipped away from a ballroom.

"Someplace I can stand without putting my elbow in a glass of punch," he said, making her giggle.

The Wasbroughs' ballroom was packed beyond its capacity, and the air thick with heavy-scented perfumes, the acrid odor of tallow candles, and smoke. The rectangular room was smaller and narrower than the ones she had mingled in on her previous stops this evening.

Fayne took a deep breath as he and Kilby stepped outdoors. "A place to sit for a while and stare at the stars."

Kilby raised her eyes dubiously at the night sky. There were too many clouds for stargazing, but she said nothing. A fragile truce had settled between them. As long as neither one of them mentioned Lord Tulley or what happened in the back parlor, they might have a cordial conversation.

He guided her away from the small clusters of ladies and gentlemen who had also tired of the crowded ballroom. They strolled to the right and off the stone terrace until they reached a wrought-iron bench. Kilby sat down and looked expectantly at Fayne.

"I think we should discuss what happened three nights ago."

Kilby's shoulders slumped at his declaration. "Honestly, I cannot see what good it will do to hash over that awful night."

An unnerving stillness assailed Fayne. "Awful?" he murmured, after a tense, lengthy pause. The muscles in his jaw worked as he swallowed. "No, that is not the word I would have selected to describe that particular night."

"Oh." She brightened, straightening her posture. "How would you describe the night when I am attacked by an ardent gentleman, and you arrive, fight him off, issue a ridiculous challenge, and then take me to task over my stupidity for being alone with the gentleman . . . Only to take his place—"

Fayne held up a silencing hand. His nostrils flared in indignation. "You cannot accuse me of attacking you, Kilby. The major difference between Tulley and me is that you *desired* my hands on you."

"Details, details," she said, blithely dismissing his arrogant observation. "Now where was I? Oh yes, and then you proceeded to dispatch my undergarments with your wickedly sharp knife, ensconce us on the sofa, and take my innocence with the consideration you might give the whores you visit in the brothels."

He winced. "Christ, you've a low opinion of my character. I'll have you know, I do not visit broth—"

Kilby was not listening. Speaking over his grand confession, she demanded, "If 'awful' does not describe the night, pray, what word does?"

" 'Inevitable'!" he snapped back. Fayne leaped to his feet. Glowering at her, he was a tower of intimidation and simmering passion. "Lady Kilby Ermina Fitchwolf, will you consent to be my wife?"

CHAPTER TEN

"What?" Kilby splayed her right hand across her breast as if she could not catch her breath. Even in the shadows, her stark white face gleamed like a beacon. "What did you say?"

Fayne had never proposed to a woman. Well, proposed marriage, anyway. Kilby's less than joyous reaction was a brutal blow to his pride. He had anticipated several responses his offer might evoke. Fear was not one of them. "You heard me," he coldly replied. "What say you?"

She shifted on the bench. Fayne tensed, wondering if she was planning to flee from him. Kilby searched his austere expression. "Why?" She helplessly gestured. "Is it because of what we did on—"

He reached down and grabbed her by the arms. Pulling her onto her feet, he could not resist giving her a shake. The blank shock in her violet gaze was shredding his gut. "If I married every silly chit I tumbled onto her back, I would be a polygamist many times over."

Kilby's face tightened. She brushed aside his hands.

"Fine," she said, crossing her arms, her eyes glittering like amethysts. "Then why me? Why offer marriage to me? I am certain if I approached the legion of lovers in your past, they would all attest that you have never felt the slightest inclination to bind yourself to a single lady."

He opened his mouth to argue, and then clamped it shut. Fayne was damned by the truth. Before his father's death, he had been utterly content to remain unfettered. The drivel about the Solitea curse had prompted his father into marriage early in life to secure his heir.

Fayne had not anticipated following the same path as his father. When his father was alive, there had been no rush to hunt for a bride. Why would he have desired such a demanding creature? His life had been carefree; there were riches to indulge every whim, and a never-ending string of beautiful ladies panting in his bed.

"Why?" she mused aloud, circling him. "Why marry your father's mistress?"

Ah, the crux of her pique. He looked indulgently at her. "We both know you were not my father's mistress." She was too kindhearted not to forgive him for making a natural assumption.

She shook her head in disappointment. "You lied to me." She raised her arms and gesticulated at the heavens. "You placated me with sweet flattery and lies while you carried forth your seduction."

"Nothing so devious or dramatic," he said, refusing to be painted as the vile scoundrel who seduced her. Fayne took her by the shoulders and pushed her back down on the bench. "My father had a well-earned reputation for bedding any miss who caught his eye."

"As does the son," she said, lifting her right brow knowingly.

His palm itched to turn her over and paddle her for her insolent remark, but now was not the occasion for play.

"What should matter to you is that I do not care whether or not you were my father's mistress. I want you."

Kilby was not appeased. "That is your misfortune. You cannot always have what you want." She tossed her head back haughtily.

There was a challenge in her gleaming gaze, which Fayne eagerly embraced. "Too late. I already have. And I will again," he said intensely.

The candid nature of their conversation had Kilby glancing warily at the terrace to make certain no one was paying attention to them. "If you are referring to what transpired on the sofa three nights ago, you are sadly mistaken."

Fayne wanted to growl in frustration. Kilby was punishing him. She was not upset about his hasty lovemaking. The breaching of her maidenhead had caused her only some minor discomfort. What she found unforgivable was that he had not believed her. A lady's pride, he broodingly mused. How was he to know when he first met her that she had not merely been playing flirtatious games with him? It was not as if he went about despoiling virgins each season.

He knelt in front of her. "Heed me well, my little wolf. I will have you again—soon and often. So our first union was a trifle clumsy—"

Kilby gave an unladylike snort of disdain.

Fayne pinned her with a resolute green stare. "Largely, I am to blame. We will improve with practice, I assure you."

He was tempted to drag her out into the gardens this instant and show her how pleasurable lovemaking could be. Regrettably, he had to concentrate on more practical matters.

"Your answer, Lady Kilby," Fayne curtly said. "And it better be yes. Will you marry me?"

"I can't believe the lady rejected your offer of marriage."

Fayne glowered at Cadd for reminding him of his humiliating defeat. Two days had passed since Kilby had thanked him politely, and then refused his marriage proposal. He had not lost his temper or created an incident the gossips would have relished. Instead, he had mockingly bowed in false gallantry, and departed.

Everod affectionately punched Fayne on the arm. "What I can't believe is that Carlisle actually made an honorable proposal to a lady."

He accepted his friend's teasing graciously. Ramscar, Cadd, and Everod had cajoled him into joining them this evening at the theater. None of them believed Fayne was truly despondent over Kilby's rejection. Years earlier, he had drunkenly boasted to all of them that he would not bind himself to a wife until he was forty. There was no point wasting his best years being leg-shackled. Fayne was only twenty-five. According to his original plan, he had fifteen years to indulge every decadent whim and vice. A man would have to be mad or in love to toss away his freedom.

Was he in love with the stubborn Lady Kilby Fitchwolf?

Madness was a kinder fate.

Ramscar stepped in between Everod and Fayne, placing a companionable hand on each friend's shoulder. "The fact remains, our dear friend behaved gallantly toward the lady and was rebuffed. Honestly, Solitea, you have astounding luck. Perhaps we should have taken you directly to Moirai's Lust."

"Later, if the hunting is poor," Cadd promised, as they strolled through the lobby of the theater.

The hunt for which the marquess was eager had nothing to do with finding a good theater box. *Les sauvages nobles* were seeking friendly companions for the evening. Fayne privately acknowledged they were an impressive group. Heads turned and the crowd parted, deferring to the four breathtakingly handsome males. They reeked of arrogance, wealth, and mischief. Very few ladies resisted the combination for long.

Except for Kilby.

From the corner of his eye, a flash of violet caught his notice. Glancing left, he met the curious stares of three very attractive ladies. The tall one in the middle clutched an open fan the exact hue of Kilby's eyes. The ladies preened and whispered to each other at his candid perusal. Fayne smiled, and the trio collapsed into one another in a fit of giggles.

"One or all," Everod whispered in Fayne's ear. "You could fuck each one in turn and they would weep with gratitude."

Perhaps it was time to find a willing lady who did not make him feel like a clumsy arse whenever he was around her. He owed no fidelity to Lady Kilby Fitchwolf. They had had a very brief affair, nothing more. There were at least a dozen ladies of whom he could make a similar claim. What had clouded the issue was her apparent innocence. Well, he had tried to make amends, had he not? The lady had firmly rejected his offer.

"The night is full of possibilities," Fayne agreed.

"Lyssa, I am not good company tonight," Kilby complained, sitting down next to her friend in their rented box.

She was not even certain how her friend had talked her into attending the theater, especially since she had resisted Priddy's invitation to watch the fireworks display at Vauxhall, followed by a very late supper at Lady Carsell's town house. Kilby had lied by excusing herself from the festivities due to a disagreeable stomach. She did not have the heart to spend the evening flirting with the potential suitors Priddy would have insisted that she meet. If she had accepted, there was the strong possibility that she might have come across Fayne. She was not ready to face him yet.

"Rubbish. There is nothing wrong with you. It is the weather that is making you melancholy," Lyssa assured her. She leaned forward and waved to a friend five boxes to their left.

Kilby sighed. Unlike her friend, she knew the real cause of her low spirits. "I hope the rain will hold off until after the fireworks. The viscountess was looking forward to them."

Lyssa sat back and smiled. "Do not fret about Lady Quennell. It would take more than a little rain to distress her." Her expression brightened at something she noticed beyond Kilby's shoulder.

Kilby turned around and saw Lord Darknell at the threshold. She looked askance at Lyssa. Her friend's scarlet features revealed she had set up this accidental meeting to give Kilby and Darknell a chance to settle their differences.

The viscount bowed formally. "Perhaps you have a spare seat for an old friend."

Everod and Cadd took the lead in their casual pursuit of muslin. Fayne was content to follow. Ramscar divided his attention between the activity being carried out on the stage, and a careful perusal of the theater boxes. Instead of remaining in their rented boxes, the foursome spent the next several hours socializing from theater box to theater box. Throughout it all, Everod and Cadd bickered over which sort of female made the best mistress.

"I disagree, Everod," Cadd said to no one's surprise, as they departed a private box. "A courtesan makes a more amenable mistress than a married lady. A lady tutored in the trade has too many benefits to simply dismiss." He began ticking off the advantages with his fingers. "They are highly skilled lovers, their sole purpose in life is to pleasure their lover, and when the affair has ended, a respectable *congé* sends them searching for a new protector. There are no regrets."

No regrets. Fayne dug his fingers into the pocket of his waistcoat and removed his watch. Fayne checked the time.

He knew he was suffering over his parting with Kilby when Cadd's arguments seemed valid.

Everod made a rude sound. "I grant you, Cadd, a courtesan is skilled. She has manipulation down to an art. The lady teases your cock until you are willing to offer her anything."

"I can afford it," the marquess smoothly countered.

Ramscar cuffed Cadd on the back of his head. "Puppy," he muttered, before walking away and disappearing through the curtain of the next box they had planned to visit.

"Hey!" Cadd called after him. He scowled at Fayne. "What did I do to offend him?"

Fayne shrugged. Ramscar was quieter, more introspective than the rest of them. It was difficult to guess at what point Cadd's diatribe had offended him. The earl had a deep affection for women. He tended to see beyond the superficial. The ladies he selected as lovers were not necessarily renowned beauties; however, they possessed an intellect that equaled his own. It was probably why his liaisons lasted longer than the others'.

"Your idiocy offends him, Cadd," Everod taunted, shoving the marquess forward toward the curtains. "Ramscar understands the risks a gentleman takes when dallying with these courtesans. While she plays the devoted mistress for you, she is bedding two or three other gentlemen to plump up her purse. Egad, you are damned fortunate your rod isn't festering in your breeches from one of those cunning bitches."

Fayne stepped through the curtain after them. What he saw had him turning away and clapping his hand over his mouth to muffle his laughter. Lost in their argument, Cadd and Everod had not considered that the occupants of the box might overhear their conversation. Ramscar abruptly straightened at their arrival. His sweeping glare encompassed them all. The ladies he had been quietly conversing with were the very conservative Duke of Hadnott's wife, her fifteen-year-old twin daughters, and the duke's eighty-year-old mother. The varying degrees of astonishment on the ladies' faces was priceless. The duke's mother raised her quizzing glass to her eye and pointedly examined the marquess's crotch.

Cadd snarled, shoved Everod away with a muffled curse, and marched off. Sneering at Ramscar for not warning them, Everod hastily followed after his friend.

Fayne could not stop laughing. He fought to keep his face sober, while the earl eloquently apologized to the ladies. His friends' antics had been highly amusing. He could not recall the last time he had been so highly entertained in the theater.

Bringing the back of his hand to his lips to hide his smile, he bowed respectfully to the ladies. As he turned to leave, he noticed something that swiftly quelled his good humor.

Across the circular expanse of the auditorium, Lord Darknell was cozily sitting next to Kilby.

Kilby sensed the viscount's gaze on her face as she watched the ballet performance on stage. Matters between them had become confusing since her arrival in London. She longed for the simplicity of life at Ealkin, the life she had had before her parents' deaths. Lyssa was winding and unwinding one of the ribbons of her reticule around her first finger, a definite sign her friend was fretting about her meddling. She could have reassured her friend that she was not angry, but decided Lyssa deserved to share a little of the uneasiness Kilby was feeling.

"Fitchwolf, are you so vexed you cannot bear to look at me?"

She shifted her gaze from the energetic dancers below to the viscount's beseeching expression. The apprehension tightening her face lessened with the affection born of years of friendship.

"There. You see?" Kilby said lightly, staring into his familiar brown eyes. "Not vexed in the least."

"You forgive too easily," Darknell chided. He clasped her unencumbered hand on her lap. "I have been deserving of your anger. The spiteful burden Archer has placed on your slender shoulders has caused you great angst. Instead of being the friend you needed, I have been sarcastic, judgmental, and overall nasty in disposition." He stroked his thumb across the back of her hand. "I offer my deepest apologies and pray you will forgive me."

"I forgave you the instant I saw you." Kilby leaned over and laid her cheek on his shoulder. "You are one of my dearest friends. We may not always agree, my lord, but I have no desire to toss away our friendship because of those differences."

Kilby straightened and squeezed his hand. She turned to Lyssa, intending to tell her friend that her meddling had had a happy ending. It was then she noticed a matron frowning at her from the next theater box. Gently she released Darknell's hand on the pretense of searching for an item in her reticule. A prickly warmth crept up her neck and face. Kilby silently chastised herself. How many people had observed her demonstrative exchange with the viscount? She had forgotten how closely the other patrons watched the activity in the boxes.

Tugging on the strings of her reticule, she discreetly looked about, fearing she and Darknell had become more fascinating than the spectacle on stage. Kilby visibly sagged in relief as she realized those concerns were unfounded. No one was paying them the slightest attention, well, with the exception of the nosy matron in the next box. She leaned back in her chair. It was then her roaming gaze paused on a box one tier down and almost directly across from theirs.

Four elegantly dressed ladies were holding court in the box, while six to eight gentlemen vied for their exclusive regard. Kilby thought several of them seemed familiar to her, but she could not recall where she had met them.

"My lord, do you recognize the ladies yonder one tier below?"

Darknell peered down at the box Kilby had directed him to. "Yes, though I daresay it is best if you avoid them."

Overhearing his comment, Lyssa inclined her posture closer to them. "Are they paphians?" she asked in hushed excitement. Her friend studied the audience in search of the intriguing ladies who had caught Kilby's interest.

"Not exactly, Nunn." Darknell seemed reluctant to pursue the conversation further. "To do so would credit them with more import than they deserve."

"Who are they? They seem very popular," Kilby said, observing one of the gentlemen offering his hand to the lady adorned in a bronze-colored dress. There was something vaguely familiar about the gentleman, she mused, as she studied him from the back. The distance and dim lighting made it nearly impossible to guess his identity.

"Ladies of the *ton,*" Darknell said, trying to sound bored. "On the right, there is Lady Silver. Next to her is Mrs. Du Toy, followed by Lady Talemon." He paused and cleared his throat. Giving Kilby a sympathetic look, he said, "And the lady your new friend the Duke of Solitea is trying to coax into a more intimate setting is Lady Spryng. If I recall, the countess was once reputed to have been the duke's mistress. It appears Solitea plans on rekindling their intimate connection."

Kilby merely blinked at the sudden sound of applause and catcalls emanating from the pit. The ballet piece had ended and a lone woman with a guitar advanced to the center of the stage.

As if sensing her regard, Fayne turned and looked directly

into her startled gaze. The bastard had the impudence to smile. Lady Spryng caressed his arm and spoke to him. Kilby's heart twisted painfully in her chest as she watched them disappear into the shadows.

"I have missed you, Carlisle," Velouette Whall, Countess of Spryng, said throatily. Her lightly accented inflections were exotic, never failing to arouse Fayne.

As they entered the private parlor that connected to the theater box, she gestured at her personal maid, who was stitching silently in one of the chairs. "Isold, take your work outside the door where there is better light."

Without looking at either one of them, the maid solemnly stuffed her sewing into a fabric bag and left the room.

Fayne trailed after the countess, who slipped off her Indian shawl. The dress she wore revealed the appreciative curves of breasts and shoulders. "I'll have you know the light in those passageways is abysmal."

Velouette faced him, her face sparkling with mirth. "I know, darling. I thought you preferred your entertainments without an audience."

Fayne knew what the countess was anticipating. While he had knelt beside her in the box, the minx had whispered the naughty details in his ear. There was something about the theater that aroused Velouette. With one of his friends guarding the curtain and a servant outside the door, how many times during their brief affair had he taken the countess on the sofa she was reclining on now?

She beckoned him with one finger. "Share your thoughts with me."

He sat down sideways on the cushion, facing her. "I was thinking about you," he answered honestly. "And the things we did to each other on this sofa."

Fayne was also thinking about Kilby. Seeing her with Lord Darknell had enraged him. The viscount plainly desired

Kilby. From their intimate pose, Fayne suspected the gentleman had grown weary of just being a close friend. Fuming
and jealous, he had sought out a woman who was a balm to
his tattered pride.

The countess purred in delight. "Oh, those were grand
times, were they not?"

"The best," he agreed, smiling slightly as she reached
for his cravat. He stopped her hands before she could ruin
the knot. "If we were so grand together, Velouette, why did
we part ways?"

The countess shrugged. "It is the way of things, I suppose." She moved forward, literally crawling into his lap.
Gazing up at him with liquid brown eyes, she said, "What
does it matter? You are here and we are together again."

Fayne curled his arm around her waist. The countess
was everything he had once desired in a mistress. She was
an enthusiastic, exotic beauty who was not afraid of her
body or the pleasure he could give her. He had never trembled in her arms, been too hasty or clumsy. Velouette saw
the advantages of being his lover, the power and wealth behind the title.

Kilby had just wanted him.

After witnessing the tragic death of his father and his
family's assumptions about her questionable character, she
had been reluctant to be connected with any Carlisle. His
wealth and position in society had not swayed her into his
bed. Once he had coaxed her there, he had lost all semblance
of control. She had run from him, wary and unsatisfied.

"You would do anything for me, would you not?" he
murmured, caressing her face.

"Anything you desire, Your Grace," she vowed.

"I could bend you over this sofa, toss up your skirts, and
fill you—"

"Yes, my darling—"

"Without tender words, no teasing touch—nothing gentle, just me inside you, pounding—"

"Yes. Please!" she begged.

Fayne cocked his head inquiringly to one side. "And if I use your body and think of another?"

He knew Kilby had seen him with Velouette. Feeling goaded by Darknell's presence in her theater box, he had deliberately flaunted Velouette in front of her. Despite the distance, Fayne swore he felt her bewilderment and anguish. Kilby was too young, too innocent for sophisticated pretenses.

The countess pouted at his question, and then shrugged elegantly. "I can be whoever you desire, Carlisle." Her nimble fingers reached for the buttons on his breeches. "Let me show you."

CHAPTER
ELEVEN

"Fitchwolf!" Darknell seized Kilby by the arm, halting her abrupt departure from the private box. "Wait! Where are you going?"

He knew what had upset her. They had both watched Fayne and his new mistress leave the box. The duke had placed his hand on the Lady Spryng's backside as they disappeared behind the curtain.

"I have seen enough theater for one evening, my lord," Kilby said, clenching her fists against her abdomen. They were standing alone in the dim passageway. Lyssa had wisely given them their privacy. "All I want to do is go home."

She refused to cry in front of Darknell. Alone in her bedchamber she would put a pillow over her head to muffle the pain and fury she was feeling. First, she had to get around her friend. "Release me. Please!"

"No." He jerked her closer when Kilby tried to pull away. "Not until you tell me what sent you scrambling out of your seat . . . why you are shaking as if cold . . . what has put tears that refuse to fall in your beautiful violet eyes."

Kilby shook her head. "You already know. Do not deny that you wanted me to see him. I suppose you took great pleasure in pointing him out as he cavorted with his mistress."

"Solitea?" Darknell sneered, his dark brown eyes glittering even in the shadows. "I warned you once that the man was like his father. Did you naïvely believe that he would behave honorably toward you? Especially since he considered you his dead father's mistress?"

She closed her eyes, blocking out his cruelty. "No more," she said, her voice cracking with suppressed emotion. "You have proven him a villain. I hope this pleases you. Now let me go."

"Never!" he said fiercely. "If I do, you will never forgive me for showing you Solitea's true nature."

Before she could disagree, Darknell lowered his head and kissed her. Over the years, he had politely kissed her hand, and on her birthday last year, he had kissed her cheek. Warm and coaxing, his mouth moved against hers, seeking a response. Kilby was too stunned by the viscount's unexpected boldness to do anything more than just stand there rigidly in his embrace. This was one of her closest friends, Teague Pethum, Viscount Darknell. He was an extremely handsome gentleman, and yet she had never contemplated exploring beyond the restraints of their friendship.

Darknell pulled back and studied her dazed expression. With the tip of her tongue, Kilby licked her lower lip, tasting the exotic flavor of the forbidden. How could she tell him that she had felt nothing?

"So Fitchwolf, now you know the truth," he said, lightly caressing her shoulder.

"My lord, I was not aware . . ." she trailed off, and shrugged helplessly.

"It was better that way. You were too young when we first met." He gave her a faint grin, reminding her of the carefree Darknell she had known at Ealkin. "I thought we had plenty of time for you to get to know me. To love me."

Her heart clenched at his unspoken question. "Darknell, of course I love you. We have been friends too long for an attachment not to develop."

The viscount rewarded her with a swift kiss. "Then it is agreed. We will marry straightaway. Tomorrow I will call on Lady Quennell and tell her that her quest to find you a husband is at an end." Darknell kissed her again, silencing her reply. He lingered, savoring her mouth. "When you first told me of the viscountess's plans, the jealousy I felt almost drove me to madness. I wanted to challenge every gentleman who dared gaze upon you."

This time when he tried to kiss her, Kilby blocked him by placing her fingers against his lips. "Darknell, I cannot marry you. It would not be fair."

"What is this nonsense? Stubbornness? Be sensible, Fitchwolf. If you do not marry while you are in town, your bastard brother will handpick your husband and you will spend the rest of your life regretting your grim fate." His brown eyes were eloquent and bright with hurt. "You spoke of love."

"I did." She glanced away. "I do. A love of a friend. Despite my great need for a husband, I would dishonor our friendship by accepting your proposal. The love you feel for me." Her throat tightened with regret because she could not freely return the love he offered. "In time, you would despise me for the lack."

She winced as his hands flexed and constricted on her shoulders. "You fell in love with him, didn't you? You love that bounder, Solitea?"

Kilby gently removed Darknell's hands from her shoulder and moved away, using the wall to guide her. "I pray that one day you will forgive me. I never meant to hurt you." She gave him her back and shoved her fist against her mouth. Rejecting him had been the hardest thing she had ever done. He deserved a lady who would love him unconditionally, one who was not simply satisfied with a lukewarm sentiment such as friendship.

"He won't marry you, you know?" the viscount shouted at her retreating figure. "Solitea might bed you out of curiosity, but you are too mundane, too practical to be a Carlisle."

His words cut her to the quick. Although Kilby deserved them, she could not resist confronting him. Whirling around, she held his pain-filled stare for the count of a dozen heartbeats. "The Duke of Solitea asked me to marry him two days ago. I kindly rejected his offer, too."

Satisfied that she had had the final word, Kilby turned on her heel and left Darknell alone in the passageway.

Within the small confines of her coach, Kilby sobbed inconsolably into the crook of her arm. It had been an awful evening! After she had witnessed Fayne smugly strolling off with Lady Spryng at his side, she had stared blindly at the stage, not conceiving that she could feel any worse than she had felt in that instant. It had been her fault, really. Her rejection of Fayne's offer of marriage had sent him straight into the arms of another woman.

Now she had devastated one of her dearest friends. His only crime was that he loved her in a manner she could not return. Darknell had looked so *hurt*. She had almost taken back her rejection because she could not bear the agony etched on his handsome face.

What stopped her from easing his pain was that he spoke the truth. He had glimpsed it in her eyes before she had.

She could not love Darknell because another had claimed her heart.

Only now did she understand the depths of her feelings

for Fayne. Her forehead bounced against her forearm as one of the wheels dipped into a deep rut. Kilby raised her head and peeked through the curtains. It had started raining when she had dashed into the coach. Raindrops clung to the glass, making it impossible to discern anything.

Kilby retrieved another handkerchief from her reticule and dabbed at her eyes. When she left the theater box, she had not bothered explaining to Lyssa what she had found so upsetting. Darknell had known. It was Lady Spryng's empty seat. Involuntarily, her gaze kept drifting back to the box. As the minutes passed, there was no doubt in her feverish imagination as to what Fayne and the countess were doing alone behind the curtain. Fayne had never resisted touching her whenever he had cornered her alone.

Kilby felt guilty for abandoning Lyssa without a word. She should have said something, but her tears had been too close to the surface. Despite Darknell's anger, she knew he would see to it that Lyssa was escorted home.

That was where she wanted to be.

Home.

However, she could not return to Ealkin. Not yet. Archer had taken her sanctuary away from her.

Her bedchamber at Lady Quennell's house was a poor substitute, but it would suffice. Kilby planned to cry until she had purged the cold-blooded rogue out of her heart. It was not until she had seen the countess gazing adoringly up at him that she realized how much she had grown accustomed to his hovering around her. Kilby was now honest enough with herself to admit that Fayne had not seduced her on that sofa as she had claimed. She had been there because she had wanted to be there.

More's the pity, she had foolishly fallen in love with the charming lothario.

The coach lurched to an abrupt halt. Kilby scrubbed her

face and blew her nose. She did not want the coachman reporting back to the viscountess that she had been crying. The rain was ruthlessly battering the coach. Drawing her cloak around her, she pitied the coachman. The poor man had to be soaked to the skin on such a miserable night.

Kilby braced herself as the door swung open. The coachman opened an umbrella. Her gaze briefly swept over his shadowed figure. She was relieved to see he was dressed appropriately for the weather. He wore a long greatcoat and a cocked hat pulled down over his eyes to keep the rain off his face.

"A miserable night to be out, is it not?" she said, raising her voice so she could be heard above the relentless rain.

"Aye, miss," the man replied, his low, raspy voice muffled by his heavy greatcoat. As she descended the coach, he grabbed her elbow and prevented her from slipping on the steps.

The coachman took a lantern off the side of the coach and used it to light their path to the door. The interior of the house was dark. Priddy had issued orders to the servants that they were not required to wait for her return. Kilby had not bothered changing the order, although now she was beginning to regret it. In the rain and gloom, the dark house was a bit frightening.

Behind her, Kilby heard a man shout out and the crack of a whip. She turned in time to see the coach rattle off down the street. "What?" She pointed helplessly at the departing coach and then at the man standing beside her. "Well, that was rude of your companion. How are you supposed to get home?"

The coachman sighed. He pushed up his cocked hat, and she gasped as she recognized the green eyes gleaming at her from beneath the upturned brim.

"No kiss for me, little wolf?"

• • •

Kilby screamed.

This wasn't a ladylike shriek. Kilby hit a high note guaranteed to make a man's ears bleed. Whirling away, she dashed off into the night.

The woman was truly daft.

Tossing aside the umbrella, Fayne charged after her. He lost his cocked hat after a few yards. Perhaps it had been too much to expect that she might have actually been pleased to see him. Actually, it probably was. She had seen him in the company of another woman, a former mistress no less.

"Damn it, Kilby, will you wait!" he yelled at her retreating figure. "You will drown in this rain."

He had not counted on her diving facefirst into the nearest puddle on the street. With a faint exclamation, Kilby had slipped in the mud and plopped facedown into the small lake forming on the street. Fayne reached her just as she was sitting up on her knees.

Kilby was crying and shaking off the water sluicing down her arms. The bottom of her cloak, bloated with water, sank like ballast. Squinting up at him with rain beading on her face, she said, "Well, this is unquestionably the zenith to an already dreadful evening."

She staggered to her feet.

"Here, let me help you," Fayne offered, taking her arm.

Kilby pushed him away. "Hands off." She swayed, almost losing her balance. The additional weight of her drenched cloak and skirts made her ungainly. "You have certainly done enough. Now skulk back to your mistress and leave me alone."

Fayne could not bear the misery and defeat he heard in her voice. He thought about offering her his greatcoat, but figured Kilby would topple over if he added more weight to her slender frame. "Who told you Velouette was my mistress?" he asked, keeping pace with her uncoordinated stride.

Kilby bared her teeth at his familiar use of the countess's Christian name. "Darknell mentioned that she was a very good friend of yours."

The sneaky villain. He should have guessed the viscount was the one who had gleefully imparted the details of his relationship with Lady Spryng to Kilby. "The countess is old news. What we shared was brief and a very long time ago."

She abruptly halted. Blinking furiously against the rain, she said, "Liar. Everyone in the theater observed you leaving the box with your very old news clinging to your arm." Kilby stomped off, heading for Lady Quennell's house.

Fayne shut his eyes and wiped his face with the sleeve of his greatcoat. Jealousy had prodded him to hurt Kilby. Seeing the hurt and betrayal in her violet eyes, he wished he had chosen a different course. For instance, confronting Darknell and breaking his jaw would have been immensely satisfying.

"Appearances are deceiving."

"No, Your Grace, *you* are deceiving," she called out over her shoulder. "As for appearances, I no longer care."

"Now who is the liar, Kilby?" he asked, catching up to her as she reached the door. Tired of arguing, Fayne scooped her up in his arms.

Kilby immediately began flailing. "Put me down!"

Fayne almost dropped the lantern as he held on to a struggling wet bundle of womanly outrage. "Stop kicking. I don't want to douse us both with hot oil," he roughly ordered, and to his amazement she stilled.

"I can walk, you know," she said tartly.

"Impressive. You can demonstrate your skills later." Fayne opened the door. "Since you were without your chaperone this evening, I assume she is still out?" He carried her through the door.

"Yes," she hissed. When he did not put her down, she began to fidget in his arms.

Fayne absently nodded. "And the servants? They had orders to retire early." Using the lantern to light his way, he headed for the stairs.

"Yes. Now will you please put me down?" Terrified he was about to drop her, Kilby buried her face in his shoulder.

Fayne smiled into her wet hair. There was something oddly comforting about her strangling embrace. Climbing unfamiliar stairs with a panicked lady in his arms was tricky business; however, Fayne was up to the challenge. He did not speak again until he had reached the second landing. "Is your room down this passageway?"

Kilby nodded, her face not lifting from his shoulder. She was shivering uncontrollably.

Fayne proceeded down the hall, passing several doors until he heard her soft plea to stop. "Open the door."

She pulled away and reached out to open the door for him. Fayne stepped into her boudoir. A wave of sorrow buffeted him. His father had died here. Fayne released Kilby, allowing her to stand. He closed the door. There was not much to see in the dim light of the lantern. He set the lantern on her dressing table.

"You must be freezing," he said, shrugging out of his greatcoat. He laid it across the closest chair. The frock coat underneath was damp, especially near the neck. Fayne removed it, also.

Kilby had moved to the other side of the room. Warily watching him disrobe, she made no attempt to remove her wet cloak. The hem of the garment was so drenched he could hear water droplets striking the floorboards.

"I will see to myself," she said, her teeth chattering. "There is no reason for you to stay."

Fayne shook his head. "I beg to disagree." He closed the distance between them. Kilby backed up against the wall, holding her hands out in front to halt his approach. He brushed aside her hands and unclasped the cloak. "Keep still, woman, I only want to get you warm."

Her dress was ruined.

Peeling off the sodden cloak, he finally understood Kilby's hesitation about removing it in his presence. The rain had turned the muslin transparent. Streaked with mud, the dress clung to her provocatively.

Fayne swallowed thickly with desire. "Turn around," he said, the curt order coming out husky.

Kilby slowly presented her back to him. The number of tiny buttons was daunting. Without asking for permission, he ripped open the back. "There is no help for it. Besides, the dress is ruined," he told her, fingering the knots binding her corset. "The laces are also wet." He retrieved the small sheathed knife he had concealed in the small of his back under his waistcoat. "I seem to be making a habit out of this," he teased, wanting to put her at ease as he sliced through the bindings.

She shivered and crossed her arms. "Fine. Play lady's maid. I doubt I could stop you anyway."

"At least we understand each other." Fayne decided swiftness was kinder. He peeled layer after layer of wet clothing off her until she was standing in her chemise. Fayne put away his knife, resisting the urge to nip her bare nape. Stepping back, he said, "There. You can manage the rest on your own. I'll see to building a fire."

Wondering what she would do, Fayne walked into her bedchamber. The lantern emitted enough light for him to make out the fireplace. Crouching down, he concentrated on bringing light and warmth to the room.

"Why are you doing this?"

Fayne hoped she was stripping off her slippers and stockings. He blew lightly on the smoldering kindling. "We need to talk."

He listened to her movements in the dressing room. "I should warn you, Your Grace. The liberties I granted you were out of necessity. What occurred between us the night you challenged Tulley will not happen again."

He mentally counted off the faint steps she took to reach the door.

Bracing his hands on his thighs, Fayne devilishly grinned into the mounting fire. "I heartily concur, little wolf."

He retrieved a small key from his waistcoat pocket. Examining it in the firelight, Fayne patiently waited for Kilby to discover the door was locked.

Kilby gave the latch on the door another useless tug. Fayne had locked the door and secreted the key. She leaned her head against the door and marveled that the duke had always been one step ahead of her.

"Come here, Kilby," he said, beckoning from the other room.

Moving away from the door, she glanced down at her chemise in despair. The thin undergarment was not enough protection from Fayne's shrewd green gaze. Striding to a small mahogany chest, she opened the lid and pulled out a long brown and white shawl. Kilby carefully wrapped it around her like a shield.

"You still wear your chemise," he chided, when she entered the bedchamber. He held out his hand, signaling for her to join him in front of the fire. During their time apart, he had removed his waistcoat and his cravat hung loosely from his neck. The duke's feet were also bare. "I told you to remove everything."

"Everything *wet*," she said crisply. Ignoring his outstretched hand, she knelt down on the blanket he had laid out in front of the fireplace. "I assume—" She paused, distracted when he leaned forward and dragged a large bowl of water he had warming on the hearth closer to them. "What do you intend to do?"

Fayne grabbed his untied cravat and pulled it away from his neck. Folding the material in his hands, he pushed the fabric into the water. "Talk." He wrung out the wet cravat. "Your face is filthy."

Kilby touched her cheek and grimaced at the flecks of dirt and other things she would do well not to contemplate on her fingertips. Annoyed, she held out her hand, expecting him to hand over the wet fabric. Fayne ignored her hand and grasped her chin firmly. Tilting her head up, he gently began washing the muddy streaks from her face.

Giving up, she said, "So you want to talk about the dirt on my face." He had gone to a great deal of trouble ensconcing them in her bedchamber. If hearing his grand confession granted her the key and his departure, she was prepared to listen.

The dimple on his cheek flashed as he gifted her with a quick grin. "No." He glided the cloth along the curve of her jaw. The soft cloth and the tepid water felt good on her face. "I want to talk about Lady Spryng."

She pulled back from his hand. "I am not interested in hearing about your good friend the countess."

Fayne sighed. "A pity, since I feel compelled to share." He dipped the cloth in the water and squeezed. "This is a first for me. I have never justified myself to anyone about anything. If you have the courage to listen, you might learn more about me than I have ever shared with another."

With his other hand, he curled his fingers around her nape and pulled her closer. He nudged her chin up and to the left with his fingertip. She felt the cloth stroke her throat. "Your assumptions were correct. When Velouette invited me to join her in the private parlor, I left the box aware the lady desired to renew our, ah, friendship."

Kilby turned her face to the right, offering him more of her throat. It also kept him from noticing her tears. Even at a distance, it was apparent Lady Spryng was stunning and exotic. The voluptuous countess was everything Kilby was not. "I see." She trembled beneath his trailing caress. The cloth followed the slope of her neck, down her shoulder, and across the ridges of her fragile collarbones.

"No you don't. Not yet."

His fingers and the cloth ventured lower. Water dripped over her breasts and her nipples were erect painful points chafing against her chemise. Under his gentle stroking, she had relaxed and allowed her shawl to fall to her waist. When the cloth slipped under her chemise and over her breast, her womb pulsed in response. The cleft nestled in the curly hair between her legs grew damp and a part of her ached for Fayne to bury his hand there, too.

"Kilby." There was longing and regret in his voice. "I need you to understand."

"What?" she asked, her eyes fluttering open. Fayne was seducing her with his slow, meandering strokes. Kilby was almost prepared to forgive him anything if he would stop teasing her and—do *more*. Turning back to him, she saw the same stark hunger glittering in his green eyes. He wanted her, too. The impressive length of his manhood was a prominent bulge in his breeches. Yet, he was holding back, resisting the chance to take her.

"Fayne?" she asked, doubt clouding the sweet lethargy his touch had evoked. "What do you want me to understand?"

His hand halted mid-stroke over her heart. "Velouette was mine for the taking. No questions. No avowals of love. No complications. She offered to fulfill my darkest fantasies, to yield her body to my wickedest commands."

Kilby placed her hand over his. Her gaze fell to his arm, ashamed by her uninhibited response to his touch. He skillfully seduced while he soothed. If she allowed him to continue stroking her with the damp cloth, she might have been tempted to blurt out similar reckless promises as his former mistress had. She nodded, her eyes filling with tears. "You wanted me to understand why you did not refuse—"

"No!" he barked sharply, withdrawing his hand from her grasp. "I want you to understand why I *did*!" Disgusted, he tossed his wet cravat into the bowl.

Her head shot up. "You . . . You and the countess—" She could not say the words aloud for fear she had misunderstood him.

"No," he said, inching closer. "What I had with her, I no longer want," he confessed, spearing his fingers through her hair, getting rid of hairpins as he discovered them.

The full weight of her hair spilled down her back. "What do you want?" She licked her lips. His mouth was hovering temptingly above hers.

"I crave you, my little wolf." Unable to hold back, Fayne crushed his lips to hers. His tongue pierced her lips, coaxing her to let him in. He tasted like rain, of reckless sin, and dark promises that only he could fulfill.

Fayne pulled back. Gently, he eased her chemise over her head. As he stared hungrily at her naked body, his thumb teased one of her nipples. "Here and now, let me show you."

Fayne sensed lovemaking with Kilby could be much more than frenzied lust, more than finding his own pleasure in her tight body. Fayne had taken her in that fashion when he had thought she had had previous lovers. Knowing that he had been her first lover, Fayne needed to show her tenderness.

"No, do not cover your breasts," he said, drawing her hands away and appreciating the pert uplift of her firm breasts. Fayne guided her onto her back.

Most of his former lovers, like Velouette, had been overly bountiful. Kilby's exquisitely responsive breasts had him reevaluating his preferences. Squeezing one of her firm globes in his hand, Fayne bent his head down and licked her swollen nipple. He nibbled the underside of her breast and she giggled.

"Like that, did you?" he murmured, caging her with his body so he could taste her other breast.

"Fayne, would you untie your queue?" she asked unexpectedly, drawing idle circles on his shoulder with her finger. "The color is so glorious. I have often wondered how your hair looked down."

"As you wish, my lady." He reached back and pulled on the leather thong. Kilby immediately threaded her fingers through the thick, dark cinnamon strands as they fell over his shoulders. Fayne preferred wearing his hair long. Women had always adored running their fingers through it. There were also some intriguing benefits. He moved down her body, allowing the spiky ends to tickle Kilby's sensitive flesh. She laughed openly, the muscles of her stomach rippling as he traced the oval of her navel with the tip of his tongue.

"S-stop," she begged, choking on her laughter. "I cannot bear it!"

Fayne parted her thighs wider. The scent of her arousal made his stomach clench painfully. No woman had ever ignited his senses as Kilby did. He lifted his head, his expression naughty. "You are only challenging me to prove you wrong, little wolf."

Lowering his face to the dewy curls between her legs, Fayne parted her tender folds and suckled the sensitive nub tucked within. Kilby cried out his name, her upper body craned upward while her hands reached for him in a feeble attempt to stop his delightful torment.

"You taste like honeydew, little wolf," he murmured, lapping the nectar.

He reveled in the distinct flavor of her. This was the way

their first time should have been. Slow. Savoring each plea-sure. Kilby squirmed against his unrelenting mouth, her thighs subtly widening, silently willing him to fill her with his cock.

Oh, he would fill her.

Soon.

His body yearned for completion. However, first he wanted to savor Kilby's climax. She was close. Dewy beads of his own arousal moistened the tip of his cock. His body was throbbing in anticipation. Repeatedly thrusting his fingers deeply into her dripping wet sheath, he suckled her clitoris, ruthlessly demanding her surrender.

Her body answered.

Kilby sobbed his name brokenly, her entire body shaking as the blinding magnificence of her first orgasm claimed her. She held him tightly throughout, overwhelmed by the powerful tempest assailing her.

Fayne was far from finished with her. Nuzzling the indentation of her right hip, he crawled up the length of her body and kissed leisurely. When he pulled back to examine her face, Kilby looked charmingly befuddled.

"What did you do to me?" she asked, her violet eyes filled with awe and excitement.

The way she was staring up at him made him feel omnipotent. He wanted to pound his chest and howl in triumph. Instead, Fayne brushed a few stray hairs from her face. "A mere taste of our passion."

Her mouth parted in surprise at his announcement. "There is *more*?"

"Oh, yes, my cuddly little wolf," Fayne promised. "An entire night of it."

CHAPTER
TWELVE

The days that followed drifted by for Kilby like a superlative, decadent dream. Since the night Fayne had carried her up to her bedchamber and made love to her in front of the fire, there had been some subtle changes in her relationship with Fayne that went beyond the physical.

Though she had no complaints in that regard!

What discomfort she had experienced in the beginning had disappeared and Fayne had proved himself to be a very inventive and attentive lover. The aches that plagued her now were the result of anticipation, of knowing what those skillful, dexterous hands of his could evoke from her body. He had somehow bound her to him with his exquisite lovemaking. She felt the pull of his absence from those invisible threads woven around her heart each moment they were apart.

His misguided offer of marriage had not been mentioned nor had he extended the generous offer again.

Essentially, Kilby was relieved that Fayne had not pressed her for a permanent union. If she felt a jot of disappointment, she reminded herself that she had already refused his offer. What she shared with Fayne was temporary. When his roving eye settled on another lady, she would not let bitterness ruin her fond memories of their time together.

For now, Fayne was hers.

They had plans to encounter each other at Lord and Lady Kennard's ball this evening. Socializing in the same circles made it simple for them to accidentally meet without gaining the *ton*'s notice. At her urging, their public assignations had been above reproach. Only Priddy had commented with a shrewd look in her eye on the frequency of Fayne's presence at the gatherings they both attended together. The older woman had wondered aloud at the wisdom of encouraging the flirtation. After all, there was that awkward business with the duke's father. She was convinced Fayne was subtly courting her young charge. Nothing Kilby said dissuaded her of the notion.

From the corner of her eye, Kilby noticed Lord Ordish's measured approach. He was leaning heavily on his walking stick.

"Good evening, my lord."

The earl made a soft disapproving sound. "Where is your chaperone? She is not doing right by you, my dear child. You are too young and pretty not to be dancing with the others," Lord Ordish said, joining her.

"How kind of you to say so," Kilby said, patting his arm affectionately. "Nevertheless, do not fret. Lady Quennell has vowed to one and all that she will have me betrothed by season's end. If her daunting ambitions do not come to fruition, I fear it will be my failing, not hers."

"Balderdash! If you do not have a dozen gents leaving their cards each afternoon, there is something wrong with the young noblemen your chaperone is presenting you to," Lord Ordish said vehemently in her defense. "Where is

Lady Quennell? I should dash off and find her, mayhap, have a word or two with her."

Kilby was appreciative of the earl's concern. However, there would be no dashing off for the Lord Ordish, not with his painful gait. "Heavens, there is no telling where Priddy might be at this moment, and I will not have you straining your leg on my behalf."

"My hip, actually. And here I thought I was hiding it so well." The earl glanced at her sheepishly, and then gruffly chuckled. "I confess I have some lingering inflammation in my right hip that often plagues me at inopportune moments. It is the sad result of a humbling tumble from my horse two summers past."

"How terrible for you," Kilby murmured sympathetically. Lord Ordish's retelling of his accident faded in the distance as her violet gaze landed on Fayne, who was entering the north side of the ballroom. A warm, welcoming smile animated her countenance. Kilby could pick him out of any crowd with great ease. His proud bearing and long, dark reddish-brown hair color were distinctly Fayne.

"Lord Ordish," Kilby said abruptly, interrupting his story. "Forgive me, my lord. I promised a certain gentleman a dance, and he has just arrived."

"Go." The earl's face crinkled in amusement as he urged her to hurry off with a wave of his hand. "Run off and flirt with your young gentleman. You have better things to do than listen to an old man's ramblings."

She curtsied. Unable to resist, she kissed Lord Ordish on the cheek. "You are not old, my lord, and I always like our chats. One of these days I shall introduce you to Lady Quennell. Though I must warn you, once Priddy learns that you are unmarried, she will never give you any peace."

Kilby waved farewell to the earl. She could hear his throaty laughter follow her as she wended her way through the crowd to Fayne. He was also moving toward her. Fayne occasionally stopped and spoke to friends and acquaintances. Although he had not looked in her direction, Kilby knew his thoughts were focused on her.

They met each other halfway.

"Your Grace," she said breathlessly, slipping down into a graceful curtsy.

Fayne bowed formally over her extended hand. "Lady Kilby. How fortuitous. Would you do me the honor of being my partner for the next dance?" His green gaze glittered intently as he held her gaze.

Kilby fought not to smile. The question itself was not amusing. It was his unspoken question that made her heart sing.

"Will you let me love you tonight, my little wolf?"

"I gladly accept, Your Grace."

"I did not think the evening would ever end, Your Grace," Kilby said, raining kisses on his face while Fayne carried her into his rented town house. Although the Solitea town house was rightfully his, Fayne preferred residing separately from his mother.

"Fayne will do nicely, love," he said, kicking the door shut with his foot. " 'Master' has a nice ring to it, too."

"Ha-ha!" She pinched his ear. "Never."

His manservant appeared from the back of the house, carrying a small branch of candles. Hedge was a somber little man with alert hazel eyes and a rigid formal bearing and whose attention to detail had made him a valued servant. Somewhere in his early forties, the slightly balding Hedge had been under Fayne's employ for six years.

"Your Grace, might I be of service to you and your lady this evening?" the servant politely inquired.

For some reason, Kilby found the servant's offer ridiculously amusing. She pressed her face into Fayne's throat to muffle her laughter. Judging from Hedge's unruffled demeanor, one might think Fayne arrived home each night with a young lady bundled in his arms.

Fayne playfully smacked her on the bottom. "Behave," he sternly warned her. To his manservant he said, "No, thank you, Hedge. I'll see to the lady's needs myself. You may retire."

"Very good, Your Grace." He placed the branch of candles on a table for them. "I bid you both a good night." The servant disappeared into the darkness.

"That was rather cheeky of you to tell your man that you would see to my needs," Kilby said, extending her arm out and picking up the candelabra.

Fayne kissed her on the nose. "How so? I don't plan to overlook a single one."

"You have utterly corrupted me, Your Grace," Kilby confessed to Fayne an hour later, not particularly troubled by her disgrace. She was feeling sleepy and sated from their earlier lovemaking. Lying naked in his arms, she rolled onto her side and braced her head with her bent arm. "No wonder gentlemen are always collecting mistresses. Though, it hardly seems fair. No doubt the matrons of the *ton* would not think kindly of me if I began amassing a string of lovers."

Fayne teased her hip with his fingernails. "Never mind the matrons." He dragged her on top of him. "What about me, your devoted lover? Have you tired of me so much that you are already planning your next conquest, you heartless vixen?" In teasing punishment, he dug his fingers into her sides and tickled her mercilessly.

"No," Kilby said, squealing with laughter, wiggling crazily against his virile, naked physique. "Stop. Fine. I am keeping you. After all, you do have your uses."

She surprised him by lightly cupping his testicles with

her hand. In response, he clenched his teeth and sucked in his breath. Until then, Fayne had always taken the lead in their passionate encounters. Willingly conceding to his devastating expertise as a lover, Kilby had never thought to challenge his authority. It had not occurred to her that Fayne's dominant nature would ever tolerate, let alone desire, her sudden impulse to control him for a change.

"There is such strength here," she observed, stroking his erect shaft from its base to the tip. His manhood twitched, lifting up to meet her caressing fingers. A droplet of his arousal welled at the slit opening. He felt like hot silk. "What does it feel like to push your rod inside of me?"

Fayne shuddered. "Paradise. I wish I could remain inside you forever."

Secretly pleased by his admission, Kilby smiled against his stomach. It definitely explained why Fayne made love to her at each opportunity. The taut muscles against her cheek rippled, as curiosity prompted her to shift lower. "And what do you taste like, Your Grace?"

Not giving him a chance to reply, her tongue tentatively flicked out to connect with the tip, tasting him. "Mmm, salty. A bit like what sin tastes like, I imagine."

"Kilby," he choked out, his fingers tangling in her black hair as her lips drifted teasingly over the hooded ridge of his manhood. "Have mercy."

She turned back to face him, her violet eyes dancing with impish delight. "Why should I? You taught me half the fun is partaking in the torment."

Lady Kilby Fitchwolf had finally awakened. The violet-eyed enchantress had just discovered her powers, and Fayne was completely ensorcelled. He closed his eyes, savoring the magic of her mouth on his cock. The untutored caresses of her hands and mouth were tantalizingly erotic. No courtesan or highly skilled mistress could have aroused him so thoroughly.

Fayne moaned. "Ride me," he said, desperately needing to be inside her when he came. The rigid control he had always prided himself on seemed to swiftly evaporate whenever Kilby was near.

She sat up partway, her hand idly stroking his inner thigh. Although it had taken some persuasion to convince her to come home with him, he liked having her naked in his bed. She looked like a wanton pagan goddess with her white skin gleaming like captured moonlight. His kisses had reddened her lips, and her long black hair flowed down about her waist in alluring disarray.

She gave him an inquiring glance. "Do what?"

"Mount me, my little wolf." He guided her until she straddled him. Fayne rubbed his straining cock against the curly thatch of her sex. "Would you not like to ride and tame your ravenous beast?"

Kilby was clearly fascinated by the suggestion. "Show me."

Fayne cupped her buttocks and positioned her sultry heat over his arousal. She knew what he craved. As she moved against him, her wetness enticed him deeper. His splayed hands on her buttocks tightened as he thrust his cock into her welcoming sheath.

"Now ride," he commanded hoarsely. Gripping her hips, he demonstrated the friction he craved.

Kilby eagerly embraced the new freedom of her position. She moved slowly at first, rolling her hips against his as she took his full measure. Gradually, exploration and her growing confidence had her quickening her pace. Fayne groaned. He reached up and his hands squeezed the pliant flesh of her breasts.

"Am I doing this correctly?" she asked dreamily.

By God, Kilby was devastating him! Each downward

stroke was exquisite. Her snug sheath was milking the head of his cock, demanding his surrender.

Fayne refused to disappoint his lady.

Pulling one of her breasts to his hungry mouth, Fayne suckled her nipple fiercely as his other hand teased her clitoris. The impetus sent her hurtling toward her release. Fayne's guttural shout mingled with Kilby's sweet, faint cry as they lost themselves in the staggering throes of their shared orgasm.

Kilby collapsed on top of him, burying her face against his shoulder. Her lithe body was shaking from their exertion and slick with sweat. Their bodies still joined, Fayne shivered as tiny quakes surged from his cock. He gently pushed himself deeper, savoring the sensation.

"Hmm," she mumbled in his ear. "My mother used to tell me that riding daily was good for my health. You have broadened my perspective on the benefits of her wisdom."

Fayne managed a weak chuckle. He smoothed her hair from her face and tenderly kissed her. "Give me a month or two to recover and we will do this again."

Kilby carefully disengaged from him and rolled onto her side. "A pity. We only have an hour or so before I must return home. Perhaps we should ring for Hedge and have him concoct an elixir for your waning stamina."

Fayne rolled on top of her and caged her face with his hands. "Waning stamina? What irreverence! Now, my dear lady, you force me to prove myself—"

"Again?" Kilby interjected, not believing he was capable of taking her again so quickly.

In reality, his violet-eyed wolf had wrung him dry. Still, there were other ways of pleasuring her. "Again," he demanded, gliding his hand up her thigh. He pressed his thumb firmly against her clitoris and the jolt had her hips lifting up off the mattress. "An hour or two will be just enough time."

◆ ◆ ◆

"Did you fall asleep again?" Fayne murmured against her ear.

She had, but she was not about to confess that his love-making had worn her out. The man was by far too smug about his talents in bed. Without opening her eyes, she rolled into him and nuzzled his chest. "Mmm . . . merely drifting." Kilby stifled a yawn. "I suppose I should get dressed."

"You don't have to on my account," he said, smoothing the stray strands of long black hair that covered her face. "Hedge could serve us breakfast in bed."

Kilby opened her eyes at his outlandish suggestion. "And become this evening's gossip? When I find the strength to search under your bed for my chemise, I will certainly hunt for your sanity!"

"Kilby," he cajoled, pressing her back onto the mattress when she tried to sit up. He used his body to hold her in place.

"Do not Kilby me, Your Grace," she said crossly, refusing to allow him to distract her from leaving again. "I cannot remain. Being here at all is risky enough."

Bracing his arms on both sides of her head, he peered down at her, his expression sober. "This is about my father, isn't it?"

They had never spoken about the night she had been with his father. Fayne had never asked, and Kilby had been reluctant to talk about those final minutes with the old duke. For some reason she could not fathom, he was demanding they speak about a night that was unmistakably painful for him and his family.

"Fayne, what is the point in discussing—" she began.

"I disagree." He relaxed his right arm and gracefully plopped down on his side. "You like being in my bed, Kilby. I'll even be so daring as to say that you love it."

"You are insufferable," she said, grabbing a fistful of his long hair and tugging sharply.

He turned his face into her clenched fist and kissed her knuckles. "No, just tenacious. Now pay attention. Lady Quennell has announced to all and sundry that she hopes to see you married this season, and yet when you get a respectable proposal from an incredibly handsome gent, you refuse him."

"Two," she said forlornly, recalling her angry parting from Lord Darknell.

"Two?" he repeated, his forehead furrowing in puzzlment.

"I rejected two offers for my hand; yours and Darknell's." Watching his stunned expression turn to anger, Kilby immediately regretted her confession.

"So Darknell found the courage to tell you that he was in love with you," Fayne mused, not looking pleased.

"You knew?" It was intolerable to learn that the viscount's feelings were visible to everyone but her. She was still silently berating herself for having caused her friend so much pain.

"A man recognizes his rival," Fayne said grimly. "The minute I saw you with Darknell, I knew he wanted you for himself."

"Not anymore," she said irritably, recalling the viscount's hurt expression. "I told him that I could not return his feelings. So that should please you."

The harsh muscled lines in his jaw relaxed at her admission. Slipping his hand beneath the sheet, he cupped her warm breast. "Oh, it does please me. You have no excuse now."

"Excuse? Excuse for what?" The man was not making any sense to her.

Fayne leaned over and kissed her softly on her unprotesting lips. He looked like a man who had nothing to lose. "Marrying me."

◆ ◆ ◆

Kilby was silent.

Now that he knew for certain that his rival for her affections was not a rival at all, Fayne was determined to convince her his offer was sincere. "I could only think of two reasons why you might reject my offer of marriage."

She blinked slowly at him. "Only two?"

So she thought at the moment that he was an arrogant arse. He could charm her out of her ire. "I thought you might have rejected me because you loved Lord Darknell."

Kilby turned away and sighed. The quarrel with the viscount had been painful. "Not the love he demanded," she said, sounding miserable.

"Good," he said, ignoring her gasp. "Then it means you are free to love *me*."

She had no acerbic response to his arrogant statement.

Fayne slid his hand up to her face, and adjusted it so she was forced to meet his steady gaze. "That leaves my family. You are worried that they will never accept you as my duchess since they believe you were my father's mistress."

"In part," Kilby conceded, her lip quivering with emotion.

"Kilby, what is it?" he asked, suspecting there was more to the meeting with his father than he had guessed. "Does it have something to do with why my father was in your private sitting room the night he died?"

She nodded and covered her eyes with her hand. "Have you ever wondered why Lady Quennell is so determined to help me find a husband this season?"

"Not really. Your chaperone does not seem any more mercenary than the other matrons sponsoring a daughter or niece this season," he teased, hoping she would smile.

If anything, Kilby appeared even gloomier.

She removed her hand from her eyes and took a deep breath. "It all began when word reached us that my parents had drowned."

He listened without interrupting as she told him about her brother, Archer, and his cruel accusations that stole her father from a grieving daughter, and severed a blood tie that prevented a brother from easing his lust with the one person forbidden. Fayne surmised the details she was reluctant to speak aloud, and the revelation made him want to kill her brother. She spoke of her fears for Gypsy, and the viscountess's plans to find a man outside Nipping's influence. Kilby also admitted her own plans to examine her mother's past through the eyes of people who knew her. She wanted proof that her brother was lying as she had suspected.

"And my father?" he asked after she was finished.

Kilby idly circled his flat nipple with her finger. "He claimed to know both my parents. Your father was the one who suggested visiting me while Priddy was out. I desired privacy, and the meeting was respectable," she added defensively. "We were in the drawing room. I had to get something from my sitting room and—"

Fayne took her fingers, which were stroking his chest, and brought them to his lips. "The old scoundrel followed you upstairs." His father would not have been able to resist an opportunity to coax a lady from her private sitting room into her bed.

Kilby looked relieved by his understanding. "Yes. He tried to kiss me, but I moved away."

Fayne laughed until the muscles in his stomach ached. "I would have thought less of him if he hadn't."

She closed her fingers around his hand. "And then he just collapsed without warning. His coloring distressed me and his breathing was rapid. Suddenly, he grabbed my hand. I think he was trying to reassure me." Kilby shook her head sadly. "I am so sorry, Fayne. Your father was gone by the time one of the servants heard my cries for help."

She buried her face in his neck and cried. Fayne's own

eyes burned. His family's pact with Lady Quennell for secrecy had placed a guilty burden on Kilby. He supposed
she blamed herself because she had not been able to save
the man who had died in her arms. Nor could she explain
to anyone the reasons why he had been there in the first
place.

"It wasn't your fault," he murmured into her hair. He
pushed back her head and kissed the tears streaking her
face. "Can I tell you a secret?"

"What?" she croaked, her voice strained by her tears.

"If my father had to die without his family at his side, it
comforts me to know the last face he saw was yours, my
pretty little wolf," Fayne said, meaning every word of it.

They held each other until the sunrise chased away the
shadows in the room.

CHAPTER
THIRTEEN

"You have a lot of explaining to do, madam," Archer said, storming into the Quennell breakfast room unannounced. Usually immaculate, his clothes were wrinkled and he had a day's growth of beard shadowing his jaw. His disposition was equally brusque. "Where is Kilby?"

Archer shouldered past the two footmen who tried to keep him from approaching the table where the viscountess sat alone. He braced his hands on the surface of the table and glowered. Priddy refused to be intimidated by the young marquess. Carefully setting aside her fork, she said with false cheer, "Good morning, Archer. Pardon me for saying so, but you look absolutely bedraggled from your journey. If you like, I could summon my butler and have him prepare a room and a hot bath for you."

"I did not come here for pleasantries, Viscountess. I came for Kilby," he said flatly.

Priddy's fingers fluttered to her throat. Her throat constricted painfully at the thought of losing Kilby so soon. She felt that she was so close to fulfilling her plans for her young charge. "Why would you want to take her away from London? The season has barely begun. Besides, your sister is enjoying herself immensely. It would be cruel to tear her away from her new friends."

"New friends?" the man bellowed, causing Priddy to involuntarily flinch. "I know what you are about, madam. You thought you had deceived me, but no longer. Bringing Kilby to town had nothing to do with her acquiring a social polish that you claimed she lacked. Your true aim was to see her betrothed to a gentleman of your choosing."

Priddy had never doubted Archer's intelligence. He was, after all, his father's son. She had simply hoped his own selfish motives would keep him believing her simple subterfuge until she had whisked Kilby safely out of his foul hands.

"My dear boy," she said, intentionally belittling him. "No one has misled you. What did you expect would happen when Kilby was introduced to polite society? Your sister is a charming and beautiful young lady. I thought you would be pleased when you learned that she has attained the regard of a few gentlemen."

"A few?" Archer seethed, pushing off from the table and pacing. "Since Kilby's arrival in town, I have received ten letters. Three were from concerned members of the *ton* who thought I should know that my sister has been observed on several occasions flirting with a notorious rake, one of the *sauvages nobles*."

Oh, dear! Her hand in her lap curved into a fist. It was inevitable that town gossip would reach Archer's ears. Keeping her expression carefully blank, she said, "And which gentleman would that be, my lord? After all, there are four of them."

"I am in no mood to parry words with you, madam." Priddy tensed as Archer circled her, his body visibly shaking with fury. "You are aware my sister has caught the

roving eye of the Duke of Solitea. What were you thinking?" he demanded. "The man is entirely unsuitable for
my pl—uh, sister."

Oh, she knew why Archer was furious about the Duke
of Solitea's attentions toward Kilby. He was not concerned
about his sister's reputation. The duke was plainly a threat
to the marquess's twisted ambitions for his sister. The Duke
of Solitea might not have been her first choice for Kilby—
that awkward business with his father had ruined him as a
possible suitor—but he was a man Archer could not control, which in the viscountess's opinion made Solitea perfect for Kilby.

"Unsuitable?" Priddy lifted her delicate brows in feigned
puzzlement. "The gentleman comes from a well-connected
family, has more wealth than Croesus, and has just inherited the dukedom. Such a match for Kilby would be advantageous."

She sensed her words inflamed him. During her forty-
five years, Priddy had had a few dreadful experiences with
violent gentlemen. She had recognized the signs in Archer's
flawed temperament years earlier, long before his parents'
deaths. She was certain Archer was close to throttling her
for her interference. Still, there were two footmen in the
breakfast room with them. She prayed Archer was not so
provoked as to attack her openly.

"I disagree," he snapped. "You do not comprehend the
damage you have wrought by encouraging Kilby in this
manner."

She exhaled softly when he did not hesitate behind her
chair and continued his agitated saunter around her table.
"Really, Archer, do you not think you are being a tad dramatic? You told me that you desire Kilby to marry—"

"A man of my choosing!" the marquess countered, ignoring her defense. "Did you forget our arrangement? No,
the Duke of Solitea will not do. The Carlisles have always

been embroiled in one scandal after another. Can you believe that one of the letters I received actually hinted that Kilby might have been involved in the old duke's death?"

Oh, this is too much! She doubted the Carlisles would stoop so low as to inform Archer of Kilby's misdeeds. One of the servants had to have gossiped to one of their betters. What good was a bribe, if one did not have the satisfaction of secrecy?

"No. No, I do not believe it," Priddy said crisply. She reached for her teacup again and took a contemplative sip. The tea was tepid, but it eased the dryness in her throat. "What are you implying, my lord? That our Kilby murdered the former Duke of Solitea so she could marry his heir? Preposterous!" She gave him a pitying look. "Honestly, Archer, your pacing is making me twitchy. Sit down and I will have one of the servants pour you some hot tea."

He ignored her offer. "No, of course not. Kilby could not harm a soul. I merely brought it up as testament to your dereliction of duties. You have much to answer for, madam, and I have traveled half the night for your explanation!"

"Well, storming into my home and threatening me will not grant you the answers you seek." She set down her teacup. Clasping her hands together, she gave him a considering glance. "The duke has been dead for weeks. If you really feared that Kilby was involved in some nasty mischief, you would have been pounding on my door sooner. So tell me, what has truly brought you here, Archer?"

Sensing she was willing to be reasonable, he calmed slightly. "If the letters notifying me about Kilby's unsavory dalliance with Solitea and your incompetence as a chaperone were not enough to bring me down to London, the other letters I received in the post confirmed it. Three of the letters were from gentlemen who want my permission to court Kilby. The other four were outright proposals of marriage. Confound it, these gentlemen are demanding to meet with me and discuss her bloody dowry!"

Priddy applauded the good news. She had anticipated that Kilby would be embraced by the *ton*. Evidently, once she had obtained the admiration of a young, handsome duke, others had been spurred to vie for Kilby's hand. The Duke of Solitea's continual interest had eased many concerns the viscountess had that the Carlisle family had viewed Kilby's association with the old duke as something reprehensible.

Priddy smiled, noting that Archer was less than pleased by this news. "Excellent tidings, my lord. You must be thrilled your sister has so many admirers," she said, awaiting his explosive response.

"No, damn it, I am not," Archer snarled. He stomped about, acting like a boy on the verge of a tantrum. "None of the bounders who petitioned me are worthy of her. If these men are a fine example of the company Kilby has been keeping, then you leave me no choice but to remove her from your care. Where is she?"

"Right behind you, brother. Were you looking for me?" Kilby asked, standing in the doorway. Her troubled gaze shifted from Priddy to her brother.

"Have your maid pack your belongings, Kilby," Archer ordered brusquely. "We have imposed on the good viscountess's hospitality long enough." He grabbed Kilby firmly by the wrist and dragged her toward the door.

Frightened, Kilby appealed to Priddy. The viscountess rose from her chair and slapped down her napkin. "Archer, you are being ridiculous." She followed after them.

"What has happened? Let go of me," Kilby said, using her other hand to free her wrist from his brutal grip. "Priddy, what is going on?"

"Your brother received some troubling letters," the viscountess said, whacking Archer's arm. "Release the poor girl at once. She has done nothing wrong. If your parents had lived, they would have brought her to London. Kilby deserves to find happiness!"

They crossed the front hall to the stairs. Archer eyed the steep incline. "I respect the long friendship you shared with my parents. However, you have no say in our family's business. Keep out of it, madam."

Kilby clutched the newel before he could haul her upstairs. "Wait! What letters?" Had someone written to him about the former Duke of Solitea or, worse, her relationship with Fayne? "For heaven's sake, stop twisting my arm and answer me!"

"Archer has received numerous letters from several gentlemen of the *ton,*" Priddy explained, rushing up the steps and extending her arms as if to bar Kilby's brother from passing. "Some were merely requesting permission to court you, and others were offers of marriage. Is that not wonderful? I told you, my dear, you are a success!"

The room reeled at the other woman's revelation. "Marriage offers. From whom?" Her brother's unexpected arrival and decision to remove her from London were beginning to make sense.

"We never got around to the names, did we, Archer," Lady Quennell said crossly. "Now that Kilby is here, do you care to share them with us?"

"I owe you nothing, madam. Especially now, since I have witnessed firsthand the results of your interference." Archer tugged on his sister's arm. "Kilby, I have no patience for your obstinacy. Release the post!"

Without warning, he maliciously bent several of her fingers back. Crying out, Kilby let go of the newel and jerked her injured hand out of his grasp. Maddened by her disobedience, he moved closer and wrapped his fingers around her nape.

His light blue eyes flickered over her terrified face contemptuously. "Forget about collecting your belongings. We leave this moment."

Kilby saw all her aspirations crumble at his decree. Once Archer had her safely ensconced again at Ealkin, there would be no chance to secure a marriage with a gentleman he did not influence, no chance to disprove his foul accusations about her mother. She would never see Fayne again. "Archer, be sensible. I cannot leave without my possessions," she argued, grasping at any excuse to delay their departure.

Priddy slowly descended the stairs, cautiously approaching them. "I concur. A lady needs her property."

"She will survive a day or so without a clean dress," he said dryly. "Come along, my sweet sister. The coach awaits." He dug his fingertips into her nape and pushed her toward the door.

"I do not want to leave. Priddy!" Kilby flung her hand back, reaching for her friend. The viscountess was rushing after them and crying. "Please, Archer," Kilby begged, though she loathed doing so. "There is no reason why I cannot remain. If the letters offend you so much, just destroy them."

Her brother scowled at the butler near the door. Several footmen stood in the hall, uncertain whether they should intervene in what was plainly a family argument. "Open the door."

"No. Stop. Please, you cannot take her away like this," Priddy sobbed, lacing her fingers with Kilby's.

"Watch me." Archer severed their clasped hands with a harsh chop of his hand. He pressed his mouth to his sister's ear and growled, "Tell her that you want to leave with me,

Kilby. Think of Gypsy. The poor child needs her sister. Without you at Ealkin, who will see to her welfare?"

Kilby went cold at his words. She understood his threat. If she continued to fight him, Gypsy would suffer for Kilby's defiance. He would lock Gypsy away in an asylum for the insane just for spite. "Monster," she murmured low, for his ears alone.

He flexed his hand at her nape, a reminder of how simple it would be to snap her fragile neck. "You can whisper endearments to me later. Why do you not ease the viscountess's mind and tell her you leave willingly."

"I will if you release me!" she snapped, and was surprised when he complied. She used the edge of her hand to wipe her tears before she turned and faced her distressed chaperone. "Priddy, please forgive me. There is no help for it. I have to go. Archer is correct. I have been absent from Ealkin too long. Gypsy needs me."

She embraced the viscountess. "I hope you understand." Kilby kissed her lightly on the cheek and stepped away. There was nothing left to say. Archer was watching her closely, expecting some kind of trickery.

"Forgive our hasty parting, madam. We have a long journey ahead of us," Archer said, positioning himself between Kilby and the viscountess. Since he had now won, a veneer of civility returned to his demeanor. Ignoring both women's tears, he bowed gallantly. "Please accept my apologies for upsetting you. In time, you will realize that I am simply protecting what little family I have left. Good day."

Archer offered his hand, his eyes warning her that it was in her best interest to accept his assistance. Accept her fate. From the open door of the coach, Kilby observed Priddy crying in her handkerchief. Belatedly, she wondered if the viscountess had understood her problems with Archer better than she had let on. Her desire to see Kilby betrothed might have extended beyond fulfilling a promise to her dead parents. None of it mattered now. Kilby saw her last chance at freedom vanish when the coachman shut and secured the door.

Fayne was in high spirits as his carriage halted in front of the Quennell town house. It was a trifle early in the day for social calls; however, Lady Quennell was making an exception for him. He had an appointment with the lady at eleven o'clock.

If all went well, he would have a cunning ally to help him persuade Kilby finally accept his marriage proposal. The viscountess was impatient for her young charge to make a solid match, and the Solitea title was old and respectable, even if the dukes were not. Once he had Kilby's consent, he would have to approach the brother. Fayne expected some difficulty from the gentleman. Kilby's hesitant confession about her perverse brother's ambitions hinted as much. Nevertheless, he might be able to convince the gentleman to see reason. A connection to his family was advantageous. Eventually, the marquess would come to appreciate the benefits, even if his soon-to-be-bride refused to.

Fayne bounded up the steps and knocked on the door. The butler opened the door and glowered at him. He was a tall middle-aged man with a robust figure that was settling around the servant's belly. The man was not pleased to find someone standing on the other side of the door. "Lady Quennell is not at home."

Unperturbed, Fayne handed the servant his card. "The viscountess will see me. I have an eleven o'clock appointment."

The butler hesitated, his face clouded with indecision. "My apologies, Your Grace. The viscountess has—"

"Gordan, who is at the door?" a woman demanded, her voice hoarse from crying. "Has Kilby returned?"

Taking advantage of the servant's divided attention,

Fayne pushed open the door and crossed the threshold. The viscountess was poised on the stairs with her hand on the railing. It was apparent the lady had been crying for some time before Fayne's arrival.

He could tell by her stunned expression that she had forgotten about their meeting. A flash of relief flickered in her eyes. She rapidly descended the stairs and took up his hands in hers. "I need your help, Your Grace. I do not know what to do. My head is so jumbled. She told me that she was leaving willingly, but I know Archer well. He did something, said something to coerce her. I just know it!"

Fayne let the viscountess ramble as he tried to make sense of her words. One thing was clear to him. Kilby was gone. "Where is Kilby?"

His question increased the lady's misery. She brought her handkerchief to her nose and sobbed. "I told you. Archer took her away."

His gut clenched briefly at the notion that Kilby might have run off with another gentleman. Fayne rejected the thought immediately. Kilby was not the sort of lady who played games.

Fayne strived for patience. "Who is Archer?" he asked, crisply enunciating each word.

"Her brother, Lord Nipping," Lady Quennell explained.

Fayne released the breath he was holding. He had forgotten the scoundrel brother's given name was Archer.

The viscountess quickly relayed to him the events that led up to Kilby's climbing into the marquess's coach. "So you see, I did not know what to do. I had no authority to prevent Archer from taking her from the house. He is rightfully her guardian. Still, I cannot bear thinking of Kilby in her brother's merciless hands."

Fayne freed his hands from the viscountess's clinging grasp. "How much time has passed since they left the house?"

"Minutes," she said, frowning as she concentrated. "Five or ten, I suppose." She followed him out the door. "What are you planning to do?"

"I hope to find their coach. Do you know where they were heading?" If Kilby thought she could leave him without an explanation or farewell, she obviously did not understand him very well.

Lady Quennell grasped the side of his carriage, while Fayne reached for the reins. One of her footmen was unfettering his horses. "Archer refused to allow her any time to collect her belongings. I assume they were immediately heading back to Ealkin," she said, her tearful expression lightening at the glimpse of hope he offered. "Will you be returning Kilby to my house?"

Fayne shook his head. If the brother was unstable, the viscountess would be unable to prevent the man from retrieving his sister again. "I think Kilby would be safer with her husband, do you not concur?"

Lady Quennell gave him a watery smile. "So I was not wrong about you. Good. Is Kilby agreeable to the match?"

"She is," he lied, seeing the older woman needed reassurance.

There had never been any doubt in Fayne's mind that Kilby would eventually marry him. He had been willing to give her a little bit more time. Regrettably, her brother had forced Fayne's hand by taking Kilby.

Even though Kilby was under twenty-one, there were legal means at his disposal for getting around a recalcitrant guardian, all of which took time, a luxury Fayne did not have. He only had one option. They would elope to Gretna Green. "I'll send word to you when she is safe."

Satisfied, the viscountess stepped away from the carriage. "Excellent. For the first time since Archer's arrival, I feel I can breathe. Will you send Kilby my love?"

"I will," he replied absently. In his mind, he was mapping

out the streets as he decided which ones Nipping might have taken.

Lady Quennell waved farewell. "Good luck, Your Grace. I pray that you find her quickly. There is something disturbing about Archer's manner toward his sister. I confess, I fear for her well-being."

They rode in silence.

Kilby had wedged her body into the farthest corner away from Archer as the coach rumbled through the streets of London. She had expected him to rail at her for defying him at Priddy's house. Archer had been eerily silent. With his chin resting on his propped fist, he stared enigmatically out the side window.

It was maddening!

Unable to tolerate a second more, Kilby said, "Are we riding straight to Ealkin?"

Archer blinked. He looked slightly startled to see her sitting across from him. "No. I am too weary to sit in the coach another day. We will spend the night at the family town house and then leave for Ealkin the following morning."

Fear clawed at her throat. The notion of being alone in the house with her brother was disconcerting. "The house has been closed up for over a year, Archer. Think of the dust. And there are no servants. If you are seeking comfort, perhaps we should stop at an inn along our way to Ealkin."

Her worries must have been transparent. The corner of her brother's mouth curved into a faint smile. "Do you fear being alone with me?"

Yes! She wanted to shriek at him. Instead, she calmly looked him in the eye and said, "No. I just want to return home to Gypsy."

"You are a dreadful liar, Kilby," he mocked, his gaze drifting from her face down to her bared ankles. "You have been plotting with the viscountess to free yourself of

Ealkin and your responsibilities to me. Those letters I received are proof of your deception."

She pressed her fingers into her tender brow and shut her eyes, striving for patience. "Archer, no one is plotting against you. As Priddy had promised you before we departed Ealkin, she merely wanted to fulfill Mama's wish and launch me into polite society. During my brief stay, I have met hundreds of people. Is it my fault if I made a favorable impression? I thought that you wanted me to marry."

"The letters I received indicate that you did more than make a favorable impression on certain male members of the *ton*," he said petulantly. "And what is this business with the Duke of Solitea?"

Kilby inhaled sharply. It took her a moment to realize her brother was not speaking of the old duke, but rather of Fayne. She had to tread lightly because she did not know what he had been told. "Exaggerations and lies, I am certain. I have met the Duke of Solitea on several occasions and he was very flattering. Really, Archer, it is so unlike you to listen to gossip."

Archer abruptly nodded, seemingly satisfied with her explanation. He leaned over and placed his hand on her knee. The harshness in his light blue eyes eased into a dreamy indulgence. "No one could blame Solitea for wanting you. You have grown into a bewitching beauty. What man can resist those trusting wide violet eyes? They make a man hunger to tangle himself in your long, silken black hair, to feel your creamy legs wrap around his hips as he spills himself inside you."

Kilby's heart was pounding in her chest. She gently shifted her knee away from his hand. "This discussion is improper, brother." This was not the first instance that Archer's conversation with her had taken a lewd and alarming turn. Usually, such talk transpired late at night after the numerous bottles of wine he had consumed had made him nasty. She had done her best to avoid him whenever the alcohol released the demon inside him.

However, this time Archer was not drunk.

Nor did he react well to her edging away from him. "Unseemly to speak in this fashion to a sister, perhaps." Gripping her knee painfully, he held her leg in place while he moved from the bench opposing her to sit beside her. "On the other hand, you and I are both aware that you are not my sister."

Kilby felt his hot breath on her cheek. "You are wrong. I am your sister and to treat me otherwise will damn your soul."

Archer dropped his forehead onto her shoulder and laughed unreservedly. He relaxed his hold on her knee. "Oh, Kilby, if you knew of the things I've done since leaving Ealkin." He idly traced the curve of her ear with his finger. "You'd know my soul already belongs to the devil. I have nothing to lose." Using his hand, he seized her chin and wrenched her face toward his.

"No!" she begged, fighting him in earnest. She felt his teeth bite into her soft lips as he ravaged her mouth with a demoralizing kiss.

CHAPTER FOURTEEN

Fayne had driven his carriage down several streets, but there had been no sign of Nipping's coach. If Kilby and her brother were heading for Ealkin, that narrowed down the possible streets they were likely to navigate. He was counting on instinct and the Carlisle luck to help him catch up with them. With each passing minute, Kilby was traveling farther out of his reach.

According to Lady Quennell, the marquess had coerced Kilby into his coach. Grimly, Fayne agreed. Kilby would not have left him so abruptly. She would have sent him a note, alerting him to her departure. He did not know Nipping personally. However, after he had listened to the viscountess's account, he thought the gentleman's casual violence toward his sister was unpardonable. Fayne did not care about the man's rights. Kilby belonged to him, and he planned to make it official as soon as he could liberate her from her scoundrel brother.

He turned left and crossed several bystreets before turning right onto a thoroughfare. Fayne barked a curt command

and tugged on the reins, slowing down his pair of dark bays.
A quarter mile ahead, a farmer had overturned his wagon,
and baskets of vegetables had scattered in the streets. The accident had drawn a mob of people scrambling for the trampled produce. Several fights had broken out, and the chaos
had brought all street traffic to a congested halt. There was a
long line of equipages blocking the street. Many of the pas-
sengers had disembarked from their coaches to get a better
view of the accident.

Frustrated by the delay, Fayne almost signaled the bays
to proceed so he could circumvent the congestion. An elegant crest on one of the stranded coaches had him pausing.
There was a chance Nipping had also turned this way and
was trapped. Jumping down from his perch, he grabbed a
passing pedestrian by the shoulder. He offered the man an
outrageous amount to guard his equipage, and once the
bargain was struck, Fayne started down the street on foot.

He was prepared to open each closed door and check
the interiors until he was satisfied. If Kilby was hidden in
one of them, he meant to find her.

Kilby squirmed within Archer's embrace. He was holding
her so tightly, she could barely draw a breath. She wondered if he was intentionally trying to induce her to faint.
The thought of what her brother could do to her while she
was unconscious urged her to fight him off with renewed
vigor.

"Oh, I like it when you wiggle your body against me,"
Archer said, panting in her ear. "With each bump my rod
grows harder."

Kilby craned her face away from his. She scored his
cheek with her fingernails. He reared his head back, cursing. His hand viciously connected with her cheek. Her head
struck the wall of the tiny compartment.

"Enough," she said, hitting him in the head and shoulders

whenever she managed to free her wrist. Every time he groped her thigh or her breast, Kilby fought down the bile in her throat.

"Enough? You stupid bitch, I will tell you when I have had enough," Archer bellowed at her, the three deep scratches furrowing his right cheek dripped with blood. He touched his fingers to his face and noted the blood. "I'm bleeding. If you've scarred me, I'll take the edge of a blade to your face and repay you in kind."

Archer tried to kiss her again. When she turned away, he wiped his bloodied fingers down her cheek. He captured the front of her bodice and ripped the front panel, revealing the swell of her breasts spilling out of her corset.

"What a fine bounty you have been keeping from me."

Kilby did not have the breath to articulate her rage in words. She pummeled him with blow after blow with her fists, but he seemed invulnerable to her attacks. As he bent his face to her exposed breasts, his hand jerked the edge of her corset downward.

"God, no—please!" she choked out. Kilby could not believe what was happening. Her own brother was determined to violate her in the coach. If the coachman heard the scuffling within the interior of the coach, he was dutifully ignoring it.

"Hold still," Archer commanded gruffly. He had bared one of her breasts. "You'll like this."

Kilby felt only revulsion as his mouth covered her nipple. At the wet lash of his tongue, she mercilessly pulled his hair. Instead of releasing her, Archer buried his teeth into her delicate flesh.

She threw her head back and screamed.

The door of the coach was jerked open. At some point during their struggles, the coach had stopped. Kilby whimpered in gratitude. She could not see her would-be knight in shining armor because Archer was blocking her view.

She did not care, just as long as the man took her away from her brother. Blindly, she reached out, needing to touch someone who was decent.

Archer lifted his head and snarled at the intruder. "I do not pay you to interfere——" Whoever was at the door was not the coachman. His next words confirmed it. "Who the devil are you? Off with you, this is not your business."

"I disagree. The lady is definitely my business," Fayne said icily.

Kilby scrambled upright and covered her breasts. She could not take her eyes off him. Haloed by sunlight, he looked like the angel of vengeance. A part of her feared she was hallucinating. There was no plausible reason for him to be standing in the doorway.

"Kilby, come to me," Fayne ordered roughly, not sparing her a glance. She need no encouragement and edged toward the door.

"You are not going anywhere," her brother told her, pushing her back onto the bench. "Who is this man to you? He snaps his fingers and you obey like a well-trained whore."

With lightning reflexes, Fayne slammed his fist into her brother's nose. Archer staggered backward and sprawled on the floor. Archer cupped his nose and howled. "Bleeding Christ, you broke my nose, you bastard!" A considerable amount of blood was dripping from his nostrils onto his cravat. Pushing off the floor, he lunged for Fayne. "I will tear you apart!"

Anticipating the attack, Fayne caught him by the edges of his frock coat and dragged him out of the coach. Archer landed forcefully on his knees. Effortlessly, Fayne picked her brother up and slammed him against the side of the coach.

Fayne drove his fist into the marquess's soft middle. "Not so mighty, are you?" He punched him again. "Bullying women. That's your cowardly manner. I should kill you for putting your filthy hands on her!"

"Fayne?" Kilby called out his name as she made her way toward the door. He was rigid with unbridled fury. She had never glimpsed this lethal side of him. Even the day at the fair when he battled Hollensworth, he still had a measure of control.

"Are you mad?" the marquess asked, stanching the flow of blood with the sleeve of his coat. "I see no reason why it should concern you how I deal with my own family. Who are you anyway?"

Fayne lifted her brother up and slammed him several more times against the coach. The back of Archer's head made a sickening thwack with each impact. Kilby covered her mouth with her hand. She had no great love for her brother. Nevertheless, Fayne's attacks were efficiently brutal.

"My apologies for not formally introducing myself. I am the Duke of Solitea." Fayne kneed the marquess in the groin and released him.

Archer gasped and dropped abruptly on his knees. Groaning, he cupped his crotch. "Solitea?" He shot Kilby a withering look. "You're not him. The man is dead."

"Not yet." Fayne seized the marquess by his throat. Archer gasped. "But you will be if you come near your sister again."

After glimpsing the violence Nipping had planned for his sister, it was difficult to refrain from killing the depraved bastard. Since Fayne could not murder him in cold blood, he concentrated on giving the man a lesson in pain. Using the marquess's ears as clever grips, Fayne smashed the back of Nipping's head against one of the coach's wheels. The man's skull made a very satisfying crack. The marquess's eyes rolled back and he collapsed facedown into the street.

It was a pity the man would eventually wake up. "See to

your lord." Fayne barked the command at the openmouthed
coachman. Kilby was quietly crying, her face pressed into
the arm she was using to brace herself in the doorway.
Without hesitating, he scooped Kilby into his arms. His argument with the marquess had already drawn enough attention from onlookers.

Striding in the opposite direction, he carried her to his
waiting carriage. As he thanked the man for looking after
his equipage, Fayne lifted Kilby onto the seat. He left her
long enough to retrieve a small wool blanket from the small
chest at the back of the carriage. Circling around, he climbed
in beside her and wrapped the blanket around her trem-
bling shoulders. Kilby had not spoken since she called to
him when she thought Fayne was on the verge of killing
her brother. Biting back a curse, he signaled the bays about
their imminent departure. A swift snap on the reins and a
low verbal command, and he turned the carriage around,
putting as much distance as he could from Nipping.

Kilby's slender figure trembled against the warmth of
his body. Fayne's heart ached. All he wanted to do was halt
the carriage and cuddle her in his arms until the tremors
subsided. Unfortunately, they needed to leave town immediately. "I need you to talk to me, Kilby. How badly hurt
are you?"

She sobbed into her hand at the question, and the muscles
in his abdomen clenched fiercely. Whatever had happened
had left her terrified. A cursory appraisal of her injuries revealed that most were superficial. The front of her dress
was torn and most of her hair had escaped the numerous
hairpins she generally used to style her hair. One of her
cheeks was reddened and her lower lip was split. It looked
sore. Dried blood crusted at the corner of her mouth. There
was also a smear of blood on her other cheek.

Fayne retrieved his handkerchief and offered it to her.
She mutely accepted it. "Come on, little wolf. If you don't

talk to me, I'll think the worst and have to go back to finish off your brother," he said, reaching over to stroke her knee. Kilby flinched at his touch. Cursing Nipping's black soul to hell, he withdrew his hand. "Speak to me. I need some reassurances."

Her lips parted and she exhaled a shaky breath. "How did you—" She intensified her bloodless hold on the blanket. "How did you know where to find me?"

Fayne scowled at her question. Kilby was not telling him what he really wanted to know. Then again, she was talking to him. "Lady Quennell. I had an eleven o'clock appointment with her. She told me how Nipping had taken you against your will."

He felt her staring at his profile as his words sank in. A tiny line formed between her brows. "An appointment?" Kilby made a face. "Never mind. We can discuss it later. Fayne, you have to take me back."

Denial flared in his green eyes. Kilby was hurt and she needed him. He did not want to hand her over to anyone. "To the viscountess? It will be the first place Nipping will look."

"No."

Huddled under the blanket, and shivering despite the mild weather, Kilby looked miserable. He was so incensed that he wanted to kick something, preferably her brother— again. "Well, if you think I'm taking you back to that madman brother of yours, his clout to your face must have addled your wits!"

She did not bother denying his accusation.

Kilby sniffed into a handkerchief. "You have to take me to Ealkin. I need to get to my sister."

"Why?"

She extended her arms in a gesture of helplessness. "Fayne, do not misunderstand me. I am grateful for your timely rescue."

Fayne did not want her thanks. Next, she would be apologizing for inconveniencing him. "I didn't do it for your gratitude, Kilby."

"I know," she said, laying her cheek on his shoulder to placate him. "You are a decent gentleman."

Fayne blinked at the compliment. Kilby was probably the only person who had ever described him in that fashion. "Why do I sense I will not like this next part?"

She sighed. "I once told you that my younger sister, Gypsy, has never recovered from our parents' deaths."

He recalled she had spoken briefly about her family the night he had encountered her at Lord Guttrey's supper. Kilby had lamented over her concerns about her younger sister. She had said very little about her older brother. Now he understood why. "You mentioned that she refuses to talk."

A spark of annoyance so much a part of the spirited lady he knew and well loved flared in her expression. "It is not simply stubbornness that prevents her from speaking. If that were true, Archer—" Kilby swiftly looked away, not finishing her admission.

She did not have to elaborate. Fayne had a pretty good idea how Nipping might have amused himself with a mute child who could not fight back. He tightened the ribbons in his grasp. "Will you despise me enormously if I end up being your brother's executioner?" he mused aloud, half serious.

"Gypsy is his leverage, Fayne," Kilby said carefully. "He knows I will do anything to protect her and he uses her to keep me in line. It is why I must return to Ealkin before Archer. He will never forgive me for leaving with you. I could not bear for Gypsy to suffer for my disobedience."

Fayne silently agreed, but he was not going to deliver Kilby into Nipping's greedy hands. "What would he do to her?"

Kilby's face crumpled in anguish as tears leaked down her cheeks. "Archer has vowed to have Gypsy declared mentally unsound and a danger to herself and others. He will lock her away in some horrible asylum for the insane." She clutched his arm, her eloquent violet gaze beseeching him to understand. "Do you see why I must get to Gypsy first? My brother will want revenge for the beating you gave him. He will take Gypsy and hide her someplace where I might never find her. Not in time."

She burrowed her face into the edge of the blanket and sobbed. His poor little wolf had been through so much. Regrettably, there were more obstacles to face before day's end. Fayne curved his arm around her back and pulled her closer. She hiccupped, and to his relief she leaned into him, accepting his comfort.

"Do not worry about Gypsy," he assured her, chastely kissing the top of her head. "I'll see to it your brother does not get his hands on her."

There was a glimmer of hope in her eyes. Still, she shook her head. "Fayne, for better or worse, he is our guardian. How can you—"

"It can be done," Fayne interjected, quelling her argument. The family name was influential in many powerful circles. He would appeal to the courts, if Nipping challenged him for either Kilby or her sister. There was no doubt in his mind that with the Solitea name and wealth behind him, he would emerge victorious.

Finally becoming aware of her surroundings, Kilby said, "We are heading in the wrong direction if we are traveling to Ealkin."

Fayne gave her an assessing look. Kilby was still shaken by her ordeal with Nipping, but the blank shock he had glimpsed was fading. He wondered how Kilby would react when she learned that they were not going to her family's country estate. It was a conversation he would rather have with both hands free and preferably not in the middle of the street. "This carriage is fine for a drive in the park, but impractical for the miles we will need to cover. We will need some provisions, and you need a clean dress."

She was pleased at his thoughtfulness. "So we are returning to Priddy's, after all?"

"No," he said, hating to disappoint her. The viscountess's residence would be the first place Fayne expected the marquess to appear. "In case your brother is already searching for you, we need a place no one will expect to find either one of us."

Her nose wrinkled in puzzlement. "Where?"

"At my brother-in-law's house."

CHAPTER
FIFTEEN

Fayne was taking her to his sister's house. Kilby had been tempted to leap out of the carriage the instant he made the casual announcement. Good heavens, of all the residences he could take her, he chose his *sister's*! She could not believe the man's insensitivity.

"Why do I not just wait for you here?" she said mutinously.

He plucked her out of the carriage and placed her feet on the ground. Hooking her arm through his, he marched her toward the front door. "Don't be a goose. You will like my sister."

Kilby locked her knees together, refusing to move. "Stop acting so *thickheaded*! Do you honestly think your sister wants to entertain in her house the last person who saw her father alive?"

He tried to soothe her by sliding his hands up and down her arms. "You are working yourself into a fine case of nerves over nothing."

Kilby held her ground. "What did you think, the first time we met?"

Fayne tucked several strands of hair behind her ear. "I was enchanted," he answered sincerely. "I knew a rake such as I was not worthy of you."

His confession was so sweet and unexpected, Kilby faltered, briefly forgetting the point of her argument. She mentally shook herself. The man had a charming way about him that was dangerous to a lady's heart. "Thank you," she said politely. "I meant, what was your opinion of me before that unfortunate encounter on the sofa."

He looked perplexed for a few seconds. Kilby saw his reply in his green eyes before his lips twitched. Fayne winced, knowing this was still a sore point of contention with her. "Christ, Kilby, will you be holding my erroneous judgment about your delicate state of innocence for eternity?"

"Probably," she said offhandedly. "You held this same erroneous opinion of me even after meeting me on several occasions."

"Kilby!"

She crossed her arms defiantly. "If that was your fine opinion, Your Grace, what do you think your sister's opinion will be? Especially when she deduces that you have been cavorting with your father's former mistress?"

Fayne's gaze heated at the accusation. "For God's sake, will you stop? It was a stupid assumption on my part. I get it. I was a horse's arse. I—"

"You will get no argument from me," Lady Fayre said from the doorway. A wiry gray-haired servant was standing beside her. "Why do you not come in and introduce me to the lady who coerces such a fascinating confession out of you?"

"Too late for escape," he murmured, reading Kilby's exact thoughts. "Come on, little wolf, you can brazen this out. I promise no one will hurt you."

Kilby did not believe him. However, Gypsy's welfare was at stake, and Fayne was willing to help. Tucking her arm into his, she entered the Brawley house.

His sister surprised Fayne by not escorting them to the drawing room as he had anticipated. Instead, she brought them to the study. The reason was not obviously clear until Fayne noticed Brawley was at his desk. He sighed. Fayne had hoped her husband was attending to a business meeting or visiting the Exchange.

"Good afternoon, Brawley," he said with false cheeriness, causing both his sister and Kilby to give him an odd glance.

His brother-in-law stiffened as they entered his private sanctuary. Three years older than Fayne, Maccus Brawley had straight black hair that he tied into a queue. He was handsomely formed with keen gray eyes and a chiseled jaw, which hinted at his inner fortitude. He was a fitting example of a lowborn man who had transformed himself into a wealthy gentleman. Not many people outside the family were aware that one of London's most influential participants at the Exchange had once made his living as a smuggler.

Fayne's relationship with his brother-in-law was based on sufferance. Mainly, he suffered whenever Brawley was around. For that reason, they usually avoided each other. It was for Fayre's sake that they occasionally tolerated each other's company. He did not know exactly what it was about Brawley that set his teeth on edge whenever the man walked into a room. It might have been due to the fact that both of them were dominating and opinionated. Fayne also privately worried that Brawley had taken advantage of his sister during a time when she had been vulnerable from another man's betrayal. Regardless of his personal feelings, his sister loved him. His mother adored her new son-in-law, and his father—well, the duke was unwilling to break his daughter's heart by not accepting the marriage.

Bracing himself, Brawley rose from his chair. "Carlisle, what brings you here? I thought the duchess's bullying was the only thing capable of making you pay a social call."

"Maccus," his sister firmly interjected, her green eyes flashing an unspoken warning to behave. "Tem has brought us a guest."

Fayne was often struck by his sister's beauty, which was a harmonious blend of both their parents. Her hair was curlier than his, but they shared the same unusual cinnamon hue and the Carlisle green eyes. She was elegantly attired in a depressing black crepe dress, a stark reminder of the family's loss.

Brawley came around his desk to formally greet Kilby. His genial expression hardened into suppressed anger as he noticed the faint bruising on her cheek and the ruined state of her dress. "Carlisle, tell me you are not responsible for this young lady's condition?"

Embarrassed by Brawley's intense scrutiny, Kilby brushed the strands of hair tickling her cheek and clutched the edges of the blanket tightly to her chest.

Fayne glared at his brother-in-law. "Of course not. Her lunatic brother is responsible." Kilby was already skittish about being in his sister's house. He did not need Brawley to send her out the door with a careless comment. "Stop fussing," he ordered her gruffly. "You are still beautiful."

"Ha," was her soft retort.

His compliment prompted his sister and Brawley to privately exchange knowing looks. It was totally out of the ordinary for Fayne to introduce his family to the ladies in his life. Equally odd, he supposed, was the noticeable protectiveness he felt for Kilby.

"Tem, perhaps you should introduce us to your friend,"

Fayre said, her delicate brow lifting as she reminded him of his lapse.

Fayne caught Kilby's arm and held her at his side before she could take a panicky step away from their hosts. "May I present Lady Kilby Fitchwolf," he said, his narrowing green eyes daring either one of them to say anything untoward.

Brawley threaded his hand through his scalp. Shaking his head, he wandered away from them laughing. No doubt the man thought he was playing some kind of twisted prank on the family.

His sister stared at Kilby in astonishment. Fayne was certain his sister could not reconcile the vulnerable woman who stood in front of her with the image of a mysterious temptress who had seduced their father in his final hours.

Finding her tongue, his sister pinned him with an incisive glance. "I need a moment of your time, Fayne," she crisply said, using his given name. It was a definite sign of her annoyance at him. "Now."

"Here," Mr. Brawley said, dangling a glass of brandy in front of Kilby's face. It was the first time the man had spoken directly to her since Fayne had pushed her into a chair, imperiously commanded her to stay, and followed his sister out of the study.

Kilby slouched even lower, wishing she could disappear, too, preferably right out the front door.

"I do not drink brandy," she said softly, feeling thoroughly intimidated. She and Fayne were also going to have private words after she survived this awkward incident.

"Neither do I," Mr. Brawley confessed. "Still, you look like you need it. Think of it as medicinal fortification."

Kilby accepted the glass and took a tentative sip. As with most panaceas, the brandy tasted foul and burned her throat. Taking another sip, she grimaced and shuddered. "Thank you."

Mr. Brawley grabbed the edge of one of the chairs and dragged it until it was positioned beside hers. He sat down, his gray eyes contemplative. "Was Carlisle telling us the truth about your brother? Is he responsible for your—injuries?"

The man was being kind and Kilby appreciated that he had bothered. "I am afraid so . . ." She trailed off, fighting back the tears. "My apologies, it has been a horrible day. I do not want to contemplate my fate if Fayne had not shown up when he did."

Mr. Brawley raised his brows at her mentioning Fayne by his given name, but he did not comment on her familiarity with the duke. "Why don't you tell me what happened?" he generously invited.

Kilby cast a wary glance at the door. She imagined that brother and sister were just beyond the door. Lady Fayre was probably flaying her brother alive for bringing their dead father's mistress into her house. "I should not be here. I told him it was not proper, but he refused to see reason on the matter."

Mr. Brawley snorted. "That is a common flaw in the entire Carlisle clan, I fear."

Kilby started at the sound of a muffled thump. She gave her host an apologetic smile. Ever since Archer's arrival in town, she had become so jumpy. Through the door, she heard Fayne's voice and his sister's sharp reply. Their words were indistinct; however, their angry tones were not.

If she had any sense, she would just get up and leave. Fayne was not resolving anything by bullying his grieving sister into helping a lady she was already prepared to hate. She could return to Priddy's house. From there she would travel to Ealkin. Fayne was welcome to join her if he caught up to her in time. She could leave him a note.

"The Carlisles are also prone to violent outbursts," the

man added sympathetically, observing that she had shifted to the edge of her seat and was poised to flee. "Give them a minute or two and they will settle down."

"Mr. Brawley, there is no point in my remaining here."

"Of course there is," he said reasonably. He took the glass of brandy out of her hands and placed it on the nearby table. "Carlisle brought you here because he thought we could help. And we will, because we're family. Do not let flaring tempers or harsh words convince you otherwise. You have too much pluck to skulk away without discussing your decision with him."

Chagrined by his calm reasoning and subtle charm, she said, "I was never his mistress, you know."

"Who? Fayre's father?" He studied her face as if the truth were glimmering just beneath the surface. Mr. Brawley nodded. "Of course you weren't. Carlisle is many things, but he would never intentionally hurt his sister."

She had never expected anyone connected to the Carlisles to blindly accept her word. Her nose began burning with suppressed tears. "Mr. Brawley?"

"Call me Mac," he entreated, clasping her free hand within his. "While we are waiting for my wife and Carlisle to join us, why don't you catch me up on what has been happening?"

"How could you be so inconsiderate, Tem?" Fayre railed against her brother. "To bring *her* above all ladies into my house. What if Mama had been visiting?"

They had adjourned to a small reading room that had connecting doors to Brawley's study. Fayne picked up a book on one of the chairs. Casually glancing at the spine, he discarded it on the floor and sat down.

"You underestimate the duchess's tolerance regarding these matters. How many former mistresses of our father's do you think she encounters in a single evening? If she were as sensitive as you claim, she would have to retire to the country." Fayne crossed his arms over his chest and stretched out his legs. He was willing to allow his sister to throw her fit. Nevertheless, he was very aware of the ticking clock and Kilby's impatience. "Besides, I know once Mother has met Lady Kilby Fitchwolf, she will adore her."

Fayre stared at him as if a pair of horns had sprouted on his forehead. "You expect too much from our mother, and you demand too much from me. If you love me, you will remove this woman from my house."

"I have not demanded anything from you, sister mine," he said, disappointed that his sister had condemned Kilby out of hand. *"Yet."* Fayne grimaced, realizing he had done exactly the same thing. "Kilby was never our father's mistress."

"Is that what she told you?" She sneered, throwing her hands up in disgust at what she perceived as her brother's gullibility. "Have you considered that since our father escaped her clutches, she is striving to get her hooks in you?"

Fayre had gone too far.

"Enough!" Fayne bellowed, slamming his palm on the arm of the chair. "There was nothing between Kilby and our father. I *know*!"

Stunned, Fayre sank into the nearest chair. "What have you done?" she demanded, her voice rich with accusation.

Fayne looked away. He was uncomfortable with his confession, but he needed his sister's backing. "Kilby was as innocent as you were when Lord Thatcher Standish seduced you. I should know since I was her first lover."

She pinched the bridge of her nose as if it pained her. "My word, Tem, you are not saying that you bedded this woman out of revenge?" Fayre paled at the thought.

"Christ, do you think me so despicable?" he fired back, jumping up when she did, stepping into her path so she had to deal with him.

Discussing Lord Thatcher Standish was difficult for his sister. Fayne had only mentioned the bastard because he knew she alone understood intimately how gossip cruelly distorted the truth, how easily a young innocent's reputation could be ruined. He had not counted on her believing that he and Standish had been cut from the same cloth.

His green gaze locked onto hers. "I seduced Kilby because I desired her. I did not care if she had been with the duke or a thousand men. I wanted her in my bed." Using both hands, he smoothed the hair back from his face and sighed. "From the very beginning, she denied being the duke's mistress. I didn't believe her, until . . ." He let the word hang in the ensuing silence.

"Good grief, Tem, when you make a mess of things you do not do it by degrees." Fayre groaned in frustration. She was not happy with Fayne. He had adeptly neutralized her unkind opinion of a lady she had been prepared to hate, and actually had her feeling sympathetic toward her. She lightly punched him on the shoulder. "You are fortunate I love you. How can Maccus and I help Lady Kilby?"

Mr. Brawley, or Mac as he had insisted that she call him, had been correct about his wife and Fayne. Their private argument might have gotten rather spirited, but it was blessedly brief. When Fayne and Lady Fayre returned, his sister actually apologized for her rudeness. Kilby discreetly glanced at Fayne, wondering what he had revealed to his sister to change her opinion.

Since she had explained to Mac the unfortunate circumstances with her brother, the men immediately began to form a plan.

"Someone needs to ride to Ealkin and collect Gypsy before Nipping thinks to use her against Kilby," Fayne explained to his family. "With your permission, I'd like to send one of your servants off to get a message to Ramscar.

The man is responsible and good with children," he added, hoping to ease Kilby's concerns. "He could slip Gypsy out from under your brother's nose if need be."

"Wait." There had been a sudden change of plan and Fayne had failed to discuss it with her. "I thought we were going to collect her? Gypsy might not go willingly with a stranger."

Both men ignored her. Lady Fayre shrugged and patted her hand sympathetically. Clearly she was used to these overbearing males. "I have my maid preparing a bedchamber for you," the other woman confided to her.

Kilby tore her gaze away from the gentlemen, who were arbitrarily making plans without consulting her, and tried to concentrate on what his sister was offering. "You are too generous, Lady Fayre. However, I would not want to impose."

"It is no trouble," Lady Fayre assured her. "I am also having her lay out a few dresses."

"But—"

Before Kilby could refuse, the other woman glanced knowingly at the blanket that concealed the damage done to her bodice, and wrinkled her nose. "Do not argue. You cannot continue your journey wearing a ruined dress. The blood splattered on the front will draw unnecessary notice."

"Forget Ramscar," Mac was telling Fayne. "I'll collect the girl."

"Do I not get a say in this matter? I am, after all, Gypsy's sister," Kilby testily reminded them. Had they forgotten she was in the room?

Mac winked at her. "Trust me, Lady Kilby. Your sister will be safe in my care."

Fayne was taken aback by his brother-in-law's offer. "There is no need to involve yourself. Once I contact Ramscar—"

"There is no time to track down your friend," Mac said

tersely. "I'll retrieve little Gypsy from Ealkin, and then bring her back here. No one will think to search for the child here."

It was a very generous offer. Still, Kilby did not understand why they could not go to Ealkin themselves. "Fayne, why do we not col—" She gritted her teeth, when he silenced her with a gesture.

"It was not my intention to involve you and Fayre so deeply," Fayne admitted, though he seemed relieved. "Nevertheless, we are grateful."

Mac accepted Fayne's thanks with a courteous nod of his head. "You are family, Carlisle. Besides, Fayre and I could use the practice."

Kilby glanced questioningly at Lady Fayre, who was blushing profusely.

A huge grin broke across Fayne's face. Whooping, he crossed over to his sister and picked her up. "And you said nothing, you little minx!" He hugged her tightly and spun her around.

"Easy, Tem. My stomach is always unsettled these days," Lady Fayre warned, her green eyes sparkling with joy. "I take it you are pleased with our news?"

Fayne gently placed his sister on her feet again. He kissed her lovingly on the forehead. "You are making me an uncle. I cannot think of any better news."

Unexpectedly, Lady Fayre looked over at Kilby. "Oh, I am positive you will come up with something," she said enigmatically.

Fayne extended his hand to his brother-in-law, and they shook. "Congratulations, Brawley. Good thing the duke did not manage to shoot you, after all, eh?"

"Something for which I am eternally grateful," Mac said wryly.

Kilby rose from her chair. "Best wishes to you both,"

she said to the Brawleys. She was tired of Fayne's ignoring her and she meant to do something about it. "Your Grace, I am concerned about the time."

Fayne always knew she was annoyed at him when she started addressing him formally. In an attempt to appease her, he came over and put his arm around her. Kilby blinked in surprise that he would so boldly declare their intimacy. She had only told Mac about her brother, and had been deliberately vague about her relationship with Fayne. What had the man told his sister?

"Yes. You are so right." He nudged Kilby toward Lady Fayre. "Is everything ready?" he asked his sister.

"I assume so. Amelie was taking care of everything." His sister extended her hand to Kilby. "Come along, Lady Kilby. Let us get you cleaned up before your departure."

The notion of changing her dress and washing her face was appealing. Still, she could not help but feel that she was missing a critical piece of his plan. "Wait. If Mr. Brawley is riding to Ealkin, what is our destination?"

"Gretna Green," Fayne said, kissing her on the mouth and pushing her at his sister. "You are about to become my duchess."

CHAPTER
SIXTEEN

Within the hour, Fayne and Kilby were under way. He had switched his light carriage for Brawley's larger travel coach. Although he was trading some speed for comfort, the enclosed compartment guaranteed their anonymity. If Nipping was searching for them, and Fayne was certain the man was, he would be searching for the Solitea crest.

"You are serious about this?" Kilby asked. His highhanded announcement still had her reeling.

The time she had spent alone with Fayre and her maid had significantly improved her appearance. She had bathed, removing all the blood and grime off her face. The swelling on her lower lip had disappeared and a touch of rouge on her cheeks had hidden the redness from Nipping's blow. Her long black tresses had been brushed until they gleamed and were swept up and pinned high on her head. The torn dress had been replaced with one of his sister's. Kilby wore an underdress of sarcenet with long sleeves that concealed the light bruising on her arms. On top of the underdress she had added an amaranth-colored velvet

Turkish robe that was trimmed with ermine. Her headdress was made out of the same material as the robe.

Fayne thought she was the most exquisite woman he had ever beheld. It mattered little that she was frowning at him. "Of course I am, love. In spite of the grief I feel obliged to give my sister's husband; Brawley is a good man. I would not put your sister's welfare in his hands if I did not think he was capable."

Kilby crossed her eyes at him in exasperation. "You are being intentionally obtuse. You know very well that I am speaking of our imminent nuptials."

He settled back in the seat. She had not screeched her refusal at him in front of his family. Perhaps it had been too much to hope that she had been resigned to her leg-shackled fate. "Oh, that. Why wouldn't I be serious? I've already asked you to marry."

"And I recall rejecting your generous offer," she countered huffily. "If I had been the seductress you had assumed I was, I doubt you would have found it necessary to come up to scratch."

"I disagree." It maddened him tremendously that her indignation over his one tiny mistake had not abated. Moreover, was he not marrying the lady? "I believe I stepped on the flowery path to marital bliss the instant I saw you."

Kilby looked skeptical instead of awed by his romantic declaration. "There have been so many other women in your life. Why would you want to give up the bachelor existence that gave you access to an assortment of lonely widows and discontented married countesses and pledge yourself to one lady?"

Fayne sensed that was not the question she had wanted to ask. What Kilby really wanted to know was if he viewed marriage as his father had done. She knew what a rake the duke had been. Was the son like the father? What she knew of his past was not comforting. A lady might be better off reconsidering her marriage to a gentleman if she thought she was fated to endure an unhappy life of turning a blind eye to her husband's numerous indiscretions.

Could he be faithful to her? He honestly did not know. No lady had ever ensnared him so thoroughly that he had contemplated pledging his heart, his honor. The generations of adulterous Carlisle males who came before him would attest that his family had not been born for fidelity. Still, he had sworn to be different. It was one of the reasons why he had planned on putting off marriage until he was in his forties. Meeting Kilby had changed everything.

"Are you demanding constancy?" he warily asked. He supposed he could say the words she needed to hear. They were only words. However, it did not seem to bode well to be offering half-truths and speculation on his wedding day.

"Many find it a virtue in marriage," she said, disappointed by his response. "Let me ask you, do you expect faithfulness from me?"

"Yes!" he replied without hesitation. The thought of her turning to another man sent a need for violence rushing through his system. "I have not been intimate with another woman since our first meeting, Kilby. You satisfy me as no other who came before you. Marriage is just a legal binding for the courts. It does not alter who I am, how I feel about you."

Kilby glanced away, not wanting him to see the moist sheen in her violet gaze. "So why marry me, if it means so little?"

Fayne was in a quandary. He was fouling things up. Just because they were on their way to Gretna Green did not mean she would marry him. "Did you think it all ended with your rejection? I told you that I intended to marry you. My timely appearance at Lady Quennell's town house was no accident. Since you were not being very cooperative, I had planned to solicit the viscountess's support for the match."

"You were declaring your intentions to Priddy?" her voice squeaked. "You should have warned me."

And give her a chance to flee? Never. "Why should I have consulted you, when you were being obnoxiously stubborn about the issue? I was counting on Lady Quennell to be more practical. I had assumed she would be able to sway your brother into accepting the match." Fayne snorted. "Well, that was before I realized he was demented."

"If you have gotten it into your head that you need to behave honorably because I was a virgin when you bedded me—"

"No, it is more than your virginity, damn it!" Fayne leaned forward and clasped both her hands. "You are rejecting me out of pride, when you need to be practical. Lady Quennell suspected it before I did."

Only because you did not tell me the truth until last evening, he thought, but kept the snide comment to himself. "You need a husband, Kilby, and I am willing. There is protection to be gained by taking my name. With the assistance of the courts, we will take Gypsy away from Nipping. We can be her guardians. I will summon the finest physicians in the country and have them examine Gypsy. Hopefully, with a little time she will return to being the little girl she was before your parents' deaths."

Perhaps it was ruthless on his part to use Kilby's feelings for her sister as a means to convince the lady to accept their marriage. Unfortunately, she did not have too many options. The lady was going to marry him. He was not above using anyone or any means to influence her.

"And what do you get out of this arrangement?"

Her quiet question took him by surprise. A mischievous grin formed on his lips as the first advantage popped into his head. "You." He slid down on his knees and began pulling up her skirts. "Permit me to demonstrate how dedicated I am to this union."

"Here? In the coach?" She was shocked by his wicked suggestion.

Shoving up yards of fabric, he settled between her parted thighs. Fayne suspected the memory of her brother's offensive groping still lingered in her mind. He hoped to replace those horrible thoughts with something devastatingly pleasurable.

In an appalled whisper Kilby asked, "What if the coachman hears us?"

Fayne nipped her inner thigh and she shuddered. "A man anticipating his bride," he murmured, inhaling the musky scent of her arousal. "Hmm . . . under the circumstances, I warrant the coachman will completely understand."

She was a married lady.

Kilby peered into the mirror attached to the wall as she prepared for her wedding night.

"I am the Duchess of Solitea," she said, still not comprehending how it had happened.

This morning she had awakened in her bed at Priddy's town house and tonight she was preparing for bed at an inn with her *husband.* She brushed over the faint mark where Archer had struck her. It barely hurt now. She pushed all thoughts of her brother aside. Indeed, it had been a strange day.

Fayne had been incredible and extremely efficient for a man who had claimed he had never thought of marrying anyone before. When they arrived at Gretna Green, she discovered that once again he had been one step ahead of her. Within his pocket he had a ring.

Kilby held up her left hand and examined the gold ring on her finger. The ring was as weighty as the title her marriage to Fayne bestowed. It was a large, exquisite oval ruby framed with clear white diamonds. After Fayne had slipped it onto her finger, he had told her that rubies had been worn throughout time to banish sorrow and ill thoughts. Diamonds were supposed to expel anger and were considered the stone of reconciliation. The ancients believed if a warrior wore a diamond into battle, he would return home victorious.

Fayne had teased that if there were a grain of truth in the tale about the stones being talismans against misfortune, then their combination assured them happiness in their marriage. It had eased Kilby's anxiety to discover he was as nervous about their marrying as she was.

Kilby stared at her reflection in the mirror. Lady Fayre had given her a nightgown to wear on her wedding night. It was designed with seduction in mind. The cambric fabric was so sheer, she might as well not be wearing anything at all. Kilby laughed softly to herself. She doubted Fayne cared what she wore. He coveted what was beneath.

Her head turned at the knock on the door.

"May I enter?" Fayne politely asked from the other side.

Kilby did not understand why she was stalling. Fayne had seen her naked, had touched her intimately. Somehow everything seemed different between them. "Of course," she said, moving to open the door just in case he thought it was locked.

The door opened just as she reached it. Fayne stepped into the room, his hungry gaze taking in the nightgown she had donned. "Kilby Ermina Carlisle, Duchess of Solitea, you are the most beguiling temptress I have ever had the pleasure of marrying."

She rolled her eyes. "That is a pitiful compliment. Especially since I happen to be the only lady you have taken as wife."

He circled around her, enjoying every aspect of his view. He was dressed informally, wearing only his shirt and breeches. "Fayre had made me promise to give you some privacy. She said that a lady needed the comfort of her personal rituals on the night of her wedding." He took up her left hand and kissed the knuckles above the ring he had placed on her finger. There was a possessive quality to his gleaming green gaze.

"Nighttime rituals were tasks I performed to please my-self," Kilby said, moving away from him and returning to the mirror. She began removing the pins from her hair. "This is the first time I have ever done them to please a man."

Fayne came up from behind and circled her waist. The heat from his splayed hand on her stomach burned her. "Your husband," he murmured, kissing her neck.

She leaned against him, reveling in his warmth. "Fayne, there is a chance Archer may try to have our marriage an-nulled. I am only nineteen. Lawfully, he is my guardian." Kilby turned her head to the side, trying to see his face.

Fayne silenced her argument by brushing his lips teas-ingly over hers. "Hush. Forget about your brother. Nipping might whine over his rights, but no court will grant them. I'll see to it. You are mine, little wolf. The marriage will stand."

Kilby wanted to pursue the conversation, but her hus-band had more important matters on his mind. Starting at her nape, Fayne massaged her scalp with his fingertips, ca-sually removing hairpins as he discovered them. There was something magical about his touch. He managed to soothe and make her ache at the same time. As her tousled hair fell down around her waist, Kilby allowed her head to fall back against his shoulder.

Inviting.

Fayne growled against her ear. The ridge of his man-hood pressed insistently against her buttocks. "The desire I feel for you consumes me. I don't want to be gentle."

Her lashes fluttered up and she locked gazes with him in the mirror. "Then don't."

❖ ❖ ❖

His new bride was a contrary mix of naïveté and wantonness. It was a potent combination sure to drive him mad with lust. "Did my sister give you this nightgown?"

Kilby turned around and faced him. "Yes. Rather conservative, do you not think?" she teased, her nimble fingers unfastening the last few buttons on his shirt.

"It is a sinful confection." Fayne helped her pull his shirt over his head and discard it. "I love it. When we return to London, I shall purchase you a dozen more."

The nightgown was fashioned to reveal rather than conceal. The rounded neck was low and adjustable. The sleeves tapered at the elbow with a flowing ruffled edge. The hem brushed the back of her calves. Whenever Kilby moved, the fabric floated about her. The glimpses of her pert nipples, the dark triangle of hair between her legs, and the sweet curve of her buttocks were a tantalizing visual treat.

Kilby laughed, her gaze shifting to his breeches. Out of respect for her sensibilities, Fayne had pulled the ends of his shirt out of his breeches to conceal his erection. His wicked thoughts about their wedding night had put him in this rather uncomfortable condition since they had sat down for supper. They had lingered over their meal of roast duck and venison, and still his unruly body had not abated. Eventually, when they rose to leave, their departure had been swift, with Kilby leading the way.

"You look uncomfortable," she said sympathetically, letting her fingers glide over the rigid bulge in his breeches. She moved closer and flicked her tongue over his left pap.

"I am. You have a stimulating effect on me."

Kilby unbuttoned the flap at his waist and widened the opening. Fayne inhaled sharply as she tenderly cupped his arousal. Freed from the confines of his breeches, his cock swelled in her hand.

He stopped her when she began to sink to her knees. Glancing speculatively at the mirror, he gave her an impish smirk. "I have another idea." Fayne spun her around to face the mirror mounted to the wall. It was a long rectangular glass that ended at their knees. "Brace your hands on each side."

Kilby complied with his command. "Are you certain my idea was not the better one?"

Her idea was a splendid one. "Perhaps later when my legs fail me," he said, removing his breeches. He positioned himself behind her.

"Should I remove the nightgown?" she asked, unsure of his intentions.

"No, leave it," he said, slipping his hands under the sheer fabric and stroking the indentation of her buttocks. "I like the teasing view the gown offers, how your nipples pebble against the fabric."

He brought his hand around and rubbed his thumb against her clitoris. As he had suspected, she moistened at his touch. Fayne nuzzled her neck. "I want you to watch me take you."

Taking his cock into his hand, he rubbed the velvet head down the cleft of her buttocks. "Spread your legs and lean into the glass," he said roughly. The hand probing her womanly folds was slick with her arousal. Unable to resist, he pressed deeper, finding her sheath.

"Fayne, if you persist, my legs will not support me."

His tongue lashed her ear. "Don't shut your eyes," he chided, deliberately heightening her senses for his penetration. Using his hand he guided the broad head of his shaft to the hidden opening of her sheath.

"Watch me fill you, *wife*." There was fierce satisfaction

in his voice when he said the word. Fayne thrust deeply, silently commanding her to take all of him.

Kilby gasped aloud at the overwhelming sensation of him filling her completely. He had never tried to take her from behind before, let alone do it standing! She did not even know it was possible. Fayne had told her to watch them, but all she could do was concentrate on *him.* Never had she been so aware of him inside her, his unyielding manhood stretching the tiny muscles as he reinforced his claim on her body.

"Am I hurting you?" he murmured, holding himself still as her body grew accustomed to his size.

"Not really. You just seem bigger if that is at all possible," she admitted, and wanted to bite her tongue when he laughed.

"Anything is possible," he said, moving experimentally while he observed her response in the mirror.

There was little she could do but shiver. In this position, Fayne was her master. With her hands braced against the wall, he controlled the pace and depth of his strokes. She could not touch him. And yet he was free to fondle her breasts and torment her by rubbing the little sensitive nubbin between her legs.

"This is not fair," Kilby said, panting, her violet eyes dark with passion. "You get all the fun."

"How so?" He pinched her nipples playfully. "This is not pleasurable?" Fayne bit the side of her neck as he flexed deeply within her.

Kilby swallowed visibly. Her nipples ached for his caress. "Fayne, touch me," she begged.

The green color of his eyes intensified at her breathy order. "Where, little wolf?"

His leisurely thrust quickened as he moved one hand from her hip to her stomach. "Here?"

She shook her head. "My breasts."

"Ah, yes. Have I mentioned how much I adore your perfect breasts?" he asked, his breath sounding winded. "I do. This position denies me the pleasure of suckling them, but I'll make it up to you later."

"Promise?" Kilby moaned.

Cupping both her breasts with his hands, Fayne drove her lithe body against him. Her fingers curled into fists as a warm heat spread through her abdomen. Kilby caught a glimpse of her reflection. Through the long black hair obscuring most of her face, she barely recognized the wanton female striving for release only her mate could give her. Craving him to end this excruciating torture, she arched her spine slightly to ease his entry, silently coax him into surrendering to his lust.

Fayne lost control. Wildly, he pounded into her sheath. Sensing her release was close, his fingers skillfully stroked the swollen nub between her legs. "This is where I belong," he said, softly grunting with each thrust. "Here. Deep. Spilling my seed in you over and over . . ."

Kilby cried out. The violence of her orgasm washed over her as her womb contracted; the sensation was so intense it bordered on pain. Fayne gave a strangled shout and pulled her hips forcefully against his. Breathing heavily, she watched her husband's face contort as he found his potent release within her body.

Fayne wrapped his arms around her waist and had curled his body protectively over hers. His embrace was the only thing keeping her from sliding bonelessly to the floor.

"I definitely see the benefits of making you my wife," he smugly said, slowly withdrawing his manhood from her.

"Really? How so?" Straightening, she turned around and sagged against the mirror.

He stalked up to her. Brushing back the tangled strands of hair in her face, he latched his mouth onto her lips for a smoldering kiss. Fayne was insatiable, she thought as his arousal prodded her belly. "Our days of sneaking around and worrying about the hour are over. Instead of watching the clock, I get to make love to you all night."

CHAPTER
SEVENTEEN

When Kilby awoke the next morning, she discovered that she was naked and alone in the bed. Half asleep, she sat up and rubbed her eyes. Stumbling out of bed, she stooped down and picked up her nightgown. Until Fayne had barged his way into her life, she had never contemplated sleeping without a stitch of clothing on. She pulled the delicate gown over her head. Moving to the door, she opened it and peeked into the small sitting room that was connected to the bedchamber.

Where is Fayne?

Glancing at the small chimneypiece, she blurrily peered at the clock on the mantel. It was twenty minutes past eight o'clock. Ugh, it was too early to be out of bed. True to his word, her new husband had made love to her throughout the night. They occasionally dozed; however, Kilby could not think of a passing hour that chimed on the mantel clock when Fayne had not stroked her body into a feverish pitch. The man could not seem to keep his hands to himself. A slight smile formed on her lips. She had never heard of anyone actually perishing from lovemaking, but it seemed like a pleasurable way to expire.

"Is that smile for me, duchess?"

Kilby turned to see Fayne stroll into the room and close the door. At some point, he had washed and shaved while she had slept. He looked rather invigorated for a man who had spent a large portion of the night frolicking in bed.

"Where have you been?" she said peevishly, feeling like a hag.

"Grumpy in the morning, are we?" Fayne teased, kissing the tip of her nose. "Ah, the things a man learns about his wife *after* the leg-shackling."

"Oh, please." Kilby rolled her eyes at him and crossed over to the satchel Lady Fayre had prepared for her. She dug around for a hairbrush. "I am perfectly amiable most days; that is, when I have had more than three hours of sleep."

Fayne was in good spirits this morning. He scooped her up into his arms and spun them around. She was giggling by the time they collapsed on the bed.

"That's better." Fayne caught her chin with his hand. "Good morning, wife."

"Good morning, husband," she said, dutifully tilting her cheek upward for a polite peck one might expect an old married couple would share.

He bent his head closer as if preparing to kiss her. Before their lips could brush, Fayne grimaced and pulled back. "You muddle my thoughts, woman. I return to you with news."

Kilby's fingers tensed, digging into his shoulders. "Have you received news about Gypsy?" Despite Fayne's efforts to distract her from her troubles, concern about her sister's fate lurked just beneath the surface.

"Yes. A messenger arrived thirty minutes ago bearing the good news we have been waiting to hear. Brawley reached Ealkin before Nipping." Fayne rubbed her back soothingly. "Gypsy is in good health. The letter you wrote her, vouching that Brawley was there at your request, eased her fears. She is now safely ensconced at Brawley's town house, and most likely is being ridiculously spoiled by my sister."

Gypsy was protected. The relief she felt was so immense, she sagged bonelessly against her husband's chest. "I owe you and your family so much for Gypsy. I—"

Fayne tipped her face upward, slightly paling when he glimpsed her tears. "There now," he crooned, wiping the wetness from her cheeks. "I understand how much your sister means to you. Besides, I could not leave an innocent child in the hands of a man like Nipping."

Fitting his lips over hers, he showed her without words the depths of his affection for her. Slowly, thoroughly, he tasted her until he filled her with thoughts and senses.

Kilby ended the kiss by turning away. Slightly breathless, she laid her head down on his shoulder. The man knew how to kiss a woman senseless. She smiled against his throat as his arousal swelled and bumped against her hip.

"Christ, you would think the beast would have had its fill," he lamented, shaking his head, chagrined at his unruly body.

She collapsed into giggles. The man was a satyr, and he reveled in his wicked devilment. "You could not possibly want—"

He brushed a kiss on her open mouth. "Yes. I do." Fayne pushed her onto her feet. "Always and often. Unfortunately, we have a schedule to keep. We need to get you dressed, a proper breakfast, and then we are off." He swatted her backside to get her moving.

"What schedule?" she asked, working the hairbrush through her snarled hair. "Our trip was unplanned."

Fayne said nothing.

She sighed. What had she been thinking? The man was always making plans. The problem was he kept her in the dark until she was soundly caught up in his schemes. Kilby paused her brushing as another thought occurred to her. "Are you worried that Archer might discover Gypsy's whereabouts? Is that why we are leaving so early?"

Fayne took the hairbrush out of her hand before she hurt herself. He resumed the task of smoothing out her hair. "Stop fretting about your brother. Nipping has no say regarding either you or Gypsy."

Fayne gave her a quick hug and handed the hairbrush back to her, and then headed for the door. "What is keeping the servant? I've ordered some hot water so you can wash. Someone should have delivered it by now."

"Wait! You never told me," she called after him before he disappeared behind the door. "If you are not worried about Archer or Gypsy, why are we leaving the inn within the hour? Is there something you are not telling me?"

He glanced pointedly at his crotch. If anyone looked at him too closely they would see a hint of his waning arousal. "With you in my arms, I could have stayed here for a month. As for where we are traveling to, you will just have to wait and see, my curious little wolf."

It appeared Kilby's curiosity was no match for the rhythmic rumbling and creaking of the coach as it traveled down the dirt road. Not even fifteen minutes had elapsed before her lashes fluttered closed and her relaxed figure slumped against him. Unable to resist, Fayne cuddled his sleeping wife in his arms. He had worn his duchess out, he thought with bone-deep contentment. Yesterday he had bound Kilby to him legally. Those ties satisfied the church and the law. Fayne, nevertheless, desired more.

There were other alluring ways a man could bind a lady to him. From their first kiss, the initial indiscernible threads had been cast around Kilby without her knowledge. Their lovemaking had strengthened those subtle bindings, tempting the lady into risking her heart and very soul.

His seductive games with Kilby had begun in light-hearted amusement. Her beauty had captivated him and the lady herself had exasperated him. Fayne had desired other women. A few had fallen in love with him. Nonetheless, when the passion had burned itself out and the moment came for them to part, Fayne had sauntered away with no regrets and his heart intact.

Kilby was different.

All the while he was seducing her, he in turn had been seduced. A man had never been caught so completely in his own trap. He could not even pinpoint his initial awareness of this intriguing development. Maybe she had bewitched him the night he had picked her out of the crowded ballroom. What he did know was that from the instant he had touched her, Fayne had been driven to stake his claim on her.

His father's death and meeting Kilby had urged him to contemplate his future. Thoughts of the damn Solitea curse also lingered in his thoughts. With the title weighing on his shoulders like a mantle hewed from granite, he knew the time had come to embrace his responsibilities and fate. Marriage was a natural step. His mother had been urging him for several years to cease dallying with his mistresses and to find a proper bride. A new Solitea heir was needed, and Fayne was happy to dedicate himself to the pleasurable task.

The coachman called out to the team of horses, alerting Fayne that they had arrived at their destination. Although he was eager to introduce his new bride to his friends and the *ton,* he and Kilby deserved a few days of solitude, giving her time to adjust to her new circumstances.

"Wake up, love," Fayne said, stroking her face. His finger traced the small bruise on her cheek. It angered him that he had not gotten to her before Nipping had laid a hand on her. Last evening when he had removed her nightgown he noticed the tiny bruises on her arms and two semicircular teeth marks near her right nipple where the bastard had bitten her. Taking Kilby and her sister away from Nipping was just the beginning. As far as he was concerned, his dealings with the marquess were far from finished.

Kilby covered her yawn with the back of her hand. "Are we in London yet?" she sleepily inquired. Her lower lip pouted in puzzlement as she pondered how she had ended up in Fayne's lap.

"I told you that we were not traveling directly to town. I have a surprise for you." He tipped her upright and shifted her off his lap.

The coach halted, and minutes later, the coachman opened the door. "Good afternoon, Your Grace," the man said, his fingers tugging the brim of his hat. "I trust it was a comfortable journey?"

Kilby smiled at the coachman, accepting the extended hand he politely offered to help her disembark from the coach. "Remarkably so. Thank you," she said, sending an amused glance at her husband.

Fayne descended the coach after her.

The coachman approached him, carrying a satchel in each hand. He nodded at the house. "Your Grace, I'll take the bags inside and check to see if everything is in order."

"Very good, Stevens," Fayne said, his indulgent gaze fixed on his wife. The man opened the front door and disappeared inside.

"This is a lovely place. Where are we?" Kilby asked, her gaze taking in the large house and wooded landscape.

He absently patted one of the horses harnessed to their coach. "Welcome to Carlisle Park. What do you think of it?"

"It is splendid!" She beamed at him. "How long has it been in your family?"

Fayne removed his hat, and wiped the perspiration from his forehead. He stared at the early Tudor and Elizabethan manor house. He had little interest in family history. However, his father had drilled into his head at a very early age the importance of knowing one's assets. "The original house goes back to the late fourteen hundreds. Before Arianrod was built, the manor was used as the family's county seat. What you see here is what is left of the southeast portion of the original house."

The house had once been surrounded by six hundred acres of Carlisle land. When the county seat had been moved to Arianrod, interest in the property had waned. Much of the acreage had been sold off, leaving the remaining two hundred and fifty acres. For several generations it had served as a dowager house. Around 1720, the house had been renovated and from that time forward it had been used as a hunting lodge, although the application was rather generalized. The game was abundant for an enthusiastic sportsman. Fayne, however, suspected many of his father's hunting trips to Carlisle Park included his mistress in the party.

"How long will we be staying?" she asked, returning to his side.

Fayne put his arm casually around her waist. It had been over a year since his last visit to Carlisle Park. Ramscar, Everod, and Cadd had joined him on his two-week stay. "Three days. My father used the place as a hunting lodge. Though the upkeep has been maintained, the house is not currently staffed."

"Oh," she said faintly, looking beset by the news. She was a gently bred lady used to directing staff, not seeing to the duties herself. "I suppose you are planning on hunting game to roast in the hearth?"

He took pity on her. "Fortunately, we are not entirely without some assistance. Before we left London, I sent a messenger north to warn the caretaker of our impending visit. I ordered him to open the house and hire a woman to cook and clean up after us daily." He hugged her encouragingly. "Not to worry, little wolf, I won't make you cook for us."

The coachman confirmed the house had been readied and cleaned for their arrival. On his inspection, he had discovered the woman the caretaker had hired was already in the kitchen preparing their evening meal. Her name was Mrs. Agnes Meadows. In her mid-forties, the robust woman had light brown hair and kind bluish-gray eyes. She had told them to call her Aggie.

Kilby decided to explore the house while Fayne assisted the coachman with the horses. The house consisted of a main hall with a groin-vaulted ceiling. Huge, carved mullioned windows adorned the front of the house. Following an ornately carved passageway led her to a stone staircase. Upstairs in one wing was the dining room and drawing room. The other wing included an Elizabethan-style gallery and a round tower, likely a relic of the original house. As she had come to expect from the Carlisles, the house like its owners was eclectic, tasteful, and lavishly appointed.

Fayne found her walking in the courtyard. "Having fun poking around?"

"Yes." She grinned at him, not denying her curiosity. "I think you have a grand house."

"I'm pleased. We shall have to make a point of coming here often."

Her stomach fluttered as a thought occurred to her. By evening, they would have the house to themselves. Aggie intended on returning to her own household each night. As for the coachman, he would reside in the stables. The large building also included sleeping quarters for the grooms.

He caged her with his arms. "Have you settled in yet?"

Kilby sniffed at the ridiculous question. "There was not much to the task since I left town with little more than the dress on my back," she retorted, slightly amused by their spontaneous adventure.

She had never embarked on a trip with so few dresses and accessories. Nor had she had so much fun. With Fayne, it was easy to forget the problems that awaited them in London on their return.

While the Brawleys had seemed to accept Fayne's news that they were eloping to Gretna Green with gracious ease, Kilby still had not met his mother. Privately, she was dreading the meeting. Despite Fayne's assurances, she doubted the dowager duchess would eagerly embrace, the woman she considered her dead husband's mistress.

There was Gypsy to consider, too. A stranger had removed her from the only home her sister knew. If she had been in her sister's predicament, she would have been terrified. Still, there was no help for it. At least Gypsy was safe from Archer's machinations. As for keeping her brother from retaining custody of Gypsy, Fayne had promised her that would never happen. For some reason she believed him.

When had she started to trust him?

Fayne brought her hand to his lips and kissed her fingers. "What are you pondering?"

"My brother," she confessed, hating to spoil their quiet time together. "You keep telling me to stop worrying. Nevertheless, I cannot seem to help myself."

"Your brother is a perverted arse," Fayne said. His anger over Archer's attack on Kilby had not diminished. "Why your father trusted him to see to your protection is beyond me."

"Archer and my father had an awkward relationship," she said carefully. "My brother stayed away from Ealkin unless he was summoned. Despite their differences, my father would have expected Archer to take care of the family if he could not. I doubt he even glimpsed the twisted man his son had become."

Fayne placed his hands on her shoulders and laid his forehead affectionately against hers. He sighed. "I wish I possessed the words to calm your fears."

Kilby rubbed her palm against his chest in a soothing manner. "You took me away from him. That is what matters," she said, praying he would not come to regret it.

"When I confront him again, I will crush him," Fayne said, the ruthlessness she had witnessed the day before shining in his harsh green eyes. "Until then . . ."

She shook her head questioningly. "What?"

He lowered his lips to hers. "I will have to dedicate myself to the task of keeping you wholly distracted."

Kilby offered him her mouth, willingly accepting the satisfying oblivion of Fayne's kisses.

CHAPTER
EIGHTEEN

The next two days passed too swiftly for his comfort. This time alone with Kilby had been extraordinary. Fayne had never been so aware of a woman before. She was so responsive in his arms. He had thought it impossible that a jaded rake like himself could be taken to such new incredible heights. He did not want the enchantment to end.

Fayne wanted to prolong their stay at Carlisle Park.

"Guess what?"

Kilby had found a scenic spot near the lake under an old willow tree to read a book she had found in one of the rooms in the house. Lost in her story, she peered up at him with a vague smile on her face. "I beg your pardon?"

Fayne plopped down beside her. He was dressed informally, wearing only his shirt and breeches. "We are alone."

She rolled her eyes heavenward at his declaration. "We have been alone for days, Your Grace."

He nimbly plucked the book out of her hands and tossed it aside.

"I was reading that!" she said crossly.

He tugged on the ribbons tied into a bow under her chin. "You are not supposed to smile at me when you scold me." Fayne peeled off her bonnet and it landed on top of the book. "Stevens just departed. It appears Brawley's coach-man is rather bored in our company. He went off to search for livelier fellowship. We might not see him for a week."

Sensing his mischief, she rolled away from him with the intent to escape. He lunged for her ankle. Dragging her to-ward him, Fayne rolled Kilby onto her back and pinned her with the length of his body.

"That is unfortunate," she said, squirming for her free-dom. "I thought we were leaving tomorrow?"

Fayne got up and pulled Kilby to her feet. "I've changed my mind. With my sister and Brawley looking after Gypsy, I have the notion of keeping you here longer just to satisfy all my private whims. I estimate that should take a year or so," he said, stalking her as she backed away from him. What he enjoyed about his wife was that she was game for anything.

"Ha-ha." Kilby made a silly face at him and danced out of his reach. Unbeknownst to her, she was moving exactly in the direction he desired. "And we are not alone. Aggie is still at the house."

Fayne slowly shook his head. "I respectfully must dis-agree. I dismissed her. I assure you, my dear duchess, we are alone. Not a single soul will hear your screams."

Kilby halted at his odd comment. "Why would I—"

Fayne exploded into action. Throwing her over his shoulder, he headed straight into the lake.

"Oh, my God, you would not dare!" she screeched at him as she pounded on his back. The water was up to his waist and he was showing no signs of stopping. "Fayne. Truly, the water is cold. You would not—"

Kilby screamed as Fayne dove into the water. Taking them under, he playfully rolled their entwined bodies be-fore surging to the surface.

She came up gasping for air. He had not taken them out too far. Kilby was able to stand with the water level barely covering her breasts. He leered at her, liking how the water had molded her dress to her body. Angling her hand, she splashed an arc of water at him. "You idiot! I had my mouth open. I swallowed half the lake when you dunked us."

"Half the lake, eh?" he asked, laughing at her exaggeration. "As much as that?"

She stifled a giggle, since she was pretending to be vexed with him. "Yes, you rat!"

They were a sight to see with their clothes plastered to their bodies like a second skin. A steady stream of droplets dripped from the sodden mass of hair pinned high on her head, making it seem as if her head had sprung a leak.

Kilby began to trudge through the water away from him toward the embankment, but Fayne seized her arm. "Where are you going? I'm not finished with you yet."

"Oh, you have done enough, Your Grace." She pushed back the wet hair plastered to her face. Her coiffure was listing to one side. "I intend to remove my soggy clothes and put on the remaining dry dress I have in my possession." She reached into the water and pulled off her shoes and stockings. Stuffing the hosiery into the toes of her wet shoes, she hurled the pair onto the dry bank.

For a lady used to changing her attire several times a day, her extremely limited wardrobe was a nuisance. Fayne commiserated with her. He had only borrowed a spare shirt from Brawley before they had departed London. "Our clothes needed a good washing anyway."

She laughed at his odd logic, and shook her head. "No, I am not going to encourage you."

Yet she already had with the coy tilt of her head and a seductive smile on her lips. "Stand still while I finish this," he ordered, opening the panel at the back of her dress.

He made quick work of the cloth tapes. Ignoring her

protests, he shoved the wet fabric down over her arms. "Step out of the dress. This is tricky business doing this task in the water."

She held on to his shoulder and let him free the garment from her legs. Kilby had not put on a corset or petticoats this morning. The remaining chemise was too sheer when wet to protect her modesty. Immediately she crossed her arms over her breasts. "No, I cannot possibly—someone might see us," she said plaintively.

He bundled her dress into a wet ball and threw it in the general direction of her discarded shoes. "I told you. We are alone. Do you believe I would allow another man to see you so?" He stripped her of the chemise and she sank deeper into the water to prevent him from seeing her.

"I never know what to think," she replied, pouting sullenly. "You always seem to be one step ahead of me at every turn."

His white teeth flashed at her as he smiled. "Why, thank you, little wolf. I do believe you mean that as a compliment." As Fayne stripped down, his shirt and breeches plopped on top of her garments in quick succession.

"Not really."

Fayne waded deeper, closing in on her. He and his sister had spent countless summers swimming in the lake. "Did anyone teach you how to swim?"

As her expression dimmed, her eyes conveyed the sadness his question evoked. "Archer taught me when I was seven."

Taking her into his arms, he silently cursed. Fayne did not want her reflecting on her brother. He threaded his fingers through her hair, shaking her loose coil of hair free of its hairpins. She whirled around, trying to rescue the pins as they vanished into the murky depths of the lake.

"Fayne! Those were the last of my pins!" she exclaimed in exasperation, striking both of her fists against his chest.

"It matters little," he said casually. "I prefer it when you wear it down anyway." To support his point, he kissed her tenderly on the lips. It came as no surprise that his cock thickened and stirred in response.

Her violet eyes blinked at him beguilingly. "Truly, everyone is gone?" She circled her arms around his neck and lifted her mouth up to his.

Fayne flicked the tip of his tongue at the drop of water on her nose. "My oath as a gentleman," he said, lowering his head for another kiss.

Kilby, his mischievous wolf, had other plans. Waiting for the proper moment, she braced her hands on his shoulders to rise out of the water and submerge him.

"Ha! You, my duke, are no gentleman!" She pushed off him and swam away.

Fayne broke the surface of the water, laughing. She was swimming several yards ahead of him, when he began his pursuit. Although she was surprisingly an excellent swimmer, his long, powerful strokes ensured that he would be the winner.

He caught her by the waist, hugging her slim figure to his own. "Take a breath," was his only warning before he sent them both under. Maneuvering her until she was facing him, Fayne locked his lips over hers. Air bubbles tickled his face as he relished the sweet unique taste of her mouth.

They were both breathless when he finally let them surface. Kilby wrapped her legs around his waist. "So you have decided to be playful, eh?"

Content to allow him to support her in the water, Kilby reached back with both hands and squeezed the excess water out of her hair to prevent it from dripping in her face.

"You deserved it," she said unremorsefully. "I sensed it when I first met you, and now I know it as fact. Fayne Carlisle, Duke of Solitea, you are a very wicked man."

The dimples in his cheeks appeared as he grinned at her.

"My darling girl, do you expect me to disagree? The Carlisle males were made for sin!"

Kilby stared at her husband, feeling warm despite the cool water. She could not refute his arrogant boast. Fayne was the handsomest man she had ever beheld. The man was flawless. His face was beautifully formed, with a strong masculine jawline that kept him from being too pretty. Then there were his eyes. Oh, those intense green orbs gleamed at her with such need. Her legs tightened around his waist in anticipation. She reached for his queue and untied the leather thong.

"You make me feel sinful, too, husband," she shyly confessed.

Sweet heaven, the things the man did to her body. She felt incredibly wanton whenever he touched her. Using his mouth, his hands, and his sex, he had branded her body, leaving her to crave him even more. The intensity of these longings for Fayne sometimes frightened her. No one had come to mean so much to her as quickly as he had.

"I'm pleased to hear it is so," he said, his hand reaching between their bodies. He was fully aroused. As he shifted her expertly, she felt the head of his manhood push demandingly at her feminine portal. "Open for me, love."

With her legs wrapped around his torso, she was utterly exposed to his penetration. Moving against her in short, rapid thrusts Fayne eased his way into her snug sheath.

"That's it," he said, the muscles in his throat visibly tightening. He grunted in ecstasy as he filled her to the hilt. "A perfect fit." Using the buoyancy of the water to his advantage, he moved her up and down him.

There was little for Kilby to do but to hold on, letting Fayne control their pace. Her wet breasts slapped against his chest as the water churned and lapped around their entwined bodies. Grabbing a fistful of his long dark cinnamon-colored hair, she pressed her lips to his cool cheek. Her tongue laved the abrasive stubble along his jaw.

"Kiss me," she said, not above making her own demands. Fayne was used to leading, of being the one in control. Each time he lost his formidable restraint with her, she saw it as a small victory, a measure of her true power.

Fayne instantly obeyed, piercing her lips with his tongue. She parried her tongue against his. Kilby loved the texture and taste of him. His tongue undulated and evaded hers, daring her to reclaim it. She growled into his mouth when he escaped her questing tongue and tickled her palate.

He drew back and bit her lower lip. Tugging on the soft flesh playfully, he reached for her left breast. "You look like a violet-eyed mermaid with your black hair billowing in the water." His thumb caressed her puckered nipple.

"If I am a mermaid, who are you?" she asked, secretly pleased by his description. As a child she had splashed in the water, wishing she could change herself into the mythical sea creature.

"Me?" Fayne brought her flush against him. Kilby strained and arched her back, trying to pull him in deeper. "I'm the man who netted the temptress."

Fayne spun them in the water in a slow dancelike manner as he rocked her against him. Her long hair swirled around them, giving his bare flesh feathery caresses. The playfulness that had prompted him to toss her into the lake was waning as the predatory male in him craved completion. The water surrounding them churned like a storm-tossed sea. His vision dimmed. Focused solely on Kilby's face, he impaled her on his cock over and over. She urged him to go faster. Fayne firmly cupped her slick buttocks with his hands and increased their pace.

A few seconds later, Kilby tossed her head back and sobbed out his name. She said his name reverently, like an

arcane incantation, unleashing his restraint. Bringing her
down on him fully, his cock flexed deeply inside her as he
climaxed inside her. His breath came out in harsh broken
puffs. He held her fiercely, his hot seed jetting into her, filling her womb.

The feeling of contentment was heady. It was too soon,
but Fayne wanted her again. "For a man living under a supposed curse, I am generously blessed."

They were fortunate they had not drowned each other in the
lake. After Fayne had spent himself into her, his knees had
collapsed and the water closed over their heads. Kilby soon
discovered her legs were not much better than Fayne's.
Wobbly from their lovemaking, they managed to stagger to
shore.

It was one thing to play naked in the water, it was quite
another to walk about without any clothes. Her dress and
chemise were too wet and muddy to wear. She was prepared
to return to the house for dry clothes; however, Fayne had
another suggestion. Shaking out the blanket she had been
using while she had read a book under a tree, Fayne laid it
out on the grassy sun-drenched banks. He had assured her
that this was a pleasant albeit lazy way to dry themselves.

Fayne rejected all her hasty excuses as to why his suggestion was impractical. Dragging her onto the blanket, he
lay down beside her. It took her a few minutes to relax.
Soon the warmth of the sun began to penetrate the icy
coolness of her skin. Lying on her side, she idly played
with the dark curly hairs on his chest. He had his arm slung
over his eyes and his breathing was even.

Kilby wondered if he had fallen asleep. "Fayne?"

"Hmph?"

"What did you mean when you said that you were a supposed curse?" A terrible thought suddenly struck her. "Is it
because of me? Are you cursed because you married me?"

He lifted his arm from his eyes and gave her an irritated look. "Don't be daft. How could marrying a woman who matches my carnal appetites so perfectly that she drains every dram of my strength be a curse? Fifteen minutes ago, if I had drowned in that lake I would have died a happy man."

"Oh," she said, confused on why her innocent questions had ignited his temper. "Then where does the being cursed part come in?"

Fayne pulled himself up and braced himself on his elbows. "No one has mentioned the Solitea curse to you?"

"Your family is cursed?" She could not recall anyone mentioning a curse connected to Fayne's family.

"It depends if you believe in such things, I suppose," he said, his lip curling in scorn.

She caressed his stomach soothingly. There was something about him at times that reminded her of a feral beast. "I take it that you do not."

He rolled onto his side and laced her fingers with his. "No. Not really." Fayne shook his head and chuckled bitterly. "At least I didn't think I did."

Kilby's lips parted. "Your father. The death of your father has something to do with this." No one could lose a loved one and not think he or she was cursed.

"The curse has been a part of the Carlisle history for so long, no one knows its origins. Nevertheless, you are right. My doubts arose after the duke suddenly died in your boudoir."

She hoped he was not going to press her for details about his father. Kilby was not prepared to talk about it to him yet. "Exactly what is this curse?"

Fayne scrubbed at his face wearily and sighed. "If you are expecting a clever riddle hinting at the wrongdoing and the salvation, there is none. All we Carlisles have are facts."

"And they are?" she prompted.

He extended his arm and made a sweeping motion with his hand. "I come from a long, impressive line of descendents. Do you know what they all have in common? Each male born heir to the Solitea title died at an early age." When she said nothing, he continued, "The men in my family are bred for reckless adventures. We live hard, embrace danger, and are too handsome for our own good."

"I doubt you will get many people to disagree with you."

His green eyes twinkled in merriment. "You may be right." Fayne tweaked her nipple and slid his hand to her belly. "We eventually marry. Duty to the family and all that. We breed our heir, and die in some outrageously spectacular manner."

Kilby frowned, sensing he was deliberately leaving pieces of the tale out of his retelling. "Perhaps it is merely coincidence?"

"I used to think so, too. My father was the exception to the dukes who came before him. He did not die a young man in his prime. He sired his children and lived long enough to see his hair turn gray." Fayne looked away, fighting the grief he usually kept hidden from everyone including her. "As ridiculous as it sounds now, I thought he would live forever."

Having lost her own parents, she knew exactly how he felt. Kilby laid her hand over the one he had placed on her belly. "No, it does not sound ridiculous. Not to me."

Fayne leaned over and kissed her. "A part of me still thinks the Solitea curse is superstitious tripe. Mostly," he ruefully admitted. "Then there is a part of me that sees that despite my best efforts, I am following the same path as the other Carlisle males."

She wrinkled her nose. Denying that he was a true Carlisle was akin to Fayne's denying that he was a virile male. "You are wasting your time trying to convince yourself or me that you are anything other than a Carlisle. Good grief, Fayne, you tossed me into the lake and made love to me with such scorching fervor I would not be surprised if our passion made the lake water boil!"

As he recalled the intensity of their lovemaking, the green flame in his eyes flared with renewed interest. The man was simply incorrigible!

"And look at us," she said, gesturing to their decadent repose. "Never in my life have I contemplated lying under the sun without a stitch of clothes on. And yet, here we are. You have totally corrupted me in true Carlisle fashion. I dare you to tell me that if you could, you would choose living your life in a less extraordinary manner."

His lips quirked into a smile at the preposterous notion. "I suppose not." Fayne lightly splayed his hand over her abdomen. "Do you realize there is a chance our child is already growing in your womb?"

His question struck her entire body like a lightning bolt. Her skin felt electrified and itchy at the thought. Was she pregnant with Fayne's child? She placed her hand on the soft curve of her belly and tried to recall the date of her last menses. It had taken place before she had first encountered Fayne.

Her eyes narrowed suspiciously at his smug, knowing expression. "You have done nothing to prevent such an outcome," she said flatly. There was no question in her inflection. She saw the answer in his beautiful, arrogant eyes.

"Not once," he admitted unapologetically.

The countless times he had taken her flashed in her mind. Fayne had come to her so demanding, so hungrily.

Fayne bent his head over her stomach and kissed her belly. "I would be jubilant if you were. As would the family be, especially my mother. I knew after that night I first lost myself in your wonderfully snug body on the sofa that you were fated to be my duchess. As the Duke of Solitea, producing the next Carlisle heir is one of my primary duties to the title and the family. I saw no reason to deny myself the pleasure." When she seemed displeased by his answer, he added, "If our child, indeed, sleeps in your womb, no court will consider your brother's claim of guardianship. You are my wife now. You and the babe belong to me."

"This pleases you?" she asked skeptically. Perhaps this was what he meant when he spoke of curses and his following the same path as his ancestors. If he had married and sired his heir, then there was nothing left but to wait for the family curse to claim him.

"Yes, Duchess, it does." Fayne rolled on top of her and settled between her legs. "From now on, I am prepared to dedicate myself wholly to my duties."

His body was so hot from the sun his flesh burned hers. Aroused, she felt his manhood prodding her moist heat, urging her to take him into her body. She shifted her legs slightly, and their bodies melded together. Any uneasiness she felt about the Solitea curse faded from her consciousness as she yielded to his pleasurable stroking and denied him nothing.

CHAPTER
NINETEEN

Someone had been watching them.

Fayne crouched down next to the set of fairly fresh boot prints he discovered near the lake, not far from where he and Kilby had made love the previous day. He stroked his jaw contemplatively as he studied the shallow imprints. Judging from the size, he knew he had not made them. Stevens had not returned from the village yet so he ruled the coachman out, too.

He owned the surrounding two hundred and fifty acres. His family had never had a problem with poachers, although it seemed the safer explanation than his first thought—Nipping had tracked Kilby to Carlisle Park. By now, the marquess had probably coerced Lady Quennell into confessing that Fayne had eloped with Kilby. If the man had a jot of intelligence, he should graciously accept that his sister was beyond his reach. He had no hope of taking her from Fayne. Kilby was a Carlisle.

Still, no one had ever credited a lunatic with rational thinking.

Fayne stood, his gaze broodingly fixed on the boot imprints that should not be there. If Nipping had been watching him and Kilby frolicking in the water yesterday, he hoped the man had realized the futility of separating them. He did not want to kill his wife's brother, even if the man unquestionably deserved it.

Returning to the house, he found Kilby perched on the edge of a chair while she brushed out her hair. She was dressed only in her chemise. Fayne raised a brow at her scanty albeit alluring attire. Aggie was not expected to arrive for several hours.

"You do not look like you washed, Your Grace," she teased, tipping her head up so he could graze his lips over hers. "Were you waiting for me to scrub your back?"

"A charming idea," he said with false cheeriness. "One I hope to pursue later. While I was near the lake I discovered some game tracks. I think I'll postpone my bath and go hunting. Besides, I like the thought of providing for my duchess."

Kilby nodded. She was unaware of the tension and anticipation coiling in his gut. "I suppose you hunt each time you stay here. Do you regret that you have been so distracted lately to spare a single moment to the hunt?"

Was she serious? No man loved hunting game *that* much. "You are a delightful distraction I would choose over hunting any day." Fayne kissed her lingeringly on the mouth. He wished he could carry her upstairs and spend the day in bed with her. Regrettably, duty came first. He needed to make certain her crazy brother was not stalking them. "What will you do in my absence?"

"Nothing very interesting," she said, trailing after him as he went to find his father's rifle. "I think I will bathe in the lake. My hair needs a good scrubbing."

Fayne paused at her announcement. If he ordered Kilby to remain in the house, she would demand an explanation.

He had been assuring her for days that she was safe on Carlisle lands. No harm could befall her if she simply planned on washing herself in the shallows of the lake. Until he knew for certain, he did not want to reveal his suspicions to her.

He tried another tactic. Pulling her into his arms, he said, "If you want to delay your bath, I will personally oversee the scrubbing of your back, and any other part of your delectable body that you feel needs my special attention."

"Hmm . . . a tempting offer, Your Grace," she said, pressing her breasts against his chest. "Still, I know *you.* I will never get my hair properly washed with you underfoot. Go on, off you go." Using both hands, she dismissed him with a departing gesture. "My stomach will indubitably appreciate your efforts later."

The second she turned away to collect the articles she needed for her bath, Fayne's smile faded. Pivoting on his heel, he focused his thoughts on the hunt.

Kilby grasped the trunk of a tree while she slipped off her shoes. Fayne had left the house fifteen minutes earlier, intent on hunting the animal tracks he had discovered near the lake. She did not understand why he had a sudden urge to hunt for game. Kilby had not even known her new husband was an avid hunter. It was another example of how little she knew about the man she had married.

With the sweet almond soap ball clutched in her hand, Kilby waded out into the lake. Despite her claims yesterday about the lake being too frigid, the water was rather comfortable once she had gotten over her initial shock. Without Fayne there to talk her into removing her chemise, she was keeping the undergarment on. Aggie was due to arrive soon and the coachman could return without any warning. Though it was flimsy, Kilby wanted something covering her.

Submerging completely under the water, she surfaced, her breath coming out in a sharp hiss. Kilby pushed her hair away from her face. How had she considered this icy lake comfortable? A moment of insanity! She wrapped her arms over her breasts and moved back into the shallower water. It was warmer there. As she knelt down, the water covered her breasts partially.

Taking the ball of soap, she began scrubbing one arm and then the other. Understanding that Kilby's trip north had been made in haste, Aggie had given her the scented soap balls on her arrival. Fayne seemed content to do without certain personal luxuries; however, Kilby was feeling disheveled and—she sniffed her left underarm suspiciously—mayhap even odorous. Disgusted, she vigorously applied the soap to her underarms.

She dunked herself deeper into the water, rinsing her body. Next, she lathered the soap in her hands and worked on her long hair. Usually, she had a maid who helped her wash her waist-length tresses. Methodically, she began working the soapy lather into her hair. The wet unwieldy mass was a handful. Kilby cried out in dismay as the ball of soap slipped from her hand and struck the surface with a plop.

"Oh, no!" She plunged her hands into the water, trying to catch the soap ball before it disappeared completely. With her fingers she gingerly probed the soft lake bottom, but the soap was gone.

As she scowled at the spot where the soap had vanished, Kilby noticed a shadow cross over her reflection on the water's surface. Good! Fayne had returned. Perhaps he could help her finish washing her hair.

The hands that seized her nape did not belong to her husband. Before she could cry out, her unseen attacker shoved her face into the water. Instinctively, her hands clawed blindly at the powerful grip clamped onto her neck.

The hold was strong and merciless. No amount of frenzied twisting allowed her to lift her head out of the water.

Bubbles of her precious remaining air escaped her lips in her panicked struggles. Kilby was running out of time. The abrupt attack had given her no opportunity to draw a deep breath into her lungs, and her ineffective thrashing was swiftly using up what little air she had left in her lungs.

She was going to die.

No! she thought hysterically, *I am too young to die.*

Kilby scored her nails across her attacker's flesh, hoping to mark her killer so Fayne could avenge her murder.

Fayne. The poor man was going to think he was definitely cursed when he returned to the house and discovered her lifeless body floating facedown in the lake.

Please forgive me, love.

She felt her consciousness slipping away and her vision dimmed. Her arms were floating uselessly in the water. There was nothing left for her to do but allow the cold, dark water to claim her.

Abruptly, the tremendous weight on her neck was gone. She was so dazed, she floated facedown in the water for a few seconds before her air-starved lungs demanded that she rise out of the water. Pushing off the muddy bottom, Kilby staggered out of her kneeling position. She coughed and choked as she dragged air into her lungs. Her hair was a black curtain of sluicing water so she parted the tangled wet mass and shoved it away from her face.

Terrified her attacker was close by just waiting to submerge her again, Kilby whirled around, her body quaking from fear and the cold water.

She was alone.

Where had he gone? As she waded out of the water, her chemise clung to her breasts and hips, hindering her steps. Kilby could not stop shaking. Her legs collapsed as soon as her feet touched dry land. She kept searching for her unknown assailant, but there was no sign of him. The world looked normal. It was as if he had never existed.

Kilby pressed her hands to her face and sobbed. She needed Fayne. Tossing her head back, she did the only thing she was capable of—she screamed.

Fayne was puzzling over the tracks he had found in the woods. The imprints were identical to the set he had first discovered near the edge of the lake. The tracks circled around the main house and buildings, but there did not seem to be a purpose to the pattern. It seemed like the trespasser had been wandering aimlessly in the woods.

In the distance, he heard a woman's faint scream.

Kilby.

Fayne broke into a run, dodging trees and obstacles as agilely as a buck. He cleared the woods and headed for the lake. Had something or someone disturbed her as she bathed? With his heart pounding frantically in his chest, he saw her sitting on the embankment sobbing hysterically. Dressed only in a wet chemise, she was hugging her knees to her chest and her head was bowed.

"Kilby!"

Her face popped up when he shouted her name. "Oh, Fayne!"

Leaping to her feet, she ran straight into his embrace. She nuzzled his chest fiercely, as if trying to get under his skin. He eased the rifle to the ground so he could inspect her for any possible injuries with both hands.

Kilby sobbed against his chest. "It was so horrible."

She was shaking uncontrollably. Her face was ghostly white and there was a faint bluish tinge to her quivering lips. Fayne held her tightly, his hands stroking her everywhere. Kilby seemed unhurt. "What is it? Did something in the water frighten you?" His gaze searched the nearby shallows of the lake, seeing nothing out of the ordinary.

"Someone was h-here . . . in the water . . . he tr-tried to drown me," she said, her teeth chattering so hard it had to hurt.

The knot of fear that had settled in his gut shifted and expanded. Fayne tilted her head back so he could see her face. "Kilby, are you certain? Perhaps a submerged log in the water bumped into you and was ensnared by your hair?"

Disgusted, she pushed him away from her. Turning away, she marched over to her shoes and the towels she had left at the base of a tree. "Your Grace, I can tell the difference between a submerged log casually bumping against me and a pair of strong hands holding me facedown underwater," she said tartly.

Kilby slipped on her shoes and snatched up the large towel. Clutching the towel to her chest, she said, "I did not imagine those hands on my nape, Fayne. Why do you not believe me?"

Her tears were breaking his heart. "I do." He covered the distance between them. Fayne reached for the other towel and carefully dried her face. "Did you see the person who attacked you?"

"No. I saw only a shadow on the water's surface before he shoved my head under. Initially, I thought you had returned from your hunt." She dropped the towel and gathered her wet hair up to reveal the back of her neck. "He was so strong, I thought my neck might snap from the force alone."

Fayne's stomach roiled when he saw the ugly red marks on her tender flesh. While he had been distracted, following a false trail in the woods, he had given someone the opportunity to attack his wife. He was so furious with himself he wanted to kick something. Briskly striding over to the rifle, he seized it and returned to Kilby.

"What are you doing?" she demanded, when he picked her up into his arms and started for the house.

"You have had a shock," he said brusquely. "You need dry clothes and something warm in your stomach." He should have ordered her to remain in the house. She might not have liked it, but she would have obeyed. It was his fault she had almost drowned.

Aggie met them at the door. "Your Grace, has something happened to your lady?" she asked anxiously, wringing her hands as she followed through the hall to the stairs.

Fayne handed the servant the rifle. "She's had a bad scare. Make the duchess some tea. I'll get her settled into bed." Not waiting for a response, he hurried up the stairs.

"Why would anyone attack me?" she wondered aloud, her thoughts echoing his own. "No one knows our whereabouts, right?"

That was not exactly true. Lady Quennell and his family knew they were traveling north. Countless servants knew their destination, too. Anyone who was familiar with the family's land holdings could have easily deduced that Fayne might bring his new wife to Carlisle Park.

He tenderly placed Kilby on the bed. Pulling up a blanket, he wrapped it around her shoulders until he was satisfied that she was covered. "I know you have questions, love. So do I. I just need some time to think about all of this."

Looking miserable and close to tears, Kilby nodded.

For his wife's sake, he was trying to remain calm; however, the façade was burdensome. Inside, Fayne smoldered with rage. How could this atrocity have occurred on his lands? Was Kilby the victim of a deliberate or random attack? If she were his intended prey, then why? Kilby was too kindhearted to have gathered a single enemy in her young life. The same could not be said about him. He had his fair share of enemies. Perhaps the attack on Kilby had been a devious way to strike at him. Her attacker had spared her life in the end. Had this been intentional, or had something frightened the man off? Fayne's head was filled with so many unanswered questions he thought his head might burst.

Kilby was still rattled. Given time, her keen mind would put order to her jumbled thoughts and she would deduce that they both knew one gentleman in particular who would be very displeased about their marriage.

Her brother.

Fayne was not convinced Nipping was responsible for the attack. Nor was he prepared to dismiss him entirely. On one matter, Fayne was certain.

Lord Nipping was quite capable of hurting his rebellious sister.

CHAPTER
TWENTY

They were returning to London.

Kilby softly sighed as she stared out the window of their coach, watching the landscape slowly change from rural countryside to the congestion of town life. After Fayne had tucked her into bed, he had returned to the lake's edge to inspect the area where she had been attacked.

Whatever he had discovered had not pleased him. He had announced that they were leaving Carlisle Park immediately. While he readied the horses, Aggie helped Kilby dress and together they packed up their few belongings. Once she was settled comfortably in the coach, Fayne drove them into the village to collect their coachman. With the exception of asking her how she was feeling, her husband had spoken very few words to her since he had joined her.

There was something troubling him. His pensive silence was beginning to fray her already tattered nerves. She had been thinking during the passing hours, too, and had reached a few conclusions on her own.

"Fayne, I am trying to be considerate to your brooding

nature. However, I can no longer bear the silence between us. Will you tell me what you found at the lake's edge?" she pleaded.

A ghost of a genuine smile eased the grim tension around his mouth. "Kilby, love, everyone will tell you that I have a merry nature. I never brood." He had removed his hat. His forehead was damp from perspiration and the shorter lengths of hair around his face curled slightly in the humid air.

She was not going to let him distract her with charm. "Stop hedging. You saw something that troubled you, did you not?"

He hesitated, probably deliberating about how much he should reveal.

She refused to be treated like a child. "I am not fragile. I already know you suspect my brother had a hand in my attack," she said, keeping her voice steady. It hurt thinking about Archer. He had proven indubitably that he could be violent. She had never thought him capable of killing anyone.

"Earlier today, I was not hunting for game," he confessed. "At least not the four-legged variety. I found a set of boot impressions about two hundred yards from the spot where we made love the other day."

"Someone might have been watching us?" she asked, sickened by the notion. "Why did you not mention this before?"

His fingers flicked aside the question dismissively. She could tell from his expression that he was angry about his oversight. "There was no reason to upset you. We cannot be certain the person who left the imprint was actually spying on us. I did not want our afternoon together to be sullied by mere supposition."

She tried to understand it from his perspective. After all, the man had been attempting to protect her delicate sensibilities. "Regardless, you were concerned enough to check the surrounding area."

"It seemed prudent," he said mildly. "I assumed our trespasser was poaching on Carlisle land. Although the buildings and grounds are maintained, the property is not always inhabited. Our presence might have startled our un-invited visitor."

He had clearly given the situation some thought. "Even so, you think it is unlikely," she prompted, urging him to tell her that he suspected Archer was the one who had tried to drown her.

Fayne flexed the hand resting on his knee in agitation. "The tracks went into the surrounding woods. I decided to follow them to see if I could pick up a fresh trail or find a clue to what the man was doing there."

"But your man was not in the woods, was he?" she said in a hushed tone. Kilby vividly recalled how it felt to be roughly grabbed from behind and her head thrust into the cold water. She absently rubbed her neck.

"No," Fayne replied, his green eyes bleak. "He wasn't." He closed his eyes and pressed his fingers into the inner-most corners. "Can you forgive me for failing you?"

"You did not fail me," she said, realizing he needed comforting. Kilby moved and sat next to him. She gently tugged his hand away from his face. "I doubt you would have permitted me to leave the house if you had suspected the trespasser might be violent."

He chuckled bitterly at her understatement. "I would have locked you in the bedchamber," he said, so implaca-bly that it was difficult for her not to be offended. "Once you were safe, I would have scoured the woods until I tracked him down."

Kilby did not have to be told what came next. Her hus-band could be ruthless when provoked. He was not the type of man to wait idly for justice to be delivered on the guilty. If he had tracked his wife's attacker down, he would have been the man's executioner.

"Just say his name," she said, leaning her cheek against his rigid shoulder. "You believe my brother was the man who attacked me."

"I believe Nipping is a possible, albeit unlikely, suspect, yes." Fayne coaxed her face up with a touch of his fingers under her chin. Latching on to her gaze with his own, he said, "Once he learned of our elopement, he could have pursued us to Gretna Green, and on to Carlisle Park."

His line of reasoning was damning to her brother. "I understand why you might think Archer is responsible. Even before I met you, my relationship with him was, uh, difficult. My brother is cruel, selfish, and yes, sometimes violent."

He crossed his arms. "You will get no argument from me."

Fayne did not grasp why her feelings for her brother were so conflicted. He had glimpsed the corrupt, violent man Archer had become. She mourned the boy she had loved and played with as a child. "I am not defending him. Nevertheless, I do not see him as a murderer. Archer's arrogance surpasses even yours!"

Fayne lifted his brows questioningly, but said nothing.

"Like you, once he learns of our marriage, he will be convinced the courts will take his side," she argued, her violet eyes eloquent. "If he was your trespasser, what do you think he would do if he caught me alone?"

He groaned, sensing where she was heading with her argument. "I am sure you will enlighten me whether I want to hear it or not."

She was determined to make him consider all aspects before he condemned her brother. "If he knew he had cleverly distracted you, that we were separated, Archer would have gagged and dragged me off, not tried to drown me." What her brother might do to her once he had reclaimed her was not worth mentioning or contemplating.

"You cannot save the man, Kilby. I saw the twisted lust

he calls affection, the violence he bestows on those who are under his protection," he said, angered on her behalf. "If Nipping thinks he has lost you, his sick reasoning might convince him death by his hands is preferable than letting another man have you."

Kilby shook her head, denying the validity of his words. Was she simply refusing to see the truth out of misguided family loyalty? She had no great love for her brother. All the same, she could not envision him as her executioner. "You cannot condemn my brother just because you do not like him."

"I grant you, I despise the man. Nothing—" He stopped in mid-sentence and amended, "Well, nothing, minus a few notable exceptions, would give me greater pleasure than to put a bullet in your brother." He sighed. "Regrettably, I confess I agree with you. While identifying Nipping as the culprit would simplify matters greatly, I do not believe your brother was your attacker."

She was torn between exasperation and amusement. Only Fayne could leer at her bosom and calmly discuss killing her brother at the same time. Kilby was also relieved Fayne was willing to see reason about her brother. "I never saw my attacker, Fayne. The hands I tried to pry from my neck were those of a man's. He was so strong," she said, shuddering at the memory.

"Oh!" Kilby suddenly recalled a detail she had forgotten about her frantic fight. "I hurt him! While I was struggling to get free, I raked my fingernails across his hands maybe his wrists. I know he bears my marks. Find the man who has scratches on his hands, and you will find the man who attacked me."

"Never fear," he said, bringing her body up against his. He kissed her on the temple. "The man who attacked you will pay dearly for his crimes."

◆ ◆ ◆

"If you are so eager to be rid of me," Kilby said stiffly, "I see no reason why you cannot leave me at Priddy's house. I have been worried about her. What if Archer returned to her house and hurt her?"

Fayne responded with a baleful stare. "That is more than enough reason to stay away. Do not worry about Lady Quennell. Brawley was supposed to send someone to watch over the viscountess. If you like, you can write her a brief note informing her of our return. I will see that it is delivered."

Kilby crossed her arms and huffed. "Are you certain you can afford to be bothered by such a menial task?"

His reasonable duchess had turned into a maddening shrew the instant she learned he meant to leave her and seek out her brother. While he had already decided Archer was not cunning enough to play assassin, Fayne thought it was time he introduced himself formally to his new brother-in-law. He had a few questions for the gentleman. Kilby was carrying on as if he planned on murdering the bastard in cold blood.

"I will have your note delivered." He grabbed her chin and tipped it upward so she was forced to meet his less than pleased gaze. "Lest you have forgotten, you are my duchess now," he explained, his tone slightly condescending. "That means you are under my protection and follow my orders."

"Without question," was her flippant retort.

"Oh, good. I am so pleased we understand each other so well." Fayne unlocked the front door to the town house he had rented, and opened the door. He gestured for her to enter. "Anyone here?" he shouted out.

No one answered his greeting.

Kilby sniffed and crossed her arms. "Nice, respectful staff you have, Your Grace," she muttered sourly.

"A lot like my wife," he shot back. "Well, there is no help for it. We are on our own for a few days."

"What?"

He gave her an impatient look. "I have never kept a full staff on hand. There was never any need since I preferred living alone." That was in the past. Unless he planned on moving them in with his mother, which he would rather not, then he needed to get his household in order. They had been living a vagabond's life since they were married. Such a way of life was not for his new duchess. "Before we left for town, I sent word to my manservant to close up the house and dismiss the staff for a week. We were supposed to be gone longer."

"Wait!" She stalled him on the stairs. "You are not leaving me alone down here."

Fayne took her hand and led her upstairs to his bedchamber. This was not how he had envisioned their homecoming. The house was dark and uninviting. The succulent, alluring smell of roasting meat was not wafting from the kitchen. What he preferred to do was strip them both of their clothes and make love to his wife. Unfortunately, he had to be practical. Kilby's attacker was out there, perhaps waiting for a chance to finish what he had started. Nipping was also roaming London wanting to reclaim his missing sisters. Fayne might not be able to lay his hands on his wife's attacker, but he could track down her brother before the man caused any more trouble.

She sat on the edge of his bed and glumly observed him as he removed his shirt. The rest of his clothes swiftly followed. "You are determined to find Archer, are you not?"

He saw no reason to lie to her. "Yes." Fayne picked up the clean shirt his manservant had thoughtfully laid out for him.

Kilby got up from the bed and crossed over to him. Once he pulled a clean shirt over his head, she smoothed out the linen and fastened the four buttons on his shirt. It was the kind of intimacy that never failed to fire his blood. "I do not want to remain here alone."

"You won't." Fayne did not want to distress her. He had let her think he was only pursuing her brother. Unfortunately, there were others in town who desired his head just as eagerly as Nipping. While he had no regrets about his life before Kilby, Fayne silently acknowledged that he had lived selfishly, loved a little too liberally, and had collected his fair share of enemies. Their early arrival was unexpected and he intended to use that element of surprise to his advantage. He would feel better when he had her tucked away someplace safe.

Kilby curled her hands around on of the end posts of his bed. "It is my opinion—"

"Enough!" Coolly, he narrowed his green gaze on her as he tied his cravat with efficient, brisk motions. The lady was too used to having her way. Fayne was planning on spending the rest of his life indulging her; nevertheless, this was one of the few instances he was insisting that she listen to his commands. "You are *my* wife," he said, stressing his claim on her. "I expect obedience from my duchess."

She looked so stricken by his harsh words, he almost took them back. Whether she realized it or not, he only wanted to protect her.

Kilby flounced away from him in a huff. She scowled at the ruby and diamond ring he had put on her left hand. "So much for marital bliss, *Your Grace*."

They had not spoken another word to each other since their argument in his bedchamber. While she had dashed off a quick note to Priddy, Fayne had hastily finished changing his clothes. Distracted by his private musings, he had silently bundled her into the coach. Her mood vacillated from hurt to outrage as the carriage bounced and rumbled down the street. She had sensed from the beginning that Fayne was a gentleman used to commanding his own fate, and the fates of those under his charge. His flash of temper and autocratic demand for obedience had disturbingly reminded Kilby of her brother's disagreeable nature. The comparison had momentarily stunned her into speechlessness. Mutinous stubbornness had urged her to remain silent.

His temper had bruised her pride. If she had desired a sullen, unreasonable husband who planned on controlling every aspect of her life, she had merely had to wait for Archer to make his selection. As she had gotten to know Fayne, a seed of hope had sprung within her. Despite their hasty flight to Gretna Green, she had started to believe that they could build a comfortable marriage from their growing affection for one another.

She had been raised with the freedom to make her own decisions. It was unrealistic for Fayne to expect her to blithely surrender to all her husband's dictates without question. If Fayne was planning on leaving her while he hunted down her brother and attempted to find out who was behind the attack at the lake, did she not have a say on where she should go? Obviously, he did not give a farthing for her opinion. The hateful man had not even bothered to tell her their destination!

It was only when she recognized the surroundings that Kilby's anger began to dissipate. Fayne had not been completely boorish, after all. He had brought her to the Brawleys' house, brought her to Gypsy. His thoughtfulness had her regretting several of her unkind thoughts. Kilby longed to see her sister again. She would have recommended the Brawleys' residence herself. However, after she had been attacked at the lake, she had considered it best that she stay away from Gypsy until they knew who had tried to drown her and why.

Fayne had apparently weighed the risks against the benefits and had concluded otherwise. She could hardly criticize the man for giving her something she wanted, now could she?

Fayne kept one hand on her arm and the other placed on her lower back as they approached the house on foot. Kilby wondered if he expected her to flee. She rolled her eyes at the idiocy of such a deduction, her lips parted as she prepared to thank him for reuniting him with Gypsy.

The door abruptly opened, and the Brawleys' odd butler with his wild wiry gray hair stood on the threshold. Kilby had encountered the servant briefly during their last visit to the town house. Slightly unkempt, coarse in speech, and opinionated, he was not the kind of servant she would have expected Lady Fayre to employ. Nevertheless, the Brawleys treated him like a member of the family.

"Oh, 'tis you. Good tidings are in order, I hear, Your Grace. You seem no worse from your adventure," the man boldly stated.

"I was fortunate, Hobbs. My bride was extremely gentle with me," Fayne said genially, unruffled by the butler's inquisitive nature. "Is the family at home?"

The servant turned his sharp gaze on her. *How odd,* she thought, *his left eye is more prominent than the other.* He also had the most fascinating eyebrows. The short spiky hair sprouting from his brow was black, except for ends closest to his wide nose. There, the hair was a long, wispy tuft of white that reminded Kilby of dandelions that had gone to seed. In his youth, the butler might have been taller than Fayne, but age and life's burdens had bowed his lanky frame at the shoulders. Becoming increasingly uneasy under his frank stare, Kilby doubted very little escaped the man's notice.

"Aye," Hobbs said, finally returning his attention to Fayne. "Leastways, they are for ye. I have orders to turn away the curious."

"The curious?" Kilby asked.

Fayne gave her an enigmatic glance since this was the first time she had deigned to speak.

"Him!"—he nodded at Fayne—"eloping with ye as he did, has caused quite a flap with the *ton,* I must say." The butler gestured for them to step into the front hall. "Not to mention the family."

"That will be quite enough from you, Hobbs," Maccus Brawley said sternly as he calmly descended the stairs to join them. "Can't you see you are terrifying poor Kilby."

"Bah!" the servant said, contorting his face in such a manner that Kilby half expected the man to spit on the marble floor. "If she's brave enough to tangle with the likes of him, I say the lass has mettle or is as balmy as the rest of ye." Not waiting to be dismissed, the butler trudged off in the direction of the kitchen.

Fayne raised an inquiring brow at his brother-in-law. "It appears Fayre hasn't had much luck wearing down his rough edges. I swear the man gets crustier each time we meet."

"That means he likes you," Mr. Brawley explained to Fayne. Moving to Kilby, he took her hand and kissed it. "Permit me to be the first to welcome you to our family." Drawing her closer, he led her up the stairs. "Now that you both have returned to London, let me forewarn you. The family will insist that a celebratory ball is planned in your honor."

Kilby glanced back at her husband. From behind them, she could have sworn she heard Fayne muttering something about the duchess and her damned balls.

"Uh"—she faltered for words that would not sound insulting to her new brother-in-law—"Mr. Brawley, while we are flattered by all the fuss, a ball is not necessary—"

"Perhaps not, but our mother will insist. It is best if we just indulge her in these matters," Lady Fayre said dryly, meeting them at the landing.

She was not alone.

Kilby's eyes filled with tears. Grabbing the front of her skirts, she dashed up the remaining steps and opened her arms. With a joyful gasp, her sister released Lady Fayre's hand and ran toward Kilby. She wrapped her arms around Kilby's waist, holding on to her tightly.

Kilby felt light-headed as she hugged her sister. Fayne had done this. With his help, they were both free from Archer. "Oh, Gypsy. How I have missed you!"

Fayne had loathed leaving Kilby. He took comfort in the knowledge that Brawley and his sister would look after his duchess until his return. Kilby had been so distracted by her reunion with Gypsy that she probably had forgotten why he was leaving her.

Ha! Not likely.

He had watched the wariness as it eclipsed her joyful expression when he had told Brawley that he needed to speak to him privately. Archer had tarnished what little affection Kilby had had for her brother. Nevertheless, he was still family. She did not want Fayne confronting her brother.

Kilby would eventually understand that he was simply protecting her, even from that perverted, idiot brother of hers. There was also her unknown assailant. If the villain wanted another chance to hurt Kilby, he would follow them to London.

Fayne still winced each time he recalled Kilby's caustic retort to his high-handed demand for her obedience. It was not difficult to deduce her dour thoughts. She had traded her overbearing brother and replaced him with a domineering husband. For a lady who had been interested in marriage out of necessity, she was probably viewing their hasty elopement as a mediocre alliance. He was going to need more than charm to get back in her good graces.

Reuniting her with Gypsy had been a rewarding step

toward his goal. When he had kissed Kilby farewell at the Brawleys' house, he had felt her lips soften under his questing mouth. His duchess was not pleased with him. Nor, on the other hand, was she wishing him to perdition.

After he hired a messenger to deliver Kilby's note to Lady Quennell, Fayne sought out Ramscar at his house. The earl was not at home. Fortunately, his butler knew where he had gone. Fayne's next stop was at Tattersall's. At the horse auction he encountered not only Ramscar, but Everod and Cadd, too.

Turning away from the horse that was currently up on the auction block, Cadd was the first one to notice Fayne. "Ho! Do my eyes deceive me or does the very married Duke of Solitea stand before us," he said, heartily hugging him and slapping him on the back. "I wagered Everod here that you and your duchess would not be seen for at least a fortnight."

"You have ruined a perfectly good wager," Everod said in mock disappointment. "I fear all of us greatly overestimated your prowess. My bet was for three weeks. Ramscar, you put down a month, did you not?"

The earl extended his hand to Fayne and they shook hands. "I did. I had assumed that your lady had you wrapped around her little finger to get a disreputable rake like you to come up to scratch." He embraced his friend briefly before cuffing him lightly on the ear. "A word to your friends might be appropriate the next time you dash off."

Everod chuckled, enjoying his friend's downfall too much. "More likely she had her silken hands wrapped around his throbbing rod to get him to hie them off to Gretna Green without a word."

Fayne accepted their teasing banter graciously. They were all recalling the night several years back when he had drunkenly lectured them all about the folly of marrying too young.

He had held his father up as an example of the price a man paid for hastily throwing away his freedom. It was only after his father had wedded and bedded his duchess that he had belatedly discovered the lady who owned his soul was the very married Lady Dening. Although he had sired a son on his lover, he had remained with his wife and the children she had given him. The duke's decision had been honorable, but it had left him with a restless heart. He spent the rest of his life bedding one mistress after another, trying to recapture, albeit briefly, the happiness he had found with the one lady he could not publicly claim for his own.

It was a mistake he had planned on not making. Almost too drunk to stand, he had proclaimed that he would not marry until he was forty. His friends had boisterously cheered his decision and had made similar outrageous boasts of their own.

"Our hasty marriage was spurred by events beyond our control," Fayne admitted quietly as he searched the faces of the gentlemen who had gathered to observe the auction. Nipping was not in the crowd.

Ramscar clamped a hand on Fayne's shoulder. "Christ, you virile, randy bastard! You've already planted your heir in her belly."

Fayne rolled his eyes heavenward. "Keep your voice down," he cautioned, dreading Kilby's reaction if the bawdy talk reached her ears. "All I need is to have the gossips counting on their fingers because my friend cannot keep his mouth shut." Thankfully, no one seemed interested in their conversation. "I am making no such announcements regarding my wife's delicate condition," he deliberately drawled. "Yet."

His friends shrewdly laughed at his slight amendment of the facts. While his wife might not be carrying his child at present, Fayne was intending to dedicate himself to insure that she soon would be.

"Then what are you doing here, Carlisle?" Cadd asked,

winking at him suggestively. "There will be no peace for you in this town. Your runaway marriage has the *ton* agog."

Ramscar cleared his throat. "And before you blame us, you can thank your family for spreading the news. Brawley told the duchess your good news, and the lady has been telling everyone."

"I believe she put an announcement in the *Times*," Everod added helpfully.

The earl nodded when Fayne put his hand to his head and groaned. He had told Brawley to circulate the news of their elopement. Fayne had assumed that when the gossip finally reached Nipping's ears, it would keep the man from proclaiming that his beloved sister had been carried off against her will. Leave it to his mother not to do things in half-measures.

"Your mother even hunted the three of us down, demanding details about your new bride," Everod said.

He could just imagine the interrogation his mother had put his friends through. "What did you tell her?"

With regard to his family, he had always been discreet about his liaisons. He had carefully avoided revealing to his family his interest in Lady Kilby Fitchwolf. Even when Fayne had thought Kilby had been his father's mistress, his primary motivation for keeping their affair a secret from them had not been shame. He had not wanted to cause his family any additional pain. Conversely, if they had learned of his intent, none of them could have dissuaded him from claiming her.

Cadd carelessly shrugged. "What could we tell her? You have been very cagey about your connection to the lady."

"Not that she believed us," Everod said, his face conveying his aggravation about their exchange with his tenacious mother.

"Well, I appreciate you all suffering on my behalf, gents," Fayne said, commiserating with their ordeal.

Before he introduced his new bride to his mother, he and the dowager were going to have to hash everything out. He did not want their first meeting to go awry because of a misunderstanding.

"I have sought you out because I need your help." Fayne glanced guardedly at the crowd. "But not here."

His friends followed him out to the street. Everod broke the silence by suggesting, "We can get one of the private rooms at the club."

Ramscar gestured at a carriage awaiting him across the street. "Cadd, why don't you tie Solitea's horse to your equipage, while he rides with me? We can all meet up at my house since it is the closest."

Anticipating Everod's argumentative response, the earl said, "If Solitea arrives at one of the clubs, half the *ton* will know he has returned within the hour." He looked at his friend for confirmation and saw what he needed in Fayne's steady gaze.

He and Ramscar crossed the street to his carriage. He slowed his stride as he turned his head back at Cadd when the man shouted out his name.

"I've had designs on your fine horse for some time," the marquess said, grinning. "Are you certain you want to trust me with the beast?"

Fayne shook his head and waved the man off. Cadd had always envied Fayne's keen eye for prime horseflesh, and his vast resources to outbid him on any beast he coveted. It was a harmless competition between them that had gone on for years.

A large black coach appeared suddenly, without warning. Fayne turned to see a team of four horses heading directly at him. He could hear the sounds of a whip cracking in the air as the unknown driver urged the team to go faster. The animals were so close he could see foam dripping from their mouths and smell their fear. Fayne threw his body to the side, just as the horses and the coach thundered over the exact spot he had been standing. Despite the near-miss, the driver did not stop, continuing down the street until it vanished from sight entirely.

Ramscar reached him first. His other friends and concerned strangers circled him, checking to see if he was uninjured.

"I never saw anything like it," Cadd said angrily. "The driver must have been foxed. It was like he was aiming the damned coach right at you!"

Fayne accepted Ramscar's hand and he was pulled to his feet. "Did anyone get a look at the coachman?" All he had glimpsed was a dark indistinct figure. In truth, his focus had been on the horses. He listened vaguely to the negative replies. No one around seemed to recall anything about the mysterious coachman.

His entire body was shaking and there was an uncomfortable weakness in his limbs. If he had hesitated, Kilby would have been a widow. First, someone tried to drown his wife, and just now he almost died under the wheels of a runaway coach. Fayne did not believe in coincidences.

He waved his hand at the dust in the air and coughed. Leaning heavily on his friend, Fayne murmured, "I think someone is trying to breathe life into the Solitea curse." He coughed again into his fist.

Ramscar nodded, signaling silently to Cadd and Everod that it was time to leave. "Let's go. I'm beginning to see your point about us discussing your recent troubles in private. If there is trouble brewing, surprise may be your only advantage."

CHAPTER
TWENTY-ONE

Kilby sat on one of the sofas in the Brawleys' drawing room feigning a calmness that she was incapable of while she plaited Gypsy's long black hair. There had been nothing wrong with the previous braid. Fussing with her sister's hair gave her an excuse to touch Gypsy. She needed the tactile reminder that the girl was safe. Fayne's family had kept their promise, and Kilby was in their debt.

From the corner of her eye, she observed her new brother-in-law as he paced in front of the window. The tension he tried to conceal was palpable to everyone in the room. Like Fayne, Mr. Maccus Brawley was a man of action. Kilby sensed he longed to join her husband in the hunt for her brother and for clues to the man who had attacked her. Nonetheless, he had made a promise to protect Fayne's new family and the man took his job seriously.

Lady Fayre, or Fayre, as she insisted on being addressed, was at the pianoforte playing a piece of lighthearted music that was meant to distract them all from dwelling on Fayne's absence. Her sister-in-law played the instrument with supreme confidence and she did credit to the sheet music. It was a pity Kilby was unable to properly appreciate the lady's efforts.

Gypsy made a soft sound of complaint.

Kilby finished tying the bow. "Fidgety, are we?" She affectionately stroked the length of the braid with her fingers. "You never could sit still for more than a few minutes."

Kilby tipped Gypsy's chin up and kissed her cheek. The fact that her sister seemed happy made it easier for Kilby to let her go. "Off you go, then. Take care not to trouble the servants."

Gypsy jumped up, her blue eyes gleaming with excitement at the prospect of exploring the house. After three steps, she abruptly turned and threw her arms around her older sister. Kilby held her close, relishing Gypsy's show of affection.

"I love you, my wandering girl," she whispered against Gypsy's ear.

Her sister broke away and slipped out of the room.

"She hasn't spoken a single word since your parents' deaths?" Fayre asked, concern marring her lovely face. She had given up on her music.

Kilby shook her head and wearily sighed. "No. Sometimes she will make sounds, and for a few seconds I start to believe she is finally recovering from the loss of our parents." She glanced down at her clasped hands, fighting back the despair that tightened her throat.

"Gypsy seems to comprehend the world around her somewhat," Maccus said carefully, not wanting to offend his new sister-in-law. "Have you considered that her silence is merely stubbornness?"

"Several of the physicians who examined my sister came to the same conclusion." Kilby's mouth tightened as the past assailed her. "With Archer's approval, these learned men subjected Gypsy to numerous cruelties in an attempt to provoke her into speaking."

Fayre gasped in horror, clearly imagining the pain that was inflicted on the grieving child. Her hand lightly rose upward to caress the silver and diamond brooch pinned to the front of her bodice as if the delicate spray of flowers and leaves brought her comfort. Standing, she crossed the room and sat beside Kilby on the sofa.

"What did you do?" her sister-in-law asked, sliding a comforting arm around her. Fayre's green eyes were so reminiscent of Fayne's that Kilby had to look away.

"I turned them out of the house." Her defiant actions had incurred Archer's wrath, but she had not cared. "I could not bear my sister's distress." Kilby met Maccus's sympathetic gaze. "If it is stubbornness that keeps Gypsy from speaking, then that will has been forged by pain and loss. Nothing will coerce her into breaking her silence, until she is prepared to do so."

Maccus solemnly nodded. There was something in his expression that revealed he was intimately acquainted with tragedy. "You and Gypsy are part of our family now. If there is anything we can do to help you or your sister, you only need to ask."

"You both have my gratitude. I do not know how I can return the favor," Kilby said, futilely wishing Fayne was at her side.

Fayre pressed a lace handkerchief into her hand. "You have already repaid us a thousand times over."

Confused, Kilby looked blankly at the young woman. "Pray, how? My connection to your family from the very beginning was an imbroglio."

Maccus crossed his arms and chuckled. "When you know the Carlisles better, you will understand they thrive on adversity," he said, earning a piercing glare from his wife. "Some of them even seek it out."

"You are not being helpful, *Mac*," Fayre warned, emphasizing his name as if the abbreviation held a private significance between them. She turned back to Kilby. "There is no debt between family. Your arrival heralded a dark period for our family."

Kilby felt shame burning hotly just beneath her skin. "I realize—"

"I do not think you do," Fayre countered quietly. "My father's death was difficult for all of us. Although he tried to hide it from the rest of us, Fayne took the duke's death the hardest. Hot-blooded . . . hurting. My mother and I were concerned that we were going to lose him as suddenly as we did my beloved father. My brother was beginning to slip away from us, Kilby, until he met you. In his bleakest days, you pulled him away from the precipice of his reckless nature. For that alone, I am eternally grateful you came into our lives."

Kilby stood up and used the handkerchief to stem the tears forming in her eyes. Fayre's words felt like a warm, healing balm over her raw nerves. She laughed lightly as her thoughts switched to Fayne. "If something happens to your brother while he hunts down Archer, you may regret your kind words."

Maccus moved away from the window and stood behind his wife. Fayre reached up and patted the hand he had tenderly placed in silent support on her shoulder. "Carlisle has too much to live for now to be careless," he said.

If she did not leave the room immediately, she was going to have a very humiliating cry in front of the Brawleys. "I should check on Gypsy. There is no telling what mischief she has gotten herself into wandering about your fine house."

"Dear me, you are in love with him."

Kilby's hand hovered over the door latch at Fayre's statement.

Fayre cocked her head inquiringly, her cinnamon-colored curls, bouncing saucily against her shoulder. "My brother thinks you agreed to marry him because you needed protection from that dastardly brother of yours. However, you had another reason, did you not?" Fayre slowly smiled as she closely observed Kilby's face. "How delightful! Tell me, is Fayne aware that you fell in love with him?"

Kilby closed the door, listening for the inner mechanism of the latch to click. Inhaling deeply, she leaned against the door and waited for the deafening pounding in her ears to stop

Tell me, is Fayne aware that you fell in love with him?

She had met Fayre twice. How could the lady deduce a revelation Kilby herself was still reconciling in her heart? Did she wear the answer to Fayre's question so plainly on her face? And what of Fayne? What did his entrancing green eyes see when he stared thoughtfully down at her?

The notion that her feelings were on the surface for everyone to see was disconcerting. It felt as if someone had stripped her down to her soul, leaving her vulnerable. After everything that had occurred, it was a prickly sensation even if it was one of the noblest of sentiments.

She had to get out of this house.

Kilby moved away from the door and strode down the passageway that led to the stairs. She had walked down as far as the first landing of the horseshoe-shaped staircase before she stopped and recalled her promise. Resting her hand on the decorative support posts, she glanced curiously downstairs, wondering if Gypsy was on one of the upper floors. At the moment, hiding from everyone seemed like a grand plan.

"Your Grace, there ye are," Hobbs said, approaching from below. "Had enough of that pair, did ye? Can't say I blame ye, with them always tickling and kissing one another in all parts of the house. No place is safe."

"Oh." Kilby glanced up in the direction of the drawing room. The butler's opinion of the Brawleys was certainly enlightening. Her gaze returned to Hobbs who was watching her expectantly. "Oh, no . . . they were not . . . I was not—"

"A bit tiring on the eyes, isn't it? We'll say no more of it," the servant assured her. Before she could clear up the misunderstanding, Hobbs offered the folded note in his hand to her. "A boy just delivered this for ye. I'm supposed to put such things on the silver salver we have for such occasions. Regrettably, I seem to have misplaced it."

She accepted the note. Opening the note, she frowned as she read the message. "Oh, dear."

"There, there . . . not to worry, Your Grace. It'll turn up one day," he said, before launching into an amusing tale about a missing cuspidor.

Kilby did not hear a single word of it.

Her gaze fell to the letter written by Priddy. Something terrible had occurred and the viscountess was begging for her assistance. She was also insisting that Kilby travel alone. Priddy feared another scandal was afoot.

Coming to a decision, she touched the servant on the arm to interrupt his tale. "Hobbs, I need to write a letter to my husband immediately," Kilby said, heading down the stairs to the library.

"Aye, Your Grace," the butler said, responding to the urgency in her tone.

"I'll need a carriage, too." Kilby folded the viscountess's note and tucked it into her corset. "And a promise," she added as an afterthought.

"You have had a run of bad luck of late, Carlisle," Cadd said somberly. "It does make one think there is something to the Solitea curse."

Fayne's near collision with a speeding coach had darkened everyone's mood, especially when it was beginning to appear someone was trying to kill both him and Kilby. He and his friends had gathered in Ramscar's library cum armory. The room was a reflection of the man's contemplative intellect and his quiet appreciation for violence when all logical paths had been exhausted.

The walls were lined with waist-high bookcases. In each corner medieval suits of armor, complete with lance, stood guard. Above the bookcases, weapons and helms accrued by the Knowden family over several generations were mounted on the walls. On the north wall, high above the chimney-piece, the skin of a leopard one of Ramscar's ancestor's had slain was displayed.

It was Fayne's favorite room in the house, and a perfect example of his friend's tidy efficiency. Since Ramscar's town house was smaller in comparison to many of the family residences, Ramscar's rooms served multiple purposes. For a gentleman who lived alone it was still a generous amount of living space.

"Is it bad luck, a curse, or is someone helping fate along?" Fayne wondered aloud. "I saw the marks on my wife's neck. Someone followed her to the lake and held her face down in the water. She could have drowned." His throat burned with acrid bile each time he thought how close he had come to losing her.

Everod sat in a large scale-patterned mahogany chair with his long legs stretched out in front of him. "Why do you think her attacker stopped?"

Fayne scrubbed his face in frustration. "I don't know. Perhaps Kilby had stopped fighting him, and he thought her dead. Or he heard something that ran him off." He slammed his fist against the wall, rattling the metal swords next to him. "Damn it, above all places I could have taken her, Kilby should have been safe on the family's lands."

"Carlisle, you have to stop blaming yourself. There was no way of knowing that someone had followed you," Ramscar said in his familiar matter-of-fact manner. He had propped his hip on one of the shorter bookcases. Displayed on the either side of him were five death masks of his predecessors. "If you were followed at all. Have you ruled out a vagrant?"

"That's the problem, Ram," Fayne said, trying to hold on to his temper. "I have not ruled out anything or anyone." Though that did not mean he did not have his suspicions.

"I wager your duchess's brother is the likely suspect," Cadd said, unsheathing a gem-encrusted dagger and testing the sharpness of its blade with his thumb. "You made an enemy when you absconded with his sister. While you were gone, Nipping has been trying to rally sympathy from the *ton*. He claims you kidnapped the lady against her will."

A sound of disbelief rumbled in Fayne's throat. No one was going to argue that his intentions were not honorable. After all, he did marry the lady. "Nipping can whine all he wants. Kilby is a Carlisle now. What he should be worrying about is what I plan to do to *him* once I am assured Kilby is safe."

Cadd slid the blade into its sheath and carefully returned it to its display. "Overall, Nipping's complaints are going unnoticed. Brawley let it be known that you had left town abruptly to marry your lady love. Dreadfully romantic and all that. The news that you have taken a bride at all is more titillating than the marquess's version that she was stolen from his care."

Ramscar scratched the tiny scar on his left eyebrow. "I agree with Cadd. If anyone does believe the lady was stolen from the bosom of her beloved family, the ladies of the *ton* will simply view your actions as romantic."

Fayne grimaced. "Wonderful." He did not want his actions seen in a romantic light. He was merely protecting the woman he considered his. "I imagine my mother will encourage the fanciful retelling of the tale."

His friends chuckled at the possible exaggerated stories the dowager might spin on her son's behalf.

"No doubt," Everod said, crossing his arms. "Besides Nipping, you must have a few other gents you would like to call on?"

"Hollensworth," Cadd interjected, sneering. "The man despises you. He insults you behind your back in hopes of provoking you into challenging him. As far as I know, he is still in town."

Fayne had also considered the baron. Hollensworth would never accept that Fayne had not played a small part in his brother's suicide. The fight at the fair should have ended things between them. Nevertheless, Fayne did not trust the man. His resentment could have prompted him to strike out at Kilby. What better way to destroy a man than take away something he valued?

"Anyone else?" Ramscar asked, his hazel eyes sweeping over them as he silently considered what they knew.

"How far back do you want to go?" Fayne rolled his eyes at the futility of singling out a single enemy. "Tulley? Burlton? Nicout? Crynes? *Pengree?*" Even Kilby's friend Lord Darknell disliked him.

It was not surprising his mother and sister had been concerned for him. Since his father's death, he had been collecting enemies like Ramscar collected ancient weaponry. Marrying Kilby was the only sane and responsible decision he had made in the past few weeks.

His face was harsh when he faced his friends. "We start with Archer, and work our way back. Something tells me whoever desires me maimed or dead is someone I have angered recently. The attacks on Kilby and me seem to be rushed and unplanned."

"Which probably explains why he hasn't succeeded," Everod quipped.

Fayne touched the earl on the arm. "Ram, I need a favor from you. I left Kilby at my sister's house. I am certain Brawley is competent in a fair fight. Nonetheless, it would ease my mind to know you both were looking after my wife and sister. Will you go there and help guard my family until I return?"

Ramscar took a lethal-looking battle-ax off the wall. He handled the weapon as skillfully as its original owner. "I will protect them as if they were my own blood, Carlisle."

Kilby's thoughts were harried and sad as she strode up the walkway to the Quennell town house. Archer had used violence and threats to get her to leave. Five days later, she was returning as a married lady.

Had her parents lived, she wondered if they would have approved of the choices she had made. Both her mother and father would have been pleased by her marriage into the influential Solitea family. Her father probably would have had a few concerns about the young duke's ability to see to his daughter's happiness. Kilby smiled faintly at the thought of her father sternly lecturing Fayne on his duties. She had no doubt that Fayne would have convinced her father of his good intentions as effortlessly as he had managed to charm her.

Naturally, her mother would have been disappointed that they had missed out on the opportunity to plan a proper wedding for their eldest daughter. A private ceremony in the small chapel at Ealkin would have been Lady Nipping's wish. Kilby had also dreamed of marrying in the beautiful old chapel with her family and friends surrounding her.

It was a lovely fantasy. Sadly, nothing was going to bring her parents back to her so it was useless to moon over things she could not change. It was trouble that had brought her to Priddy's door. Kilby reached up and rapped on the front door.

No one came to the door.

Tapping her foot in agitation, she knocked harder. Priddy's note had been brief and to the point. While the viscountess had been enjoying a visit from Lord Darknell, Archer had broken into the house. He intended to confront Lady Quennell again about the whereabouts of his sisters. Insults were exchanged between the two gentlemen and a violent fight ensued. Lord Darknell had subdued her brother, but a decision had to be made on whether or not the magistrate should be summoned. Priddy was concerned how the Carlisles might view this latest incident.

Priddy was correct. Fayne would not be pleased, when he learned of Archer's conduct.

Kilby glanced around the area, searching for the man who was supposed to be watching Lady Quennell's house. If the man was close, he was doing a magnificent job of hiding himself. Kilby knocked on the door again. Where were the servants? Priddy knew she was coming to her assistance. She had not come all this way, risked Fayne's ire, for nothing.

Certain the viscountess would not mind, Kilby opened the door and marched into the front hall. Hearing muffled voices coming from the drawing room above, she climbed the stairs. As she came up to the door, Kilby recognized one of the speakers as the viscountess. The low murmured response was decidedly male. Nor did the conversation seem hostile.

Kilby flung open the doors, and gaped at the unexpected intimate encounter she had interrupted. Priddy was leaning forward, pouring Lord Ordish a cup of tea.

"Oh, dear! Lady Quennell and Lord Ordish, I do beg both your pardons," Kilby said, resisting the urge to back away and shut the door. "No one answered the front door. I thought, after I received your note, that you might need me."

"Kilby! What an extremely prompt girl you are!" the viscountess exclaimed with insincere joviality. "You would never believe the afternoon I have endured." She glanced nervously at her companion. Lord Ordish seemed to have been made rather uncomfortable by her arrival. Embarrassment had reddened the poor gentleman's face to an uncomplimentary hue.

Priddy set down the teapot and rose from the sofa she had been sharing with the earl. Crossing the room to Kilby, the two women embraced. "Your letter took me by surprise! I did not anticipate seeing you and your husband for another week."

The viscountess was unaware of the attack at Carlisle Park. Kilby had wanted to share the news in person. She glanced curiously at Lord Ordish, slightly puzzled by his presence. "I left the minute I received your note. Pray, where are Lord Darknell and my brother?"

The viscountess's light blue eyes welled with tears. She took up Kilby's hands within her own and squeezed them, overcome by emotion. "How considerate of you to be thinking of me, especially now, when you should be thinking of yourself."

Priddy was acting oddly. Kilby stepped into the room, her violet gaze giving the interior a casual glance. Not a single stick of furniture was out of place. If Archer and Darknell had fought, it was not in this room.

Lord Ordish stood slowly, using his walking stick. His hip was apparently still paining the poor man. "Indeed. I hear congratulations are in order, young lady. Lady Quennell was just sharing with me your good news about your recent marriage to Solitea."

Kilby gestured for the earl to sit. "Thank you, my lord. Please sit down. I consider you a friend, and we do not need to rigidly embrace formality. I see your injury is still bothering you."

"Yes," the man confided, chagrined his limitations were so noticeable. "I must sadly confess that my days of walking without the aid of my walking stick are over." He beckoned both women to join him. "Where is that new husband of yours? Pray do not tell me the man has already abandoned his new bride for the comfort of his clubs?"

Ire flared briefly in the viscountess's gaze. "Solitea is an honorable gentleman, Lord Ordish. Why would he abandon Kilby when he went to great lengths to secure her as his duchess?"

Priddy's anger was so aberrant in contrast to her congenial nature that she gaped at her former chaperone as Kilby selected one of the chairs directly across from the earl. The viscountess sat down in one parallel to hers.

"Our hasty departure prevented my husband from attending to several obligations that needed his immediate attention," Kilby explained, sensing the tension between her two companions.

What had she interrupted?

Unable to keep her concern or her curiosity at bay, she shifted in her chair to address the viscountess. "Priddy, what has happened? Where are Darknell and my brother? Your note mentioned a fight. And by the bye, where is Gordon, or any of the servants for that matter? I was surprised to find that no one was tending to the door."

"Yes, Lady Quennell, why don't you tell the girl all about Darknell and her wayward brother," Lord Ordish pressed, his eyes glittering.

With shaking hands, the viscountess reached for her tea. The cup had remained untouched for so long that the tea had to be cold. "Give me a moment, Kilby. This day has been such a jumble, I am not sure where I should begin," she said, sounding as perplexed as Kilby felt. "When I sent Gordon off on an errand, I told the remaining servants that I did not want to be disturbed. I suppose no one saw any point in opening the door."

"An incompetent staff reflects poorly on their employer," Lord Ordish chided. The viscountess visibly bristled at his criticism, but did not defend herself.

Kilby frowned as she realized this was the first time she had encountered the couple together. "My lord, I must confess I am a bit surprised to find you here. I was under the impression that you and Lady Quennell were not acquainted."

Lord Ordish chuckled and wagged his finger at her. "Ah, yes, the viscountess and I never could quite meet up, despite your best efforts," the earl said, wheezing slightly as he laughed. "In your absence, I was forced to take matters into my own hands."

"Honestly, Kilby, you never even mentioned Lord Ordish to me. I was not aware that you two had been introduced," Priddy primly said, setting her teacup down with a clatter.

Guilt rippled through Kilby. Since Lord Ordish knew she was curious about her mother's past, it had been her intention that they should never meet.

A disparaging sound rumbled from the earl's throat. "You were not attentive to many things, madam. Unless your notion of chaperoning is akin to a petticoat merchant displaying her prized virgins before every lusty rake who has enough blunt to impress you."

The hostility and contempt Kilby heard in the earl's tone toward the viscountess was bewildering. He had just met the lady. "Lord Ordish, I take exception to your condemnation of Lady Quennell's character."

"Kilby," Priddy quietly interjected.

"No. I will not sit quietly and permit him to speak such utter slander." Kilby was not exactly sure what had occurred before her arrival; however, she intended to find out. "I have valued your opinions in the past, my lord. Nevertheless, I cannot allow you to insult a lady who has my utmost respect and love."

The earl's gaze hardened at her censure. "You have picked up the Carlisle arrogance quick enough."

Kilby felt the implacable pressure of Priddy's fingers on

her arm as the older woman tried to prevent her from standing. "On the contrary, Lord Ordish, my arrogance was bred into me, passed on by my father."

"Are you so certain? It seemed to me that you came to London with a few doubts," he said silkily.

"Enough, my lord," the viscountess said, her anxious gaze switching from Kilby's to his. "Please."

"Oh, very well," Lord Ordish sourly replied. He gestured at Lady Quennell. "Why don't you tell her about Darknell and her brother? By her expression, I can see the girl has a dozen questions rattling around in her head and it is cruel to keep her in suspense."

There was an awkward pause of silence.

Kilby did not like how the earl was staring at Priddy. He eyed her as if she were his prey. "Where are they? Did you summon the magistrate?"

Lord Ordish chuckled. "Maybe it will all make sense if I explain. Actually, it is an amusing tale, one I think you will enjoy." He reached for the teapot. "But first, permit me to make amends for my earlier rudeness by pouring you the cup of tea Lady Quennell neglected to offer you."

"There is no need . . ." Kilby sighed and gave up. If drinking cold tea would hasten them both into explaining Priddy's odd note, then she would graciously accept it.

Unused to the task, the earl shifted his position in the chair, using his walking stick as a counterbalance. His hands trembled with the added weight of the teapot.

"Here, my lord. Allow me to assist you." She steadied the teapot quaking in his grasp by holding it from the bottom so he could pour. Whatever had transpired in this house, it appeared that it had ended long before her arrival. Once she was assured that Priddy was not in any danger, Kilby intended to return to the Brawleys. With luck, Fayne would never know she had left the house.

As Lord Ordish flexed his wrist, Kilby caught a glimpse

of the bared flesh exposed between his glove and the cuff
of his sleeve. She cried out in surprise, her hands recoiling
from the teapot. Unprepared for the abrupt loss of her support, the porcelain teapot slipped from Lord Ordish's hand.
The fragile teapot shattered, along with the cups and saucers
arranged on the silver tray. Shards of porcelain and tea splattered in all directions.

The earl muttered an oath, retreating to avoid the mess.

"Good heavens! Are you hurt, my dear?" the viscountess demanded, moving around the low table to her side.
Using her handkerchief, she brushed the bits of porcelain
and tea from Kilby's skirts. "What happened? Did you get
scalded?"

Kilby still could not credit what she had seen. Shaking,
she concentrated on the top of the viscountess's coiffure.
"No. Truly, Priddy, I am fine. Pray do not bother," she said,
urging the older woman to stop fussing with the wet tea
stains on the front of her dress.

"Pridwyn, step away from the girl," Lord Ordish snapped.
His harsh command and his informal usage of the viscountess's first name had both ladies glancing at him. "The
tea has long gone cold."

He reached into his frock coat. Instead of producing a
handkerchief as Kilby had assumed he was groping for, the
earl pointed a small flintlock pistol at her. "Your upset had
nothing to do with the tea. Am I not correct, my dear?"

Kilby thought of the raw bloodied scrapes she had
glimpsed on the upper part of his hand. Scratches she had cut
into her attacker at the lake. "You are right, my lord. I am
not concerned about the tea."

CHAPTER
TWENTY-TWO

There had been no sign of Nipping.

Fayne, Everod, and Cadd had first gone to the Fitchwolf town house in hopes of catching him there. The residence was locked up and the furniture was covered. If the marquess was staying there, he had not bothered to hire any servants.

The trio moved on to some of the more popular private clubs. By the time they had entered White's, Fayne was convinced the task was pointless. Nipping could be anywhere. Maybe he had underestimated the man. For all he knew, Nipping could be discreetly watching Fayne chase his bloody tail all over London while the marquess sat back and laughed at his mischief.

Cadd approached him, shaking his head. "Nipping is a member. Though no one has seen him recently."

Everod strode over to them. "You have made the betting book again, Carlisle," the viscount cheerfully announced. "I counted three new entries since I entered one almost a fortnight ago."

"Betting on me, Everod?" Fayne softly mocked, understanding nothing short of severe beating would stop the man from profiting off his friends. "Do I even want to know what the wager was?"

The viscount grinned at him sheepishly. "I wagered Cadd that you would be able to resist bedding Lady Spryng this season." Everod shrugged, unrepentant of his actions. "After you refused your chance at having both Lady Spryng and Lady Silver, I was positive another lady had you by the rod."

How was Fayne ever going to be able to polish his tarnished reputation in the eyes of his duchess if his loyal, uncouth friends were going to keep reminding everyone of his misdeeds—or his temporary lapses? "If Kilby ever hears of that tale, Everod, I will see to it that you will be unable to hold a pen or your cock in your hands permanently!"

Everod backed away, his hands raised in surrender. "She won't be hearing anything from me, Carlisle. I swear, you are positively becoming stodgy now that you are a married gent. Next you will be expecting us to play uncle and bounce your drooling heir on our knees."

"A babe in Everod's arms." Cadd snickered. "That'll be the day."

Everod and Cadd stared at each other in silent accord. From the marquess's swaggering grin, Fayne guessed the pair had thought up their next wager. Fayne was tempted to spoil their fun by telling them that he no longer viewed marriage as a punishment best relegated to old age. He was not even blanching at the thought of becoming a father. If his suspicions were correct, he anticipated that by autumn he would be able to place his hand on the softly rounded swell of Kilby's belly and feel the tiny life they had created together flutter beneath his palm. As for granting Everod a chance to hold his heir, that was an entirely different issue.

His grin faded as a door to his right opened; and Hollensworth stepped into the lobby where they were standing.

The baron's expression grew insolent when he saw Fayne. "I thought you ran off with your father's whore, Solitea?"

Before his friends realized his intent, Fayne lunged for the man.

No one had moved since Lord Ordish had brandished his flintlock weapon. Suddenly, Priddy burst into nervous laughter, as if the pistol pointed at them were a jest. Kilby was just figuring out how deadly his intentions actually were.

"Put the pistol away, my lord," the viscountess said, waving her hand regally as if dismissing his actions as harmless. She sat down in her chair. "Who are you planning to shoot? Kilby? It was an accident. Spilled tea and broken crockery is no reason to shoot anyone."

Kilby placed her fingers against her brow. "Good grief, I fell neatly into your hands, did I not?" She straightened in her chair and gave herself a shake to clear her head. This was not the time to lose her composure. "Archer and Lord Darknell . . . they were never here."

The earl watched her closely, waiting for her to work it all out. "No."

"And the note?" With sorrow-filled eyes she faced the viscountess. "Priddy, I recognized your distinctive hand. What part do you play in Lord Ordish's ruse?"

"I had no choice, Kilby, I swear," Lady Quennell said, placing her hand over her heart. "He was already here when your letter arrived. He forced me to write that note." She glared bitterly at the earl.

The earl waved the pistol at Priddy. "She speaks the truth. I must admit, the lady is very dedicated to you. There was a moment or two when I thought I might have to snap sweet Pridwyn's neck. In the end, I was rather disappointed that she eventually agreed."

"You have managed to surprise me, Lord Ordish," Kilby said, eyeing the seven-and-a-half-inch barrel warily.

"I thought we were friends. I would have never suspected that you were the one who tried to drown me in the lake."

Priddy clasped her hand over her heart. With her light blue eyes wide with horror, she said, "What? What is this? Kilby, child, are you hurt?"

"Obviously not," Lord Ordish said, his lips twisting in distaste. "You twit. If I had succeeded, I would not be obliged to finish the task." He sighed wearily. "Things would have been simpler if you had not seen the scratches."

The memory of those frantic moments as she struggled beneath the surface of the cold lake water repeated over and over in her mind. Kilby could still feel those unseen hands at her neck, pressing her deeper into the murky depths. It was difficult to reconcile that those powerful, implacable hands belonged to Lord Ordish.

"What did you intend to do? Serve me tea and then shoot me in the head?" She shook her head, feigning her disappointment. "Forgive me for saying so, my lord, but it is not really a good plan. Think of the mess, not to mention a witness." Her gaze deliberately slid from the earl's to Priddy's shocked expression. The viscountess's face changed from white to gray at Kilby's implication that her life was also at risk.

The barrel wavered, a sign of his agitation. "Do not speak to me of plans. You thought you were so clever, did you not? Thinking you could get me and the other gentlemen of the *ton* to do your bidding." He turned his scornful gaze on the viscountess. "And you . . . pathetically ambitious and totally oblivious to the mischief the girl was stirring up behind your back."

Lord Ordish's expression was truly frightening as he glared at Priddy. What had she and the viscountess done to deserve this man's hate? She cleared her throat, drawing his focus away from the older woman. "What mischief?

I told you when we first met that I had discovered a few old letters belonging to my mother and I desired to meet some of her old friends. Nothing more."

"Oh, Kilby." Priddy groaned and pressed her hand to her forehead. "You do not know what you have done."

What had she done? "My parents are dead," she said defensively. "My curiosity is natural. Asking questions and talking to a few old acquaintances of my mother are hardly examples of criminal conduct." If the viscountess was unhappy about Kilby's curiosity, then the lady was going to have an apoplectic fit when she learned the true reasons that had prompted her interest.

Priddy lifted her head abruptly. Bitterly, she said, "Curiosity is one thing. Sharing confidences with *him* is quite another!"

"You never could manage to introduce Lady Quennell to me, now could you? Did you ever wonder why?" The earl paused, letting the question hang between them. "Then again, I doubt you tried too hard. If you had introduced me to your chaperone, I might have accidentally let something slip, alerting her to the fact that you were doing more than whoring yourself to Solitea. I think we both can guess how the viscountess will react when she learns why you were prying into your mother's past."

He was bluffing. How could he know anything about her past? "Have you been listening to Archer? Whatever he told you was a lie!"

"Ho! So your brother knows, as well." Lord Ordish's keen eyes might gleamed, considering the ramifications. "Your parents were rather sloppy to leave incriminating evidence for others to find."

Priddy was tiring of watching the earl play with Kilby as a cat plays with a mouse. "What does Archer know?"

Lord Ordish ignored the viscountess's question. Concentrating on Kilby, he said, "So it was the young marquess who put you on this fool's quest. How tragic. Though I suppose the man had private reasons for whispering his lies."

"What do you know?" Kilby asked in a hushed voice.

The earl glanced impatiently at her. "You still have not figured it out? You were asking the wrong question all along."

The agonizing question had given her countless sleepless nights. She had come to London hoping to find the answer. "Was Lord Nipping my father?"

The viscountess made a choking sound and sank into her chair.

Lord Ordish nodded in approval. "Believe it or not, I think you have suffered enough for the truth." He leaned forward. "I will answer your question truthfully. Yes, Lord Nipping was your father."

Kilby was so relieved by his reply that she burst into tears. The viscountess did not react to his revelation. She merely stared blankly at the wall. Kilby wanted to comfort Priddy, but the pistol aimed at her heart kept her in place.

Her elation faded at the earl's next words. "On the other hand, the more intriguing question you really should be asking yourself is, who is your mother?"

Everyone began shouting as Fayne seized Hollensworth by the coat, sending them crashing through the door the baron has just exited from. The gentlemen sitting in the private room leaped out of their chairs as Fayne and Hollensworth fell against one of the card tables, tipping it over. Cards, chips, and money scattered everywhere. The men rolled on the ground, each trying to clip the other in the jaw.

Fayne broke the baron's hold and rolled away, climbing to his feet. "Spreading lies, Hollensworth? Everyone knows Lady Kilby Fitchwolf was not my father's mistress. I have been discreetly courting the lady out of the public eye for months."

Blood was welling on the baron's swollen lip. He spat

on the floor. "I heard rumors your father paid nightly visits to your bride."

When this was over, he intended to hunt down the source of these rumors and express his displeasure. "There is nothing untoward about my father visiting his future daughter-in-law." So he was rewriting history a bit, but Carlisles were known for changing the world as it suited them. "If I hear you utter another unkind word regarding the new Duchess of Solitea, I will give you what you have been wanting since you arrived in town."

Hollensworth knelt on the floor, glaring at his enemy. "And what is that? A fair fight?" The baron lunged upward at him, swinging his arm wildly. Fayne blocked the punch with his arm, and drove his knee into the man's groin. Making a low keening sound, Hollensworth grabbed his crotch and dropped to the floor.

"No." Fayne panted, breathless from the swift violent scuffle. He waved away Everod and Cadd. "You want an honorable death. A fitting punishment, don't you think, for a man who failed to save his only brother."

The baron roared in anguish and surged to his feet. Maddened by Fayne's words, Hollensworth charged him. Prepared for the attack, Fayne locked arms with the man and they spun into chairs and tables, knocking the furniture over. Having a slight edge in strength, Fayne shoved the baron onto the surface of an upright table. He did not want to fight the grieving man. Nevertheless, if Hollensworth was responsible for the attack on Kilby, he would kill the man.

"Let me up, you bastard!"

Fayne held him down. "I spared you once because I understand a thing or two about family loyalty. It is simpler to blame me for Mitchell's death."

Red-faced, Hollensworth struggled against Fayne's restraining hold. "You are to blame. He never played so deep until he sat down at your table."

He made a tsking noise. "Is that how you comfort yourself at night? Haven't you figured it out yet, Hollensworth? If you didn't have me to blame, then you would have to admit that your brother was a disgrace. He was a spendthrift and a cheat. Instead of making amends to his family and creditors, he took the effortless way out of the mess he had created and killed himself, leaving you to clean up after him."

Satisfied he had made his point, Fayne released the baron and stepped out of striking range. Hollensworth remained on his back. Bringing his hands to his eyes, the man broke down and cried. Fayne was not proud he had publicly stripped the man's grieving heart bare by forcing him to accept that the brother he loved had been far from perfect. Deep down, he suspected the baron had known the truth all along.

"I never wanted to fight you," Fayne said solemnly. "However, if hating me gives you some measure of comfort then, by all means, continue to do so. My wife, on the other hand, is a different matter. She has no part in your vengeance. If I learn that you were the one who tried to drown her, your life, sir, is forfeit."

Hollensworth pulled his hands away from his face and glowered at him. "Drown you wife? Are you mad? I have not spoken two words to the lady."

Fayne looked at Everod and Cadd. He could tell by their expressions that they were thinking the same thing. Unless the baron was a consummate actor, he did not know anything about the attack on Kilby.

"My mother?" Kilby could not believe she had heard the earl correctly. "I do not understand why you are trying to hurt me, my lord, but in this I know you lie. My mother was Ermina Fitchwolf, Marchioness of Nipping. I was given her name. My entire life, people were always commenting on how much we looked alike."

She turned to her mother's closest friend and silently beseeched the woman to tell Lord Ordish that he was wrong. "Priddy, tell him that he lies," she commanded, when the other woman said nothing.

"Dear girl, you look like you might faint." The earl chuckled, and waved the barrel of the pistol in the general direction of the sofa. "Sit down before you collapse."

Kilby sank onto the sofa cushion. Lord Ordish slowly sat down and shifted his position to an angle from which he could aim the pistol at either lady with ease. "I am certain you are unaware of this. However, watching you flutter about the *ton* this season has been a great source of amusement for me."

"How sweet of you to say so, my lord. All the same, the last time I checked, killing people who amuse you is not precisely a sign of sanity," she said sarcastically.

Priddy gaped in horror at her young charge's audacity. "Kilby!"

"Let her be. Her spirit is refreshing," Lord Ordish said, unperturbed by her cutting remark. "Another lady in her situation would be mewling and pleading for me to spare her life." He took a deep breath and exhaled, thoroughly relishing the power he had over his two companions. "You are curious about the past, Kilby. Would you like to hear an old tale?"

The viscountess started to rise in protest until she recalled the pistol. She sat back down. "My lord, I beg you to reconsider," the older woman said, gripping the carved wooden supports of the chair. "Lord and Lady Nipping are dead. What good can be accomplished by digging up the past?"

The earl gave her an incredulous look. "Why, absolutely none, Pridwyn! You should know that better than most." Keeping the pistol aimed at Kilby, Lord Ordish raised his walking stick and slammed it down on the table bearing the shattered tea set. Pieces of sharp porcelain bounced with the impact. "Not another word from you, my lady, else the next thing I smash with my stick will be your thick skull."

"You wanted to tell me a story, my lord," Kilby prompted, not liking the flat, hostile gaze that hardened the man's face each time he stared at the viscountess.

Some of the enmity in his expression faded as he blinked and focused on her. "Ah, yes. It is a sad little tale that I believe you will find fascinating. The story is about a man and his beautiful wife. The couple had been fortunate enough to find one other in their youth and had fallen deeply in love. The man respected his lady, and proved his commitment by marrying her."

"This man and woman," Kilby interjected. "Are they my parents?"

Fierce denial flared in his eyes. "No. They were happy for a time. How could they not be? They were blessed with love, companionship, and constancy. The only burden they carried was that the couple remained childless. With each passing year, the woman grieved her womb was barren. Her husband quietly accepted God's decree, and was content. He loved his lady dearly. Nothing, not even a child born of their love, could have strengthened his devotion."

He paused, and leaned slightly forward, subtly excluding Priddy. "Shall I tell you a secret about the man? Something his wife never knew?"

Kilby shrugged nonchalantly. Her thoughts were focused on counting the hours that had passed since Fayne had left her at his town house. She suspected that despite their awkward parting, he would not leave her alone too long. When he returned and read her note, Fayne would come for her. As far as she was concerned, Lord Ordish could regale her with obscure tales for days. She would listen attentively to every word as long as it distracted him from pulling the trigger on his elegant flintlock pistol.

"The gentleman secretly loved another lady," Kilby

helpfully suggested. She glanced meaningfully at Priddy. It was important that they kept the man engaged in his story. However, the viscountess, too frightened by his earlier display of temper, seemed withdrawn from their conversation.

"No!" Lord Ordish harshly bellowed. "He loved only her, more than life itself. His passion burned in his soul like a white flame, pure and unwavering." He visibly calmed, the wrinkles near his eyes lessening by degrees. "No, the truth was, the man was secretly pleased his lady was barren. And why not? A child is a fretful, demanding creature, sapping its mother's strength and dividing her affection."

Kilby wisely did not debate the issue. It was apparent Lord Ordish had an affinity for the man in his story, and shared his dislike for children.

"While the man privately rejoiced, his wife continued to despair over what she viewed as her unnatural state. The lady grew melancholy. The bliss she had initially found in her marriage bed withered, and her selfish obsession drove her husband away." Lord Ordish peered at the viscountess. "What say you, madam? Did the lady deserve her husband's coldness or his compassion?"

"I dare not offer an opinion, my lord," Priddy said quietly. "You are the storyteller. Why do you not tell us?"

Lord Ordish tilted his head, scrutinizing the viscountess's bleak expression. If there was veiled belligerence behind her words, he had not detected it. Nodding, he continued, "It had been a grave error on the man's part to distance himself from his lady. He had thought if he gave her distance, she would gradually accept her childless condition. However, what man can grasp the illogical workings of a lady's mind? Perceiving her lord's silence for rejection, in her loneliest hours of despair the heartless wench turned to another man. Her lover used her traitorous body for a time, and the lady pretended she was in love. In spite of her wiles, she could not seduce her lover into pledging his love for he knew she belonged to another. Like most men, her lover was content to sample the pleasures of a lying whore. It was quite another matter to give the bitch his honorable name and protection. Eventually, the man encountered a lady worthy of his name and affection. In a callous act, he discarded his mistress. Refusing his lover's tearful entreaties to continue their affair, the gentleman married his lady and forgot the whore who had been merely an entertaining diversion."

Kilby felt sorry for the three people in Lord Ordish's tale. All of them, whether it was calculated or not, were responsible for the sorrowful turn in their lives. "You are right, my lord. It is a sad tale."

"Partly," the earl conceded. "In shame, the woman returned to her husband and begged his forgiveness for her perfidy. What could the man do? He loved his lady, so he forgave her and opened his house to her again. For a time, he even blamed himself for her confusion."

"The man was lying to himself and his lady," Priddy tersely muttered, startling them with her exasperation. The older woman had seemed so wholly distracted, Kilby had wondered if she was paying attention to the earl's story. "No man forgives betrayal."

"A man in love might, if his unfaithful lady had truly cast aside her sinful nature," Lord Ordish sharply retorted. "Alas, the lady in my tale did not. Rejecting her husband's sage counsel, she attempted to conceal from him the tangible proof of her betrayal, allowing it to flourish in her womb. With each passing month, her belly swelled with iniquity, until her devoted husband could not look upon her without wanting to strangle the wanton bitch for her fickle affection."

The earl abruptly stood and aimed the pistol at Priddy. "I was a tolerant husband, was I not, Pridwyn?"

CHAPTER
TWENTY-THREE

"Solitea, a word if I may!"

Fayne turned to see Lord Darknell grimly approaching their carriage. Irritated by the delay, he felt the muscles in his jaw tighten painfully. He really did not like the gentleman. It was only out of respect for Kilby's friendship with this man that he did not order the coachman to drive on. "What do you want, Darknell?" he said, trying hard to forget that the viscount had offered to marry *his* duchess.

Darknell frowned at Fayne's unfriendly tone. "What you said to Hollensworth—"

The way this day was going, Darknell was probably on the verge of challenging him. Fayne held up a silencing hand. "Sir, I do not have the time or inclination to listen to your diatribe on what you witnessed. Suffice to say, I've been amazingly tolerant toward the man who has, since his arrival, tried his best to maim or kill me. My apologies if he is a good friend of yours. However, I—"

"I'm not here on Hollensworth's behalf," the viscount said bluntly. "I'm here for Fitchwolf."

His announcement had Fayne's green eyes narrowing on him warningly. Realizing how his declaration could be misconstrued, Darknell scowled, saying, "Don't be daft. I haven't come to challenge you. Fitchwolf has chosen her champion. I can respect her choice, even if I do not agree with it." Even though Darknell had claimed he was not challenging Fayne's right to Kilby, his stance was rigid and poised for attack. "What I want is a few answers. You practically accused Hollensworth of trying to drown Kilb—uh, your wife. Solitea, differences aside, the lady is a beloved friend. If she is in danger, I want to help."

What irritated Fayne about the viscount's offer was his blasted sincerity. His affection for Kilby was genuine. While Darknell might have relished watching Fayne being trampled under the wheels of a speeding coach, he was an honorable gentleman who thought nothing of offering his support to a rival if it protected a dear friend.

By God, he detested the man.

"Then you are welcome to join us." He nodded at the already crowded carriage not far away. "I haven't the time to stand here and chat."

Fayne longed to return to Kilby. Only a few hours had passed, and already he was yearning for her. When she saw him, would she greet him coolly? If his duchess was still miffed at him for his angry outburst, he could think of several diverting ways of persuading her to forgive him.

His sister's house was as good as any for all of them to plan their next step. "If Hollensworth was not responsible for the attacks on Kilby or me, then our speculation returns to her brother. If Nipping is the villain, I want to put an end to it."

The viscount kept pace with him as they approached the carriage.

Darknell made a derisive sound in his throat. "You think Archer would stain his hands with blood? Improbable,"

Darknell said. "I have no love for the little worm, but Nipping is too cowardly to be your villian. He preys solely on weaker quarry. Attacking Fitchwolf is essentially taking on the entire Carlisle clan."

As much as he hated to admit it, Lord Darknell's reasoning was sound. The attack on Kilby had to have been a means to strike at him.

Lord Darknell climbed into the carriage, murmuring brief greetings to Cadd and Everod. Waiting until Fayne had settled down into his seat, Darknell grimly added, "Besides, the man has a certain affection for his sister."

"An affection that will get him castrated if he persists." Fayne called out to the coachman to drive them to the Brawleys' town house.

Lady Quennell had been married to Lord Ordish? "Priddy?" Kilby asked, needing the woman to deny it.

The viscountess cringed as the earl moved around the low table that was thwarting him from his prey. From the corner of his eye, he noticed Kilby's dazed regard at his sinuous movements. "Forgive me, dear girl, for deliberately misleading you on the extent of my injuries. While I did fall from my horse last season, I must confess, I have fully recovered."

Keeping the pistol aimed in their general direction, the earl backed up until he reached the door and turned the key in the lock. He slipped the key into the inner pocket of his blue waistcoat.

Kilby watched him as he strolled unhurriedly to Priddy's side. "Why did you lie?" She had been so gullible, her initial impression of the gentleman so flawed.

"I needed to avert any suspicion that might be cast my way," Lord Ordish explained, lowering the end of the barrel and pressing the cold metal against the viscountess's jugular. "I really owe you a debt of gratitude, Kilby. Until you

charmingly introduced yourself to me, I had no idea what
had become of my dear wife." The viscountess whimpered,
turning her head to avoid the barrel painfully prodding her
throat. "The Church had readily approved my separation
from an adulteress. How could they not? It took influential
friends in the House of Lords, and a veritable fortune in
discreet bribes to buy me the divorce I deserved by Act of
Parliament. Afterward, sweet faithless Pridwyn vanished.
I should have guessed the unrepentant whore had spread her
thighs for another fool and enticed him into marrying her."

"You had no idea your—uh—Priddy had married Lord
Quennell?" Kilby convulsively swallowed. She was sickened that she had inadvertently revealed the viscountess's
whereabouts to her former husband.

She silently willed her friend to look at her.

*Not once did you ever mention that you had been mar-
ried to a lunatic. Pray forgive me for leading him straight
to you,* Kilby thought as their frightened gazes met.

"Lord Ordish and I have not encountered each other in
almost twenty years." Priddy's voice quivered, her eyes
shifting from the pistol at her throat to Kilby. "It came rather
as a surprise when my butler announced him. I—I had
heard years ago that he had forsaken his homeland and was
traveling abroad."

"The rumors you heard were correct," he said, his breath
hot against the side of the other woman's face. Priddy
shrank lower into the chair. "I have traveled rather exten-
sively over the years. Is that why you thought it safe to
reemerge into polite society? You believed me out of the
country?"

"Or dead," the viscountess said, some of her former
spirit strengthening her voice. "You cared little about polite society. Twenty years ago, neither one of us were important in the eyes of the *ton*. You had yet to inherit the
earldom when we parted ways."

"Very true. Like you, I have always preferred the countryside to town life. When I returned to England two years ago and encountered Lord and Lady Nipping, I should have guessed you had not strayed very far from your baseborn whelp." Lord Ordish concentrated his fierce, loathing gaze on Kilby.

Suddenly, the confusing jumbled pieces of the past fit together for Kilby. Taken aback, she stared at Priddy in stunned silence. None of this was true. Where was Fayne? Why had he not come for her?

Lord Ordish made a soft sympathetic sound. "Dear me, you mean you still have not guessed? Lady Quennell is your mother."

"Kilby is gone?"

Fayne had not really posed it as a question. He just could not comprehend Kilby's audacity to ignore his simple instructions. Nor could he beat down the terror he was feeling that she was out there alone and unprotected. Brawley was upstairs comforting Fayre and Gypsy. Hobbs, the traitorous servant who had secured a carriage for Her Grace, was in hiding from Fayne's wrath. He had wanted to take the man apart piece by piece after he had learned that Kilby had left the house unescorted. He, Everod, Cadd, and Darknell had just arrived at the Brawley town house ten minutes earlier. They had found Ramscar sitting on the stairs with his ax at his side. He had Kilby's note in his hand.

Her note had been brief. It read:

Your Grace,

Sitting here in your sister's house awaiting your return, I have discovered I am not a patient woman. If you consider this a serious flaw in my character, then I predict we shall be facing many difficulties in our new marriage. Regardless, I cannot sit idle when Priddy pleads for my assistance. Fayne, please understand. The viscountess is part of my family. If all is well, I shall return forthwith and promptly burn this letter. That way, you will never know what a rebellious creature your lady wife is.

Forever yours,
Kilby

P.S. I pray you will refrain from berating Hobbs too harshly for his part in my escape. He is an exemplary servant and was merely following my orders.

Fayne rudely snorted as he read the last line. Hobbs? An exemplary servant? The butler was surly and disobedient to his betters. The more likely explanation was that Kilby had bewitched the ornery man into doing her bidding.

His duchess possessed a spirited nature that reminded him of a vibrant, inexhaustible flame. He had been drawn to her glowing warmth from their first meeting. Fayne did not want to quell her adventurous spirit. Nonetheless, they were going to have to reach an amiable compromise for both their sakes.

His heart stopped beating as he realized something. "She never returned to burn the note."

Fayne handed the note to Darknell. "Kilby thought she could respond to Lady Quennell's summons and return before anyone realized she had left the house. Hobbs told Brawley and my sister that Kilby was lying down. No one would have checked on her for hours. Only Ram's arrival prompted my sister to check on her."

Fayne watched as the viscount read the note and passed it on so Everod and Cadd could also read it.

"How long has she been gone?" Cadd asked, handing the note back to Fayne.

Too long. He glanced at Ramscar. "I was never meant to see this note. Whatever the reasons for the viscountess's summons, Kilby never intended to remain there for long. Knowing my stubborn wife, she just wanted assurance that her dear friend was fine."

"Something delayed her," Darknell said, his face harsh with concern.

Or someone.

Ramscar grabbed the banister and stood, the ax in his hand dangling at his side. "I'll summon Brawley. We will need more weapons."

Priddy was her mother.

Kilby stared at the woman who had been her mother's dearest friend, trying to see something of herself in her. She did not look like the older woman. Where was the connection a mother and daughter had? The one she had with her real mother, Ermina Fitchwolf, Lady Nipping? Lady Quennell's light blue eyes gleamed with bright, unshed tears as the viscountess mutely pleaded with Kilby. For what? Understanding? Forgiveness? In that instant, Kilby was so overwhelmed she barely felt anything at all.

"I never truly cared about your fate," Lord Ordish said, bringing her attention back to the man who captivated them with his righteous fury and his very lethal pistol. "Whether you lived or died was not my concern. I only thought of punishing my wife. She was not going to keep her lover's child. Minutes after the midwife had pulled you from your mother's womb I took you, and left the house. With Pridwyn's screams ringing in my ears, I rode to Ealkin. Your father had just married his marchioness, and I thought it rather poetic that I present his bastard daughter to him with his bride at his side."

"Why did you bother, my lord?" Kilby asked, numbly thinking how her birth had negatively impacted so many people's lives. "Since I was newly born, you could have exposed me to the elements. No one would have known."

Lord Ordish chuckled. "I had considered it. You were nothing but a mewling abomination. Tangible proof of my lady's betrayal. I could have snapped your flimsy neck and ended my torment."

A wordless sound of denial escaped the viscountess's lips. The earl silenced her by grasping her hair and ruthlessly tugging her head back. "If I had given in to the impulse, Pridwyn's grief would have been too brief. My pride demanded vengeance, and Lord Nipping was surprisingly helpful."

"You are lying," she said, staunchly defending her father's memory. "My father was a decent man. He would have never helped you hurt anyone."

"Oh, but he did. Lord Nipping granted me the revenge I craved by keeping you. Each day you lived was a day my adulterous Pridwyn was denied a mother's love." He jerked Priddy's head back so he could look into her terrified gaze. "Is that not so, my lady? Did you grieve for your bastard daughter?"

"Every day, my lord, for more than nineteen years," she brokenly sobbed. "Taking my child hurt me more severely than any blow ever delivered from your fist."

"And yet you thought you had thwarted me, did you not?" Lord Ordish painfully wrenched her head back, a small reminder of his authority. "Despite my efforts, you figured out a way to be part of your child's life, after all. What did you do? Blackmail your lover? Or was it your plan all along to continue the affair once his wife accepted his bastard as her own?"

"Why should I tell you?" she shouted at him. "You will twist anything I say into something vile." He released her hair, disgusted that he had touched her. Priddy sniffed and sobbed into her handkerchief. "What you speak of occurred almost twenty years ago. No one recalls our connection, my lord, and you have had your revenge. Lord and Lady Nipping are dead, and with them any proof of the true circumstances of Kilby's birth."

"Not quite," Lord Ordish said crisply. "It is your fault, you know. If you had left matters alone, this all would have ended when I killed Lord and Lady Nipping."

It appeared that Kilby had been correct all along to worry about Lady Quennell, Fayne thought as he stealthily crept up to Nipping from behind. When no one had answered the front door, he and his companions had decided to search the perimeter of the house. Ramscar spotted the marquess clinging to the iron railing on the upper balcony. His neck was craned as he tried to glimpse through one of the drawing room windows.

Nipping was so distracted that he never sensed the men approaching him. Fayne grabbed the man's leg and unbalanced him from his precarious perch. The marquess hit the ground hard, knocking the breath from him. "I have been looking for you, Nipping," Fayne said, standing over him.

The marquess expelled a hoarse yelp of fear as Fayne ruthlessly seized the man by his frock coat and dragged him away from the house. He did not want to frighten the women. Besides, he thought he and his new brother-in-law deserved to get acquainted without Kilby's interference.

"We need to talk," Fayne said, once he was satisfied no one within the house could hear them. The other men circled around them.

If Nipping intended to cry out, he thought better of it. Cadd stroked the keen edge of the battle-ax against the man's soft belly, while Darknell and Ramscar aimed loaded pistols at his head. "What d-do you w-want from me?"

"I vote we just kill him and toss his body in the Thames." Everod sneered. Knowing his friend well, Fayne thought the viscount was probably serious.

"It's over, Nipping. I know what kind of sick game you were playing with your sisters." The man's neck was in his hands. Fayne could throttle Nipping just as he tried to hurt Kilby. No one would try to stop him.

"Arrogant bastard!" Nervous laughter burst from Nipping. "Over? Nothing is over."

Ice settled in Fayne's stomach. "Have you hurt Kilby?" His arm pressed into Nipping's throat. "If you have I—"

"I haven't touched her," he blurted out. His face was pink from Fayne's constricting arm, and the bruises from his previous beating were prominent hues of deep purple. "I doubt you will get the same assurances from the armed gentleman inside with your wife."

"You murdered my parents!" Kilby screamed. She jumped off the sofa, intending to attack the man who had caused her family so much pain.

Lord Ordish pushed the rising viscountess down into her chair as he aimed the pistol at Kilby's heart. "Sit! I will shoot you." He gestured at Priddy. "Now or later, it makes no difference to me. As a matter of fact, the notion of Pridwyn sitting here helplessly as the red blood pumps fiercely out of your shattered chest is beginning to appeal to me. Do not force me to end our revealing little chat so abruptly."

"Please, Kilby, think of your husband," the viscountess begged, her beautiful face ravished by her tears. "Sit down."

Kilby slowly slid back down onto the sofa. "My parents drowned while yachting," she said crossly, daring him to refute the facts. Something the earl had mentioned earlier had her silently counting the months on her fingers. "You said that you saw my parents almost two years ago. That was when they—"

"Yes, my dear girl. That was several days before their unfortunate accident," he said, pleased by her reasoning. "Can you believe that after all that transpired between our families, Lord Nipping and his wife greeted me warmly, as if I were an old friend?" Years later, he still seemed perplexed by their reaction.

"Lord and Lady Nipping never glimpsed the true monster in you. You were the gentleman who brought home their beloved daughter. They were grateful for your generosity," Priddy bitterly mocked. When the earl lifted his hand to strike her, she shut her eyes and braced for the blow.

It never landed.

"It was a moment of weakness that spared you, Kilby. When I took you away, I should have fed you to my pigs or left you in the fields to die of exposure," he said, his brow furrowed in regret. "I knew my failings had long-reaching consequences when I met your parents again. Do you know, all they could talk about was you? Oh, they had such plans for you. They told me all about their plans to bring you to London for the season. It was time, Lady Nipping said. You had grown into a beauty, your father boasted. Both were anticipating that you would contract a respectable marriage."

Kilby was flabbergasted. "They were planning a season in London for me. That was their crime? The reason you killed them?"

"Yes, yes, yes!" he yelled at her, keeping a firm grip on the viscountess. "At first I thought they were mocking me. How could they be serious? In a moment of weakness I let you live and this was how they repaid me?"

"They did nothing wrong. I am no different than the dozens of other young ladies who come to London each season seeking a solid match," Kilby argued.

"Wrong?" Lord Ordish lashed his foot out at the table and sent it careening into the side of the sofa. Shards of broken porcelain flew everywhere. Kilby winced as it collided

with her legs. "There was nothing *right* about their plans.
Your father was pretending the sin born from his adulterous affair with my wife was a gently bred lady. How could
I permit them to foist a lie on the unsuspecting gentlemen
of the *ton*?"

"How did he lie, my lord? I was his daughter," she said,
trying to reach the intelligent, rational gentleman she thought
was still beneath the rage. "Lady Nipping was my mother.
In all ways." Kilby did not want to cause Priddy any more
pain, but this was how she felt.

"Not by blood, girl. Marriage is all about merging
bloodlines and wealth," he said, his eyes narrowing. "You
think you were clever, but unlike your incompetent chaperone, I have been watching you from afar. I know the wicked
games you have been playing with the young duke. I will
admit that you are sharper than the sniveling whore who
birthed you. You parted your thighs quickly and beguiled
him into marriage. How do you think Solitea will react
when he learns his noble lady is baseborn?"

"Fayne will not care. He loves me," Kilby said dismissively, realizing she believed that she spoke the truth. Leave
it to her, she mused, to choose the most awkward moment
to figure out something so important about her husband.

"Already carrying his heir, are you?" Lord Ordish said
slyly. "Shrewd girl. I had wondered what you did to get him
to hie you off to Gretna Green so swiftly. I have tried to discourage Solitea's interest in you, but you have the man so
thoroughly spellbound, nothing short of death would keep
him from you."

Kilby felt the blood drain from her face. Her anxiety
was unfeigned as she gathered a fistful of fabric from her
skirts and released it, carefully covering a jagged piece of
porcelain the length of her hand that had landed next to
her on the sofa. She had come to London seeking answers.

Listening to Lord Ordish, she understood the truth was likely to cost her her life.

And Fayne's.

Had the earl ambushed her husband? Her heart pounded in her throat at the terrible thought. Was that the reason why he had not come for her? "What do you mean by 'discourage'? If you have done anything to Fayne, I swear I will—" Kilby grasped the porcelain shard in her hand.

"Calm yourself, girl," Lord Ordish said, speaking over her feeble threats. "I have no quarrel with the Duke of Solitea or his family. I just arranged a few accidents, hoping to distract the young man from his lustful pursuit of you. The family believes they are cursed. A few scrapes with death should have reminded him of his duty. He should have abandoned his idle pleasures and directed his ambitions to finding a virtuous lady for his duchess."

"Good grief! Are you insane?" She cringed at her dumb question. "You could have killed Fayne with those so-called accidents!" No wonder Fayne had begun to believe he was truly cursed.

His eyes smoldered and his rigid body shook with fury as he recalled his failures. "Solitea should have cast you aside. I could not save him. The man was blinded by his lust. He did not see the evil cleverly hidden within you." Lord Ordish took a menacing step toward her. "You should have remained at Ealkin. I thought with your parents' deaths, all aspirations for you coming to London would end. Do you understand why I have to kill you? Your marriage to Solitea has given me no choice."

"Dear God, Grennil, she is blameless," Priddy said, sucking in her breath as she felt the cold barrel of the pistol against her skin. "If you crave vengeance, then kill me! I am the one who betrayed you. You wanted to kill me all those years ago, but some shred of humanity in you stilled your hand. Please. Do whatever you must with me. I beg you, please do not harm her."

Beneath her skirts, Kilby's hand curled around the sharp edges of her crude weapon. She felt an unpleasant sting as porcelain sliced into her flesh. She and Priddy had run out of time. In his zealous state, Lord Ordish had convinced himself that both ladies had to die. By killing her, the man believed he was actually saving Fayne and other foolish gentlemen from her insidious charms. The moment had come for her to use the intellect Lord Ordish credited her with. The earl could fire only a single shot. It would take him time to reload, a luxury she had no intention of allowing him to indulge.

"You are willing to die for your bastard daughter. You love the girl that much?" the earl whined.

"Yes! Please, Grennil," the viscountess pleaded, blatantly using his family name in order to reach the man who once had loved her. "Kilby is nothing like me. She understands the meaning of honor, compassion, and loyalty. Nor will she betray the husband she loves. You can afford to be generous. No one remembers or cares about our past mistakes."

Lord Ordish relaxed his hold on Priddy's hair. Both ladies held their breaths, awaiting his decision. Kilby tensed, preparing to move if the earl aimed the pistol at her again. In his highly agitated state, she was counting on his finger to instinctively pull on the trigger. She was also hoping he would miss.

"No." The man shook his head sadly. "*I* remember. Forgive me, Pridwyn," he said over her frantic pleas for mercy. "I have it all planned out. When I have finished here, everyone will believe an argument between you two was the cause of the senseless violence the servants will eventually discover. With my reluctant help, the *ton* will learn the tragic details. By tomorrow morning, everyone will know that in a fit of rage, Kilby killed you after hearing the news that you are her mother. There will be rumors circulating that you and Lord Nipping never ended your relationship, and the conclusion, I am sorry to say, Pridwyn, is that you were responsible for the Nippings' accident. Kilby, so horrified by your actions and the ensuing scandal, will do the honorable thing. To spare the Soliteas more heartache, she will turn the pistol on herself."

"Fayne will never believe I killed myself," Kilby said confidently.

Lord Ordish laughed at her vehement denial. "Your husband fears he is cursed, madam. Your gory death, delivered by your own hand, will confirm his suspicions."

Kilby took a deep breath. She was not entirely defenseless, she thought, as her fingers constricted around the jagged edge of broken porcelain, still concealed beneath the folds of her skirt. "There is only one problem with your plan."

"And what is that, girl?" he demanded, annoyed that she might have indeed found a flaw.

"I intend to live, you mad, stupid man," she said, throwing the daggerlike porcelain at his face.

CHAPTER
TWENTY-FOUR

"For God's sake! Now!" Fayne shouted to Darknell and Cadd. Together they charged and rammed the large, heavy barrel into Lady Quennell's beautiful glass French doors. The destructive sound of splintering wood and tinkling of shattered glass was extremely satisfying to Fayne's ears as they burst into the drawing room.

Their violent entry into the house only added to the pandemonium in the room. The drawing room was in disarray. Overturned furniture and broken glass was scattered all about them. On their arrival, Ordish pulled the viscountess into a standing position by her hair. Originally, the pistol had been pressed against Lady Quennell's throat. Struggling to keep hold of his fighting captive, the earl was straightening his arm to aim the weapon at Kilby. Shaking the glass off him, Fayne erupted from his crouched position and dashed toward his wife.

In the distance, he could hear Ramscar and the others breaking down the other door. Fayne hooked his arm around Kilby's waist and tackled her. She cried out as they hit the hard floor. There was quite a lot of broken crockery scattered about. However, not getting either of them shot was worth the risk.

From the corner of his eye, he saw Darknell and Cadd cautiously close in on Ordish and Lady Quennell.

"Damn you, Kilby! I told you not to leave the town house," he roared, his suppressed ire over her disobedience exploding as she continued to struggle in his arms.

"Let me go!" She strained against him. He rolled her over, using his body as a shield just in case Ordish fired his pistol. "He is going to kill her!"

"Never," Fayne fiercely vowed.

The door leading to the hall shattered on its hinges and Ramscar rushed in with a pistol in hand. Everod and the viscountess's butler, Gordon, entered with Nipping in their custody. Everyone seemed to freeze in place as Lady Quennell struggled and fought the earl as he tried to bring his arm up and aim the pistol at the viscountess's face.

"Ramscar, shoot the bastard!" Fayne growled.

"No!" Kilby cried out, frightened for her friend.

Ordish whirled around to confront Ramscar, ruining the clear shot at his back. Lady Quennell did not spare a glance at anyone. She was wholly focused on using all her strength to keep the pistol away. It was a battle she had no hope of winning alone. "If you discharge your weapon," the earl boasted triumphantly, "you risk hitting the lady. And I so do want to claim that pleasure for myself."

Kilby was going to hurt herself if she continued to fight him. Resigned, he crawled off her and hauled her onto her feet. "Christ!" he swore viciously under his breath when he noticed the blood dripping from her fingers. Her palm was a gory mess. Kilby, who seemed determined to escape him, did not seem to be aware of her painful wounds. Pulling out his handkerchief, he thrust the linen into her hand. It was the best he could do until someone managed to get the pistol away from Ordish. He had his hands full keeping his wife from throwing herself on top of the earl's back.

Ramscar's arm was steady as he took aim. "I'm an excellent shot, my lord." Still, he hesitated. The deadly shifting dance the older couple seemed to perform as each one grappled for the upper hand prevented him from pulling the trigger.

"You will have to be, sir," Ordish countered, knowing he was surrounded. Although he had lost his chance to coldly murder Kilby, he could have his revenge on the viscountess. "Anything less than a kill will not stop me from putting a large, ugly hole into Pridwyn's face."

"She is my mother, Fayne," Kilby said, her desperation vibrating through her slender figure. "He will kill her for that fact alone."

Lady Quennell surprised them all by taking the matter into her own hands. Abruptly releasing her grip on his arm, she drove her fist into Lord Ordish's hip, the one he had injured last summer. The earl cried out at the sudden burst of pain and his leg gave out. The couple fell to the floor.

Fayne, Darknell, and Cadd all lunged for the man, attempting to separate him from the viscountess. Whatever had driven Lord Ordish to violence was ending, but the man was determined to fight them all until he had his revenge. He brought the pistol up to Lady Quennell's throat, his finger poised on the trigger.

Instead of forcing his hand down, the viscountess instinctively shoved his hand higher, away from her neck.

Kilby's scream could be heard over the deafening discharge of the pistol. Dispelling the billowing smoke with her hands, she helped Fayne drag Lady Quennell away from Ordish.

Shaken by the explosion, the older woman stared blankly at the unmoving earl while Kilby hugged her. "Is—is he dead?"

Fayne's grim gaze met Ramscar's. Curtly nodding, his friend lowered the pistol to his side. Discreetly positioning himself between the ladies and the earl's body, Fayne crouched over Ordish.

There was no doubt the man was dead. The proximity of the discharge from Ordish's own pistol had ruined his face. The lead ball had entered the earl's left cheek, shattering his right eye socket, and the lethal fragments had pierced his brain. "Yes," Fayne called back over his shoulder. "Ordish won't bother anyone again."

"Fayne, she should be in bed," Kilby whispered to her husband.

Once he had announced that Lord Ordish was dead, he had picked her up into his arms, ordered his companions to assist Priddy, and had carried her into the library. There, he had pushed a glass of brandy into her hands and harshly demanded that she drink it. Kilby tentatively took a sip. A barrel of the stuff was not going to blot out her memories of Lord Ordish.

"Kilby, you do not have to fuss," Priddy lightly chided, when she joined them. She seemed remarkably calm in spite of her horrifying ordeal. If her dress had not been splattered with the earl's blood, one might have thought they were enjoying a social call. "I understand, Your Grace, your friends will eventually return with the constable, and everyone will have questions."

"It can all wait until later, can it not?" Kilby said, exasperated, knowing she was being difficult. She could not seem to resist. Ever since they had left the drawing room, she could not prevent the anger from overwhelming her. Nor could she seem to stop shaking, which in turn made her even more incensed. "Lord Ordish is certainly not going anywhere."

"Kilby," Fayne growled.

It was only the three of them in the library. Ramscar, Everod, and Cadd had left the house to gather the appropriate authorities, while Darknell and Gordon remained below in the front hall with Archer. Kilby had not had a chance to ask how her brother'had gotten involved in this mess.

"I think we need to discuss matters before we speak to the authorities," Fayne said, sounding practical and sane. It was all Kilby could do not to grit her teeth.

"I concur." Priddy covered her mouth as her eyes filled with tears. It took her a few minutes to get control over her emotions. "Forgive me. You have been enormously patient with me, Your Grace. More than I deserve, considering that Kilby almost died because of me."

Fayne took the viscountess's hand and squeezed it comfortingly. His green eyes shifted to his wife's, hardening slightly as he shook his head ruefully. "No, madam, Kilby has a knack for getting into trouble all by herself."

Kilby brought her chin up haughtily at his remark. She and Priddy had just fought off a madman. If she had hoped his anger over her blatant disobedience would have waned in the face of adversity, she was sadly mistaken. "On a few issues, my husband is correct, Priddy. I should have mentioned Lord Ordish."

"You should have mentioned a hell of a great deal more, Kilby," Fayne said, causing her to wince at his biting tone.

He was furious over her rebellious decision to leave the Brawleys' town house.

"Do you understand the danger you were in as a result of your reckless actions?" Fayne asked, staring at her as if he were tempted to paddle her backside in front of the viscountess. "Your lack of faith in me put you tidily into the hands of a madman."

"I did not exactly . . ." Kilby trailed off with a weary sigh. "Well, not really . . . at least not for long anyway, thanks to you and your friends."

"The note he forced the viscountess to write preyed upon your fears. You know me well enough to know that I care little what the *ton* thinks. Even if anyone had believed your brother's lies about your questionable parentage, do you think it would have mattered? You wouldn't have been the first duchess in our family to be embroiled in a scandal. You disappoint me, Duchess. You should have trusted me to handle your brother." He stood and rubbed the stiffness in his neck.

Priddy flashed Kilby a sympathetic look, hoping to ease the sting of Fayne's criticism. "Your Grace, I beg of you to strive for patience. Archer has been influencing Kilby longer than you. Her brother took every opportunity to abuse his position, cruelly attempting to justify his perverted nature. Lord Ordish had heard rumors about how Archer had taken Kilby from my house, and had deduced that Kilby would come to protect me. In truth, I am to blame for this debacle."

Kilby's shoulders slumped in despair. "I just thought of something. If Lord Nipping is my father, then Archer is truly my brother." She was not pleased by the revelation.

"Blood tie or not," Fayne said forbiddingly, glaring at the closed library door as if he could see through it down to the troubled marquess. "It will not spare him, not even for you, Kilby. I may consider leniency, if your brother willingly surrenders his guardianship of Gypsy to me and does not contest our marriage. If he wants a fight, I will take him to the courts. The Carlisles have the wealth and influence to break him."

Priddy cleared her throat, taken aback by the vehemence in the duke's vow. No one doubted that Fayne would bend Archer to his will. "Rest assured, my girl, Lord Nipping was your father. Lord Ordish told you essentially the truth, though his resentment clouded his perception."

Kilby set her glass down. She had a thousand questions

to ask Priddy. The pain of what she had lost rose up within her like an all-consuming wave, leaving her devastated. "Why was I not told the truth? After my parents' death, you could have told me." Fayne's silence was very telling. Kilby wondered how much of the truth he had gleaned on his own.

"What truth?" Priddy asked. "The moment Grennil pushed you into Ermina's arms, you were hers. If I had been given the choice, I could not have picked a more loving, superior lady than my dear friend Ermina for your mother."

She had such conflicting emotions battering her insides. Priddy was right. Lady Nipping was her mother. To think otherwise was a betrayal, especially now that she knew the true circumstances of her birth. Then there was her friend Priddy. She loved the viscountess. The lady had suffered silently, giving up the child she had clearly desired. Fayne seemed to sense her torment. Putting his personal annoyance with her aside, he gathered her into his arms and settled them both down into the chair. Kilby leaned against him, craving the strength and heat that radiated from him.

Priddy's light blue eyes grew distant as she spoke of the past. "Knowing Grennil, I assume he had expected Lady Nipping to coldly reject her husband's bastard daughter. Maybe he had hopes of ruining their marriage. I do not know. He was certainly capable of it." The viscountess quietly sipped her brandy. She lifted her head, bracing her shoulders. Speaking of the past had always been difficult for her. "My brief affair with your father was not as sordid as Lord Ordish purported. I thought my marriage was over when I encountered Lord Nipping. His first wife had just died and he had an infant son to raise alone. For a time, we turned to each other for comfort. It was only afterward that I realized I was with child. By then, your father had met Ermina, and had fallen in love. I was still married to Grennil so I saw no reason to ruin their happiness."

"Were you in love with my father?" Kilby asked, before she could censure the unbidden thought.

Lady Quennell briefly reflected on the question. "It was a difficult time for me, my dear. Lord Nipping was so unlike the gentleman I had married. He was generous and romantic, and for a while, I suppose I did think myself in love with him. That, naturally, changed when he met your mother. They were so perfect, so wonderful together."

Tears shone in Kilby's violet eyes. "I know." Her parents had loved each other with an enviable passion. That love had encompassed their children. The blood ties Lord Ordish had claimed were so important, had not mattered to the woman she had believed was her mother. Kilby glanced up at Fayne. She lightly caressed his beard-stubbled jaw. He shuddered and leaned into her hand.

"Ermina saw you as the miracle you were. It immediately became apparent to your parents that even if they had tried to return you to me, I could not keep you, not even acknowledge you. Grennil was abusive," Priddy confessed, she glanced away, ashamed. "You would not have been safe in my care. My husband could not forgive my betrayal. When he took you from me, he broke my spirit in ways I never thought possible."

She reached out for the viscountess's hand. "Oh, Priddy." With hands clasped, Kilby ached for the older woman. Lady Quennell had always been part of her family's life. The beautiful, elegant lady with a flirtatious smile had visited Ealkin several times a year laden with gifts for the Nipping children and adventurous stories to amuse her parents. "You were always a part of our lives, and yet I never guessed."

"You were not supposed to," Fayne murmured, cuddling her closer. "The arrangement protected not only you from Lord Ordish's wrath, but the viscountess as well."

"You are correct, Your Grace," Priddy conceded with a subtle nod.

"Call me Carlisle," Fayne said, shrugging gracefully. "Or Tem, if you prefer. It is what the family calls me."

The viscountess's face crumpled, overwhelmed by her new son-in-law's kindness. "Very well—Tem." Her breath quivered when she exhaled. "Your astuteness serves you well. Grennil was never quite rational after he surrendered Kilby to the Nippings. Even after he was granted the divorce, I feared him. I left England for several years, hoping he would forget about me. It was your mother, Kilby, who kept in touch. When word reached her that Grennil had left England, she urged me to return home. Your family by then, was living quietly at Ealkin. Your father never had any patience for the *ton*. In those early years, discreet visits to Ealkin by an old friend of the family went unnoticed. Eventually, Grennil became Lord Ordish, and I married my Lord Quennell. It was simpler, and perhaps kinder, to distance myself from the sorrowful lady who had been forced to give up her baby."

Kilby slipped away from Fayne's embrace. Kneeling beside her newly found mother, she said, "No one is blaming you, least of all me. You deserved to be happy, Priddy."

The viscountess cupped Kilby's face with her hand. "I have made mistakes. I should have told you the truth about me, about Grennil, after your parents' deaths. If I had, you would not have believed Archer's lies or encountered Lord Ordish—"

"Or become my duchess," Fayne said dryly. "Or found *you*. To embrace the joy in our lives, my lady, we must resign ourselves to the bad. In my case, it is Kilby's brother. However, with Ordish permanently out of the way, I have high hopes Nipping will soon follow."

CHAPTER TWENTY-FIVE

"Perhaps we should have taken Priddy up on her offer to remain at her house?"

Kilby sounded nervous. Fayne knew her anxiety had nothing to do with the shocking discovery that the lady was her mother. Kilby already loved the viscountess. In time, she would understand that accepting the lady as her mother was not a betrayal to the memory of the lady who raised her. She was fortunate to have had two mothers who loved her, who thought only of her happiness.

Fayne gave her a playful nudge up the pathway, which led to the Solitea town house. "No. Ordish's body was removed and the authorities are satisfied. Priddy told you that she planned to go to bed and recover from her ordeal. With luck, I anticipate doing the same. Perhaps the urge to paddle your backside will wane in a month or two."

"Are you frightfully angry at me?" she asked in a faint, slightly childish voice.

Fayne felt himself soften, despite his resolve not to let her off so lightly. "What do you think? You disobeyed an order meant only for your protection and then shared tea with your would-be killer. How angry do you think I should be?" he muttered crossly. He had not been married to the lady a week, and already he was losing his sanity. If the Solitea curse did not claim him, chasing after his errant duchess was likely to put him in an early grave.

Still rebellious, Kilby pouted. "Not so angry as to feed me to the dragon."

Fayne halted, thoroughly perplexed by her reasoning. "What the devil are you talking about?" With the exception of some cuts on her hand, Kilby had escaped the fate Ordish had planned for her and the viscountess relatively unscathed. Her nonsensical chatter was making him reconsider his opinion.

She glowered at the Solitea town house. "I am talking about you handing me over to your mother. I suppose I deserve whatever punishment you deem appropriate. Frankly, however, I am exhausted and not quite up to being devoured by your mother this evening."

So much had happened, he had forgotten Kilby's concerns about his family. "Little wolf, my mother knows I have married. She knows *who* I have married."

"And probably fearful of your life, considering your father's tragic fate," she added tartly. Kilby seized the edges of his coat. "Please, Fayne, can we go someplace else? Your town house? Who cares if there are servants or not? Or—or your sister's house? Or even sleep on the bank of the Thames? I am not fussy."

Fayne gathered his wife close. Kilby had taken on a murderous earl, but the thought of meeting his mother paralyzed her with terror. "The duchess is harmless," he said, guiding her to the door. "Wait and see. She'll come to love you as much as I do."

He pounded on the door. Almost immediately the butler

opened the door. "Good evening, Your Graces. The household was not expecting you this evening."

Fayne smiled at the servant. The butler had been in his family's employ for years and was well acquainted with their eccentric tendencies. "Good evening, Curdey. I trust you have room for me and my duchess for a few days."

Stepping back, the butler opened the door wider. "Of course, Your Grace. If you would follow—"

Kilby held out her arm, blocking his way. "Wait! A moment, if you please, Curdey." She looked up at him, her violet eyes shimmering with diffidence. "You love me?"

"Evidently. I married you," he retorted, half convinced his duchess had struck her head. "I do not make a habit of marrying every lady I—"

Kilby tactfully clamped her hand over his mouth. "I love you, too."

His little duchess was striving to make a good impression. Fayne could have told her the servants had by now surmised that there was nothing *good* about a Carlisle.

"Curdey?" his mother inquired from above. "Who is at the door?"

Fayne grinned impishly as Kilby did her best to crawl into his waistcoat pocket. "I thought you'd like to meet the lady who ruined me"—he ignored Kilby's ruthless jab to his injured ribs—"for all others."

The dowager duchess was not what Kilby had expected. A few years older than Priddy, her resemblance to Lady Fayre was uncanny. Instead of the Carlisle green, the dowager's eyes were a tranquil blue. Still dressed for an evening out, the older woman gestured for them to join her upstairs in the music room.

"Come up. We have just returned." The woman warmly embraced her son. "Oh, how I have missed you."

Fayne cursed when his mother tugged on his ear sharply. "What was that for?" he bellowed indignantly.

"For your impatience!" the dowager snapped back. "What was this business of scampering off to Gretna Green? You are just like your father, I vow. You hold off for years, ignoring all my attempts to pair you with a decent lady." She glanced at Kilby, seeking sympathy for the troubles a devoted mother suffered on her children's behalf.

Kilby gave the woman a faint smile.

It was all the encouragement the dowager needed. "And then without a word to anyone, you pick out your own fine lady and marry her."

Fayne winked at Kilby. Appearing offended, he said, "And you are not pleased?"

The dowager gave his ear another punishing tug. "Tem, don't be a goose! Your bride will think she has pledged herself to an idiot."

Kilby coughed delicately, using her fist to conceal her laughter.

"Why could you not have married by special license?" The dowager gave him an aggrieved look. "You know how much I would have loved having you two marry in the gardens. Did you give your poor mother a single thought when you whisked your lady away without even a proper introduction? I suppose like most men all your thoughts were dedicated to the wedding night."

"Christ, Duchess, no man is thinking about his mother on his wedding night!" he said, looking cornered.

Observing Fayne squirm under his mother's blue gimlet stare was immensely pleasurable. Perhaps it was wicked of her, but the man had been always one step ahead, unobtrusively maneuvering her in the direction he chose. It was not surprising it took a Carlisle to best a Carlisle.

Kilby decided to take pity on him. "Fayne, are you ever planning to introduce me to your mother?"

Fayne's green eyes flashed with heat. "Oh, for heaven's sake, not you, too?" Lacking his usual grace, he belligerently gestured at Kilby. "Mother, meet my duchess. Something tells me she will be a fitting addition to our lunatic family."

The dowager pulled Kilby into an affectionate embrace. "Welcome to our family, Kilby. I am pleased to see my son does actually possess some sense when choosing his bride, after all." The older woman surprised her by giving her a quick conspiring wink before leading them to the music room. "If you had encountered some of those horrid, gaudy creatures that were always trying to get their conniving hooks into my dear Tem, you would understand a mother's despair."

"Enough, Mother," Fayne said, catching on to her game. "Kilby is aware of my disreputable past. Fortunately, she managed to ensnare my roguish heart before she regarded it irredeemable."

A respectable Duke of Solitea? It seemed like an impossible task. "Oh, I suppose with Priddy's help, I could have you respectable, in what? Say, fifty or so years?" Kilby teased. Truly, she would not want to change him. She loved Fayne exactly the way he was, his sinful flaws and all.

"Probably more like eighty, but I'll make the dedicated effort worthwhile," Fayne said, pausing in front of the door. He pulled Kilby against him and kissed her lingeringly in front of the dowager. "I promise." Her toes curled at his husky vow.

"Well." The older woman beamed at them, her eyes becoming unquestionably misty. Even if Kilby had been slow to recognize her husband's love, his mother had immediately noticed the wondrous changes in her son. He was not mockingly contemplating the cursed fate of the Carlisle males as he had done in the past. This particular Duke of Solitea was looking forward to a long future with his duchess.

Fayne was the first to notice the room was occupied and barred Kilby's entry with his arm. "What are they doing here?"

Two very handsome gentlemen turned at Fayne's irritated query. The dark-haired gentleman sitting in front of an ornate gilt harpsichord abruptly stood. The tallest of the pair was standing in front of a huge scrolling rococo-style pier glass. Like his elegantly attired companion, he had black hair and blue eyes. Both gentlemen were young enough to be Fayne's older brothers.

Unperturbed by her son's surliness, the dowager introduced her companions as Vinson Savil, Marquis de Quaintrell, and Alain Kewell, Comte de Merieux. "We had decided to enjoy an evening at home for a change. Before your arrival, the comte was entertaining us with his marvelous skills."

Kilby tried not to gape as the comte kissed his hostess's hand, and then boldly kissed her cheek. "Do you know these gentlemen?" she asked her husband.

Fayne was not pleased to see that his mother had guests. "No. I have no desire to be acquainted with them, and neither do you," he said curtly.

How very autocratic of him! And this was coming from the man who once changed mistresses with each passing season. "Heavens, why not?" Kilby demanded, smiling at the marquis. "They seem to be good friends of your mother's."

She was not going to start off her relationship with her new mother-in-law by being rude. They still needed to explain a few things to the duchess, such as why Fayne despised her brother, Gypsy's guardianship, her newly found mother, and why Lord Ordish had been trying to kill them. Fayne had often told her that his family was eccentric. Somehow, she suspected that their past week exceeded even a Carlisle's standard for outrageousness.

"They always are," Fayne muttered under his breath. "I brought you here because I wanted you to meet my mother. *Tomorrow.* I had assumed the Solitea town house was one of the few places I could get you alone for more than a few minutes. I certainly did not bring you here so you could flirt with the duchess's new lovers."

"Lovers? *Both* of them?" Simply astonishing. Awed, she peered at the dowager with new interest.

Fayne, noticing his wife's keen regard, scowled. "My mother prefers collecting them in pairs. And don't ask me why, it is not the sort of conversation I ever intend to have with her. Nor should you. I will not have you picking up her bad habits."

The dowager, who had been sharing whispered confidences with Lord Quaintrell, glanced up, surprised to see them still standing in the doorway. "Tem, darling, do not dawdle. Kilby, you must sit beside me. Merieux has the most incredible hands. You can almost feel—"

"That's quite enough," Fayne said, cutting his mother off. "Kilby will have to marvel at the comte's impressive talent another day. It is time I put my wife in bed."

The man undeniably had no tact. Kilby refrained from digging her elbow into his sore ribs. "Fayne! You are embarrassing me," she hissed.

His devilish grin should have tipped her off that he was up to mischief. "Apparently, I have not made myself clear." Fayne hoisted Kilby up and flung her over his shoulder. "Forgive us, Mother. Gentlemen. Another evening perhaps. My new duchess needs a few private lessons in obedience." He smacked her backside affectionately. "I expect you will not see either one of us for days."

"Days?" Kilby echoed, mortified that she was dangling upside down. The man had to learn he could not haul her about like a sack of onions. It was so undignified. She caught a glimpse of the dowager and her male companions.

They seemed very amused by Fayne's high-handed antics. "What do you think you are doing?"

Heavens, the man has me screeching!

"Hmm." He stroked the curve of her buttock posses-sively. "Someone has to take your waywardness in hand, little wolf. Who better than I?" he huskily drawled.

Her lips parted for a scathing reply. Kilby paused, and then closed her mouth. There was no man who loved her more than Fayne. He was wicked, passionate, and adventurous—and he belonged to her. Life at his side would never be dull.

"Absolutely no one, Your Grace."